# BEYOND THE SHADOWLANDS

GEORGINA FLEMING

# BEYOND THE SHADOWLANDS

ORION

First published in Great Britain in 1993 by
Orion
An imprint of Orion Books Ltd
Orion House, 5 Upper St Martin's Lane, London WC2H 9EA

A CIP catalogue record for this book is available
from the British Library

ISBN 1 85797 015 2

Printed and bound in Great Britain by
Butler & Tanner Ltd, Frome and London

# ONE

Alice Brennan dreamed as she walked along. Sometimes she went very far in her wanderings. It was a little like tramping the sky, among the stars. Childish, oh yes, but then she'd never felt like a woman – grown up. It was more as though she had inadvertently stumbled into the wrong house and felt odd in it.

She'd never been able to love anyone in a proper, adult way, either.

She had always been different. Even as a child she'd been different, suspecting that nobody else, deep inside, felt as tumultuous or explosive as she. Perhaps she had failed to survive because she lacked the skill to dull the mind and the senses, she'd never learned how to pretend real feelings weren't there. Yes, perhaps that's why. Even as a child she used to look about her and wonder if anyone else was really happy – or just pretending, as she mostly was.

She'd spent most of her childhood afraid – of herself. Afraid of what she might do next. And looking fearfully round for approval.

Nothing had really changed.

Love, hate, resentment, fury – forbidden behaviour – she'd coped with it all in silence, smiling. A woman must be pure and true and clean, like the heroines she read about in novels. There'd been an awful lot of pretending in those days, pretending that her mind was not invaded by those wistful, shadowy longings . . . and, oh yes, it is so easy for a woman to be branded as mad once she steps off the accepted pathway. She'd always taken herself too seriously, that was the whole trouble, Milly said – Milly, that large, obstinate, disapproving woman who knew more about reality than she did. That, and too much of a wild imagination.

Too much day-dreaming.

1

But she wished Milly was here with her now, wiping her big red hands on her apron.

The autumn sun came pale through the white mist of evening, turning everywhere into nowhere. Valley melted into valley, tree into sky, and the woman who walked was thinly dark upon the horizon. Only she could feel the vapour of fear, tight like a winding sheet, constricting, twisting, that made her step and turn, step and turn, and feel a pleasure real enough to make her smile when the white moon shadow finally fitted to a fold of sky.

'I need to get as far away as I can. But this time I have to get further away from my dreams than my dreams.'

The web in her head was fragile, she must not break it. But she was safer. Night was coming. Soon the sun would turn red and sink, the clouds would change into violet, and with every footstep she left her terror a little further behind her. All day long it had plagued her until gradually it had become the firmest thing about her, while she herself, sunk deep in her cloak and hood, was just a figment of it. Real. It was so real. If she let her mind slip she could see so clearly the terrible place of torment she had left so recently behind her . . . the place where she'd perfected the trick of keeping her eyes so they looked at nothing. She could hear it and smell it and then she found herself playing with the terror, almost juggling it from hand to hand as a child might play with a paper ball on the end of a string, trembling. And what would happen if she lost control? What if she dropped it?

She felt puny and frail in the face of such terror.

Again and again she pushed back the fear and thought of her children. She must walk on, for their sakes. She must not tire, she must not take notice of her blistered heels or the chafed ankles so recently chained, or the shadows that threatened her or the distant dogs that barked at her, knowing of her approach, her coming and her passing.

2

If only she could make Shilstone tonight . . .

There was nothing to weigh her down as she traipsed the gentle Devonshire hills. She bore no luggage, just the heavy black cloak, the ill-fitting boots, the child in her arms, and her fear. Oh yes, there was the child, but he was no weight at all. And although everything else might only be in her head – for how many times had she woken up at night running away from monsters – her baby was all too real. He was part of her still; she was used to the shape and the carrying of him. The terror felt much heavier than her human burden, and only herself, and the wild things in the hedges she passed, sensed that.

Sometimes she patted her own hand, in a solitary gesture of comfort. To give herself hope, a little love. But it felt like a claw, a beggar's hand.

The wind was cold, hard and raw. The skin on her face grew tight and chapped for she was not used to the open air. Her path was uneven, full of hollows and hummocks. Limping slightly she dipped with the earth and rose with it. She curled round the edges of small woods. When she came to streams, she didn't cross them if she could avoid it, listening to the chattering of the water as it laughed its way over silver stones. The sound made her shudder. This countryside could have come from the page of a fairy-tale book, with its little squares of watery colour, its slopes and triangles, its farms and cottages. And oh, how she had dreamed, as a child, of living in one of those fairy-land pages. What would she be if she lived there – a queen or a witch? Whatever she made herself, there was no doubt about it that one day her prince would come and save her, come along on his horse and whisk her away. Take care of her. For women were nothing without men. Every book she read told her that, on marriage, life began. She nearly laughed. That was almost funny!

She avoided the streams, the carriageways and the farm-tracks, keeping to the darker places even if this meant taking a longer route, making a detour or climbing a hill. While she moved her eyes were watching and they were wild like animals' eyes sensing a trap. Sometimes, unaware of it, she murmured a brief phrase of song, as mothers do when they fear for a waking child. But then she would fall silent again, only able to hear her own laboured breathing.

The grass turned spongy and water oozed through the holes in her boots. The larger stones cut through them. She came to the stile and climbed it, clambering over and pulling the muddy flaps of her cloak on after her. The hedges rose, tall on either side of her, wintry with thorn, and no sign, now, of the foxgloves and wild flowers, no sign of the tiny pimpernel. While she climbed, for just an instant, her eyes ceased to watch the darkness, but concentrated instead on the obstacle before her. Her hand slipped on the wet wood and her heart lurched when she almost stumbled. She regained her balance but before her eyes could focus once more on the sloping distance ahead, before she had fully adjusted her stance, the voice came quietly on to the silence.

'I'll have the child now, Alice, please.'

The woman froze, hating the moonlight that peered at her through the elms. She coiled up inside like a snake. Running away – it should have made her invisible, dark and secret like the night. How strange that someone could see her . . . how strange that she was real! All hope gone, now there was only horror. At once her body became just an extension of the wooden structure she stood on, angled, dead and devoid of all purpose. Time ceased to be and her head was so heavy now, full of tears that refused to flow. But the baby moved, at first just a gentle unfolding – its arms and legs were firmly swaddled – it stretched its neck and flexed the muscles of its face, making a tiny pout before it opened its eyes and gasped at the ferocity of the moonlight.

'I said I would take the child now, Alice.'

His voice came like the wind in a cave, through stone

lips. It was courteous but firm, a voice that, although clearly tired was yet prepared to be tolerant before it achieved what it demanded – instant obedience. She used to feel safe giving instant obedience. She used to worship those who demanded it of her. But now she had a child . . . a real one, and it needed her to be a grown-up person, *to be a mother*.

Alice, frozen there, half-on, half-off the stile, searched the darkness with her eyes but the rest of her face, still hidden under the hood, was pale and stiff with shock. Where to go? Where to run? *Think, Alice, think* – the thing she had so rarely done in her life was think! It had not been expected of her. *Think*! Should she go back? She narrowed her eyes in order to see him better although she did not want to, oh no, she did not want to.

'For the love of God . . . ' she began.

The child began to whine; the feeble cry of the newly-born went well with the silent night, echoed eerily into it like one more breeze through the grasses. Hugged so close to his mother, he could not fail to sense the tension that came off her in trails of dark, making her breaths come as sobs, wet as the leaves that dripped their dew on to the frosty earth, and froze there. It was old – this sorrow of hers, it was so old.

The man who, until then had been merely a shadow, came out of the mist leading his horse behind him. Edward Brennan held the reins loosely in his hand and walked towards his wife.

He was big, powerful and forbidding as always. 'How did you know?' she asked, her eyes fixed on him. Nicholas, her son, was the only one who could possibly have told him, and she had trusted Nicholas with her life. The betrayal drenched her, took away the last of her courage. Suddenly sick, stunned, her limbs were shaking and she had no control over them.

'The child,' he said, stepping nearer so she could smell him again. She shuddered with a familiar pain. He smelled of so much sorrow. He smelled of her own exhaustion. 'Give him to me.'

5

'If I could plead with you . . . if I could beg you, Edward . . . '

He laughed then. She remembered the farm dogs barking. She remembered hearing a dog fox, howling upon a hard granite midnight. She thought she saw his teeth bared, she thought the moonlight caught them. And his eyes flashed at the same time and she saw the hatred there.

'You know you have no option, not now, not any longer. You have ceased to be a person, Alice . . . '

'You saw to that!' she sobbed.

To this Edward Brennan did not reply, but lowered his eyes to stare at her. That old stare . . .

'He will not live,' she started to say. 'He will die without me, you know it.'

'I think not, Alice.'

'You will not take him, Edward. Not this one. I will not give him up.'

He repeated himself, his voice contemptuously easy. 'You have no choice.'

She tried to plead, knowing her words fell on stony ground. 'Just for a while, let me keep the child, just until he is weaned, perhaps . . . ' She dared a glance at Edward's face, saw hard pebble eyes, stony ground where nothing grew, where nothing had ever grown but a fierce and brambled cruelty. Her dread of him consumed her.

He spoke to her in the manner the sane use to speak to the mad, and Alice had grown used to that. 'And how would you live, Alice? Have you thought of that? How could you possibly care for a child – any child – let alone one so vulnerable, one so young. You have always needed so much help with the others.' And he held out his hand to touch the baby.

Alice flinched from the devil. 'You have the others. You care not a jot for the others. You keep them, not for their sakes, not for their welfare, but in order to punish me!'

'You are mad, dear Alice. Mad. You are not fit to

6

care for children, let alone a newborn infant.'

At the word 'mad' she closed her eyes and held them shut to try and stop hearing more, as if she could shut out his terrible words, their menacing meaning, with such a simple gesture. Keeping them closed, herself closed against him, she said, 'You know that is not true.'

''Tis not only I who says it.'

'It was you who told the lies. 'Twas you, with your vile purposes, who made up the stories, who has turned even Nicholas against me.'

'Nicholas is a man now,' Edward Brennan smiled at the mention of his son, 'and well able to make up his own mind. What did you think, Alice?' and his voice turned gently mocking. 'That you would confide in Nicholas, manipulate him as you have so often done in the past, persuade him to take part in your pathetic little plan? Hah! Did nothing in that poor, vacant head of yours tell you that perhaps Nicholas was at last astute enough to know, and come to me with his suspicions? If that does not convince you of your own miserable shortcomings, of your own madness, I don't know what will.'

She was down from the stile now. She must try to keep him talking like this, convince him that eventually she might be prepared to do his bidding. She must answer him calmly, not become excited and tearful, het up by his goadings, a habit which had let her down so badly in the past. She must defeat that old urge to fling herself on his mercy, knowing how futile that was, how he scorned and used that behaviour against her. She remembered how his eyes had watched her . . . years ago, he had started to watch her, turning her into the cowed, defeated creature eventually she had become. She hated herself like this – hated hated hated. She kept her voice low and quiet, free from emotion, as very slowly she took account of the new surroundings, the way the ground fell, the angle of the hedgerow, the soft dip of the gulley in the distance. She would wait

7

until his horse wandered around to his left-hand side and then she would move to his right . . . and go! Fly!

'Your cruelty does not mark you,' she said, keeping her voice quite light, keeping the dull hopelessness she felt out of it. 'I find this incredible, but so. I would have thought it would have scarred your face, pulled down your mouth, veined and dulled your eyes. But no, Edward. You are still just as handsome. No one would know of your darkness – it stays well hidden inside you.'

'And you, Alice.' He returned the compliment slyly between smiling lips. 'Madness makes you more lovely. It is painful for me to see you like this. If you only knew . . . '

She turned her face away from him. 'You followed me all the way?'

'I had no need. I knew you would come this way so I waited here.'

'For how long?' She imagined his cold, impatient vigil.

'For no longer than half an hour.'

Stealthily she began to edge her way to the right, making it seem as if she was merely adjusting her cloak or her tiny burden. His horse munched the grass, stepping along every so often to find something fresh, steaming in the mist like a dream horse and quite unperturbed by the drama. Its ears flickered, the reins lightly jingled. Every second passed slow as a year . . . every heartbeat was a clanging bell. She couldn't swallow, her tongue was stuck.

And then she picked up the heavy material, arranging it, and fled. She gripped the wailing child and she ran. She heard Edward shout but she did not catch his words. She ran from him, from Deale, she ran from memories and she ran from herself. She imagined him pulling his horse around, wicked with anger, impatiently mounting, gripping his whip and shouting. Which is what she hoped he would do, for it gave her the few precious seconds she needed to make for the gulley, deep in shadow. He must lose sight of her just for a moment. He might imagine she'd followed the hedge, that she had not been so reckless as to cross the open field.

She ran. She tore over the roughly-ploughed earth, twisting her ankles, losing pace, desperately trying to break through this dream. She did not know if the baby was crying, there was too much noise in the air to detect individual sounds. All sense of time and direction was gone. She came to a hedge, and wrapped the baby like a parcel before tearing through it, uncaring of briars and brambles, the cruel little spikes that rent her skin and her clothing. She had no breath left to use but this didn't matter. She was animal now – pure, wild, mad animal. She would kill her child rather than give him up to Edward. But this thought was merely a cool, thin ribbon that unwound deep in her fading consciousness – not important. Nothing was important except to escape him. The horror of him gave her a strength that was new and full of power. There was no point in pausing to listen or watch for him. He was the cause of her flight and yet he no longer existed. There was only her and the night and the child, the red-hot energy inside her and the white glow of the moon. There were scents of earth, soil, blood, birth and terror, the wild, primitive scents, they drove her.

She had never disobeyed Edward Brennan in her life before. She liked to be childish, she liked to be told childish things and be able to believe them. Because everything else was so dark . . . vanished in all the darkness.

God help me – oh, God help me! She threw herself down and huddled, panting and breathless, in the place where she was, pulling branches round her. The wind whispered in a ring of trees and, gasping convulsively, she whirled her head around. Nothing. No sign, no sound of Edward. With trembling fingers she undid her bodice and pushed the child on her to suck. He did so with wide open eyes; with moon-eyes he stared at his

9

mother, his wild, terrified mother. And yes, she could have been a wolf, a stoat, a weasel, and he her cub . . . safe briefly, which is all the wild things ever are and all they can ever hope to be.

A tawny owl hooted in a far-off wood. She passed her hand over her baby's head. She let it trace the small warm outline of the blanketed body.

The only sound was running water.

She waited.

She listened.

But she no longer trembled.

For there was nothing more she could do. If Edward came, he came. She would hear him coming and have time to squeeze the life from her baby before he could take him from her.

And, in so doing, finally kill her.

# TWO

'Did I lock the door, or didn't I – or maybe I should keep it open?'

Milly did not know best any more. She didn't know what was going on any more and now she had time to wonder if she had ever, honestly, known best.

The pear tree in the garden dripped like a broken fountain. Beyond it the small cottage bulged, and the light at the one downstairs window made a track across the tangled grass. The curtains had not been drawn. The place was in waiting.

Charlotte was evil, through and through, and Edward in spite of his posturings, was nothing more than a fool. Dear Lord . . . when she thought of the things she had heard today.

Within the house Milly Toole paced the floor, waiting. Waiting for the worst, cursing herself for the idiot she was. The grandmother clock that fitted between the two largest beams up the wall, ticked and tocked brownly to her plodding footsteps. Her hands ran over her body, smoothing her apron down over the place where there used to be a waist but now was merely a continuation of ample folds. Yesterday her aching old body had felt spry and eager with hope. How foolish to be so naive as to believe Edward Brennan could be outwitted. Foolish to allow herself to be filled with the hope that she and Alice might get away with it.

Would she come, even yet – would she come? And she remembered her words of old: 'Come to Milly, my darling, come to Milly!' She clicked her tongue like fast knitting needles.

She paced, and every now and again she glanced nervously outside into the darkness where she saw motion, furtive and threatening, everywhere. Between the nervous smoothings of her apron, she patted the cap

11

that sat, starchly erect on her swept-up, cottage loaf hair. Grey hair now, and coarser than it had been. She readjusted a pin here, a comb there. Milly had always needed an armoury of wood and metal to keep the heavy mass in place, even now, even at her advanced age. She felt at her neck for wayward strands but there were none. Desperately, she needed to fiddle in order to pass the time, to turn her concentration, however briefly, to something else. She would have liked to sink into the chair by the fire and pick up her knitting, but she couldn't do that. Her concentration was quite gone.

Poor little Alice was out there somewhere, with or without the child, unless Edward had caught her already and taken her back. Milly set the many lines on her face so that they straightened and crossed it with anger.

When Master Nicholas went off to visit his mother that afternoon, Milly had squeezed up her eyes as tight as her hands to pray. She had gone to Winterbourne House to give Jane a hand in the nursery. When she was told of the young man's destination she had prayed with her hands steeped in warm washing-up water, swishing them round and searching for crockery which she brought up finally between red fingers like wet white bones. Like a witch-doctor rattling bones she had prayed: 'Alice . . . do not confide in the boy. You love him. You trust him. But look at his eyes, Alice my dear. For the love of God take a moment to look in your young man's eyes. He is on the side of his father, God help him, and who can honestly blame him for that, after all the dark lies and stories?'

But Nicholas had returned from Deale Asylum this evening with a smug, closed look on his face. Milly, waiting there at the house, had watched from the nursery window, through narrowly parted curtains. She had seen him crossing the courtyard in haste, leaping the steps three at a time and then making straight for his father's study.

12

Milly, following him, had crouched in the passage outside the thick oaken door and had managed to hear, 'The child was born this afternoon . . . ' before the door closed and cut out all sound like a heavy wooden footstep stamping on words.

Milly had done a good deal of stealthy listening just lately. And she had not liked what she heard.

Oh Lord, Alice, we are both such fools! And Milly, feeble now and rheumatic, had become so agitated she couldn't think straight, cursing her inability to warn poor Alice. For once again it seemed that they had lost. There was nothing to do but return to her cottage in the grounds and wait, hoping against hope for a miracle, keeping strictly to the plan, trying to dismiss her doleful conjectures and telling herself again and again that this . . . this wickedness . . . was none of her doing and that there was nothing she could have done to prevent it.

But could she?

And now it was far too late.

When she'd first seen the Hospital she had shuddered. No heart. No soul. Just stone – massive, a monstrous mausoleum of a place with tall, barred windows and mile upon mile of corridors and stairs. Even the narrow windows looked sick – like bilious yellow eyes. Half this grim building was put to use as a house for the destitute poor, half as a hospital for the insane.

Milly had only once been to visit Alice in Deale, and her lack of stamina, her inability to overcome her horror and go again, sickened her. But to see someone you love so much . . . to experience such helplessness in the face of such appalling conditions . . . to come to terms with that had proved too much. Was it any wonder? She had spent her life trying to protect Alice from anything ugly. And now look . . . shadows, bells, and that heavy odour . . . But Alice, in spite of all that hideous humiliation had been understanding, watching her nurse's face and knowing so well its every expression. 'It's better, Milly, if you stay away. You can't help me here. Seeing me like this you suffer even more than I do.'

Milly, too distracted to talk much, had turned away, had closed her eyes to the shiny white walls, to the bed that was not a bed but a straw paillasse tucked up by the wall of the thin, mean cell. White gas lighting spluttered from iron rods in the ceiling, bathing the sights she saw in a cruel, unforgiving harshness and whispering terribly of horrors Milly could only imagine. She had closed her ears to the sounds of moaning, to the tormented screams from the unwashed, hysterical creatures in the ward, screams that echoed along the freezing corridors like trapped voices from Hell. She had closed everything up inside her and held the small hand of Alice.

It was cold. Cold and frightened.

And Milly remembered how people had started saying, 'Alice is over-emotional. Alice is such a nervous child!'

'He is a devil,' Milly had whispered as she sat there, glinty-eyed and hunched over. 'He can't get away with this. Someone, some time, will punish him for what he has done. No one can get away with this.'

Alice's voice was brittle and cheerful but she'd been crying, Milly could tell. 'He has convinced everyone of my sickness. All the friends I once had, my family, his family, even the doctors are afraid to question him – and why should they?' Milly winced because no one had bothered to do Alice's hair. No one had brushed it or combed it, so that she began to look like a madwoman, sitting so listlessly. Milly tried to smile kindly but knew, instantly, that she had failed and grimaced instead.

'And trying to convince strangers of your own sanity, ah, Milly, that is a task that should never be forced on anyone. For in the end it becomes impossible. When people look for madness, they find it.' Alice had finished off with blank eyes and a voice that lacked any anger or blame, 'And I think, by the end, that I probably was mad.'

'Driven to it by that demon,' said Milly. 'He had his ways. He was ever a clever, devious man – but never a match for Charlotte.' And she placed both her own hands over Alice's, preventing her from plucking at her fingers, hating to see her do that.

'When I have the child they will move me from here. They have told me I'll be moved to the lying-in room next door. Then I'll have my chance to escape.'

Milly interrupted, 'You're talking about six months from now. How will you ever survive six months of this? How would anyone?'

'I have no choice.'

'There must be a quicker way. You should not be allowed to give birth in such a place, I find it unendurable to imagine you here left to the ministrations of these people. And the birth certificate . . . it will give this bedlam as the place of birth. It will leave a stigma on the child that'll stick as cruelly as any disfigurement.' And what on earth had they got her dressed in – some dreadful old rag. Milly concentrated hard on Alice's face while she tried to block out the other sights, but there was no consolation in the younger woman's face. It was desolate. Her eyes were careful.

Alice started to talk again, but stopped, and when her voice trailed to nothing her hands moved on as if to finish her sentence for her. She pulled at the ends of her fingers; she bit at her uncut, fractured nails. Gathering strength from somewhere, she added, 'And I truly believe he imagines that my situation, the birth, the waiting in here, might fulfil his wildest hopes, might make his horrible insinuations come true. I know that my memory plays me tricks . . . ' And then she burst out, 'There's nothing for me to behave well for now, it doesn't matter in the least what I do!'

'It would drive the sanest to madness,' said Milly.

'You'll wait for me, Milly? You'll help me? Even though you could lose your cottage and the income that Edward allows you each year?'

15

'You've no need to ask me those questions. You know that I'll be there. Haven't I always been there?'

Alice's laugh was bitter. 'Edward might have convinced even you by then.'

'You insult me, Alice. You hurt me when you talk like that. I know you, and I know Edward. I have known him since he was fourteen years old.'

'Then you know that I am the world's best forgetter and that one day, even this will fade like a dream.'

For a little while they fell silent. Alice's deep blue eyes were dark in her skull and sadness sat in circles round them.

She said, 'But Edward has been good to you, Milly.'

'That's his way and that's half the trouble but he doesn't impress me! People look at him and they see a generous man who donates gifts to charity and to the church, who looks after his servants well. Oh yes, my darling, but he is not his own man. He is driven, he is led down devious, treacherous paths by Charlotte.'

'But you do see why it's important you don't come to visit me again?'

Milly's little shudder of repulsion gave strength to her words. 'I will find it quite easy not to come to this place again. There will be no great hardship for me in that. But don't you think that Edward might suspect that all is not right? After all, in spite of everything, I've never abandoned you before.'

'Oh Milly, this time we've got to be as devious and cunning as he is. Somehow you've got to make him think that you believe him. You must change your attitude towards him because if we're to succeed then it's essential Edward believes he has convinced even you.'

Milly worried. 'But what attitude should I take towards the children?'

'Say nothing to them. Don't contradict their father. There'll be time enough, later, to explain the truth to the children. You must do this, Milly, for my sake. All that's important to me now is that I get free from this

16

place. While he has me here I am powerless.'

Milly had promised her, adding, 'I'm sure Nicholas does not trust Edward, he loves you too much for that. At the moment he's confused, heartbroken, he wants you home. He has great arguments with Edward. He demands to know why, if you're ill as his father insists, he doesn't employ a nurse to care for you until you're better. He's fourteen now and Nicholas is feeling his feet. He refuses to whisper around your illness, he shouts about it instead, often at mealtimes when he has to be dismissed from the table.'

'And Kate and Laura?'

'Jane has been ordered to tell them you have gone away to be looked after for your own good. She tells them you're not well . . . '

'And Edward? What does he tell them? Does he say when I'm coming home?'

There was nothing for it but to confess to the truth. Milly had not prepared a lie and she was not quick enough to invent one. Afterwards she would wish she had. 'He tells them stories about you, as if you're a memory or a legend, someone that was, once, but is no longer. I heard him say that you'd gone to some-where beyond the shadowlands – he makes it sound like a magic place – where no one and nothing can reach you.' Then, overcome by the horror of it all, she blew her nose on an enormous white handkerchief.

Brilliant tears shone in Alice's eyes. She gripped her lip with her teeth, her hands tore through her hair. Milly thought of an exotic animal she'd once seen, pacing in a zoo. 'He is making me disappear! And Kate and Laura, what do they say?'

Milly folded her handkerchief into a tiny knob. 'Kate's a dreamer, like you. She said that one day she'd get a rowing boat and row across to the place where the shadowlands were, and shout so loudly and so piercingly across the moat and through the fog that you'd hear her. Laura told her not to be silly, that there was no such place. Edward didn't answer.'

17

'Oh Milly, what's going to happen in the end? How is it possible that I'll ever escape from this sort of evil, this amount of hatred? What have I done? What did I ever do to merit this?'

Milly's attempts at comfort were useless. She tried to collect her wits and find something positive to talk about. She brightened her face and her voice, urging Alice to listen. 'Before this happened we didn't know how far they were prepared to go to achieve their ends. That's the difference. Now we do know. We know the depths to which Edward Brennan will sink if Charlotte goads him, and that makes it easier for us.'

'Does it, Milly? Nothing feels easier to me. It feels like a crazy haze and I can't even see my way out. I only know I am me in this place because of my own smell!'

'Don't talk like that, Alice. You know how I hate to hear you talk like that. Your husband is driven by this ferocious love he has for your sister . . . he is obsessed by her. She has cast a spell and told all sorts of lies . . . '

'Don't speak to me of her, not now, not here.'

Milly tried to interrupt, knowing honesty was all-important. They really ought to talk about this. But Alice prevented her, covered her face and muttered through her hands, 'I won't speak of Charlotte, I don't want to hear her name. Please, Milly, I have enough to bear just now without that.'

'She still sleeps in his bed . . . the brazen hussy!'

'Milly – enough!'

And so they had not discussed Charlotte that day. And Milly had done as she'd been asked, and had not visited Alice again in that terrible place. Not a day went by when she did not think about her, worry about her and pray for her, especially as the birth of the child drew nearer. How would she escape, and who might pursue her? How would she travel the twenty-mile distance from Deale to home without being seen? She would be weak from childbirth, cold, hungry and afraid. As the months crawled slowly by Milly tried to be less antagonistic towards Edward. She hadn't spoken to the children about their mother, but she had watched and listened, she'd hung about stealthily in quiet places. Milly knew most of the secret things that went on at Winterbourne House. She was convinced that Edward Brennan would never suspect his wife could escape from Deale and dare take sanctuary so close to home.

They might be granted a little breathing space. Time to make plans.

Yes, Milly was convinced – almost. She paced – backwards and forwards, backwards and forwards. Would Alice come tonight? Would she bring the child? Milly rubbed the window once more and put her eye to it. She felt the chill of the outside air against her warm, rosy skin. And yet didn't Edward Brennan know as well as she did, that Alice had nowhere else to go?

Milly listened. She kept on listening, but the only noise the night made was the sound of running water.

# THREE

Alice waited until the autumn night froze into stillness, until her breathing became painless once more and the cold whine of silence was louder than the beat of her heart. But her eyes did not close, they continued to stare – hot eyes, they might be red – only dropping their gaze for brief moments on the face of the baby, resting on him for refreshment, before assuming the direct, frightened glare of the sentinel once again.

Edward was not a man to give up so easily, *Edward, Charlotte, Edward, Charlotte.* He would be out there somewhere in the darkness, as silent as she, as watchful as she. And he would be white with anger, for he hated to be outwitted; it was a situation he was quite unused to and one with which he had never been able to come to terms.

There ceased to be such simple things as days – named and sectioned like Wednesday and Saturday and Monday. Time was measured by a clatter of pails, a scrubbing of brushes, and jingling of keys and a banging of doors . . . and bells clanged the time, even breaking into the hush of the night. And you couldn't name time that was measured like that any more.

When Alice's labour started they came to move her. Waves of nausea and faintness flowed over her, leaving her desolate, engulfed by a terror so great it was more like despair. It was hard to get along. She couldn't move quickly and she found walking difficult because she was cramped and stiff from a week of being chained to the wall; the hard leather strap they had used on her ankle had caused her leg to swell and her foot throbbed painfully. But they loosed her and she hobbled along, following the hard-faced woman who led, heckled by

20

the second nurse who followed. If Alice lagged behind, clung to the wall for balance, or bent to rub her aching leg, she was pushed and cursed. 'We have not got all day to be bothering with women who are nothing but trouble-makers and who sneer and refuse to eat when their fancy takes them!' The woman's breath reeked of gin – replacement wages for tired workhouse employees – and her face was a hardened purple like that of a man who has spent all day in the fields, labouring. With hard eyes she continued to watch as Alice paused, bracing herself for the next step, steeling herself against the next stab of pain.

The dream feeling was there, in Deale, just as it was outside it. She made herself dream in Deale for there was no other way out. They tried to chain her to reality. They chained her to stop her pacing the ward by night. She must learn to do as she was told, they said. She would never get out of here if she did not comply with their wishes and try to help herself. 'Nights are for sleeping,' they said, with their tired, resentful eyes.

What sense was there in sleeping? 'But I can't sleep for the noise. The long nights are nothing but torture and I can't get comfortable on the bed with the weight of the child pressing down on me. And the mattress is so hard . . . '

'Bah! You imagine it, because you're not well. Other people manage to sleep – you are just trying to be difficult.'

Talking in Deale was futile. No sound came out of your mouth. Joshua Myers was not interested in reasons. Edward had told him, 'You'll see how these complaints are all part of her sickness. She imagines that people are deliberately trying to make life hard for her. She thinks that they are conspiring together to hurt her. It is all to do with her anxious, hysterical state of mind, and for years her family and servants have had to try and cope with her constant neurotic complaints. So naturally, Myers, she will continue to behave in the same way in here. I am merely warning you . . . these

21

whinings are all part of the sickess.'

They were saving her, in spite of herself. 'We can't have every patient taking it into her head that she can get up when she likes, go to bed when she likes. Sleep when she likes. Eat when she likes,' the fat doctor said softly to Alice.

What sense was there in eating, speaking or sleeping? They chained her and she would not eat.

Anyway, you'd have to be starving to eat the food in here – she was not trying to be difficult. She gagged on the greasy soup, she rolled up small pieces of hard bread and soaked it, but even then it was hard to swallow; it stuck in her throat and then lingered like mud in her chest. Meanwhile the others slopped and grunted, pushing the food into their mouths as they dribbled and drooled, or sat, staring at it with intense concentration, fidgeting with themselves, until forced to eat by strong-armed nurses with no patience and filthy hands. Food meant dribbling, blubbering, and sitting amongst inarticulate sounds. There was vomit on the table and excrement on the floor.

And then there were always the watching nurses—workhouse women who couldn't find work elsewhere. They understood cruelty well. She tried to be quiet and compliant, for she feared the hot baths they forced her to take when they accused her of becoming hysterical, she feared for the life of the child. The baths were nothing like a nightmare, they were far, far worse than that. She tried to be calm, to avoid as much violent handling as possible as they lowered her into the water. She closed her eyes and willed herself away from this place, craving oblivion. She tried not to see the vast bathhouse with the vaulted iron ceilings, the rows of baths, the confused heads that stuck up like various pale species of flower through the cloying steam, the smell of bodies, the stench of fear. She railed against the baths, hammering on the wooden lid they screwed down over her until her hands were raw and bleeding, until she was nauseous and feeling as mad and out of control as the others around her. But sometimes

22

her feelings of terror and frustration, the horror of the thought that she might never leave this place, overcame her. One day she sank into swamps of black desolation, the next she raged against her own impotence, hating herself for what they had done, for what she had let them do. And then she would search for a place to be alone, where they would not find her, but oh it was so hard to find such a place in the turmoil of Deale. There was nowhere here to bathe or get clean without hot eyes watching, strong arms waiting. Sleep? If you slept you were startled awake by a shriek and a face and fingers which clutched at your bedding and tore at your clothes. Manic. Frenzied.

She lived in a cliff of grey brick and a chill draught blew down the long, scrubbed corridors and lofty halls, bringing the damp, cold smell of a cellar with it. Those wretches who were not frantic with madness sat dull and mute, listlessly staring with hopeless eyes, or wandered inanely from one end of the ward to the other, scratching. There was no peace. Her room, cell-like, with walls that stopped just above eye level, had no door, only a curtain which ran along clattering rails and added to the wild, mad music of this devilish place. They would not allow her to sleep with the curtain drawn. Whenever she closed it they looked in and accused her of being devious.

Beyond the ward was the place where they kept the dangerous lunatics, those who would do harm to themselves and others. Alice could hear them at night–those sounds made sleep impossible. The nurses threatened that, if Alice did not behave herself, she would be put in there with them.

Behave herself! By being in Deale she had lost all status, was denigrated to a condition more helpless than childhood. Yet that had happened immediately after her marriage to Edward, at eighteen years old. She was used to that.

Alice pleaded with Myers to allow her some books. 'It would help pass the time.' And immediately she'd

23

felt like a mutinous child, daring to ask an unpardonable question in the presence of adults.

'Books stimulate the mind too much,' he said, in the cold unemotional voice of the sane, that fishy-eyed man with the pudgy fat hands that he kept flatly on his desk at all times, not even moving them to pick up a pencil. There was nothing human about those hands. He added, with triumph, 'And that leads to trouble. Sick minds should not be set to churning, they should be left restful. Books would be of absolutely no benefit to somebody with your condition.'

'But what is my condition?' she stuttered. So much depended on being supplied with books but the asking for them was a shocking indecency. The doctor's eyes directed themselves on her restless hands and she calmed them. This time she did not demand to see the governors. There would be no begging or pleading, no appealing for mercy. 'Isn't it time you came to some decision and gave me a name for my malaise?'

The doctor closed his eyes, sat back slightly, and signalled the end of the interview by joining his fingers to form a steeple. Was God there, over the top of his fingers, was he pointing her to God? The nurses led her back to the ward.

It was curious to be alive and yet be unable to smell green things, feel the wind along the top of the woods, see the scuttle of a grey squirrel in the treetops.

Edward came. She tried to refuse to see him but they wouldn't listen. They led her to a small, square room off the ward where wooden benches were nailed to the walls and there was nothing, not even a shadow to hide behind.

'No, no, I'll be ill if I have to face him! He is the reason for me being in here . . . he has spent years trying to drive me insane! I beg you, let me alone, I cannot see him.'

They did not bother to listen. Had he deliberately chosen to be late? The wait was unendurable. Time after time she imagined she heard the key turn in the

24

lock, heralding the sound of his voice . . . his presence . . . his terrible nearness to her! He said she was insane and yes, while she waited she knew what madness meant. She trembled. She muttered to herself as she tried to rehearse a conversation, tried to choose the words which might sway him, an idea which might mollify him. If he would agree to her freedom she would go away . . . far away . . . and never see him or go near him again. Anywhere! It didn't matter.

And the children? He would be bound to ask about the children.

Oh, she would agree to anything . . . absolutely anything in order to get out of Deale.

But how could he marry Charlotte with his wife still living and sane? Adultery was out of the question. Madness was much easier . . . an asylum for life . . . poor man. He could renounce her eventually and people would understand and sympathize.

And yet when they had married she had been so eager to please him, so unsure of herself that she had not realized what was happening. She had even begun to believe that she was truly losing her mind! No, Alice had never had the confidence, the cool, calm assurance or the cunning of her sister Charlotte.

She cowered by the wall, a madwoman, waiting for him.

Edward came. The doctor left them alone. She dragged herself up and stood with her back to him, staring at the wall. Humiliated, helpless. She was tortured by his presence and afraid of what she would see if she turned and looked in his eyes.

'Well, Alice, and how are you?'

She squeezed her hands together, hot and wet and sticky like her heart, pumping wildly. She raised her head. She stared at one brick in the wall. It eyed her back, glossily.

'I thought I would come and assess the situation. I have spoken to Doctor Myers. He says you are not making the quick recovery he hoped for. He says you have not settled well.'

Chattering teeth. She clenched them. She would not turn round. He was a monster! And he was here with her now; they were alone and she just as helpless as she ever was.

'I see that your behaviour is still curiously incongruous,' he said softly in precise, clipped tones. 'I see that that has not changed.'

Alice would not be drawn.

'Alice! For pity's sake! What do you look like!'

It was then that she whirled round. He had used that expression so often in the past and it never failed to upset her. There, in her institutional rags she faced him, smoothing the hideous grey material, trying to untangle her hair with her fingers, horribly aware of the picture she must be presenting. He was seeing her exactly as he wanted her to be!

'How do you expect me to look, Edward, incarcerated in here with no way of taking care of myself, no mirror to look in except for the window when the lights are on and it's dark outside. I have no underclothes . . . my dress is laundered once in a fortnight! I am allowed no brush, no comb.' Her face crumpled, her body slumped. 'There is rarely clean water to wash in. My God, and now you come in here and criticize my looks!'

Then he smiled. And she realized how high her voice was, how she had coiled herself, how her hands, done with her hair, rested in it as she spat out her words at him. Shaking, she wrapped herself in her arms and let herself drop to the bench where she huddled, trying to warm herself against all the freezing cold that was Edward, her husband and her persecutor. There was nothing in her head now. She had nothing to say.

'The children are well. They continue to ask after you. Especially Kate.'

Alice hugged herself tightly. She clamped her top teeth down on her lip. He looked . . . fine. Neat and orderly in his well-cut brown coat, knee breeches and

26

boots, the silver watch-chain dangling below his long waistcoat. A handkerchief, done in a flamboyant bow, came from the frill of his cuffs and he carried his wide-brimmed hat in his hand, as a gentleman would when visiting a lady. That same contempt was stamped on his face, a smiling contempt, an expression he often wore. His full side-whiskers started below his ear, just where his thick hair curled to a stop. How wonderful she had once thought that thick brown wavy hair, those knowing brown eyes, that wide, sensuous mouth . . . how safe she had thought him. Not now. She saw him now as he really was – a weak, selfish, self-obsessed man.

She would not speak again. She would not. He could not goad her into another of what he liked to call her performances.

'Alice? Can you hear me? Are you listening to me or are you deliberately trying to provoke me?'

She lifted her eyes to him then, and stared at him.

'You realize that everything that is being done for you here is for your own good? You realize, at last, how sick you are, how much we have all endured in order to keep you at home. How, finally, it became too much for all of us . . . you were having such a bad effect on the children.'

How convincing he was! He almost believed his own words. She stared on, her blue eyes cold and unblinking.

'The Doctor tells me that he's going to try other treatments. He has asked for my permission and I have, today, signed the papers. I told him that everything must be done in order to cure you – no expense, no attention spared.'

How had she ever loved him? How had she ever believed him, trusted him?

'I gather that Milly has not repeated her visit. She has come to see that nothing more can be done to help you from mere well-wishers. Yes, even she has come to her senses. Even she has had to believe the truth when it stared her so starkly in the face. Poor soul. She has gone all glum on us. She rarely visits the nursery now, only when especially asked by Jane when she is exceptionally busy.'

All Alice wanted to do was crouch like a tormented animal, away from him in the corner. She wanted to cover her head with her arms, but she would not do that . . . she would not give him the pleasure of seeing her so wounded.

'When the child is born I will come for it,' said Edward Brennan pleasantly, as if to relieve her of some burden she could not carry. It was horrible – he could almost be confiding in her! Even his hand came forward a little, as if he wanted to give her some gesture of comfort. Alice flinched. 'The authorities will inform me of its arrival and I will come for it. Charlotte is already eager, looking forward to receiving the poor scrap into the bosom of the family. You can rest assured she will care for it, bestow upon it the same devotion which she gives the others.'

Out of the woodenness of despair she found a dull strength. She got up, aimed very carefully, raised her head high and spat at him. She watched with satisfaction as the wet blob slipped down his cheek, caressing like a careless finger, until he pulled out his handkerchief and wiped it off, along with the smile from his mouth, the humour from out of his eyes.

Edward Brennan started to breathe heavily and, oh yes, she recognized the start of his anger.

Then, out of her mouth, came a small giggle that surprised her. It came as slickly as her spit, it was well-directed and full of venom. 'Now go,' she said. 'Now go. Now go. NOW GO. NOW GO.' And her screams were so loud that the nurses came to escort her out, but before they reached her she had time to watch Edward leaving the visiting room. He was walking unsteadily backwards, and a queer smile forced its way through the frown, put itself in the highly-curved eyebrows, and Alice realized that she had played straight into his hands once again. As she always did. Every single time. Even knowing what she knew . . . realizing what he was . . . she still could not control herself when faced with the reality of him.

They dragged her back to the ward and she wept. Perhaps she *was* mad. Perhaps he had really driven her mad a long, long time ago, and everyone knew it but her.

The wind rustled the grass, her baby moaned, but other than that the night was eerily silent. Little milky-white bubbles softened the lips of the sleeping child and, satiated, his mouth hung slackly open. Love for him was all that warmed her; everything else in her world was frozen hard. She lacked resolve. All she wanted to do was lie down here and cuddle him, possibly for the last time. Maybe she should try to move on. It must be late–morning would soon be here and Alice did not want to resume her journey by daylight. The darkness was dangerous enough. Would Milly be waiting, as promised? Was Milly still her friend, could she trust Milly not to betray her? She'd believed she could trust Nicholas, oh God, she had felt certain she could always trust Nicholas. She'd had such hopes of him. Through her son, Alice had vainly believed, she might, one day, be able to find some justice before it was too late.

# FOUR

The terrible feelings of solitude were worse than the cold and the damp. Alice was numbed by the kind of subservient terror she recognized from old. Her recent encounter with Edward had taken the spirit from her, and the brief rest had not benefitted her for now she could feel every ache in her exhausted body. As dawn came, trailing whitely over the hawthorn hedge that had provided her with a few hours of shelter, she saw a farm in a hollow and was overcome by a frantic desire to make straight for it. How she longed to be warm and dry, to quench her unbearable thirst, to staunch the pangs of hunger. But stronger than this was her need to find a sanctuary, to be spoken to with understanding, held in friendly arms, made safe.

Weak to the point of collapse, Alice had used up all her reserves of strength and endurance. In her distressed state she expected to see Edward taking firm shape before her like the rest of the world, and his would be a dark black shape that blanked out all the others. The sky became streaked with light, the grey trees were turned into black, and slowly, separately, the smells of the night turned into the hotter, more earthy smells of the day. Alice had managed to stay free for twenty-four hours.

If it was not for her child she would have stayed where she was and slept. But he was real and he needed her. She no longer cared for herself, but for the baby's sake she had to try. Blindly, wearily, hardly aware of what she was doing, just that she had to make Shilstone, she rose, stiffening, waiting for the voice, Edward's voice, claiming the child once again.

Keeping to the hedges, her dark cloak wrapped tightly round her, Alice gathered the last of her resolve and set off, alert at all times like a mangy cur might cower but continues to listen for the whistle of its detested master.

Over the months Alice learned to accept the ways of Deale Asylum. She learned that by helping the nurses, obeying orders, dealing with the other patients, time passed more quickly. She tried to forget the way they had wrapped her first in freezing cold blankets, then in blankets so hot she could hardly bear them, they blistered her skin. She used to fear desperately for the safety of her baby. She tried not to hear her own screams; they rent her somewhere too deep in her head, somewhere she was afraid to go. Shivering one moment, breathless with heat the next, after that they used to bind her so tight in that cruel canvas jacket she could not move her joints. Sometimes they left her like that, in the dark, all night long and all she could do was blink and swallow. And think . . . but that was most dangerous of all. Only by turning off her brain could she lie still and submit and, in so doing, relax.

Yes, she behaved herself. She helped to restrain the flaming-eyed women who railed in bursts of excessive violence. She helped wrap the head of the young girl who constantly banged herself against the wall so that her wild, straw-like hair was sticky with blood. She bound the hands of the old granny who scratched herself until the blood ran and her old wounds festered, smelling evilly. She scrubbed floors, she collected the filthy laundry, she tended to the dim and dying old hags who lay all day in their beds, gasping. Some had spent their whole lives here . . . would she? *Would she?* And in this way the intolerable place attained a shape and form with a dawn, a midday and a dusk that was not something you could just look out and see through the windows. However, the fear never left Alice . . . for you never knew when they were coming to get you, and you never knew what they would do.

It was hard not to go mad when they came to take you for treatments. And then Alice had found it impossible to sleep and had taken to walking the ward at nights.

But then it was nearly over.

She recognized the first uncomfortable pangs of labour and told the nurse. They were eager to get her off the ward as quickly as possible and down to the lying-in room where she would become the responsibility of others. They removed the straps from her ankles and she shuffled after them through the doors and down the steps. She did not take anything with her for she had nothing at Deale that was her own.

It was a long walk. At the place where the hospital ended the white gave way to red brick and the workhouse began. As Alice followed the nurses, descending the stairs, moving along warrens of corridors, the place became darker and dingier and the smell changed subtly, somewhere in the journey between, from urine to cabbage. They passed across the courtyard and Alice breathed fresh air; she looked up and saw a blustery sky. The wind was blowing! She had forgotten about the wind. She had seen rain on the blank windows, she had compared the rain to tears, the way they dried there dully like the tears that smeared on the old women's faces, but she had not been aware of the wind. Here there were people . . . free people . . . free to leave this stinking place and go outside if they wanted. But the looks on their faces showed they had lost all desire to do so. They backed into the walls as Alice and her escorts passed by, and Alice wondered if this was because of her outlandish appearance – wild-haired, so obviously pregnant, and garbed in that shapeless garment which was little more than a rag. At least here the inmates wore clothes–shabby and patched, admittedly–but still recognizable as clothes. And they wore boots. They did not go barefoot like the patients upstairs.

She halted, exhausted, but they pushed her on. 'We have not got all day to be pandering to you.'

The floor of the room was bricked. On it there was no rug or covering, nothing so frivolous to relieve the

stark task for which the room had obviously been designed. Two iron beds stood in the centre. There was
a stone basin in one corner and a wooden crib by the
wall. The window was tall and high and frosted with
opaque glass that provided a pale dulled sunlight. The
thin black gas-pipe wound its way round the walls and
finished, a one-eyed observer, on the high ceiling between the two beds.

Alice was ordered into the nearest. 'Wait there,' said
the first woman, impatience coarsening her voice. 'Get
in, and the nurse will come.'

And then . . . and then . . . for the first time since
they had forced her from the house at Edward's orders
over seven months ago, Alice Brennan found herself in
a room with an unlocked door. She found herself, at
dear last, completely alone.

# FIVE

'I would give anything in the world to have prevented you from seeing me lying here like this. After so long, Nicholas . . . please believe me, I would give anything.'

So fierce was the memory of the meeting with her son, that as she recalled it, walking along at snail's pace, heaving one foot before the other, passing over the last hill before she dropped down to the village of Shilstone, she spoke her words out loud. The baby stirred. She shushed him.

For twenty-four hours she had struggled, most of that time in a red-hot pain, mostly alone save for the infrequent visits of the midwife and the whey-faced maid with the hare lip who helped her. 'Gentry,' sniffed the midwife. Tiny and buzzing, her words were sharp at the ends, like a wasp. She droned on to her much larger, dim-witted assistant, 'Bound to be trouble. Not used to toil and effort, all rigid and locked from lack of a decent day's work. 'Twill be hours yet, mark my words, and a great fuss'll be made of it if my experiences are anything to go by.' The midwife's mouth was a tight hole and her eyes were stinging points of light. The whites of her eyes were yellow, the colour of old smoke.

The girl hardly moved but stared with wide, awed eyes, and jerked like a clumsy puppet when ordered to carry out instructions by her sharp-faced mistress. She could be no older than twelve.

There were curious gaps in Alice's consciousness when she sank into darkness feeling there was now nothing to lose and that she was no longer involved in any of this but just a casual observer. Somewhere there was a clear, white space high above the pain – if only she could reach it. There were times between when she dozed, and then awoke to the sweat of another contrac-

34

tion and her underfed body recoiled from it, tensing in terror against it. She willed herself to relax, to let the pain take her. She knew that her distressed state of mind prolonged the labour. She remembered her first born . . .

Sweat made her wet like a fish, and oily. She thrashed like a fish while the pain ripped her apart. None of the other times had been as bad as this. And all the while the girl, Nancy, sat watching from the second bed, catching nits from her hair and cracking them with her nails. Alice studied the skin on her face and on her hands, wondering about that, wondering why it was so pale, almost translucent, and wanted to stretch out an arm and touch it. She tried. Her arm was heavy and not her own. The girl jumped away from her, startled, suspicious. She stood up and started walking round the room, regaling Alice with a spluttering of words.

'I'll call Mrs Bates if you don't lie still. I will, I will, I'll call 'er back. An' 'er won't be too pleased, I'm tellin' 'e.'

She thinks I am mad. She is afraid of me. She does not know me. And Alice wept . . . to have someone near her who was not a stranger, who loved her . . . she mourned her missing children while the new one came into the world.

Oh, for some other feeling than fear. Anger would help, anger was nearer to the ground, was easier to grip and had energy in it. But who was there to feel anger at? Edward? What she felt for Edward was not anger. Any rage she felt was directed at herself – so helpless, so full of self-pity. There was no point in looking backwards; there was only one way to go.

Love? No, that was too dull, too far away, too full of pain. So all she was left with was the fear. Fear was debilitating, it was like birth, it hobbled you before it took everything away. What she wanted, what Alice would have liked to have found, was pride.

She dreamed away the agony. The gripping in her

abdomen was another part of the whole anguish of life. Once men has vied for her attention . . . had given her roses, and she had long silk dresses, flowers in her hair, and was beautiful. She was the heroine of all the stories. But all this, it seemed like a secret now, a secret or a lie. Because all Alice could remember was the way people started staring.

Oh, it was taking so long . . . so long . . . and afterwards she would need energy if she was going to escape from this nightmare. There was not even a clock in the room, no ticking to mark the passage of the time.

But time did pass. Her labour intensified. She gripped the sides of the bed, she cried out for water, she thrashed and she flailed but the only sound she would remember later was the quick click of Mrs Bates' boots on the floor and Nancy's moanings. Something left her womb in a rush, hot and piercing. It must have been around mid-afternoon when the midwife held up two mottled legs, shook them as if they belonged to a freshly-skinned hare and cawed, 'It's a boy.'

'Please let me see him. Please give him to me.'

'Why do you want to see the child? You have to sleep now, after we've tidied you up and moved out the paper padding. And 'tis best to leave the child to sleep. Nancy will put the binder on.' Mrs Bates made a great play of struggling with two buckets. Her hands were red raw and Alice knew them to be freezing cold.

'If I could just hold him while you clean up . . . '

'Oh yes, madam, no madam, certainly madam, whatever your bidding, madam. Just say the word and we are only here to obey, aren't we, Nancy?'

Alice's voice trembled with exhaustion. 'I don't mean to sound arrogant. All I'm asking is to hold my baby.'

'Your baby?'

Behind the nurse's smile was the reminder that, in a few hours' time, Alice would be returned to the ward where children were not allowed. It was the slow smile that served to remind the patient that she was mad. Alice tried to sit up, worried about what Nancy might be doing, for the child set up an angry squawling where she dealt with it on the empty bed. Mrs Bates firmly set her hands on her hips and spoke in a high-handed manner. 'Used to the administrations of a nanny, I've no doubt. Shouldn't think you know the slightest thing about children . . . '

Alice lay back, quite silent, done with protesting but her arms felt empty. The pull she felt for the baby pierced her. She wanted to hold him, take care of him, but she would not whine now, now that it was all over. She would not cry or beg any more. And she was used to having her babies taken away. They brought her water. She drank it. They brought her bread. She ate it. And the child lay sleeping in the wooden cot across the brick floor.

Later, it was still afternoon, not yet dark, when Mrs Bates returned with the incredible news, 'You have a visitor. A right fine dandy of a visitor. I should make yourself ready.'

Who? Not Edward again? He would not come for the child so soon! He could not have been informed of the birth! Carefully Alice sat up, wincing, wishing she had pillows because the iron bedstead forced her into an agonized upright position. There was blood on the sheets and she was so sore from the tearing that it was purgatory to slide herself along. She used her hands to lever herself into position. She had no time to straighten the stained night-shift, to smooth her tangled hair or attempt to cross to the basin for water with which she might clean her face and hands. For Nicholas, taller than ever she had imagined him, and more handsome – not at all the gawky, awkward lad she remembered – came striding into the room with his face set grim, ready for anything and then stood, a careful five feet away, looking down on his mother.

On Nicholas, not now, not like this.

Alice caught his eyes and smiled into them.

There was no answer from his own. They were veiled. She noticed the slight tic at the side of them: it gave his apprehension away.

It was then that she said, 'I would give anything in the world to have prevented you from seeing me lying here like this. After so long, Nicholas . . . please believe me, I would give anything.'

'This place!' he said, spluttering, gazing around him in horror. 'I never imagined such a place!'

Alice smiled weakly, patting a place on the side of the bed, hoping he might come to her. 'It is something you never get used to. I, too, cannot get over the horror of it.'

'They say the child is just born.' He stared at her, not bothering to conceal his shock. He kept himself uneasily in the same position, not backing away nor coming any further forward either. He played with the hat he held in his hand, nervously shuffling it round through his fingers. How often had she seen him like this, unsure of himself and embarrassed, as a small boy. She was surprised to hear how sure and true his voice was, deep and even, like his father's.

'That is the reason I look as I do. They don't think that a woman might want to freshen herself up, to make herself look respectable for such an important visitor.'

Nicholas said, 'I wish I had not come.'

She had not imagined the dreamed-of reunion would start like this, but then she reminded herself that this was quite a natural reaction. What, after all, had she felt like on first entering Deale? She'd been full of revulsion. It had taken days for the shock to wear off.

She looked at him, saw the faint flush on his young skin, the slight pout of his mouth, the soft depths of his brown eyes and the way the lashes shadowed and scooped the skin beneath them. She felt so proud of him. He was tall, broad-shouldered, and he stood squarely with a kind of natural defiance, defending himself from the place . . . from her? She said, 'I have longed to see you. I am so very glad you decided to come.'

'I had to see for myself,' he muttered.

She wanted to laugh, for his discomfort was obviously very great. She wanted to hold out her arms to him as she would once have done, to take away his uncertainty, reassure him that all was well. Let's pretend, oh let's pretend that this messy woman with the sallow skin and the disordered hair, sitting so tensely on the bed, had been the one he had run to as a child, had been the woman to whom he brought flowers, small achievements, night terrors. But for all those things he had gone to Milly. Her children had always gone to Milly . . . she had never been allowed . . . She wanted to say, 'It is not what you see, Nicholas, I am still me underneath. And if only you knew what good seeing you is doing for me!' But Alice Brennan did not say that. She asked him, 'What did your father say about your coming?'

His expression turned sharp. 'Why do you ask me that?'

She felt herself under attack. She said, 'I feared you might have had some difficulty persuading him to allow you to visit me.'

'Not so. Not so in the least. Father positively encouraged me to come.'

Alice felt surprise. 'Well, that's good. I'm glad you didn't have to fight your way here.'

Nicholas said, 'You have been ill for a long time now, Mother. Do they treat you well in here? Are the doctors helping?'

Alice closed her eyes. She let her chin sink to her chest. She breathed out slowly. 'There is no question of me being ill, Nicholas. It is a far more complicated situation than that. I am here against my will. I am here because your father wishes it, because it suits his convenience.' She lifted her head, opened her eyes and saw he had moved across the room and was standing above the cot gazing down at the child. 'What does he look like? Is he fine? Does he resemble either of the girls when they were just newly born? Oh, but I suppose you will not remember.'

Nicholas looked round. He played with his hat behind his back and she watched how fast he moved his fingers. 'Why do you ask me these questions? Surely you have seen him?'

Alice shifted painfully in the bed, straightening her legs. 'They would not let me see him. As soon as he was born they took him away.'

Nicholas looked into the cot again. Quietly he asked her, 'Why did they decide to do that?'

'It is just their way. They do not give much thought, in here, for a mother's wishes. Would you lift him up and bring him over to me, Nicholas?'

Nicholas hesitated. He peered down at the sleeping child. He looked across at his mother and thought before he spoke. 'I think it is probably better to leave him where he is. He is asleep. It would be a shame to wake him.'

Confused, but suspecting he did not want to betray his manhood by lifting the child, afraid of his own clumsiness, she left it alone. She was afraid of pushing him too hard. But once again she patted the bed. 'Come and tell me, Nicky,' she said, feeling such joy at having her boy so close once again, 'tell me about Kate and Laura. How are they? Did they send any messages?'

Nicholas cleared his throat as he approached, but he stayed in his first position and started to tap his boot with his riding crop. He kept his eyes down, concentrating on his own gesture. 'They didn't know I was coming. I decided it was best not to tell them.'

There was much that Alice did not understand, and she saw that this was bound to be the case. She had been away from home for seven months; Milly had given her some ideas but she did not know for certain what stories her children had since been told. Once again she was a stranger, separated from her own son, and the ground between them was a void that was vast, full of dangerous waters. It would take time for them to meet again, to establish the sort of relationship she had always wanted but that had been, from the very beginning, denied her. But it would happen . . . it would . . . and it would not be long now. Alice needed to make this clear, to make quite certain he understood she was not just someone who would always look like this, could only be visited in such a place, that she did not intend to remain the wretched scarecrow he must see when he looked down on the messy bed . . .

'It will be all right soon, Nicky. You will not have to come here again. It will not be long before I am away from here, free, and with a life of my own. Don't take this image of me away with you. It is, almost already, a thing of the past.'

'Freedom, Mother? I don't know what you mean.' He looked at her sharply.

'I intend to leave Deale very shortly . . . '

He cast a quick glance behind him in case someone was listening, 'What about the child?'

'Oh, I am taking the child with me.'

'Father did not say . . . '

'No. Edward knows nothing of this and obviously I am expecting you to keep my secret.'

'Your secret?' His frown was quick, like an imp, leaping, hardly there before it was gone into hiding again.

'I have no alternative. If I don't leave here I will go mad like all the others. I have this one opportunity, and I have to take it.'

'Mother, you are weak and ill. Look at you! You are nothing but skin and bone and you have just borne a child.'

'What would you have me do, Nicholas? Abandon the child and meekly allow them to lead me away up the stairs again?'

'But all this . . . ' he stopped tapping his boot and gestured round the room with the end of his whip.

41

'Surely you endure all this . . . surely this is being done in order to help you. Charlotte says . . . '

Alice held her chin in her hands. Look at her nails! She noticed her torn, untended nails. Ashamed, she folded them in her palms when she interrupted him. 'You must not believe what Charlotte, or your father say about my illness. I know it is hard for you, but one day you will understand . . . '

Nicholas coughed like a gentleman. He left his fingers at his lips, just two, about to send a kiss. 'When do you intend to leave here, Mother? And where would you go? Have you the money you need?'

'I daren't tell you where I'm going, save to say that I still have friends and I'll not need money. All I need is strength, stamina and determination, and a little encouragement from you, Nicholas, would not go amiss.'

'You know I have your welfare at heart. That is why I have come. But I don't think this plan of yours is a wise one. In the state you are in . . . '

'I have no choice–it has to be now. I can't bear to be parted from yet another of my children, nor can I bear to spend another night and day in this madhouse. You have listened to me, Nicholas, do I sound mad? Do I sound as if my mind has gone, as if there are no thoughts in my head, as if I need to be kept behind bars for the rest of my life?'

'Mother! I fear for your health should you attempt such a reckless journey. Surely there must be another way. Have you spoken to the doctors?'

Alice laughed. She burned between her legs. She flinched. The laugh turned into a sob when desperately she explained to the innocent before her, 'They do not listen to me. They have never listened to me! They only listen to Edward.'

'Who loves you.'

'No, Nicholas, no! That is not the case. That has never been the case.'

'I don't want to hear any more. You put me in an

42

impossible position. I want to stay loyal to both of you and yet by supporting one I upset the other. I don't think you should take such an ill-conceived course. I don't see how any good can come of it. I think that in time, all will be well . . . '

'Nicholas, you do not understand. Listen to me!'

'I can't, Mother. I can't.'

'But you will keep my secret?'

Nicholas stared at his mother, that witchy woman he saw lying there, scratching herself with her long nails, blood-soaked linen trailing down the side of the bed, eyes bloodshot and wild as she pleaded, dirty hair matted–undressed, messy, wild. He hardly recognized her as the mother she had been. In a voice that was gentle he said, 'I will keep your secret.'

And so Alice smiled, patted the bed once again, and this time he came and sat beside her, not wanting to touch or be touched, but she felt the nearness of him, the fresh, outdoor smell of him, she traced his hair, the contours of his face with her eyes as she dare not do with her fingers. And she loved him, oh she loved him, and she trusted him implicitly.

And then Nicholas had gone away and betrayed her. As simply as that! He had betrayed her. And Edward must have decided not to inform the Asylum of her intentions, hoping the journey would do his work for him and kill her. With an awful certainty Alice knew that, if he had succeeded, he would have taken the child from her, and left her alone to endure the night, frozen half to death and maddened with sorrow.

She would not have survived.

She was down from the hill, and in the lane that led round the back of Shilstone village. Dawn – a dangerous time, and she saw the first spirals of smoke from the cottage chimneys touching the chill air with trailing blue fingers. Soon people would be up and about, the farmworkers, the farrier, the waggoner's boy, the milkmaid. She must be careful to avoid the drunk who

43

might even now be dragging himself up from under the wall in the sombre light of daybreak. A solitary cat ran stealthily across the lane and stopped to regard her slyly before padding away into the mist.

She willed the baby to stay silent. She had only to cross the road, pass by the churchyard, go through the gates of Winterbourne House and up the beechwood track to Milly's cottage. Safety! Oh, how she craved it. But never had so simple a task seemed so immense.

The earth breathed out a frosty white smoke as she reached the churchyard. The steeple disappeared half-way up, giving way to the sky. The wet grass dripped and soaked her skirts. Her boots were no protection from the damp or the cold. They did not fit–they were stolen boots, as was the cloak, and underneath she wore the same thin night-shift in which she had given birth.

After Nicholas left, swearing secrecy, Alice had spent the night resting but waiting for dawn, for that was the time she had chosen. She prayed that she'd find the door unlocked, that they would consider her too weak to need guarding. When the dark began to change and the first feeble cold light began to shine through that frosted window, she had risen quietly, crossed the floor and picked up the child, hardly looking at him before cautiously opening the birthing-room door. She had crept along the passageway, felt her way along it, struck by the desolation of this noiseless, deserted place. Her feet were quickly frozen and her limbs ached with the cold before she found the arched front door and the pegs, on which hung a selection of shabby cloaks; just two pairs of boots were lined up underneath. She had no time to hesitate, or be choosey. She had dressed herself as well as she could, had eased open the door, cast not a glance behind her and stolen away, heart beating as though she were a thief, darting out into freedom clutching her baby.

Just twenty-four hours ago.

Now the weakness she had held at bay for so long during the endless journey crept up on her. She stumbled, and clutched at a gravestone for balance. She clung to it and sagged, before attempting just a few more futile steps. Not now! Don't let me give up now!

But it was no use–she could not go on. Alice sank down beside a marble angel. It loomed huge above her; the cold grass soaked her thin dress and she stared up at the statue, attempting a prayer. But it stared back coldly, accusation chill on its face; its arms were outstretched, but to whom? It offered no comfort.

She closed her eyes. The child cried. All was lost. She had tried, she had tried her best and failed. She could do no more. She was bound to be found, and nobody in this village would think twice about betraying her to Edward. News of her madness had travelled far further than this and for anyone to see her in her present state, well, they would need no confirmation. She knew what she must look like. What her shuddering sobs must sound like.

She was finished.

So when she heard the footsteps she did not immediately look up. She just lay where she was and dropped a kiss on the head she held so tightly against her. She expected to feel arms dragging her up, hear a rough voice enquiring, see a face full of distaste and lacking in any understanding. Nothing. The footsteps had stopped. The owner was not about to make any sudden movement.

Eventually, squinting against the first real rays of sunlight, Alice looked up. There was no hope in her glance. Beside the angel was a man, dark as the angel was pale and casting as large a shadow, but the expression he wore was nothing like that of the statue.

A gardener, come early to work? No, he had not the gentleness, the patient features of a gardener. She gave a small smile – God, then? Inspecting His ground before there were people about? Oh no, this man was not the God of her childhood . . . he could be cast from bronze with his weathered skin, tight black curls, the velvet facings on his coat and cuffs and his hat at a rakish angle. She noticed his coat had a shiny white lining . . .

He did not ask the expected question. It was in his eyes . . . his coal-black eyes which he rested mildly, quietly surprised, first on her and then on the child.

There was one chance. Only one. Before she fainted Alice took it. She summoned up what strength she had left and she whispered, 'I need to get to the cottage of Milly Toole. For the love of God please help me.'

And then, mercifully, she knew no more. She sank into a velvet dream that was shot with colour and full of voices, a make-believe, fantasy world so deep and so vast it was like nothing she had experienced before. She closed her eyes and she let it take her.

# SIX

Milly Toole crossed herself when she saw the shadow darken her door. It is Edward, she said to herself. That black devil Edward has come to wait with me!

She crouched and contorted below her small window as she tried to see who was knocking. She rubbed the pane. She muttered quietly to herself, calming words . . . 'Milly Toole, get a hold of yourself. Pull youself together. Your foolish flushed face and your unsteady breathing will give everything away.'

Perhaps if she pretended she could not hear?

She glanced at the grandmother clock. Half-past six. Any good woman would still be in bed at this hour, not hovering here waiting, tense and quivering like a hunting dog.

The knock came again. She would have to open that door eventually, the tone of the knock told her so. This visitor had no intention of going away. If she did not go to the door soon he might come to the window and look in and find her . . .

She crossed the room, entered her tiny hall and felt the gusts of cold air coming under the door. She gathered her courage, straightened her back, set her face and opened the door.

Her eyes widened in fear. It was not Edward. She crossed herself again, only half-aware of the man's horse which was tethered to the gate. She saw the limp burden he held in his arms, she heard the cry of a child from the saddle, and Milly stepped forward and held out her arms.

'Oh, blessed Jesus, it's her. She's come, and what has happened? Take her inside quickly, take her in by the fire, and the little mite . . . ' Milly stepped aside, allowing her dark visitor through before hurrying down her path. The child was wrapped and strapped to the

47

saddle-hook as though he might be a pouch of spare clothing. She stretched up on tiptoe to her full height, bit her lips hard in her struggle to release him. Catching the baby in her arms she bustled back to the cottage, anxiety crumpling her face almost out of all recognition. She exhaled a huge breath of relief when safely inside again, and she closed and bolted the door behind her.

Alice was laid on the chaise by the fire, and Luke Durant was on one knee beside her, drawing up the patchwork blanket, glancing around him as well he might . . .

Deftly Milly laid the child in the chair and began to unwrap him. 'There's water in the kitchen, newly boiled.' She cast her quick words over her shoulder. 'Go fetch it and bring it to me, and the towels beside the range. There's good hot stock in the pot, thick as soup, so add some brandy to that and see if you can't get some down her throat.' And then, inspecting the child so closely that she missed not a mark, not a wrinkle in the tiny body, she added, 'And put some of the water in a ladle of milk from the churn, and bring it to me. I will get him to suck from my finger.'

The voice that answered her was doleful, tinged with only slight amusement. 'And what would you have me do first, Mrs Toole? What has gone wrong with your own lazy hands?'

She turned. She had to raise her chin very high in order to meet his eyes. She said, 'They promised that if you ever came back here they would hang you.'

'They say many things, Mrs Toole, for words are cheap and easy to give away. Putting their brave threats into practice is an entirely different matter.'

Milly sniffed at his insolence before lowering her gaze. Ignoring her, Luke disappeared into the kitchen and she heard him moving around in there, obeying her instructions. Just for a second she thought, how bizarre . . . nobody would believe her if she told them. Here she was in her little cottage, issuing instructions

48

to a wanted man as if she did it all the time, as if there was nothing remotely strange about it!

She picked up the now naked child and went to sit by the mother. 'Alice,' she whispered gently, stroking the matted hair back from the pale face, letting her fingers follow the cheekbones, round the face and back again. Softly. Lovingly. 'Alice, you are safe. Your baby is safe. Milly's got him now, see here, Alice . . . see here.'

Not once during all those terrible years had Milly seen Alice looking so gaunt, so ill. Her hair, once honey-gold and beautiful, was almost colourless now. Her face was so thin that every bone was pushing out, trying to break through the skin, but failing and leaving a shadow instead. But in spite of all that, she was still lovely to Milly. Unaware of what she was doing, Milly gently attempted to wipe the marks of travel off the woman's face. She kept the action going when the eyes opened, and, startled, afraid, Alice tried to sit up. Immediately Milly held up the child. Free of his wrappings, he held out his tiny arms, making small fists on the ends of them. His legs curled up and kicked like a tadpole. 'Here he is, darling, here he is. Now let me put him inside your blanket with you. It's all over. Wake up, Alice, come on now my dear, wake up.'

'Milly! Oh, Milly!'

Milly sat back and allowed Alice to weep. She wept as she stared at the baby, fingering his body, resting his flopping head in one hand while with the other she opened his fist, stroked the bottom of his foot so that his toes curled, caressed the minute shoulders. A tuft of gold hair stood to attention; she wept as she smiled at Milly and blew on it. And when Luke returned to the room, looking like a doctor with a towel over one arm and a basin in his hands, she continued to weep.

'You,' she said, gulping between her tears, opening her eyes wide and looking up. 'The man in the churchyard! And I thought you must be the Devil . . . '

Milly tutted but thought it more prudent to say nothing.

'And I? Could I be forgiven for thinking you must be the gravedigger's first job of the morning? Left over, perhaps, from last night?'

'A corpse?' And Alice wept and laughed at the same time. 'You were brave then, to pick me up. I could have been carrying fever.'

'Madam,' he said, bowing slightly, 'your skin is too smooth to ever have been touched by fever.'

'Tut,' said Milly Toole, and Alice watched with fascination as expertly Milly dripped milk on to the tongue of the child who sucked hard at the old woman's little finger.

Alice tried to sit up, 'I can feed him . . . '

'You have given him enough for now. You rest. Leave him to Milly.' And Milly nodded so that Luke passed over a wooden mug into which he had broken white bread. 'Get that hot soup down you. And when you have both finished I will bathe first the child and then his mother.'

Tears still flowed from Alice's eyes. She stopped trying to staunch them because the effort was useless. The food tasted of early childhood . . . soft, savoury and home-made, comforting every inch of her as it went down. She took in every corner of the homely cottage with her eyes. It is marvellous what madness can do . . . and the will to go on dreaming, no matter what. Nothing had changed here, it was just as she wanted it. It was the one place on earth which had not changed, not since they came to Winterbourne House fifteen years ago and Milly had insisted on being given a cottage, 'So that I can keep my independence. It is important to me. And I want to know I have somewhere to go in my old age, in my dotage.'

'You would always be welcome here in the house. I have never considered you as my servant.'

'You're a married woman now. You don't need a nurse in attendance at all times.'

'But my children will need a nurse.'

'And I need a home of my own,' said Milly.

50

Edward had backed her up. 'I can understand that. I know the perfect cottage, far enough away so that you will feel private, and yet near so that we can call on you when you are needed.'

Reasonable, ah yes, but then Edward was always so dauntingly reasonable.

Had he, even then, made his plans? Was he eager to get Milly out of the way? Even now Alice wasn't exactly sure when it had all started – but what did that matter now? She was safe in her head, safe in a place of her own making. She let her eyes move round this safe place, this haven. How often had she come here for sanctuary in these past years, knowing that here she would be listened to, knowing she would see no criticism in Milly's eyes, that Milly would understand and support her. She let her eyes rest on the gentle watercolour on Milly's wall, the beloved clock, the rag rug they had made together, the nursery chaise from home where she had been laid for rests when she was little, the silver candle-holder, the embroidered fireguard. These familiar things were balm to Alice's eyes. So real! So real! And yet still she wept, as if she had not done so for so long she had much to catch up on and knew that this was a safe place in which to do so. The only unfamiliar thing in here was the tall dark man with the jet-black eyes and the wry smile. He was wrong . . . he was far too large for this small room. And why had she conjured him up?

She knew why. She needed a man for the feeling of safety. If the circumstances had been different she would be amused by her own cunning.

Milly had called him Luke. But Alice noticed the odd way in which Milly reacted to him, motherly and yet not so, familiar and yet withdrawn . . . almost as though she feared him – and yet how could this possibly be? Luke Durant was her saviour. Without him, Alice would either be lying in the churchyard still, or taken by some villager to Edward, who would be waiting. That was probably what was really happening, so

51

terrible that she'd managed to block it all out. She had learned to perfect the trick. She must concentrate hard on her dream, she had to. The dark dream man was adding more logs to the fire and bringing warmed strips with which Milly was wrapping the baby. And yet he did not look comfortable in this role. He did not seem comfortable, confined indoors. He seemed to be nervous in this place.

As Alice gradually began to relax, as her tears began to dry while her baby was put in a padded basket beside the fire, she only knew that it did not matter what happened any more. As long as she could stay in her head, as long as she could see Luke Durant, she was safe. It was essential for herself and for her baby that she never, ever, wake up again.

# SEVEN

While Milly Toole bustled around in a motherly fashion, settling the infant, tending to the mother, nagging Luke to move his horse from the front of the cottage to the back in case of unwelcome visitors, the dawn left the comparative darkness of the village, and rose and travelled, concentrating instead upon the vast open spaces of Winterbourne Park.

The high iron gates were crested with a shield of scarlet and gold. Dead leaves rustled under a belt of trees, scattering the rabbits. When the rabbits disappeared nothing moved. The half-bare branches met across the carriage drive. To meet the dawn, dogs began barking, cocks in the grain-strewn shippens of the farms began crowing and a small light in the big house at the end of the drive moved restlessly from window to window.

The man who wandered the large rooms was wrapped in a silver dressing-gown. His face was drawn and colourless, his eyes red with fatigue. When the light began to permeate the tall windows he snuffed out the lantern and placed it on a spindly-legged table in the drawing room. He pursed his lips with annoyance when the girl came apologetically into the room to tend to the fire.

'Can't that wait?'

The little bow of her apron bobbed; she paused in the action of shovelling ashes into a covered bucket. 'When will I do it then, sir?'

'Oh, never mind, I suppose you must.'

Edward Brennan returned to his study. He was not yet ready for interruptions. He sank into the leather winged chair beside the fire he had kept alight all night. So, Alice had managed, temporarily, to defeat him. Huge was his humiliation when he had returned to

Winterbourne soon after midnight after a wasted two hours of searching around in the darkness, feeling a fool, steeped in an angry sense of failure. He had tried to convince himself that it did not matter. He had seen her weakly condition . . . it was more than likely she would not survive. On that score he was not worried, but he was concerned about the child. A boy child, too. It was not so easy to cast a son upon the whims of nature, to abandon a son to the ministrations of a doubtful mother who was facing a task almost too daunting to be feasible. He had become far too self-confident of late, and for that he blamed himself. Things had started going too well, and one's wits are not at their sharpest when lulled into a comfortable sense of security.

He would have gone straight to the hospital and collected the child soon after its birth if he had been allowed his way. It was Charlotte who dissuaded him. 'Think, Edward!' she had said. 'Stop for a moment and think. Since Nicholas' visit this afternoon we know that Alice is planning to take the child and flee. We know the route she is likely to follow because there is only one place she can possibly go. We have this information, now let us not waste it. Would it not be far kinder to allow her to follow her foolish plan, remove the child from her when she is out in the open and vulnerable, and force her to face the rest of the night alone? Consider, Edward, her state of mind after that. Consider the possibilities, my dear. Neither of us enjoy the thought of her spending the rest of her life in Deale.'

But – death? To leave her there and allow her to die? Was it really kinder?

Edward blanched, but as usual, Charlotte was right, or would have been right had he succeeded in what they both saw as a simple task. Alice would make her way back to Shilstone, hoping for sanctuary in the cottage of Milly Toole, for no one else would take her in. In order to get there, she would have to pass through the Drewstone Gap and down through the

Wideacre Valley. He had only to wait by the stile to set up his snare, his simple trap.

Edward had underestimated Alice's desperation, had been deceived by those patient, submissive eyes.

But since his arrival back at the house in the cold of the moonlit night, Edward had not been lazy. Immediately he had dispatched James, the head groom, to ride to Deale and inform the authorities there of Alice's likely whereabouts. Edward had failed, and so now it would look much better if arrangements for her speedy return were made above board in the broad light of day by others. And to Edward and Charlotte, it was especially important that things were seen to be done properly.

It was the right thing to do. It was the only course to take. They couldn't be expected to keep her at home any longer. Edward had not liked Charlotte's idea. He had muffed it. And now the day was coming, and soon he would have to face Charlotte's wrath; he would have to see that vivid look of contempt in her eyes, submit to the sarcastic edge to her voice.

How strange it was, the way their love had become almost more pleasurable because of their common loathing of Alice, so that, at first, whenever they met it was to recall some tiny incident, a sentence or a word that would intensify their bitter dislike and so bring them together more closely. For years now they had been bonded by it, and the more positive actions they took, the more ferocious the need to be rid of his wife had become, until it began to feel to Edward that this need was almost completely out of his own control. Like his passion for Charlotte. But he must keep a grip, he must not allow that to happen. There was danger in being driven by pure emotion. Charlotte was more likely to be influenced by that than he was for he, in his own opinion, was a cool and calculating man. It was only in this one respect of his life that his emotions threatened to overpower him, to force him to overplay his hand.

No, let the authorities deal with the situation. He had wanted that from the beginning, but Charlotte had overruled him. Now, as he sat studying the fire, watching the dull flame with dry, tired eyes, he convinced himself that the situation was far more satisfactory as it was. Once more Alice – fate – was playing straight into his hands. He held them in front of him and stared at them.

Edward Brennan smiled. Charlotte had promised him that one day she would be his for always and now that time was surely much nearer. Alice's madness had become more and more obvious as each day went by so that by the end everyone noticed; even the servants reported little incidents to him. He ought to feel sorry for his wife, sick like that, but he didn't. Sitting there, Edward thought of Alice and he watched his white hands clench into fists of their own accord.

The woman had been forever apologizing . . . promising to try to do better! And of course this timid behaviour of hers served to incense Edward more: he felt it perfectly acceptable to punish her.

She had tried to deceive him from the start and if Charlotte had not warned him, he might never have found out the truth.

God! Edward brought his fist down hard on the arm of the chair. The set of his face was severe. They should never have married in the first place. It had not been his wish . . .

And she had shown him so much desire. She had brought it with her to bed – even on their first night together, she had been unable to disguise the sort of woman she really was. It was easy for Edward, back then, to take her, to exploit the needs of a woman so ready to give, so horribly keen to give, for her abandoned behaviour went against all he had ever been taught. 'You behave like a whore, Alice! Like a woman of the street or a courtesan! Have you been taught nothing? It is not seemly for a wife of good breeding to be so needy, to display herself wantonly in this fashion! And you disgust me. It is vile!'

How she had wept. 'If there is something wrong with me then you must teach me,' she beseeched him. 'I did not know it was so wrong to allow you, my husband, to know my true feelings. I do desire you, Edward, I love you, and I cannot help it.'

'Modesty, Alice, please, my dear!' Edward had risen up from the bed and gazed contemptuously down on her nakedness. 'Did they not teach you the value of modesty? I truly wonder what goes on in that head of yours and yes, I have to say this, I wonder if you were truly a virgin when I first took you.'

And he had watched the quick flush that covered her face.

Alice had covered her body with the quilt, her face with her hands, flushed with shame. 'Oh Edward! I want to love you. I want us to be happy. I want to be the kind of wife you desire.' But she had been unable to deny his accusations. Even she didn't have the nerve to do that.

He had kept his voice harsh. He should have loved her. Everything about her cried out for love. She was sweet, she was charming if a little too unsure of herself, and she was a lovely woman. Oh yes, with her satin-smooth skin and her fresh young innocence, there'd been many men who had wanted her. He had thought about Charlotte and of what Charlotte told him to say. 'There are ways for a cunning woman to falsify even that act. I am not a fool, Alice. Now please, for decency's sake, exercise some self-control!'

She had clung to him then. He had disengaged her, finger by finger, put on his robe and left the room.

It had been easy to play with such need as hers, to pretend he was coming to her one night, and not the other. She never knew if his words were true, whether, if he came to her room he would stay, if he roused her whether he would satisfy her, or leave the room filled with disgust and a strict admonishment on his lips. But he invariably wore a smile after he closed the door and

57

went to find Charlotte.

However late he was, he knew that Charlotte would be there waiting, along the corridor and in the bedroom next to his own – the room she had occupied from the very beginning, from her first day at Winterbourne. Oh yes, Charlotte would be waiting, but not in the easy, obedient way Alice waited. Not knowing what her mood would be, this not knowing whipped Edward up into a kind of ecstatic fever so that he trembled violently whenever he entered her room. If he tortured Alice, then Charlotte certainly tortured him . . .

That was how it had started. He had used Alice's love as a weapon against her – she had to be punished and dealt with strictly, Charlotte said, or her behaviour would get out of hand.

And guilt? Edward Brennan smiled grimly into the fire. Yes, he ought to feel guilt, but what other option did he have, what other course could he possibly take? He was not, at heart, a bad man. He was as human as anyone else, wasn't he? He watched the forests flush from brown to red, breathing deeply and knowing how good it was to feel alive. He saw the lilac and may blossom come out, he caught his breath when he saw buttercups dancing over the fields. He stared at the sky, stupidly, sometimes, drenched with the beauty of it all. Yes, he was human. And sometimes the actions he was forced to take had hurt him. A great deal. There was much that he regretted.

Now Edward leaned forward and poked the fire with violence. Alice had brought her misery down on her own head, whether she could help it or not. She forced him to behave as he did. And now, finally, he had no other recourse than to send her away to the madhouse . . .

'Edward, my dear!'

Edward sat forward in his chair and the poker went stiff in his hand. He had not heard Charlotte open the door. The clock on the mantel struck seven.

'I have ordered tea. I was told you were in here.' She

bent over and touched his hand. Even in the morning she smelled enticing, she rustled out scents of bed, warmth and excitements. 'You are frozen! How long have you been sitting here? I am disappointed you did not wake me as I instructed you to, immediately on your return. What happened?'

Charlotte, dressed already and looking fresh as he was dowdy and rumpled, seated herself in the opposite chair. She was not beautiful – even his bewitched eyes did not see her as beautiful, not in the accepted way in which Alice was beautiful. Her features were too sharp for that, her forehead too smooth, too broad, her chin over-narrow, her mouth too prim. She was striking but severe, and the force which was hers came from some-where within. With a pure, cool intensity the wonder of her came from within. Her gaze was clear; the ques-tion alerted her face with a curious eagerness under which Edward recognized a hidden but fearful delight. He felt dumb and stupid before her.

He said, 'They are riding out to fetch her back this morning. Alice will be at the cottage of Milly Toole if she has not already succumbed to the cruel weather.'

Charlotte sat forward, gripping the arms of the chair. She was small-boned, and her hands were small, al-most as tiny as a child's hands, as Laura's hands. 'You failed to find her, then?'

'I found her.' He could not lie. He could never lie to Charlotte. She saw through him, right through to the very marrow of his bones. 'I found her and I lost her.'

'Don't play games with me, Edward. You let her go – out of a misguided sense of pity?'

Quickly Edward reassured her. 'No, I did not let her go. She ran, and her actions were so unexpected, and I was burdered by my mount and by the darkness and so by the time I had gathered myself again there was no sign.'

Charlotte's voice was sharp like a bite. 'Weak, ill, afraid – a woman fresh from childbirth, and yet she escaped you? Where were your wits? How long is that

59

woman, my sister, going to be allowed to plague us?'

Edward shook his head, wincing slightly, waiting for the next angry retort. But they were forced to remain silent because the maid, frail and subdued, opened the door and carefully brought in the tea, setting the small table before the fire and unloading the tray on to it with maddening slowness. Charlotte was silent and Edward could feel the silence across the fluttering white tray-cloths, between the silver, freezing as cold steel, piercing him, like her blue eyes pierced him, holding him. As they had always held him.

By the time the maid left he had gathered his senses. 'We cannot change the situation,' he said, putting a firmness in his voice that he did not feel. 'It is as it is and nothing can change it. I did my best. I have been up all night, thinking. We have a far more satisfactory situation now . . . I would never have felt happy with Alice's death on my hands. The authorities will fetch her back. Alice will never again have an opportunity for escape, they will make sure of that.' He saw Charlotte's questioning eyes. '*I* will make sure of that. They will bring the child here . . .'

'But all this takes so long . . . so long . . . ' Charlotte stroked her forehead with a white, tapering finger.

Edward lowered his voice as he sat forward, trying to say the things that he knew Charlotte wanted to hear. 'And remember, there is always the chance that she did not make it, that they will find her out there in the cold, exhausted . . . '

'Dead,' said Charlotte, in a voice that was dispassionately flat. 'There is always the chance that they might find her dead.'

He watched the neat movements of her wrist as she leaned to lift the teapot. Her dark blue dress was tight at the wrists and at the throat. Her head was forced high by a sapphire brooch, and this gave her a look of pride, separated her from the menial task as she had always appeared to be separated, no matter what she did. Even in bed Edward felt he had never really

60

touched her. She who is so emotional, Edward thought to himself, is almost beyond emotion. She never failed to fascinate him.

'You did not succumb to some foolish sentimentality, seeing her there, with the child, so helpless?' She turned the handle of the cup round to face him, to make it easier for him.

Picking it up he said, 'You know me better than that.'

'Do I?' asked Charlotte, her back very straight as she sat with her hands together, contemplating him out of cool eyes.

'By now, yes,' he said between sips. The liquid was hot. It burnt his lips. 'I think, Charlotte, that you know me better than I know myself. I think you have always known me, and I you. Even, fancifully, I imagine we knew each other before we were born.'

'We were meant for each other,' she said, a little more softly, giving slightly.

'And soon, my dear, we shall have each other,' said Edward Brennan. 'This business cannot go on for much longer.'

Charlotte sat straight, watching as he set the cup carefully on the saucer. 'We shall have to see,' she told him. 'You have to prove your love to me, Edward. Every day I have to see it. I do not accept second best. Last night, with your foolishness, you let me down badly. I shall be interested to see what this day brings.'

And Edward Brennan turned to the door and frowned when he heard the voices of his children, knowing that Charlotte would be further annoyed to hear them so excitable, so loud in the morning.

# EIGHT

Even in a dream you can ache, your heart can break. Alice ached to see her two small girls. She was so close to them now, not half a mile away. How their faces would light up if they saw her! How they would laugh with delight as she folded them into her arms. And then, in her mind's eye, she saw the disapproving face of Charlotte. She saw it over the top of the children's golden heads, chin raised, eyebrows arched, and she imagined she heard her thin voice saying, 'For goodness sake, Alice, curb yourself! Where is your self-control? No wonder they are so overexcited all the time, and unrestrained. Discipline, Alice! If you cannot find it within yourself then try to instil some into your daughters. They have been in your charge for too long. And Milly is no better. Between you, you have ruined them!'

And Alice would force a smile to her face although she felt like crying, knowing that Charlotte, as always, was right. Certain that, yes, as a mother she was too demonstrative, forever wanting to romp and play, to read books to her children, play the piano for them, help them with their games and their lessons. She had put her own arms behind her back and grasped them at the wrists. She must learn. Edward and Charlotte were quite right to chastise her.

And so she had naturally agreed to allow Charlotte to become their teacher.

'Go to your room,' Charlotte scolded, 'and find something worthy to do with your time. Do not involve yourself entirely with your small children. It is not seemly. It is, in fact, quite embarrassing.'

An hour ago Luke Durant had left the cottage, 'To make the necessary arrangements,' he told them. When he returned he explained that there would be a short wait. 'But everything is all right,' he said to the shivering Alice. 'Everything is well in hand and you must not worry.'

Alice watched Milly prepare a bag for travel. She watched Luke closing the cottage, fastening the shutters, dampening the fire, and she heard him moving the pans from the kitchen range. For two hours she had dozed. She was clean, and dressed in one of Milly's afternoon frocks. It was far too large, ludicrously unfashionable, and she'd had to ask for a belt to prevent the garment from falling off her. But after the clothes she was accustomed to wearing Alice felt like a queen. Milly had cut and filed her nails. Milly had spread ointment on her sore legs and bandaged them. Milly had washed her hair over a basin of warm water. It was the first time it had been washed in months. And Alice had cried out and protested when Milly straightened the tangles. She had felt just like a child again, and Milly had chided her just the same. 'Milly knows best. We must get these out, Alice my dear, we cannot have you going around looking wild as a gypsy child.' And all the while Luke sat in one of the fireside chairs, sipping the ale Milly gave him, listening to the stories they told him with various expressions of surprise or disbelief, fascinated by the woman who lay on the chaise, whose smile was not a real smile and whose tears were not real tears.

Why had he picked her up and done as she asked him? It was not only her beauty that drew him – for it was there, beneath the pain, even her torments had not extinguished that – it was her whole being and manner, as if she inhabited some other world, and he wondered how she could bring herself to speak of the man who had given her so many years of suffering.

Edward's first plan had been foiled, but they would come. Soon, someone would come, they would not leave this woman and her son. Luke was prepared for them, but he would rather get the women and the child away first. What he could not understand, and what he found himself forced to ask, was why Alice had submitted for so long. How had she not realized what was going on? How she had allowed these terrible things to be done to her?

Alice, listening to Milly talking as she packed a travelling chest, picking up bits and pieces she said she could not bear to leave behind, was asking herself the same questions. And still she could find no answer, no answer convincing enough to give this man who expanded with anger as he listened to the small incidents they related as they called them to mind. Why had she allowed Charlotte to dominate her like that? Why had she given up the care of her own children? Why had she allowed herself to be treated like a child?

'And you must have known,' said Luke, one leg folded over the other, far too large for the chair, and uncomfortable in it, 'you surely must have known of your husband's relationship with your sister. Can you have been blind on top of everything else?'

'Leave her alone!' said Milly sharply. 'Hasn't the poor soul been through enough without having to put up with your ignorant accusations?'

'Perhaps your overprotective manner did not help the situation at the time,' Luke replied shortly.

'And since when have you been in a position to criticize the behaviour of others, Luke Durant?' And Milly gave him a knowing look that passed Alice by.

What was he? Who was he and why had she chosen a man like this? He was roughly dressed, but not, Alice knew, in common clothes. His garments might be travel-stained, well worn, but they were of rich material and his boots were of best leather. He wore his black hair too long, it curled to his collar, and he had the rugged complexion of an outdoor man and yet his hands were not rough or workworn. She could not place him. He did not come into her terms of reference, she had never known such a person. Milly knew him, and yet was unwilling to draw too close to him. He was an enigma and she wondered if she would be able to touch

64

him. Dream or no dream, she didn't want him to know what had happened. She did not want him to think her a silly, empty-headed woman, manipulated in such a humiliating way by others. But she could not prevent Milly from talking, and Luke was eager to know.

Alice supposed she had always been a little afraid of Charlotte. Not only afraid, but guiltily aware, since she had been constantly told so, that she had everything while Charlotte had nothing. That had been the way their childhood had gone. Alice was the first-born. There was no son, so the lands and estates would go to her . . . the beautiful, demure, elegant Alice, while Charlotte would have to do the best she could with her plain looks and her gauche ways. And yet Charlotte was bright—she had outshone Alice in the schoolroom, in wit and in conversation. Charlotte's manner was always brusque, brisk, and her nature devious and underhand, while Alice, pretending and hiding in day-dreams, appeared to sail happily over the top.

So she had always tried to do right by Charlotte, to make up for the benefits her sister lacked. She could understand why Charlotte was bitter and moody—wouldn't anyone be so, under such circumstances?

'And the circumstances were slow to change.' She tried to explain it to Luke, but he remained unconvinced, making her feel feeble and ashamed of herself for her weakness. 'It is not as we tell it, is it, Milly? Time is a funny thing. I think you can achieve anything if you have time on your side, and Edward and Charlotte were not in a great hurry.'

'Who knows, and what is the use of talking now? What's done is done, and what we have to face now, is the future.' Milly was growing anxious as time went by. She kept glancing nervously at the clock and repeating, 'Are you sure they will come? Will they pass by our house? And will we be safe with them, whoever they are? Why do you still refuse to tell us, Luke? Can we trust you, or is this merely one more of your hair-

65

brained schemes?'

Luke remained calm, but underneath it was obvious that he wanted to be away . . . that as soon as he could he would be out of that chair and doing. Impatiently he tapped his fingers on the glossy top of Milly's mahogany table. The energy of the man, even as he sat there, filled the room. It flushed, it overpowered Alice, and yet there was a certain gentleness about him . . .

'I don't think you have much choice, Mrs Toole, other than to fall in with my plan. From where I stand it seems that you can either stay here and be taken, or attempt flight by yourself with a sick woman and a newly-born child, but you'd not get far. Or you can trust me.' He smiled when he said this, knowing that his last suggestion and the way it was put would annoy Milly. Alice was startled by that smile and the effect it had on his sparkling eyes.

'We are so grateful for your help,' she started. 'Without you I cannot bear to think what would be happening to me now . . . '

'Save your gratitude for later,' snapped Milly.

'But Luke had no need to remain with us this morning, or to help with the packing, or to listen to the distressing story we have told him. There must be other, more pleasant pursuits with which he could be passing his time.'

Alice asked because she wanted to know. There was much that she wanted to know about Luke Durant. All her senses were keen. Some colour had returned to her face and it touched her cheekbones and brought out the blue of her eyes. The cause for most of this renewal of her beauty was fear. She listened. She willed Milly to hurry. She cursed her own weakness, sitting there when there was so much to be done. At any moment she expected to hear a knock at the door . . . and see Edward, or Dr Myers with two brawny nurses at his side and the Asylum carriage at the gate. Alice shivered. She glanced at the child asleep in the basket. She held out her hands and saw that they trembled.

But whenever she aired her fears Luke reassured her, 'I swear to you, please believe me, that with me here they will not take you. Even if they come they will not take you. It's hard to wait, there is nothing worse than waiting, but to act out of haste would be foolhardy. We have the child to think of, and you in your condition. I would rather this be done properly.' And he smiled up at Milly again when he repeated his words, 'You have to trust me!'

Milly responded with a tight-lipped sigh.

'I should never have come here . . . ' Alice began.

'You did not know that Nicholas would betray you and I had no way of warning you. You were right to come here. In normal circumstances we would have had the time to make proper arrangements. We could have left in a dignified manner . . . '

'But even without Nicholas, Edward would have known I would come here. He would have found me eventually.'

'There was no other course you could have taken,' said Milly with finality. 'And you're here now, and Luke is here, and we have no other recourse than to go with him.'

Luke was the first to hear the wheels on the path. He leapt to the window and, for the first time, Alice noticed the two guns at his belt as he flicked back his coat. Who was it? She thought her heart would burst from her chest. Milly's first reaction was to pick up the baby, and then she moved quickly to Alice's side.

'Who is it?' Milly's whisper came out as a growl. They could hear horses now, and heavy springs creaking. There seemed to be many, but only one paused at the gate. 'For the love of God, Luke, speak to me! Who is there outside?'

Luke relaxed. He saw the panic in the faces of the two women and he smiled. 'Come and see,' he said, holding out his hand to guide Milly. She approached the window. She bent, peered, and her face fell slack with astonishment.

'But . . . that's a circus,' she said, aghast. 'That's the fair that has spent the last week on Shilstone Green. Was it to them that you rode after breakfast? You said it was friends you were contacting. Who are these people . . . and how are we expected to ride with them? You have the Lord Venton's daughter in your keeping, and you expect her to ride in a circus wagon!'

'It's a damn sight better than the madhouse van,' he said, smiling even more broadly. 'And a travelling fair is the last place Edward would think of looking. I'm certain such people are so far below his contempt that he hardly sees them.' Purposefully he moved across the room into the hall and opened the door. Astonishment kept the women silent. When Luke returned he was accompanied by two brutish men who said nothing but picked up the luggage effortlessly and hauled it away. 'It is a most high-class circus, Mrs Toole,' said Luke, still smiling. 'We draw huge crowds wherever we go. We are actors, mummers, jugglers, clowns. I must warn you that there are freaks among us, too, and wild animals. But the quality of our plays is of world renown!'

'Well!' Gasping, Milly turned to Alice. 'I had not imagined this.'

But I would. I would imagine it. Alice was eager to be gone. She pushed back the covers, stood up, swayed and almost fell. Luke Durant was immediately at her side. He caught her, lifted her up like a doll and smiled into her eyes. 'How does the daughter of a noble lord feel about her new mode of transport?' he asked her, and his eyes were black and twinkling.

Milly would not go out without her hat. Before the mirror she removed her cap and replaced it with a mannish affair, a lark's wing swathed round the band. She turned the key in the lock before she walked down the path, nervously looking this way and that, following Luke and his precious burden. She carried the sleeping child. Briefly she looked back at the cottage. When will I see you again? she asked silently. What will become of us now? At my age I am too old, too set in my ways

68

for an adventure such as this. And yet she had no alternative but to go. Apart from the fact that she would not have dreamed of allowing Alice to depart by herself, let alone with someone with a reputation such as that of Luke Durant, she knew that Edward's revenge would be vicious. She would be driven from her cottage anyway. She might lie, she might pretend that Alice had never been here, that she had not seen her or heard from her, but Edward was not a fool. He would not believe her, of that there was no doubt. No, she would be driven out, and her things thrown after her, with nowhere to go and not enough money to keep herself alive without the few pounds a year given her by Edward as a retainer.

And Alice still needed her Milly. More than ever now she needed someone to take care of her and nurse her back to health. She could have found no stronger protector than Luke, no matter what Milly might think of him . . . what the world might think of him. He would always get by on his cunning and charm, and money was not a problem to a man such as he. But a circus! A travelling troupe!

Milly Toole sniffed and made clucking sounds of disgust as they helped her into the back of the caravan which was gaudily cushioned and, even she must admit, most comfortable. It was complete, a miniature home. The baby remained asleep. They were alone with plenty of room to spread out. Milly helped Alice inside, sorted out something suitable from a garish array of covers, and wrapped her up. The two men who had come for the luggage closed the back of the caravan, but if she sat up in her seat at the back, Milly could just see out.

They set off. With a comfortable exhortation to the horse, not so much an instruction but a short burst of song, the driver set a steady pace. They fell in with the rest of the wagons, red, green, blue, yellow, a curling, travelling, dusty rainbow. Milly saw the church spire disappearing, getting smaller and smaller until it folded

69

away in the hills. Where was Luke now? Why didn't he come and inform them of their destination, put them in the picture? Why did he have to be so secretive? Annoyed, Milly supposed he was forced into it by his scandalous way of life.

She looked across at Alice and, for the first time in forty-eight hours, Milly smiled. Alice looked almost happy, certainly relaxed, and some of the fear had gone from her face. Well, Luke had succeeded there. He had charmed her as he charmed all women. But to trust him, ah, that was a different matter. Should Milly warn Alice, inform her of his reputation, of his past? Milly frowned. She could not do that, not now. Alice must rest, learn what it was to be peaceful again. The nightmare of these last years was over, however temporarily that might be, and why should Milly be the one to raise more problems? She looked around her wryly. Hadn't they enough to cope with at the moment?

The horse clopped along, the wagon rolled and creaked sleepily leaving the cottage and the village of Shilstone further and further behind. It started to rain; the heavy pitpat of water rattled the caravan roof. Milly was glad they were dry and sheltered. The place felt safe, like a cocoon. She blew her nose powerfully on her handkerchief, overcome by sudden, silly emotion. She could do with a comforting tot of rum. Milly was exhausted after her hours of worry, her two nights without rest. It was not long before she, like her mistress, was fast asleep, travelling through the narrow Devonshire lanes to goodness knows where. They did not travel fast–they had no need to. What did anything matter? Nothing could be worse than what they had left behind them. From now on they were in the arms of fate and would have to go where it, and where the scoundrel Luke Durant, decided to take them.

# NINE

The messenger rode up the drive towards Winterbourne House. He was a dour, thickset man on a sturdy white cob, and he had travelled from Deale with the doctor's party, setting off in the early hours of the morning to arrive at the cottage just one hour ago. Jack Corbett was his name and his title was gatehouse keeper at Deale Asylum. A man of little sensitivity and less culture, he eyed the great house with a mixture of awe and suspicion as he approached it.

He mounted the steps and rang the bell and a middle-aged woman appeared at the door with a bunch of keys round her waist. Dignified, and dressed all in black, she took one look at him and said, 'Round the back.' She sniffed, and attempted to shut the door. Corbett was quick to insert his boot. 'Deliveries, hawkers, hikers, I said round the back,' she repeated.

'I'll thank you to afford me a little more respect than this,' said Corbett, who was accustomed to a certain amount of subservience in the small circle in which he moved. 'I have an important message to pass to the master of the house. I am lucky to be here with my life, such a business has gone on this morning and no one, certainly not the Doctor, expecting it. Unprepared we were, totally unprepared for it.' And Corbett hawked and gobbed upon the step.

'What business is this that you speak of?' Mrs Webber's attitude changed. She sharpened up like a needle, all inquisitive now. She opened the door to its full width, to indicate her willingness to listen as well as admit him, and Corbett peered inside, his small eyes opening wide at the grandeur he saw there.

Now he could afford to be disdainful, Corbett took full advantage of the change in the situation, which gratified him greatly. 'It is no business of yours. It is a

71

matter I can only discuss with your master and now, if you would care to show me the way . . . I do not mind waiting.'

'I'm sure,' said Mrs Webber, jingling with metallic indignation, and she showed him through to the front parlour and deliberately took her time when she went upstairs to locate Mr Brennan.

Corbett, humbled by his surroundings, removed his hat. He was fingering the porcelain, assessing its worth, when the door opened and Edward Brennan, dark-suited and in a long frockcoat, strode into the room followed by a stiff, bird-like woman in blue. Immediately Corbett noticed that the man's face was expectantly anxious while his companion's was blank, so tight it showed nothing at all. It was hardly lined. She took a chair, arranging herself in it daintily and even the folds of her dress fell stiffly, but Edward stood before the fireplace, his hands behind his back and his chin up as if to take a blow.

'You say there has been some difficulty?'

Ah, thought Corbett, so we are not regarded as high enough to be granted the courtesy of introductions. Knowing his information was precious, Corbett played upon his host's impatience and insisted on introducing himself.

'I know, I know,' said Edward dismissively, 'I have seen you at Deale, I know very well who you are, but what part did you play in this morning's matter?'

'I act as general assistant,' explained Corbett. 'On these occasions it is often necessary for extra support to be required, and so me and several of my colleagues accompany the party in the conveyance . . . acting as outriders, just in case, you understand.'

'I see,' said Edward, his hands wrestling behind his back, unseen by Corbett who thought the gentleman extremely calm under the circumstances. 'And so you travelled to the cottage to find my wife and escort her back to Deale?'

'Where is she now?'

The interruption by the beady-eyed woman disconcerted Corbett, as did the chill in her voice. He had rehearsed his story on the way and had decided on the most dramatic way to tell it. He had no intention of being persuaded to start at the end.

Corbett thought that the least they could do was offer him a chair. He looked around him pointedly, but the only chairs he could see were spindly, uncomfortable-looking pieces of furniture covered in pink velvet which would offer little comfort anyway. Corbett preferred a wooden chair, with stout arms and legs he could trust to hold him.

'We arrived,' he started. Was there to be no refreshment, either? It would seem not. Edward Brennan stared at him hard and Corbett disliked the man's eyes. They were shifty . . . and he had seen some shifty eyes in his time. 'The cottage appeared to be deserted. There was no answer when the Doctor knocked at the door and the shutters were closed. The gate was hanging open,' said Corbett, frowning as he remembered this small point, 'as if someone had recently left in a hurry.'

'Go on,' Edward Brennan cleared his throat, aware of the harsh impatience in his tone and too late to correct it.

'The Doctor ordered us to break down the door. The deserted look of the place could be a device to deceive us, he said. So we fetched an axe from the woodshed behind the cottage and broke the lock. We went inside, we searched the place from top to bottom, we even turned out the cupboards, but there was nobody there. The water was still hot in the pans, and there was warmth in the fire. We could only have missed them by a very short time.'

'And you went outside and searched the lanes and the fields?' Again the thin woman interrupted, tense behind her question.

'We were just about to do that when they came,' said Corbett. 'On God's honour, ma'am, I have never seen

73

such an army of burly great brutes. Armed with picks and staves they were, like a peasant gathering in revolt, and before we could stop them they had hobbled the horses and wrenched off the wheels of the carriage with their iron bars. Roaring and cursing, they were, savage men with brutal faces. We were greatly outnumbered, there was nothing we could do to stop them. And then a raffish gentleman, well-spoken, not such a ragamuffin as the others, well, he demanded to speak to the Doctor. Now Doctor Myers is a fine man, sir, but not the bravest when faced with such extreme circumstances. And he was cowering round the corner beneath the wall, but they found him, and a group of brutes dragged him into the garden, put a rough noose round his neck and made as if they were about to hang him from the pear tree.'

'Where is she now?'

Damn the woman, thought Corbett, resenting her interference. I will tell it as it happened. Corbett had been badly frightened; he wanted sympathy and a little admiration, for hadn't he been involved in a fracas that could have turned very nasty?

'Hush, Charlotte.' Edward Brennan's voice was careful. 'Let him explain it.'

But Corbett sensed that they considered him a fool and too stupid to deliver the information in a more direct way. He bristled, he adjusted his belt which had dropped from his waist to his stomach. He inserted one hand inside his jacket and stroked the linen shirt that stretched across his broad chest. He was aware that, while the man listened only to his words, the woman watched every movement. She appeared to consider Corbett distasteful.

'They had the Doctor,' Corbett went on, trying to ignore her. 'And the leader of the ruffian band seemed to be conducting a trial, and oh, he was enjoying himself. We could do nothing but stand by. Every one of us was guarded by one of the foul-smelling brigands. If we moved we were poked back into position again,

74

not gently. And every time the Doctor refused to answer, because, of course, he took as dignified a manner as he possibly could in such circumstances, the cocky brigand touched him up sharp with his riding whip. So that in the end the fine Doctor was reduced to a state of nervous shock by this offensive behaviour; he was almost weeping as he stood there with the noose round his neck, over a branch, and a group of disreputable vagrants pulling on the other end of it.'

'What were the questions this man asked?'

Ah, thought Corbett, satisfaction fattening his face. At last I have her interest.

'He asked why Alice Brennan was being held in Deale against her will. He asked what mental condition she was suffering from, and under what law she was being kept in the Asylum. He asked how many others were restrained there like that, and did the Doctor consider himself a doctor or a jailer, there for the convenience of husbands who were eager to be rid of the nuisance of their wives.' Jack Corbett allowed himself the pleasure of a small smile as he watched his listeners' faces.

He went on, 'Of course Doctor Myers assured his rude inquisitor that this was nonsense, put about by sick women with ideas of persecution . . . all part of the sickess, Doctor Myers said. And he asked the instigator of this pantomime what he thought ought to be done. Should he open the Asylum gates and flood the countryside with lunatics and imbeciles? But the gang-leader, well he just put back his head and roared with laughter, but it was not true laughter if you understand me, and the Doctor, all of us, we recognized that. It was not the sort of laughter to be laughed along with, if you get my meaning.'

'Carry on.' But Edward Brennan's voice lacked conviction now, and his eyes seemed heavy with fatigue.

'Then they stripped him completely in spite of his protests. We all protested,' Corbett hurried on to add. 'They left him with not a shred of dignity, standing on

75

his toes with the rope stretched taut above him and his hands tied tightly behind his back. We dared not cut him down at once as we were afraid they would come back, as they had threatened they would. So we stood about, waiting, while the Doctor pleaded and cried that he could not draw another breath unless we loosed him, so tight was the knot, so cruelly had they treated him.' Corbett brought out his pocket watch and held it to the light in order to read it better. 'We must have waited all of ten minutes before we dared remove the good man. He was not eager to remain in the area for much longer, so we put him in the back of the carriage where the patients usually travel, and I left them trying to repair the damage in order to return to Deale. I was dispatched out here to give you the news, and I came,' said Corbett, 'hot foot. No dawdling.'

'So nobody spent any time checking the area afterwards?'

Corbett shook his great head. 'No. That we did not do.'

'And apart from these swarthy brigands you speak of, you saw no one else?' Edward asked him.

'There was not another soul in the vicinity.'

'And there were no faces among your attackers that you recognized?'

Once again Corbett shook his head. 'They were strangers to all of us. They were not local men.'

'Give him a shilling and send him on his way,' said Charlotte to Edward, casting a look towards Corbett that told him she thought him scum. He even saw her checking his feet as if they might be dirty and he could be soiling the fine carpet.

Edward was not quite finished. 'And the Doctor, he had no idea of who the leader of this band might be?'

'He did not say, sir. But then he was in no fit state to say much after his ordeal.'

'Well, thank you, Corbett, for your time and trouble,' said Edward, delving into his back pocket for coins. Corbett swivelled his small eyes round this posh,

76

plush room, at the heavily gilded mirror over the fireplace, at the intricately carved cherubs on the ceiling, at the ornate frames round the oil paintings, and then he took his eyes back to Edward himself, that fine figure of a man with his lordly gestures and confident bearing. And then he turned his attention to the woman in the chair, to her bright, bird-like eyes, the pupils of which could be beads in her head, to her sharp mannerisms, her quick, unwarranted attacks. And Corbett thought of his own wife, that homely brown woman who waited for him in the one room which they shared, for ever counting out the pennies on to the table and wondering if they could afford meat this week, fruit the next.

'I am thinking that there could be some truth in what that villain was saying,' said Corbett, in a change of tone that pitched his voice lower and sent his great booted foot wheeling in a circle on the carpet. 'That there might be nothing wrong with your wife, that there could be reasons for her being held at Deale for so long against her will. Poor soul, forced to escape, and with a newborn child in her arms. It do not paint a pretty picture, sir, if there were anything in the blackguard's insinuations, truly it do not.' And as he went on Corbett's voice began to rise, turned into a wheedle, his smile broadened and he bowed obsequiously as he fumbled with his hat.

'Get him out of this house,' ordered Charlotte, and the last word she used ended in a hiss.

'That is enough, Corbett, thank you,' and Edward tugged the bell-pull to summon Mrs Webber back once again. He was glad that the housekeeper had opened the door and that it wasn't one of the maids. Mrs Webber was not so likely to gossip, but even so . . . this was proving to be most difficult. Damn Alice! Damn that sly old faggot, Milly. But most of all Edward damned himself for failing in so simple a task. And he knew that Charlotte, sitting there so coldly still, would blame him also.

77

'I was merely suggesting . . . ' Corbett had the nerve to whine on while they waited.

Edward dangled the silver shilling. Corbett raised a questioning face, covered with ill-shaven, early morning bristles which the sun rays coming through the window turned to a spine-like silver. 'It would be most unfortunate if this incident should spread round about the place,' wheedled the man. 'You know how some characters enjoy a gossip, and how a suggestion can quickly become a rumour and then fact. It do happen. Oh yes, many times I have seen it happen.'

Edward regarded Corbett with such a glare of disgust that it would quell the bravest of souls, but Corbett was not a sensitive man, and he saw his chance slipping away. 'If I was to receive just a little bit more than this for my pains, not a bribe, mind, nor a payment of that sort, more of a gentlemanly agreement between two involved parties, then I might feel it expedient to make sure this occurrence were not talked about. I am not a man without influence.' Corbett rose to his full height but he was broader than he was tall and was therefore forced to raise his head in order to meet Edward's cold, narrowed eyes.

Edward held out the shilling. 'I do not know what you are talking about, Corbett,' he said. 'You take this shilling or nothing at all and let that be an end to it. My wife is a sick woman, a poor, tormented soul who needs treatment and care. That anyone should take the slightest notice of the vile insinuations cast upon my character by some passing good-for-nothing this morning, that anyone should take such suggestions seriously, is quite monstrous. And well you know it, Corbett. Do you realize that by casting such evil aspersions upon me you are also blackening the name of your employer, Doctor Myers? I do not think he would be pleased to hear of the slurs you seem so glibly to cast upon that man's professional skill and private character.'

Corbett allowed the shilling to drop into his hand. He followed the straight back of Mrs Webber as she escorted him out. He cast angry glances over his shoulder as he rode down the drive on his way back to Deale where he would have to face the Doctor's anger. There would be an enquiry into the incident, and Corbett and his men would not come well out of it. And if he lost his job over it . . . Corbett thought of his wife again and did not allow his mind to dwell upon that dire possibility.

Back in the parlour, Charlotte's gaze was steady and cool. For a while she said nothing, and Edward continued to stand by the fire, clenching and unclenching his fists, staring at the closed door as though he wished Corbett was still there and available for him to direct his anger on.

Eventually Charlotte said quietly, and her fingers curled in her hand, 'Who was their leader?'

Edward got out his handkerchief and wiped his forehead. 'I do not know.'

'Clearly he knew Alice. He was well informed. And worse than that, he cares enough, for some reason, to defend her, to take risks in order to protect her.'

'It was hardly a risk to waylay and torment a hospital party going about their business.'

'No,' agreed Charlotte. 'Not much of a risk, all right, but why did he do it?'

Edward replaced his handkerchief. He held his hands stiffly in front of him, in an attitude of hasty prayer. Doggedly he spoke, 'Do not ask me these questions, Charlotte, when you know full well I have not the answers.'

Charlotte stared at him directly. 'No, you do not have the answers, and neither do I. But one thing is certain, that you must find the answers, and quickly, just as you must find Alice and see that she is taken back to Deale before this whole business gets quite out of hand.' And then Charlotte's face turned to contempt. Edward, seeing this, sighed, stared out of the window, preparing himself for what was coming. 'You see how easily a fumbled situation can lead to events out of our control? If you had succeeded this morning, Edward, and the task, we are agreed, was not a difficult one . . . '

Edward did not find the view outside restful or even slightly comforting. He rested his eyes on the woman he loved . . . hated sometimes, feared, but truly loved. Without her approval he was nothing. Without her support he was a frightened man, not the confident, calm, suave gentleman he presented to the outside world. Without her Edward Brennan was an empty shell, or a shivering child terrified of noises in the darkness. So now he told her, 'I swear to you, I swear upon the lives of my children, that I will find Alice and the child and bring them back, that nothing more will go wrong, and that all I have and all that I am will one day, legally, be yours. I love you, Charlotte. I live and I breathe for you.'

And Charlotte folded her hands in her lap. She looked up at Edward vacantly and gave him a small, cold smile.

# TEN

Half-asleep and half-awake, confused somewhere between the two, Milly opened her eyes and looked at
Alice, comfortable between banks of cushions. So
sweet, so childlike. Oh dear, they'd been through so
many terrible times, like the one when . . .

Milly remembered how youthful Alice had looked in
that slim silk gown the colour of ivory; the breast was
beaded with pearls and the sleeves were small and
puffed like a milkmaid's. Her golden hair was piled
high on her head and decorated with ribbons.

'Where is the money I left on the mantelpiece, right
here, under the lamp?'

'I do not know, Edward, I did not see it.' The ribbons quivered, the small slippers slid nervously one
over the other.

'Oh, come now, Alice, who else would have moved
it, who else has been to the house today? Surely you
cannot be blaming the servants? Surely you are not
suggesting that one of them would come in here, spy
the money and risk her position here in this house for
the sake of one guinea?'

'Of course I am not accusing the servants,' said Alice
mournfully. 'You are always putting words in my
mouth.'

Charlotte spoke then, from the fireside chair opposite Edward's. Alice and Milly shared the sofa beside
the wall. The lamp, which should have softened her
features, only served to highlight their sharpness, and
Milly compared her face to a ferret's when she heard
her say, 'There are too many things going missing in
this house of late, and it is becoming too much of a
coincidence to be called accidental.'

'You think that someone . . . ?' Alice began.

'I think we shall have to enquire into this without any

further delay.' Edward moved towards the bell-pull, the look of enquiry on his face shadowed by a sorrowful, knowing acceptance.

'On no, Edward. For goodness sake, don't call the servants.' Alice stood up, her hands gripped together, and only Milly saw how she trembled. Charlotte's expression was hidden, but she remained seated in that chair by the fire with her feet set neatly together.

'It was me,' said Milly, so suddenly that she surprised even herself. 'I saw the money there and I thought someone had forgotten it, or had been careless, so I took it upstairs and put it away in a safe place.'

'Oh?' Edward's hand hesitated on the bell-pull. While Milly watched, that padded, crimson pull turned into a snake, and Edward into a sly-eyed charmer who was forced to calm it for the sake of his audience. Milly saw the questioning glance he directed towards Charlotte, but for once Charlotte was not answering. She kept her eyes cast down. Reluctantly Edward returned to his chair, saying, 'I think it might have been more considerate, Milly, if you had spoken out earlier. It would have saved a great deal of unnecessary fuss . . . '

' . . . and worry,' added Charlotte, looking up with a look of pained unhappiness.

'Well, I've spoken up now,' said Milly firmly, 'because it is quite clear that you were trying to blame Alice. And why you should have immediately jumped to the conclusion that Alice took that money is quite beyond my understanding. What use would money be to Alice? She rarely goes out, and if she needs money she asks for it. Always has.'

Edward cleared his throat softly. 'Perhaps you would fetch the money, Milly, if it is not too much trouble.'

'Certainly,' Milly replied. As she left the room she was aware of Alice's anxiety. Alice, who knew that Milly had not taken the money, and who feared that she did not have it to return. Ah, but Milly sent her a reassuring smile before she closed the door because she did have the money – she had one golden guinea hidden away for good luck amongst the buttons in her button box. Flushed with triumph she returned to the room holding it up between finger and thumb as though it were something most rare and precious. She saw Alice relax immediately. There was even a little smile on her face . . . wan, but the smile was there.

Edward's stare was a weary one, full of tired understanding. He rose from his chair and took up his favoured position before the fire with his hands clasped behind his back. Charlotte was so silent there could be a scream coming out of her. Edward made no attempt to take the money, although Milly held it eagerly towards him. 'The money to which I refer was in small coins,' he said softly. 'So why do you bring me this, Milly? Who are you trying to protect?' And without further ado, without waiting for any stumbling explanations Milly might try, Edward walked towards the bell-pull and tugged it.

Oh yes, Edward Brennan had always been a trouble-maker.

Even then.

And Milly Toole, who had a lifetime's experience of assessing children's faces in order to encourage, quell them, or placate their moods, knew it instinctively the first time she saw him standing down there, not slim, but thin, in the great hall under the crystal lights of the chandelier. His eyes were little bits of coloured glass made sharp.

Broughams, barouches, victorias and phaetons were still arriving, swishing pink gravel as their pin-prick lights wavered far down the distant drive, seeming to come and disappear again as they navigated the avenue of wind-thrashed beeches. They left the park behind them and swept on under the arched gateway, wheels spinning backwards. They cut between the gas-lit domes and came towards the dignified steps of Venton Hall. The coachmen, top hats jammed hard down on

their heads, climbed down, opened the doors and lowered the steps for the luxuriously dressed guests who
hurried out, beleaguered but chattering brightly under
the dubious safety of great black umbrellas. Some of
the ladies, their dresses swinging like bells, screamed
and gave little moaning noises as the weather attacked
their feathers and furs. Clouds scudded overhead
across a frantic white moon which tried to peer
through, and slanting needles of rain were silvered by
the arc light at the door.

The laughter from the hall reached upstairs, along
with expensive scents, all of it interwoven by the magic
threads of a Viennese orchestra.

Extra maids and footmen were needed to take the
cloaks made heavy with water that night. They piled
them over their arms before ferrying them down to the
kitchens where they would attempt to dry them over
the racks above the enormous ranges – hopeless work.
Even they seemed excited tonight, red-faced, bright-
eyed and breathless.

'What a terrible night!'

'Isn't it awful? I feared that the bridge by the cattle
road might be under water but Sefton said it was safe
to go on . . . '

'Terribly good to see you. I think the Everards have
arrived. You'll find them if you care to go
through . . . '

Lord and Lady Venton, the perfect hosts, greeted
their guests after haughty announcements, at the top
of the ballroom steps.

Milly, dry, warm and crisply uniformed, and smelling as usual of cosy ironing, was bunched up fatly on
the first landing, her large face peering down through
the banister railings. Beside her were her three girl
charges, frilled and angelic in their lacy nightgowns
with their long hair loose and brushed a hundred times.
Her sweet things, Milly called them – Alice, Charlotte
and Lucinda. Alice pointed a finger through the bars
and spoke loudly so as to be heard above the music. 'I

84

know who that boy is! That's Edward Brennan from Winterbourne. Sometimes I've seen him out riding with his papa.'

'Don't point,' said Milly. Alice's wrist was frilled. Withdrawn so quickly like that, burnt by her sharp admonishment, Milly was put in mind of fish spying danger and darting to hide behind a rock. Immediately she was sorry she had spoken to Alice so sharply, and then annoyed to be made to feel in the wrong like that. Sometimes the child could be too sensitive for her own good.

They gazed down through the branches of the Christmas tree, through the haloes of white light cast by the candles, through the resin-scented green that was not green at all but crimson and emerald and a magical, fiery blue. In the candlelight the colours blurred and became a deep midnight for the silver stars. One star, larger than all the rest, was tied to the topmost branch of the tree and if you leaned forward dangerously enough, Milly was sure you might be able to touch it. Her responsible position made it impossible for her to attempt it.

Milly had already noticed the Brennan lad, the way he handed his cloak to Jarvis at the door with a flourish, the way he cast his cool eyes around the hall, smiled aloofly when spoken to by Katy, frowned as his mother – a hatchet-faced woman decked out in feathers and trailing navy-blue silk – bent to explain that he could stay at the ball until ten o'clock when they considered he would have had enough, and then would it be all right for him to join the rest of the children upstairs?

'Well, of course it will be all right,' said Milly, when asked by Mrs Gurney the housekeeper, a flustered woman with hair so creamy fine it looked like the whipped-up top of a fancy pudding. 'But I'd rather have been given some notice.' Milly was ever a plain speaker, she prided herself on that.

Although the nursery wing was at the top of the house there was no way, that night, of getting away from the music. It seeped, with all the pungent kitchen smells, and even clung to the velvet and damasks of the curtains, the tassels and the tapestries, to take up its strident position in every bend and corner. It was no good pretending there was no excitement, that the ball was not going on downstairs. Milly's charges would not sleep, no, not even when their drowsy eyes drooped so their lashes met and they could no longer see through them, not even after they'd discussed it over and over between themselves, exhausting every last detail, picked it like kittens at a chicken bone. Milly didn't mind at all. They were having a wonderful time and so was she. She gave them hot milk with sugar in it – Milly added just a touch of brandy to her own, it being Christmas – and endeavoured to keep their voices down for there were younger, visiting children, asleep in the night nursery and Milly did not want them disturbed.

They brought the boy, Edward Brennan, up at half-past ten.

Milly discouraged stressful atmospheres in her so strictly defined domain. This started at the top of the second-floor staircase and went on up until it reached the foor to the servants' attics. But Edward brought one in with him. She couldn't ban it like she would have banned a catapult or a jar of maggots or a toad in the pocket . . . that was a little boy's way and Milly, even though her charges were girls, could easily cope with little boys. No, the atmosphere came in with him. It *was* him. It was in his sneer and his defiant stance and his toffee-nosed attitude so that, for the first time in her life, Milly Toole was thrown off-balance by a child. She didn't know what to do with him. And where did this unpleasant arrogance come from, anyway? His father might be rich, but the wealth was newly-acquired. The Brennans did not have the quality, the easily detectable nobility that had been bred through the generations into the Ventons.

After twenty years at the job Milly did not know how to handle a child.

86

For child he was, there was no doubt about that.

He wanted to stay downstairs. He had no wish to be up here with the Venton girls. With scorn he proclaimed his position loudly, demanding to be taken down or given a separate bedroom. With a thumping heart Milly made herself tall; she stiffened for battle with crossed arms and glittering eyes. It would do her no good to have her authority challenged. Not here, not in the nursery.

'I expected a guest bedroom next to my parents. I did not expect to be brought to the nursery. I think there must have been some mistake.' The boy's tone was high-pitched, precocious.

He brought the finery of the ball upstairs with him, too – quite the gentleman with his squeaky black boots and his fitted black trousers, his flared jacket with its tiny waist, and wide cummerbund. He brought the scents and sounds of it in on the ends of his fingers like coloured streamers of excitement, and Milly saw the eyes of her sweet things open wide with admiration. Decked out like a little man he was, and his gestures were those of a little man, but there were two red spots of anger on his cheeks. Milly was tempted to slap them.

'Did you bring us any food? Not even a plateful of comforts, not even a taste of Turkish Delight?'

'Hush, Lucinda, jumping around like that! You do not want the young gentleman to think you are a pig!' said Milly.

Edward Brennan, aged fourteen, allowed his eyes to rest on the little girl but he did not deign to answer. He cast them about to choose a chair and he took the rocker beside the fire. Milly's chair. And there he sat and rested his feet on the fender as if this was his own place, as if he always sat there like that in command of this nursery ship. His hands, Milly noticed, he slipped together, so that his fingers fitted evenly between one another, and these he watched, with a kind of marvelling vanity, as he stretched and clenched and clicked his bones, viewing the fire with a disdainful expression, over the top of those hands.

'Well,' said Milly. 'Young man, I think it is past your bedtime. I'm sure it's well past everybody's bedtime. And if you don't require a hot drink then I'll show you your room and you can get yourself into bed so that you are fresh and up ready for Christmas morning.'

'It is merely eleven o'clock,' said Edward Brennan, and his voice was cool, not argumentative, more like the master's voice commenting upon the weather or the hcight of the river or the headlines in the newspaper. Casual, like that. Not brooking argument.

Milly Toole felt her cheeks flushing and against the white of her apron she knew they would go very red, for her colouring was naturally that of bacon, and changeable, and her hair was the shade of lightly-fried rind, rising up on her head in the massive shape of a loaf. 'It's up to you,' she said impatiently, 'but if you stay here you will be alone in the dark. I shall turn down the gas and the fire will die, and all by yourself in here you will be cold and unable to see. It is your decision, Master Brennan, you are too old for me to manhandle, so you had better be quick and make it.'

Milly's sweet things were watching the proceedings with incredulity on their faces. Alice's wide blue eyes were full of admiration for one so unquestionably brave. Pretty Alice, so keen to obey, so eager for approval, if Milly read a disturbing fairy story she closed her eyes and covered her ears, unable to bear to hear any more. So shy, so nervous was this ten-year-old child that she was fearful of being summoned to the drawing room to play the harmonium for her mother, terrified of being ordered to the study to read to her father, and she had nightmares when forced to face the morning riding lessons that had been insisted upon of late. She flitted like a moth from fear to fear, glad when she came to rest in the darkness of some small corner. The nursery was Alice's sanctuary where, alone with a book and curled up by the fire, the poor little mite could stroke Abernathy, her marmalade cat, and dream her dreams undisturbed.

Poor Alice. Poor Charlotte, and only eleven months between them. Small for her nine years, and wiry, Charlotte's hair was wispy and dry, the fawny colour of grass, parched after a summer without water. It was hard hair to curl, for it singed too easily, and Milly was nervous of doing it. And Charlotte's eyes were the palest blue; her nose was too thin and her chin was too pointed, her forehead was domed like a learned man's. She was shrivelled like a wizard and, aware of her looks, she hunched her back and tried to curl into herself if Milly gave her the chance. 'Walk tall, Charlotte!' Milly used to call. 'Straighten your back! Throw out your chest! Take up some space! Make yourself important!'

'Why should I?' was Charlotte's reply. 'I am not important in this house. Alice was born before me. It is Alice who is important.'

And Milly found it hard to answer that. For certainly Alice was her mother's darling. And Lucinda, well, eight-year-old Lucinda had picked up the roses of good looks and quick wits as if by simply trailing behind she had found bunches of these on the grass dropped by her two older sisters.

Now Alice's frightened eyes were scuttling from Edward to Milly and back, little grey mice afraid of their own shadows, pleading for help from them both.

'Go to bed if that is your habit at this early hour. I shall be quite happy sitting here,' said Edward Brennan sourly, adjusting his blue-white cuffs like a man.

'Don't be so silly,' said Milly, bustling about picking bits off the floor that nobody else would notice for the floor was quite clean. 'I'll get the girls to bed and then I'll come back for you. And if your attitude has not changed by then, there'll be trouble, I promise you.'

'I'm not going,' sang Lucinda. 'I'm not going to bed until Edward does.'

'It wouldn't be fair, would it?' argued Charlotte in her most reasonable voice, with one sly eye upon Edward as she tried to impress him.

'Don't be ridiculous,' remonstrated Milly. 'Master Edward is much older than you and should have a later bedtime anyway. And quite apart from that, it is immodest for you young ladies to be parading about in your night attire in front of a young man.'

'It's all the same now,' said the innocent Lucinda, normally so reasonable but driven, tonight, by tiredness. 'Bedtimes are done with tonight. It is already after eleven and so we are all even. We should all go to bed, or no one at all. And I want to wait until midnight so that we can go down and hear the carollers.'

At that point in time, under normal circumstances, Milly would have clucked and said, 'Well, I'm going and you can just please yourselves,' and taken herself off. She would have said that if it had not been for Alice. She could not abandon the timid Alice there, with them, with Edward Brennan ruling the roost and tapping his fingers on his knee, making Alice feel disloyal and uncomfortable, and if Alice sided with Milly and went to bed obediently on her own the others would mock her in the morning. And Alice cared about things like that. Milly felt a twinge of hot annoyance towards the child she loved best, for making the situation into one which must be settled firmly. And now.

Before the arrival of Edward Brennan Milly had already decided to allow them to watch the carollers. Now it was all spoilt. Now it was all different.

Threatening to tell Lord Thomas and Lady Sarah Venton, her employers, of their daughters' disobedience, was not an option open to Milly. They left the care of their children entirely in Milly's hands and did not deign to take any part. Thomas was not, in the ordinary sense of the word, a strict father, or a kind one, or an interfering one . . . he was a totally uninterested one, on account of the fact that he had not, so far, been able to get his wife to bear him a son. When he summoned his eldest daughter down on a Monday morning to hear her reading, this was done very much from a sense of duty. She went for an hour, and came back after an hour. They did not converse, or laugh together, or drink tea. Alice came back to the nursery stuttering and pale-faced. The new child his wife expected was a source of great hope to them both . . . Lady Sarah carried herself about in nervous expectation, half-showing her pregnant state one day in a tight-fitting gown, half-hiding it the next beneath shawls. A male heir to the name, the house and the estates was what Thomas craved. Perhaps he would take more interest in the nursery if there was a boy inside it.

Across the cushions from Milly, lulled by the gently rolling caravan, Alice was not quite asleep either. It was natural that they should both be sharing these thoughts of that early Christmas, of the first time Edward came to the house, and Alice kept her eyes closed as she remembered, trying to dilute the pain.

You could see that Edward enjoyed the situation by the way one side of his mouth was curled, and by the not-quite shuttered look behind his brooding brown eyes. He even sneered at the stockings that hung on the mantelpiece . . .

But he was handsome, Alice Venton saw that, too, and so confident . . . in this house, full of such pale, simpering fairness, they were not used to dark, brooding people. His skin was smooth and tight over perfect angles and every now and then he lifted his hand to slick down his thick, wavy hair. Then he tapped his fingers on the tight material at his knee, and waited.

Alice could have wept for Milly. She'd had a heavy day and she was tired. She'd fed extra children at teatime, she'd had to bath two babies, settle them down and put them to bed. Oh, Cherry the maid had helped her, fetching the water and filling the bottles, but Milly liked to do things herself so that she knew they had been done properly. Alice, of all the children, valued Milly. Alice was the one who remembered Agatha, the nurse they had had before, the one who had been forced to leave because of her gin-drinking and other, what her mother called, 'appallingly loutish habits'.

Neither Charlotte nor Lucinda remembered Agatha. Well, Lucinda had only just been born when she left and Charlotte a peevish toddler.

Alice remembered her. That's why she wanted Milly to be happy. She desperately wanted Milly to stay. Never in her life had Alice loved anyone in the soft, gentle, companionable way she loved Milly. And the extraordinary, almost unbelievable fact was that Milly loved her back. Yes, even though she lisped sometimes, and was scared, and hid behind curtains if she could, Milly loved Alice very much, even when Alice was quiet and only wanting to cuddle up with her book not feeling she wanted to speak to anyone. Even this was all right with Milly. Milly cuddled Alice and whispered to her and told her secrets when she put her to bed at night, and sometimes she whispered to Alice something so precious Alice could hardly believe it . . . 'You are the special one. You are Milly's special child. You know that, my pet, don't you?' But she was not special to Milly in the rather strange way she was special to Mama or Papa, because she'd been born first, and was pretty. She was special to Milly just because she was herself.

So when Milly said that, Alice had to nod, smiling shyly. She told Milly her own secrets, too, her most frightening, most difficult secret of all, and Milly said, 'Hush, no one need know if you really don't want them to.'

'Not even Charlotte?'

'No, my darling, trust Milly. Particularly not Charlotte.'

And Alice did trust Milly. Completely. Utterly. But now, incredibly, there was this boy sitting in her chair who actually wanted to hurt Milly!

It was awful. But Alice did not hate the boy; she could not help but admire him. He was behaving in ways she so often wanted to behave, but dare not . . .

it would not be seemly behaviour for a girl.

And tonight, just for fun, Milly had demanded they put silver candlesticks on the supper tray. It was little things like that that made Alice love her. Oh, and the coming of Edward Brennan had spoilt it all. How Alice wished he would comply and take himself off to the shake-down bed in the schoolroom that Milly had set up for him. Papa would not allow anyone, not even a guest, to use the specially prepared bedroom next door to their own with the cradle in it, the room that would belong to the new baby when it arrived. Milly had gone to great pains to assure the girls that when the new baby came they were all going to share the looking after it.

'Now Miss Lucinda,' said Milly. 'You make a start and lead the way for it's getting cold in here and if you leave it too long even the warming pans won't take the chill off you. And, what is worse, if you do not go to bed now Father Christmas won't come . . . he'll look down the chimney and see you still up and he'll pass straight on to the next house.' And without another word Milly bent low and swept up the angry Lucinda, setting off a violent kicking and struggling as she did so.

Edward Brennan continued to sit there and stare at the fire, showing them that he was above all this.

Alice picked up the love of her life, Abernathy, and kissed the hard, knobby bit on the top of his head. He was the only one in the world who knew what really went on in her mind. Sometimes, she used to look in the mirror and wonder at the face that stared back at her. None of her fears and terrors and secret, wild excitements showed on it. It was the face that everyone wanted to see, pretty and obedient. She used to smile at it, and thank it for not telling of the times she felt like stripping naked and dancing, or running wild over the fields, or lying on the floor and shouting her head off. Her world was so small, and her secret emotions so huge, that sometimes she felt choked by it, hemmed in by all the constrictions and rules, the propriety expected from her. But Abernathy knew. He knew everything. He went limp and purred in her arms. He left golden strands on the lacy front of her nightdress.

'Alice,' said Charlotte, 'I think we should do as Milly says and go to bed.'

Alice stared sharply at her sister. Was she feeling just as uncomfortable about all this? And only a moment ago Alice had thought Charlotte was enjoying herself.

Charlotte came to stand beside her, and looked up at her older sister through eyes as slit as the cat's. 'How would you like to give me Abernathy for Christmas instead of that scarf you have knitted me? If you did that, then we could both go to bed straight away, and put an end to the trouble.'

Alice tensed, well aware of the bribe. The squawling of Lucinda grew louder as she escaped from Milly's clutches and started back towards the day room. Edward lost his bored air. He was watching them now.

'And if I gave you Abernathy,' asked Alice slowly, astonished, 'you would agree to go to bed?'

Charlotte nodded. Alice imagined the alternative. Lucinda would be returned to her bed again and again, and every time she escaped she would become crosser. Milly would grow more and more flustered, het up and unable to cope so that everyone would be tired in the morning and Christmas Day would be ruined. Charlotte would absolutely refuse to move until, in the end, and near to tears, Milly would let them have their way. They would stay up, listen to the carollers, maybe even persuade Milly into letting them have some of the three o'clock breakfast . . . yes, that's what would happen. But to do it that way would make it sad. Milly would not be enjoying it and neither would Alice. And there would be no fun left in Christmas.

And giving the cat to Charlotte would not really be giving him away. He would remain in the nursery – she would still be able to see him, feed him sometimes, and hold him. And no matter what Charlotte tried to do, Abernathy would still love Alice.

Their exciting visitor watched them, lowered his legs

94

from the fireguard and crossed them.

'You would have to swear not to ask for him back tomorrow,' said Charlotte.

'I have not decided to give him, yet,' said Alice warily.

'But you will,' said Charlotte. 'Now, swear on something very important.'

'The Bible?' asked Alice.

'The Bible is in the schoolroom,' said Charlotte. 'And I'm not sure about the Bible. I need you to swear on something very important.' And Charlotte looked round the nursery as if in search of something small and eminently precious like a ruby or a pearl that might have got caught on a window ledge or under a rug. 'I know,' she exclaimed, brightening, enjoying the game in which Edward was somehow involved, also. They could hear Lucinda's cries getting louder. 'Swear on the new baby's life.'

Alice blanched. There was something sinister in that, something too daring and not nice – dealing with the unborn felt like witchcraft. But Alice, persuaded by Charlotte and by the hard, watching eyes of Edward, made her promise.

'I swear,' she said, pulling Abernathy's claws free and forcing him into a shape that would fit Charlotte's smaller, stiffer arms.

'Say it properly,' said Charlotte, playing up to Edward. 'Say it in full.'

So Alice said, 'I swear on the new baby's life that I am giving you Abernathy for ever and that I will never ask for him back.'

Red-faced and screaming, Lucinda, a bundle of fury, burst into the room followed by Milly who was sighing. 'See what you've done!' she shouted at the boy. 'See what mayhem you have caused here! If you had done as I asked you and gone to bed, these three little ones would be asleep and happy by now.'

Edward Brennan lifted his chin and smiled.

Charlotte's voice was firm as she carried out her part

of the bargain. 'Lucinda!' she ordered, 'stop making that noise and go back to bed! I am going. Alice is going. And it's up to Edward to decide for himself what he does. Stay here if you like, but if you stay you'll be all on your own. And with him!'

Lucinda's false tears ceased abruptly and she wiped her wet nose on her sleeve. Her little bare feet looked sweet and angelic below the long white nightgown.

'Well, and this is a change of tune,' said Milly, hands on hips and bemused, puffing a wisp of hair off her forehead and scattering hairpins. And then she stood back and watched in surprise as the angelic procession, led by Charlotte with the cat in her arms, wended its way through the day nursery door and towards the bedrooms.

Five minutes later she went to tuck them up and tried to remove the cat from Charlotte's arms. 'He is mine now, and I want him with me,' said Charlotte. 'Alice has given him to me for Christmas.'

Milly frowned and looked across at Alice's bed and the white mound in it which lay perfectly still. She shook her large head, puzzled. 'I thought she had made you a scarf for Christmas. I don't believe for one moment that Alice has given this cat to you, Charlotte. Why would you want a cat? You don't even like them! Anyway, cats can't sleep on beds, that is one of my strictest rules. Cats sit on children's heads and smother them in the night.'

Charlotte released Abernathy, knowing she could not win this, one of the oldest battles. 'But it's true that he's mine, isn't it, Alice? Tell Milly you gave him to me! She thinks I am telling lies.'

'I gave Abernathy to Charlotte,' said Alice, forcing herself to sound happy, taking the tears out of her voice for already she was regretting her impulsive action, already she was wondering with what she could buy him back. Whatever she used, the bargaining would have to be conducted under the careful veil of indifference, for Charlotte would never give him back if she

96

knew how badly Alice wanted him. 'Don't put him out tonight, Milly, please. It's wet and it's cold and it's windy and he might get crushed by the carriages. Let him stay by the nursery fire.' Alice had given her pet away and that was bad enough; let him not have to endure the cold as well.

Rocked by the gentle motion of the caravan, Alice slept, relieved of any more memories, taken over by happier dreams. The caravan moved on, the rain patted the roof, and it was Milly whose memories continued so dreadfully clearly.

'As it's a special night, Abernathy can stay indoors this once,' said Milly, bending to tuck in the naughty Lucinda. It was hard, now that the child was lying in bed sucking her thumb, to compare her with the hot sticky bundle of squawking indignation she had been dealing with only moments before.

Milly read her sweet things a story before tiptoeing out and turning off the gas. She kept a night-light burning on the tallboy.

She checked that the nursery kitchen was clean and ready for Cherry's arrival in the morning. She looked in on the sleeping babies.

As she passed along the short corridor beside the window, Milly heard the voices of the carollers coming from way below, across the ivy-clad front of the house beside the main door. Cold, sweet voices blown by wind and rain, voices lit by lanterns . . . the chestnuts would be handed out, would be juggled about in cold hands. Shame it wasn't snowing. Milly would have loved to have led the children down to the landing again; she would have loved to have watched their faces . . .

Edward Brennan had spoiled all that.

She ignored the boy who sat on beside the fire, save to tell him quite coldly, 'Your room is down there, and I'll leave the light on so that you can find your way. The bathroom is through that door there. I shall be coming in early, at six o'clock, in order to fill those stockings. I shall expect to find you gone by then.'

Sighing heavily, for she had worked hard that day. Milly Toole laid the still-sleeping cat on the rug by the fire instead of opening the door to the back staircase. How strange that Alice had given him away. Abernathy had been rescued by Alice as a kitten when she had found him tied up in a sackful of dead brothers and sisters, gasping his last out of saturated lungs in the tall green reeds by the lake. A moth-eaten thing, he would never overcome his bad start in life, never acquire that sleek fat contentedness of his more fortunate brethren. And Alice loved him the more because of this . . . in the same way Milly loved Alice best, she supposed, as she wedged the day nursery door gently ajar so she could hear any waking babies and made for her own large, spartan room.

Milly undressed quickly, leaving her wrap on her bedside chair in case she should have to rise in a hurry. She climbed into the familiar twanging of her high canopied bed. Sighs, cries, whispers in the night, Milly swore she was so well tuned to night noises by now that she could hear mice, even spiders, if they moved around the nursery at night. Probably, Milly thought, as she rested her great aching feet in the warm circle of sheet by the pan, probably Alice loved that cat so much because Abernathy, wretched though he was, puny though he was, even a little bit smelly, was sweet and gentle-natured. And he needed her.

Funny how everyone needs to be needed.

Yes, it was strange that Alice had given that cat away.

Milly Toole spat on her fingers as the wind rolled round outside and the rain lashed the windows, and she snuffed out her bedside candle.

It was in the morning that they found the cat, draped among the furs on the downstairs hat-stand. He had been strangled.

Milly jumped as a horse's head appeared at the opening above the caravan door. It broke into her day-dreams with a sparking cold shock. She had forgotten where she was. She must not spend so long in the past . . . the future was what was important now.

'I have looked in several times,' said Luke Durant, bending low to see through to the back, 'and every time I have heard your snorings.'

'I was resting,' said Milly, 'not sleeping, so I could not have been snoring. Where have you been? Where are we now? How long are we travelling and where are we going?'

'Is she all right? Have you everything you need? Are you quite comfortable?'

Milly looked across at Alice. She was asleep. The child was asleep. All was as well as it could be.

'We are calling at the castle before we leave the county,' said Luke casually, as if there was no danger involved at all in visiting his old home.

'Oh – and is that wise? Surely they search for you there?'

'The circus always camps within the Bellever walls. It is an old tradition . . . it dates back well before the time of my father and his before him. We will be quite safe there, if it's safety you crave.'

'So be it,' said Milly, as the impudent face disappeared and the horse snorted and foamed at the mouth before jingling away. And she hoped the journey would not last long, for her stomach was rumbling loudly and the wagons were travelling unbearably slowly.

# ELEVEN

That fatal Christmas when Edward Brennan paid his first visit to Venton Hall, and entered into his first little conspiracy with Charlotte, was not significant for that reason alone.

Many things were going on downstairs long after the children finally went to sleep in the quiet of the nursery, events that would prove immensely important for the future of everyone involved.

Thomas, tenth Lord of Venton, was entirely dependent on the income from his lands. And in spite of the fact that he was encouraged to do so by his friends, he had taken too long to disperse his wealth, to place just a few of his eggs in a different basket. 'You can see what's happening, you only have to look around you. Sell some of the smaller farms, Thomas, and put your money in shares . . . tobacco, coal, gold. Now is the time, man.' And, just this year, Thomas had done so, but his investments were not looking good. He should have taken no notice of his friends. He ought to have pulled in his horns and prepared himself for the invevitable crash. But Thomas took no notice; he was too proud, too set in his ways to change, and he continued to live in the grand manner despite the fact that his labourers went hungry.

He was a nervous man, quick-tempered, and an inveterate gambler. And if houses reflect the image of their owner, by Christmas 1843 Venton Hall was certainly beginning to do that. The Hall was not so large, nor so grand as the Brennans' home at Winterbourne. And it was much older. The stone they used had weathered, it was softer. The inside was riddled with passageways and secret staircases, and the great hall, which they used as a ballroom, retained its original musicians' gallery. Most of the rooms were wood-panelled and quite dark, the staircases creaked and were flanked by ornate wooden banisters, and the ceilings were low, unlike at Winterbourne, where every room was so vast and high that the fires did nothing but provide the suggestion of warmth.

Venton Hall smelled of woodsmoke, wet dogs and damp tapestries. It smelled like its owner. It was lazily littered with comfortable sofas and armchairs. It was easy-going, faded and old-fashioned.

Tradition was all-important, therefore Christmas was always the same. On Christmas Day the guests would eat, drink, sleep and play games such as Blind Man's Buff and Charades. On Boxing Day night the over-worked servants would be rewarded by their own dance in the great medieval barn, while the house guests sat back exhausted after a long day's hunting.

So at half-past two on Christmas Day morning Lady Sarah Venton edged closer to the firmly closed doors of the smoking room from where she could just hear the sound of men's voices . . . not what was said, but the tone of the conversation, and it rose and fell between the bars of Strauss. The smoking room adjoined the billiard room, quite unlike the rest of the house and decorated in a Moorish style, the rooms connected to each other by an arch. It was unfair of Thomas to go off and neglect her like this, knowing how tired she became these days, how overwrought from having to entertain such large numbers of people all night, and knowing that Christmas Day would bring little relief from it all.

She allowed herself to sink to the safety of the small settee where she fanned herself with ostrich feathers and wished she could kick off her shoes or loosen her corset just a little. She thought that Anna her maid must have laced her too tightly. Sarah, thirty years old and looking, she thought, every minute of them in spite of her careful ministrations, had never been a truly sociable creature, not deep down at heart. All she did when faced with an experience such as this was dream . . . dream of the

101

moment when the last of the Christmas guests would be gone, not until the day after Boxing Day . . . when she could go to her room and be by herself, knowing she would not have to rise up and put on her smile. Sarah, after five hours of feasting and dancing, longed to be alone, either in her room with the curtains drawn or walking out through the wind and the rain with the dogs at her heels, savouring the solitude.

She covered her bulging stomach with her hands, and inside her the baby seethed and heaved. It was always restless when she was tense. Could it sense her unease tonight? Sarah did not want this baby but she had been given no choice. Thomas was desperate for a son. She had argued, 'The firstborn child is the entailment . . . if we make sure that Alice marries well, then nothing will be lost!'

'Never, not in any previous generation, has the Venton heir been a girl,' Thomas had told her, accusingly.

The ball was going very well, as she'd known it would. It was detail that carried the day and no detail had been overlooked. She had ordered the best old wine up from its sawdust, the house was decked with garlands of holly and mistletoe. Even Thomas' hounds had tinsel woven between the studs in their collars. The house looked warm and happy. It always lent itself marvellously well to Christmas – an applewood yule log spiced the air and fir cones burned merrily. The ten-course meal had been perfect, and Sarah wished she could congratulate herself and sit back, but an early breakfast would be served in half an hour. The thought of more food made her feel ill.

'Are you feeling all right, my dear?'

Sarah put a rigid smile on her face as Florence Brennan, smelling of violets, came to sit next to her. The figure of the tall woman loomed over her like a shadow. 'I am feeling fine, Florence, but I hear that a group of gentlemen have closeted themselves away with cigars and brandy in the smoking room and I fear they are not smoking at all, but gambling.'

'It is Christmas.' Florence was a dour-faced, stiff-backed woman who carried herself royally at all times and grimaced whenever she bent. 'And men will be men.'

'You make it sound as if, at Christmas, anything is acceptable.'

'Just as long as it's in moderation,' said Florence, holding down her crinoline as she prepared to sit. Her eyes were quick with suspicion.

Sarah felt she was at a fancy-dress ball, as though her face was masked. How she wished this woman was someone in whom she could confide. How she wished her companion was not Florence, but one of her friends who had come to find her, someone wise, whom she could trust and talk to without the fear of whatever she said being spread round the house like fire. Moderation? By mistrusting her husband like this, Sarah felt she was betraying him and this feeling horrified her. It horrified her so much she almost got up and moved away, because she did not want to know, she did not, but at the same time she had to. Thomas had promised her he would never take up gambling again, and as far as Sarah knew he had not, until now . . . until this night. She might be wrong. And even if she wasn't wrong, perhaps one relapse did not mean a total slide, perhaps he was more in control. After all, he was older now, and the former troubles had taken place many years ago.

Sarah flinched as she remembered the resentments, the bitterness that had grown and grown between them until it had corroded everything, the terrible silences when they tried to pretend that nothing was happening. Sarah's father had bailed him out then . . . but he was no longer alive, and what would they do if it happened again? Who would rescue them this time? Thomas had sworn to her afterwards, he had fallen on his knees and crawled towards her, burying his head in her lap. He had sworn he would never bring his family so close to penury ever again. Lately, with his money

103

worries, her husband had become restless. She recognized those awful signs – irritation, pacing up and down at night, that gaunt look about his face again. She shook her head. Pregnancy was making her fearful.

But Thomas was delicate, he was too highly-strung.

'You are shivering,' said Florence, showing an awkward concern.

'It is nothing,' said Sarah, smiling weakly, 'just someone passing over my grave.'

'How long have you to wait until the child is born?'

'Only a month now, but I feel as if I've been pregnant for such ages . . .'

'You should have no trouble this time,' said Florence Brennan, taking her hooded eyes down over her companion's body, assessing it, 'as this is your fourth. But after I had Edward they told me, no more. I was ruined as a woman, ripped and torn, inside and out,' she said.

'The doctors say I should have no trouble.'

'Well, I have to say this, but you don't look at all blooming to me, my dear. You looked puffed, and doughy. It is not a good sign at all. And I expect you are wanting a son?'

'Thomas is sure it will be a son this time. But,' and Sarah added this last bit lamely, 'he has been certain of that every time. And disappointed.' And then she noticed her swollen ankles.

'We cannot always have what we want in this life,' said Florence Brennan firmly in her monotonous voice. She fluttered a little with her fan and Sarah saw beads of sweat on her upper lip. Sarah wondered what Florence wanted and had been unable to have, and unkindly she considered it was probably good looks. For the woman was large-boned, raw-skinned and with the thick eyebrows of a man no matter that she had plucked them and drawn thin arches there instead. A neatly sectioned woman, dominated by commonsense, Florence Brennan would never understand how anyone could be flawed by anything so trivial as lack of moderation. Her own husband, Henry, made money

104

in the city; he was not dependent on his flagging estates as Thomas was. Florence was a sensible woman and she had made sure she had married a sensible man. No wonder she was unworried about Henry in the smoking room. Henry would come out the winner; people like Henry always did, while Thomas . . .

Sarah had insisted they invite the Brennans. Thomas had urged her against it. But, 'They are our neighbours, Thomas, whether you like it or not. Some of their land even borders ours. And we cannot ignore them no matter how distasteful you find them.'

'I do not find them distasteful. Invite them if you feel you must, but the man is arrogant as hell and the wife is totally without humour.'

Sarah cast worried eyes towards the smoking-room door. Her nerves were frayed. She felt sick – how she longed for this night to be over! The dancers whirled before her eyes, even to watch them made her feel dizzy. Perhaps she could forego breakfast and retire to her room for just a short rest. After all, everyone knew and sympathized with her condition. If Thomas would only come out then Sarah could relax.

'*Fifteen hundred on a son!*'

The double doors had opened only momentarily. The words Sarah thought she heard gusted through on a cloud of cigar-rich air as a neighbour came back to the party.

'*Fifteen hundred on a son!*'

Sarah, unaware that her mouth was open, that her cornflower-blue eyes were filled with fear, turned to her companion whose fan had suddenly stilled. It must be a joke – some terrible joke – and she was unaware that she still vaguely smiled, as though endorsing her husband's words. She felt foolish, desperately foolish and vulnerable sitting there fiddling with the ribbons in her dress. If only she had chosen to rest somewhere else, then she would not have heard. For the voice that came through the door so chillingly clearly, so raucously drunk, was unmistakably that of her husband, and

105

it had been followed by the gusty guffaws of men having fun . . . paper notes on a table.

'No, Thomas, no!' The words were out of Sarah's mouth before she realized she was thinking them, staring into the critical grey eyes of Florence Brennan. Sarah struggled to her feet and somehow moved her aching body to the double doors which were on the point of closing when she pushed through. The fumes of cigar smoke were as thickly brown as the cushions, as the rugs on the floor. She held herself up, a beautiful woman in silver with blue feathers in her golden hair, pale, exhausted.

'Dear God, no! Thomas, no!'

Her words, clarion clear, pierced the heavy atmosphere in the room and her elegant husband, seated, his complexion greenly tinged by the baize table, rose to his feet, leanly intense with his slick blond locks. After pushing back his chair it took him five strides to reach his wife and to catch her before she fell.

# TWELVE

Ah yes, of course. Her happiest moments had been spent in books. This was the spice of her dreams.

Beyond the shadowlands – not even delicate, what she had done was bold, brash and shameless. Alice Brennan sat up, peered out of the caravan door and remembered Edward's sinister story, for here was just such a place. They had travelled all day and now it was evening, and a thin white mist spiralled around the crumbling towers. The fading sun flushed the granite with the soft pink of honeysuckle, accentuating the atmosphere of age and mystery that settled all around them.

The horses had slowed as they trundled the steep, ancient road that approached the castle, a road that would its way up a wooded hillside. The wheels rumbled woodenly as they crossed the bridge over the moat which flashed in the broken light, and on past the gatehouse. Once through the inner gateway, they arrived in the great courtyard. Here the wagons creaked to a halt and, forming a circle around the huge oak in the centre, men jumped down and eased the horses from their shafts before leading them out to the fields and rest.

Alice smiled, appreciating the perfection of her scene. The troupe must camp here regularly because the routine was expertly performed. Immediately women climbed down their caravan steps, flanked by excited children, firewood was fetched, efficiently and quickly, and a great iron pot was hung from a three-legged spit which was sturdily arranged above the flames. All this, Alice saw through the caravan door. She saw the people as shadows cast by the firelight. But she heard herself ask, 'Where can we be, and what is happening out there? Ought we to be helping? Where is Luke?'

And Milly answered, 'I do not know these people, or the ways of them. They might not accept us into their company as easily as that. From what I do see they look like a ragged army of tramps and thieves, and I think we had better remain where we are.'

'But you knew Luke Durant. You must have known that he was one of these travellers!'

Milly's eyes closed her face. She swept away a dismissive explanation, hoping Alice would not pry further. 'I knew him many years ago, when he and his family lived in this place. Since they left I have not seen him.'

'How extraordinary, then, that he should have been in Shilstone churchyard.' Waiting for me. Just waiting.

Milly did not have the time to reply for the man they spoke of opened the door, made a small bow, and invited them down the steps. 'It is rough and ready, but it is safe,' he assured them, helping them down. He held Alice's arm for an unnecessary length of time. Milly shivered, carrying the child, and Luke led them straight to the fire. Before they could converse further an ancient man of indiscernible age and wild white hair came through the castle door, crabbing along like a cripple but with a wide beam on his face. 'Luke! Luke, you cursed young rogue! If only you would give us some warning!'

Luke clapped the servant on the back, hugged him so hard he lifted him from the ground and confessed, 'I never know, Seaton, or else I would. You could light all the fires and prepare me a banquet. You could warm my bed and bring out the wine!'

Seaton hesitated. 'Well, my old friend . . . I do not know if I could aspire to all of those, given the difficult circumstances . . . '

'Exactly, Seaton! So now what would be the point of informing you of my arrival?'

Seaton grinned from ear to ear, his old blue eyes watering happily. 'There is plenty of wine still in the cellars, well-hid. I will bring out the glasses and make

108

sure there is enough for all. The least we can do is toast the master's return!'

Luke Durant clapped his hands. Before the bent old man could disappear he pulled him aside and enquired, 'Have they been asking for me?'

Seaton assumed a secretive glance, tugged the lobe of his whiskery ear and spoke in a low voice. 'No, no, not since last year. No one has been here. I think they are losing the will for it . . . so much time has gone by.'

'Never underestimate the doggedness of authority,' Luke replied. 'They will never give up, not so long as I remain a free man.'

The women round the stewpot left their preparations to simmer and clustered around the baby. A few little girls touched him with grubby fingers. Milly attempted to cover him, suspicions of their intentions stiff in her face, for some of these women were gypsies whom she knew to be dirty and untrustworthy folk . . . just the kind of people among whom Luke Durant would hide himself.

'What is his name?'

'He is so tiny, he must be newly born!'

'Look at his bright eyes . . . he misses nothing, already! Surely he is listening to us.'

'What is his name?'

'What is your baby's name?'

'Yes,' Luke came towards them. 'What is the name of the child?'

Alice looked up at him blankly. She was wrapped in a gypsy shawl of gold and black, fringed with opal beads. The firelight played on her face, accentuating its pale fragility. As always she spoke quickly, nervously, and her voice was sad when she said, 'I have not thought of a name. I have not had the time. And his birth will go unrecognized because I took him away . . . ' Her voice shook. This new feeling of safety was almost too much to bear, the natural acceptance of these people, Luke's kindness, Milly's care. She had been fighting for so long. Could she relax at last, and

109

if she did relax, would she wake up? How strong were her images: could they be trusted?

'We must recognize his birth in the Romany way!' A burly woman, flushed like a newly-boiled ham beneath a flowing skin of sable fur pushed herself forward and spoke in a tone that would brook no nonsense. 'While he travels with us he is one of us. We must carve his name on the tree, right here in the courtyard so that all the world will know of the birth of one of nature's children. But in order to do that, and it must be done properly as is the custom, you must give him a name. Every child deserves a name.' The flamboyant feather in her tall black hat fluttered with indignation.

Milly swelled with disapproval and croaked like a disturbed frog. 'But we are not gypsies, and this child is the son of a noble Lord. We cannot scratch his name on a tree as if he were just another poor traveller passing by!'

'We are all doing that, Mrs Toole. Surely, to think any other way is to give to human beings far too much importance.' Luke spoke softly, and he was staring into Alice's eyes.

'I would like that.' Alice was disconcerted. Never had she felt so vulnerable in the face of an honest stare, and when he smiled that easy smile she saw the reflection of herself, not as she perceived herself to be . . . ugly, hopeless, afraid . . . but a beautiful woman, desirable once again, someone whose voice was important, whose person was to be respected.

'The poor mite wants feeding,' remarked the large woman, whose earrings dangled to her shoulders and whose hair came out of her hard black hat in tatty whirls like horsehair stuffing.

Alice flushed. She made to take the child from Milly. 'I had better take him back to the wagon.'

'What is wrong with feeding him here, beside the fire and under the stars? Why take him indoors and hide your love from everyone, turning it into a secret thing?'

Now the gypsy's suggestions were too much for

110

Milly. These people, they might behave as animals do, but they knew no better. She stood up, folding the child away in her arms, and advised Alice, 'I will come with you. It will not take long. Some things are personal and ought to be conducted in private! We will return to the fire when we have finished.'

But Alice was held by the questions in Luke Durant's eyes. She remained seated on one of the chairs they had put by the fire; she undid her bodice, she held out her arms for the baby and Milly stared round for support. There was none – just flat, bemused glances. 'We do not have to stoop to this level in order to be accepted here,' Milly whispered urgently. 'We have to keep a sense of proportion. Remember who you are!'

'He is used to feeding in the open air,' Alice said simply, because anyway, this was not real, nothing mattered. And for decency's sake, to cover her mistress, Milly was forced to return the child. He sucked at his mother greedily, plucking the air with his arms, and Alice thought that nothing had ever felt so right; she had never experienced such a deep sense of satisfaction and pleasure as she did just then, sitting in a ring with the gypsies in the castle courtyard, her baby at her breast and Luke Durant gazing down at her with that interested look in his eyes. How horrified Edward would be if he could see her now! She thought about Charlotte, saw the expression of distaste on her sister's face. She had only to dance at home, to waltz round the room to incur their immediate disapproval. But here she had no need to rebel. Here was real freedom, she told herself, staring up at the night, and Alice was so tired of restrictions. If she named the child now she would remember this moment for ever. 'I am calling him Davy,' she said, 'for no reason other than I like the sound of it. I have known no one by that name, and it pleases me.'

She fed her baby and she watched as Luke moved across to the tree. His boots rustled through deep piles of leaves as he approached the giant trunk. He took out his knife and dug deep in the bark as he carved out the letters. *Davy Brennan – 1867*. Every movement he made, every gesture, every word fascinated Alice.

'Davy, Davy, my little Davy,' she whispered to the child. 'And is that legal?' she asked Luke. 'Will that be accepted anywhere?'

'That will be accepted among people who matter,' he told her. 'And only you can decide who they are.'

When eventually Seaton hobbled out carrying a tray laden with glasses, Luke stepped forward and picked one for himself and the other for Alice. 'To Davy,' he said, taking his glass to the child and then holding it to the tree. 'We won't wish him anything more, other than his name, in case we are casting our own dreams upon him, and he will want to find his own.'

'A simple toast then,' said Alice, well aware of Milly's distrust. She wished her nurse would bend more easily; she wished she did not have such firm views and that she was slower in her assessment of people. Once Milly had an idea in her head it was an almost impossible task to change it.

While they waited for the food to cook, the wine flowed, the men brought out their home-brewed ale, the children played games, and two jugglers practised in the shadows behind the fire, tossing flaming torches to each other. Three fiddlers sat on the steps of the front caravan and played. Again Alice smiled, amazed by her own imagination, her power, her skill. By now she was probably back in Deale; she would wake up in a minute and feel that hard mattress under her heavy body, would hear the screams of the lunatics, would reach for her precious bag of salt, the only way of killing the ticks in the bed. How terribly important that had seemed . . . oh yes, the patients paid dearly for the luxury of salt, brought into the workhouse next door by wandering tramps whose boots were never searched, by tradition. She would wake up and Luke Durant would be gone, replaced by Dr Myers, the medical officer, bending over her, or one of the witchy nurses.

Her escape was nothing but a wild illusion.

But Luke's voice was very real, and his breath was warm when he came so close to her ear in order to speak above the music. 'The food is ready now. Are you hungry?'

She prepared herself to say no, out of habit, for how long was it since she had experienced a real, healthy appetite? But she was hungry, she was starving hungry, for she had eaten nothing since the little soup she had swallowed at Milly's cottage. The stew tasted like nothing on earth . . . rabbit, she supposed. It was spicy, dark and hot, and stuffed with an assortment of unfamiliar vegetables. The children raked hot potatoes from the ashes of the fire. Alice ate and felt life returning. A cool wind moaned round the castle courtyard but she did not feel the cold. The fiddlers played and several couples started to dance. Seaton, on a step-ladder, had lit torches set high on the castle walls. The oak tree in the centre of the courtyard dripped with stars.

'We could dance,' said Luke softly. 'At the edge, away from everyone else.'

I have made magic. And oh yes, Alice wanted to dance, but she was not yet strong enough for that. Tears stung her eyes as she refused him. What was this . . . what was happening to her? Was it her magic, or gypsy magic? And she did not know this man who looked at her so intently. He was a rogue . . . he looked like a rogue . . . he was everything she had ever been warned against. Look at him! Bronzed, dark, with those insolent eyes that missed nothing. Even his dress was rakish – she noticed his crimson velvet waistcoat and the rings upon his fingers. Edward, so po-faced and conventional, would be appalled! But, real or unreal, he had saved her; without knowing who she was he had picked her up and carried her to safety. And if she never had anything else she had this wonderful night . . .

He refused to take no for an answer. 'And I want to show you around my palace!' he said. Alice hesitated, knowing what Milly's reaction would be. She was already wearing her tightest, most suspicious expression and her chins folded down to her chest like a series of bulging stone steps. Alice stood up, straightened her back in defiance and handed the baby to Milly, who was too taken aback by the suddenness of all this to refuse.

Luke took Alice's hand and she followed him through the castle door and into the great hall beyond. 'This is almost all that remains,' he told her, his voice echoing up and rumbling round the exposed rafters. 'No one lives here now but Seaton, who acts as a caretaker. And when Seaton is gone I suppose it will crumble completely, be quite overrun by briars and become a home for jackdaws.'

Alice looked up at the near-derelict place, overcome by a sudden sadness. Her tone was reduced to a whisper, and the echoes took it and made it loud. 'What happened? Why was your home abandoned? Why can't you return and make it into a home again?'

Luke pulled her on. Holding a lantern before him he urged her under arches and through chambers, up twisting staircases, high on to the parapet at the top of a well-preserved tower. Their footsteps echoed roundly as they climbed. Milly's dress flowed overlong behind her. Alice picked up the trailing material and gave thanks for the belt. Suddenly they seemed to step into the sky. Together they stood and peered down into the courtyard, over the wall and across into the night. 'One day I will return,' he told her, his face strangely tight and his words very soft. 'It is not from choice that I travel, although the life suits me and I don't regret a moment of it. I have travelled most of the world and back again, always back again. I have to return to this place, you see. It draws me back.'

'You are running away . . . ' Alice started.

'Just as you are,' he said, turning towards her.

'But there are people after me,' she said, her eyes large and wistful. 'Cruel people, who want to hurt me.'

Luke did not answer immediately. 'The only way to

escape your enemies is to confront them,' he said.

'I could never confront mine,' said Alice. 'They have too much power over me and I am too weak before them.' Again . . . that feeling of yearning for a protector. She used to do it, putting on her little-girl ways, thinking that's what they wanted, for her to be obedient, biddable and helpless, willing to do anything in order to be loved.

But Luke was saying, 'Then that has to change. If you want to survive, that has to change.' And the music of the gypsy fiddles weaved softly with the scents of the night. He faced her. Gently he let his hand run over the shape of her face, stroking her forehead, her eyelids, her cheeks and her chin. A soft breeze stirred her hair. Alice shivered. She tried to pull back but could not. He took her chin in his hand, held her still as he kissed her. He let her go – not surprised, not sorry. He spoke softly. 'And are you going to let me help you fight your battle?' he asked.

'But you have your own.' Alice could hardly speak. A pleading confusion was in her eyes, and she moved her lips uncertainly. She was very aware of the height, the great fall below her, the vast sweep of the granite walls behind her. She was very aware of the unreality. She could fall now and be happy to do so. This was what she loved . . . to be made to feel strong by somebody else so she could let go and be merely a leaf, trembling, about to flutter out in the wind and be taken away. 'I do not know you, Luke,' she said. 'And you know nothing about me. How can this be happening?'

'What is happening?'

'It is caused by the music and the night. Nothing more. This is as unreal as any dream.'

But he kissed her a second time, touched deeply by the lonely helplessness of the fragile woman beside him. Why did she not respond? Why did she stare at him like that, smiling like that, as if he was not really there? It felt as if she was asleep. How could she sleep through this? He summed up her beauty with his eyes,

115

seeming to gather it up in them and hold it before he approached her again, letting his hands trace the shape of her body, ignoring her moans. But her eyes stayed tightly closed.

She felt his fingers trace fire through her dress and she said again, 'Nothing is happening. Nothing.'

Everything Alice Brennan had learnt, understood, or been deliberately taught within her strict Victorian up-bringing, told her that these thoughts were wrong. She was a married women with four children, quite old enough to know better and yet here she was, imagining herself ready to be loved by a stranger. She was shocked by her own reactions. For Alice knew that if it was not for her so recent childbirth she would be happy to love him now . . . here . . . in the middle of the night, high up on the parapet of the castle tower. They were only dreams, and yet these fantasies of hers made a madness more real than any Edward had so tamely suggested. These were wilder reactions, and more shameful than anything she had seen at Deale . . . they had contrived of no restraints, nothing powerful enough to contain this.

And when finally she followed him down, twisting round the tower that was Seaton's, back through the hall and into the courtyard, she found it inconceivable that everyone gathered there did not stare astonished, knowing what had happened. The change she felt in herself made her utterly different.

And then she saw Milly, saw the look on Milly's face, and she knew that what she feared was quite true. She *was* different, and the difference was one that Milly Toole instantly, and angrily, suspected.

In a curiously mechanical voice Alice whispered to Milly, 'I have done nothing wrong, Milly. I assure you I have done nothing wrong. It is not the same, believe me, this is quite, quite different. This time you are right and I know that nothing is really happening.'

# THIRTEEN

Milly Toole noticed the shining eyes, the flushed face and the breathless way of speaking. 'It is late,' she hastened to say, not deigning to look at Luke, 'and you need your rest, my darling.'

Alice badly wanted to dance, to prolong the dream, remain in the magical courtyard, enticed by the night, to sway to the music with Luke, but her own tired body and Milly's stern insistence were too much for her. Milly helped her to bed, and then she settled Davy, recognizing the likeness to his mother in the curve of his cheek and his brow. Alice had never been any good with her children – too dizzy, too silly. Milly nuzzled his neck and his warmth consoled her. And soon he was drowsy, then sleeping, immune to the music as Milly was.

The night deepened. The carpet of pine needles in the adjoining woods sent out a scented fragrance that mingled with the woodsmoke. It was a winter smell, and Milly shuddered. How much easier would all this be if it were summer. Milly had enjoyed her stew, had been pleasantly surprised to be handed a spoon, for she feared she would have to scoop up the mess using her potato. But she was not yet ready for sleep. She was worried. So she sat up beside the fire, preoccupied with getting warm, talking to Bella Pettigrew Lovett, the large bangled gyspy, with whom she found she had much in common in spite of her nervousness of her. The two women stared into the flames as Bella explained how this troupe, 'Ah yes, so different from any other, for it has developed over the generations like a huge snowball turning,' had gradually changed from a band of travelling Romanies to a circus that included all types. 'Tinkers, Didecois, Pinkies, and Gorgios like yourselves. We do not buy and sell as others do. We

117

are performers, artists, freaks, anyone who wants to join the show. And all led by my man, Nathaniel, who is an artist to his very soul.'

Milly's tongue was loosened by relief, by wine, and by the knowledge that Alice was safely asleep in the caravan. She could smell sour alcohol on Bella's breath, but she feared hers must be soaked with the same. 'That might well be, but what have I to do with all this? At my age I fear this violent change of circumstances will prove too much for me. I have always been a creature of habit, I don't mind admitting that, and I enjoy my home comforts. I have always liked to know where I am going, and this life, well, it seems to prohibit all that.' And Milly thought of her little house with the fire gone out and the shutters across the windows and the bed gone damp and cold.

'Not so at all,' said Bella, and Milly did not approve of the vulgar way she sat with her legs spread wide like that, as she caressed the long, curved stem of her pipe with one horny finger. 'You must try to look at it in a different light. Every morning when you wake up you know exactly where you are going. You might not get there, or you might be diverted, but you know where you're aiming for. Now I don't think you can say that for the Gorgio way of life . . . as far as I can see that is a matter of sitting and waiting and never knowing where the wind is taking you.'

How had the woman painted her face like that? Two dabs on her cheeks were a violent red, and her flaky lips were a crimson-purple. There were bright blue wings above her eyes. 'I am not thinking about tomorrow, or the day after,' Milly confided, glad to find someone to listen, even though the woman disconcertingly insisted on nodding her head and tapping her large booted feet to the music. 'I am more concerned with what is going to happen to us after that. We cannot go travelling for ever. We must stop some time, and find us a home where we can settle, for the sake of the child if not for mine.'

118

'You cannot manipulate the future,' said Bella. 'To live for the day is the gypsy code. If you look too far ahead you might not get there.' Bella blew smoke rings into the air and watching them, said, 'This life is a dream. After death we will wake . . .'

Milly pursed her lips and looked round her, taking everything in. She couldn't say, 'Nonsense!' for she was a guest, so instead she said, 'This is no way to live.'

'This is one night,' Bella told her, looking puzzled. 'This is not a way of anything. Why don't you just try to enjoy this one night?'

But how could Milly enjoy it? She stared hard at Bella, at the wisdom she saw there under the paint, at the knowing black eyes with the laughter so near to the edges that followed the wings of blue. Behind her was the rise and fall of murmured conversation, the occasional chuckle of happy laughter, the cries of children, the sharp impact of a tin spoon on a plate. But the people were a complicated pattern of lights and shadows woven between the firelight, sometimes moving nearer to spoon more stew from the steaming tureen, sometimes raking the ashes to find the last of the hot potatoes before moving off again. The clearest thing about them was the whites of their eyes. Gloomily she contemplated, gypsies and thieves, and here she was sitting comfortably down amongst them. She was nervous of those shadows. Little feathers of candlelight tickled the windows of some of the caravans where the tiny curtains did not quite meet. She could smell wild animals, and every now and again there was a sleepy roar from one of the cages and the dung, which men with long forks had piled in one corner of the courtyard, had begun to steam – horror. Disreputable-looking dogs of uncertain breed slid to their bellies beside the fire and laid down their thin grey noses. For goodness sake, what sort of a world was this to find yourself in? Eventually, after several minutes of silence when the fiddles replaced conversation, Milly said, 'I am afraid for my mistress.'

119

'Yes. I can understand that.'

Milly stiffened. She turned quickly to glance at Bella – had she guessed – but she puffed at her pipe and stared at the fire in apparent contentment. Only the feather on top of her hat bobbed slightly, stirred by a gust of heat.

'I am afraid because she is still such a child, protected from life's hardships. All her life, until recently, she has only experienced a sheltered existence, surrounded by comforts. Oh, she has suffered, she has lived the last few years persecuted by a cruelty beyond all description. Her husband, Edward, is a man without scruples, vicious, cold-hearted and cruel . . .'

'There are many men like that. Perhaps your mistress should not have stayed.'

Anger stirred Milly. She sensed some criticism of herself here, and her voice was agitated when she responded, 'That is easy for you to say. You are used to your freedoms, but the world Alice comes from is very different from the one you understand. First she was a child, then she was a wife and, as the firstborn, duty always came first. And now we find ourselves in this extraordinary situation and with no way out of it that I can see. And I am afraid Alice is easily influenced. Her emotions . . .' Milly automatically reached for the silver crucifix she wore round her neck. She was never without it. She was not a religious woman, and the touching of it was more for good luck than anything else. There had been times, she had to admit, when she had taken it off and set it on her dressing table and knelt down before it, unable to justify what she was doing, but using the symbol as a point of reference . . . something on which to concentrate. She fondled it, from habit, whenever her problems threatened to overwhelm her, just as she fondled the pins in her hair.

'You are nervous of Luke Durant?' Bella Pettigrew Lovett noticed the crucifix but did not smile.

'I am nervous of him because Alice sees him as her saviour. She has a sweet personality, she is giving,

120

loving, a little impulsive sometimes, and absurdly grateful towards those whom she considers to be her friends . . .'

Bella shifted round on her chair so that she faced Milly. Her feather waved backwards and forwards. 'You speak of her as though she was still a child. She has children of her own – she is no longer a young woman.'

'To me,' said Milly firmly, 'Alice will always be a child.'

Bella tapped the tobacco from the bowl on the sole of her boot. The hem of her long sable coat was crusted with mud. Under the coat Bella wore a thin dress of gold; it was indecent the way her pendulous breasts bulged out from over the top of it. After all, Bella must be approaching Milly's age. 'And you do not trust Luke Durant?'

'I knew him once . . .' said Milly.

'And you feel he betrayed you? There are those who consider what he and his family tried to do round here was a sincere attempt to right matters. The fact that they tried and failed, the fact that the rich landowners came and burned his home in retaliation, in order to drive the Durants away, makes some folks consider that Luke Durant should be given a knighthood, not be hounded for his life. His own father died in gaol. His mother was killed, his wealth confiscated by the state. See . . . look around you. See what they did to his home.' Bella's painted face crinkled into a frown. 'Twenty years ago they came, and Luke only just becoming a man. They ransacked his home and they set it alight. And all this they did in the name of progress.'

'We did not speak the name of Durant. From the nursery to the kitchens, the name of Durant was forbidden in the house. Alice knows  nothing about him . . . we made sure the young ladies were not concerned by such violent matters. Such ideas – a charter for the people! Those men were a menace to respectable society.'

121

'Huh! Gentry! They had much to lose . . . cheap labour . . . they brought in their damn machines. They enclosed the last of the common land. They refused to give alms to the poor and instead they condemned them to life in the workhouse.' Bella spat into the fire. She blew her nose between her fingers and wiped them on her sleeve. 'Look what has happened to the people since then. Starvation, pitiful wages when they could find work, and now they have been forced away from the countryside and they live in squalor in hovels, nothing more than rat runs in tenements in the towns. Their lives are poor, restricted things, their children die in the mills and the factories in spite of efforts to improve conditions. Or they work on the railways as navvies in gangs, treated worse than animals. The Durants had the courage to see what was happening and to fight against it with the Chartists.'

'That may be so,' said Milly stiffly, for she had never heard this point of view before and it disturbed her. 'But that does not redeem the man's reputation. He took women where he wanted them, and left them broken-hearted. His wild ways were talked about as much as the other damage he and his family did.'

Bella sighed. She delved deep in her vast coat pockets and offered Milly a black cigar. Milly stared at it coldly before shaking her head. 'He was a young man then, with fire in his heart, and he came from a turbulent family with a history of violent campaigning. There has to come a time when one forgives the faults of the child and looks hard at the man.'

'I have looked long and hard at the man,' said Milly. 'And I see the same, glib-talking charmer as I remember when I foolishly invited him into the kitchens at Venton Hall whenever he used to ride by. Years ago,' said Milly. 'That was years ago.'

'Maybe you have not looked hard enough. He rescued your Alice – surely that must count in his favour?'

'It is his intentions that frighten me. And Alice is so naive!'

122

Bella did not answer and Milly saw there was no point in arguing the rights and wrongs of Luke Durant any further. She feared that Bella was probably an excitable woman, easily roused – she had the strange habit of widening her nostrils, and they were bristly with hair – and Milly did not relish the prospect of that. So she asked instead, 'And does Luke travel with you all the time?'

They closed their eyes against a hail of sparks and a sudden gust of smoke. 'He is sometimes gone for long periods, helping his friends who fight in the law courts for his rights. Influential people are working to right the injustice. But he comes back. He knows he is always welcome here. He enjoys the life. In fact,' and Bella turned and smiled, 'he is one of the best actors we have although he firmly denies it. And he and Nathaniel have always been the best of friends. They fight, they argue most of the time, but this they thoroughly enjoy. Yes, they are the best of friends. Luke Durant will always be welcomed here.'

A loud burst of laughter came from the leading caravan and Milly whirled round in surprise. Down the steps came the largest man she had ever seen, and the most extraordinarily dressed one, quite shocking. It was hard to see, as he descended the steps and grew larger, how he had ever fitted inside that timid-looking wooden frame. Milly was certain the caravan steps buckled underneath him. He, too, wore a long coat of moth-eaten fur, and his long grey beard seemed to tangle in it and get lost, an exact match. On his head was a spangled turban of the kind Milly knew that Indian princes wore, but this was askew; a gold sovereign rested on his forehead and a long silk scarf of a violent yellow was wound round his neck several times before it descended all the way to the ground amidst the folds of fur. He clapped his huge hands against the cold, in time to the music and then he rubbed them gustily together as he peered around. Even Luke, who had followed the man down the steps, looked small beside him.

'Nathaniel,' said Bella, sniffing and wiping her nose on the back of her hand. 'He's come for his coffee. And he'll want me to tell him tomorrow's fortune.' She leaned forward and lifted the lid of the black kettle before her. The sour smell that came from it almost knocked Milly back off her chair.

'God keep you safe,' said Bella, as Milly hastily made her excuses and disappeared off to her bed.

# FOURTEEN

Before she laid herself down and pulled the gaudy coverings over her, Milly checked on Davy and his mother. It was habit, really. She did not like the unnatural flush on Alice's face, and she thought the little mutterings as she turned over, and the flutterings of her lashes were bad signs. All this is proving too much for Alice, thought Milly nervously, and she wished Luke Durant would ride off and see to some other business. What Alice needed was peace and quiet and time alone with her child. She ought to be given a breathing space in which she could recover. If only Milly could take her off to some quiet place where they could be by themselves.

Milly's eyes lingered longer over the child. She watched him carefully . . . he was so very vulnerable and tiny. Another time, another place, and there had been another baby. A boy child, too, and it should have been a time of great rejoicing, for wasn't a boy exactly what everyone at Venton had been waiting for?

It had not been like that, not at all like that.

Christmas – huh! It had marred all other Christmases for her since.

Deany Cook, one of the parlourmaids, had found Abernathy's body hanging limply amongst the pile of furs belonging to their guests, the marmalade incongruous and sad beside the minks and sables. Alice had shrivelled and gone quiet then, leaving Lucinda to the hysteria and Charlotte to apportion the flaming blame. Immediately Charlotte summed up the situation in order to suit herself and she set up a screeching that would have impressed the most furious fishwife – you'd never believe she was only nine years old. 'Because she did not want me to have him she killed him! You broke his neck, didn't you?' she screamed at Alice, backing away, pointing with her finger, as if at a murderess. 'You've always been sly and cruel. Well, this time you have outdone yourself!'

Lucinda crooned over the broken body of the cat which Milly laid in a hat-box decked with a cheery red ribbon. Lucinda pulled at the ribbon, promising to replace it with a more suitable black one and her tears were flowing freely.

But Charlotte carried on relentlessly. 'How could you hate me so much? How could you be so vicious?'

'Now, now, Charlotte, don't take on so. How can you accuse your gentle sister of something so dreadful as this? You know full well that Alice loves Abernathy, she'd be the last person on earth to do anything to hurt him! After all, that cat would have died along with the rest of its family if Alice hadn't taken him in and nursed him and reared him with all that caring and all that love.'

'Milly, be quiet! How can you be so blind as not to see what is happening? All the time you protect her, just because she is pretty and sweet and quiet like a little doll! No one ever believes wrong of Alice. That is how it is here, she is never blamed for anything, it is always either me or Lucinda!'

'I think you've just condemned yourself out of your own mouth,' retorted Milly firmly. 'You are jealous of Alice because of her uncommon good looks and her sweet disposition. You have to fight your temper, your darkness, and you resent the natural innocent ways of your sister. And I think you also resent the fact that your parents consider her special because of who she is.'

'Now the truth is out!' Charlotte's features contorted with anger and Milly stepped back, astonished that such malice could manifest itself on the face of a little child. 'Go on . . . blame me . . . blame me! Make up your reasons and continue to defend her! But you defend a monster, Milly Toole, and one day you are going to realize that and be sorry!'

Alice's voice was small, her face was pale and her wide blue eyes were full of tears when she tried to defend herself against the wild accusations of her sister. 'You think that I would kill Abernathy? You think that I would kill a dear creature that meant so much to me?'

Charlotte, unable to contain her fury, hissed at Alice through bared teeth while Lucinda let her golden ringlets fall upon the dead animal. Alice stood watching the scene, wretched, pale and tense, her small hands clenched at her sides.

'Pull yourself together now, Charlotte,' Milly huffed. 'How can you say such things, and it's quite time you stopped abandoning yourself to your temper like this. Tomorrow you will be sorry you said . . . '

'I will never be sorry,' cried Charlotte. 'Look at her eyes, Milly. *Look at her eyes* . . . There is no pity in them – they are hard blue, like the glass eyes of a doll.'

'There are tears in them, Charlotte, if you care to look.'

'Crocodile tears, easily conjured up, for Alice is an expert at these guileless performances and yet you cannot see it!' The hatred on Charlotte's face was chilling. 'How long are you going to go on believing her, protecting her? Tell me, Milly, tell me. Answer me that! Dear Alice this and dear Alice that. She has always been your favourite – I have even heard you telling her so – but how long are you going to go on convincing yourself that Alice is what she is not?'

It was impossible to say how long that awful attack would have gone on, with the cat stiffening in the box and the Christmas stockings unopened on the mantel, and the rocking chair empty – for Edward Brennan had taken himself off in the night, much to Milly's relief and she did not much care where he'd gone. But she did suspect it was he who had killed the cat. Well, who else could have done it, unless it was one of the guests who could not cope with the drink . . .

But then Thomas Venton had stalked into the room in the middle of all the drama. 'What do you mean by

127

this behaviour, this undignified racket coming from the nursery when your mother has been taken ill? For goodness sake, have some respect. As if I have not got enough on my mind at the moment without having to hear such screams! Milly, what is happening here? Please establish some control. I cannot abide chaos!'

Thomas strode away from the door leaving a cold draught of justified anger behind him.

The boy, the long-awaited son and heir, Neville Venton, had been born a month early. He arrived on Boxing Day, pale blue, wrinkled and puny, and swaddled in tight blankets, he was handed to Milly on the night of his birth. By then all thoughts of the pitiful Abernathy had been put from their minds, overshadowed by the illness of Sarah Venton. The guests left early and without them there but with the decorations still up, the house went strangely quiet, garbed already in a garish, obscene kind of premature mourning. The gardeners came with ladders and stripped down the evergreens which they piled on a bonfire beside the high park wall. Milly watched the smoke from the nursery window as it whisked up greyly into a sky of steel, and thought of an ancient funeral pyre. A sense of foreboding filled the place; it was in the servants' soft tread and in the lowered eyes of the grooms and gardeners when Milly took her sweet things outside. They had to put up with the company of Cherry the nurserymaid because Milly dared not stray further than the back door. She could not leave the cradle.

And during all that was left of that Christmas, the wind wailed and blew like a lost soul and the rain lashed the windows and brought out the patches of damp high on the wall above the nursery fireplace. Yellowy damp, with patches of speckled black fungus that made your hair crawl when you looked at it. It was hard to keep warm for the draughts. Would it never end?

It was an exhausting, terrible time. And Thomas Venton spent the days cradling his head on his arms, slumped on his desk with a bottle of brandy beside him, in spite of the fact that his wife called for him constantly, in spite of the fact that his newborn son whimpered weakly upstairs. Friends tried to rally him; the bailiff, Jenkins, spent hours sitting with him, the chaplain tried to pray with him, but Thomas Venton would have none of it. He waved them away with his long-fingered, distraught white hands. He drank more deeply and his eyes went sour, dark and heavy.

When the news of his wife's death was broken to him he looked up, bleary-eyed, his mouth sagging open, and it was suspected that he did not at first comprehend. And then he put back his head and howled like an animal in anguish.

'You have a son,' said the chaplain wearily, two days later. 'And you have a family of little daughters who are all depending on you.'

Thomas Venton dashed his glass into the fireplace and watched while the dregs of brandy flared. 'I have a son,' he commented bleakly, 'but for how long? How long can this losing streak of the Ventons' persist?'

Such a tiny motherless thing. Milly attended the child day and night until she didn't know if she was sleeping or waking. Her sweet things were good as gold; mending their differences over the cat they took turns to watch the child when Milly was forced away for brief sessions of sleep.

'Will he live, Milly? Is it true what they say, that Neville is too small to survive?'

Milly clicked her tongue. 'Oh Alice, how can I answer that? How can I promise you that, my darling? All we can do is tend him and love him and pray to the Lord . . . '

'The Lord has killed his Mama.'

Milly turned to look at her favourite child as she stood there behind the cradle, one little hand on the canopy, gently rocking. 'Bless you, don't think like that. As you know full well, God has His reasons. All will come well in the end.'

129

So Milly sat with the baby for hours, trying to coax him to take the bottle into his feeble mouth. He had no suck and there was no power in his limbs. He was not a proper baby; he lay and stared for too many hours, not sleeping, nor properly waking either. Milly wished she could breathe life into him as easily as she flamed the fire with the bellows. That's what he needs, she thought to herself as she sat, stiff and cold, in the rocking chair, with the limp life warmly wrapped in her arms – a good old blast of life. Death . . . damp and cold, was threatening to win this terrible battle.

The loss of their mother made little difference to the everyday life in the nursery. The children had spent scant time with her, but even so, the knowledge that she was no longer there left them fearful and tearful, empty inside. Part of them had been wrenched away too soon. Milly hated to see her sweet things dressed in black. It did not suit their fair complexions, it made them look pale and ill and Milly was tired of illness. The stiff, coarse material, new and made up in a rush, was badly-fitting and chafed at their wrists and ankles so that Milly had to rub cream in.

Sarah Venton was buried in the family cemetery, a high-walled place of dark green, sombre with shadows of leaning tombstones, thin with gaunt railings. Stiffly ranked, the railings made Milly think they were bars dividing Heaven from Hell. Dominating the whole miserable ceremony was a black marble angel with wide-spread wings and a face so hard, so lacking in compassion it was terrible to behold. Well, if Heaven is filled with people like that, thought Milly, shivering with cold, she was certainly not looking forward to being there. Leaving Cherry with her tiny charge for just one hour, Milly stood respectfully at the back on the opposite side to the family so she could keep an eye on the children. Clasping her hands together she suddenly realized, as she felt the damp wind on her face, just how long it was since she had been outside other than to wave off the girls on their walks with

130

Cherry. She allowed the rain to slide down her cheeks unchecked; the wet drops found old furrows and followed them to the corners of her mouth. She wanted to step forward and comfort the children . . . she considered it a most unsuitable pastime for children to be standing beside the open grave like that. Given the opportunity, she would have forbidden it. They were too young. Charlotte's small shoulders were shaking and little Lucinda was sobbing aloud. Someone should put their arm round her. But their father stood like a slab of granite, slightly leaning like one of those tall tombstones, staunch and unbending. Alice showed no sign of emotion. She stood beside the grave looking in with an expression of calm on her face in the way she stared at water, her lips tight together and her eyes half-closed, a little bit like that angel, while the chaplain's prayers were blown away like dead leaves in the wind, up and over the wall and out to the open parkland. Milly's heart fluttered with them. Milly understood. Milly knew that Alice could only weep in privacy, quite alone, afraid to let her feelings show. When they got home she would comfort her. Perhaps that's why the angel looked so hard and cold; perhaps the statue, also, was trying to conceal a sorrow so deep she did not dare to reveal it.

'If my son dies, Milly, then that is the end of the line.'

Yes, at the most unexpected times, day or night it did not matter which, Thomas Venton took to visiting the nursery. Having him standing there beside her was most disconcerting. For he rarely spoke, save to bark out odd declarations such as that one, and his dour, hopeless attitude did not help much. He was nothing but a bag of nerves. Milly wasn't nursing the child because he was 'the end of the line', 'the last of the Ventons', 'the last chance for carrying on the family name'. Milly was nursing him because he was little and helpless, because she loved him. She lifted her head to face Thomas Venton, stern, tall, grim-faced, a tortured

131

presence that reeked of tobacco and alcohol, and she returned her gaze to the child in her arms, warm, smelling wetly of birth and regurgitated milk, as he lay there with his little fingers curled round her thumb.

If only Thomas would take some notice of his daughters. They were only little children, they needed their father now. It must be hurtful for them to see him striding past them, not a nod of recognition, not even the most formal of greetings, let alone a kiss or a cuddle or a romp on the floor. No, haggard, determined, he always made straight for the crib. Not for weeks had he sent for Alice to do her morning reading. It was as if, now he had what he wanted, Alice ceased to matter any more, was no more important than Charlotte or Lucinda . . . just one of the group. Even the dreaded riding lessons had stopped. Everything in the house appeared to have stopped, to be holding its breath and waiting for something. Sometimes Milly worried that she was neglecting her sweet things, giving so much of her time and attention to the sickly baby boy.

'The Doctor said that he seemed a little sturdier today,' said Milly.

Thomas Venton grunted. 'I am sparing no expense,' he said.

Huh. Milly knew that the life of the mite had little to do with expense, and a good thing, too, for rumours had started to spread. Thomas was reeling from the effects of his ill-advised, catastrophic investments. A good many shareholders had lost their money, and that was the way these things went. But she knew that the kitchen bills and the farm bills were late being paid. The villagers who depended on Venton for their livelihoods, the farmworkers and the labourers were hungry and restless. There were torchlit processions at night, meetings which thousands of people attended. One night Milly looked out of her window and saw a long low glow upon the horizon, like an early sunrise, creeping along. Some of the landowners had received threats . . . and these unruly mobs were led by wild men hell-bent on the destruction of everything that was safe, was traditional and good. Last year these men had even sent a petition to Parliament. Nothing seemed to be right any more. Everything was changing.

She wished Thomas Venton would go away and leave her alone. She wished the wind would cease its moaning, that she could skip a few months and wake up to find herself basking in spring, in the soft scents of buttercup breezes.

And then came January.

Milly would always blame herself because she was not in the room when he died. She had been gone only a second – merely a second – to check that Cherry had filled the coal-bucket before she retired for the night. Such a silly, unnecessary errand, really, but three times just lately the slatternly maid had forgotten. So three times Milly had been forced to ring downstairs after ten and withstand the bad grace of the lamp boy, Lloyd, who had fetched up the coal under greasy-faced protest.

When she got back the baby was lifeless, white as a china doll. He had even closed his own eyes, she noticed, as she leaned down wearily to pick up his pillow.

For a moment Milly just sat there beside him and smiled, relaxed for the first time in weeks, letting something unknot from the tangle of emotions way deep inside her. She had known he would not live, that it was merely a matter of time. The fight was over. But if only she had been in the room so she could have held him in her arms. Such a small bundle as that should not set off alone on such a long journey.

As Milly had sat there, limp and forlorn, her mind jumped suddenly to the cold black angel in the cemetery. A shiver, cold as any death, passed through her. And then there was Alice in her long nightgown laying a trembling hand on her shoulder, and there was the calm, drawn face of the child, knowing, understanding, fixing the baby with that intense gaze of hers.

'Oh!' exclaimed Milly, her hand to her heart. 'My

goodness, you made me jump! I thought you were in your bed and sound asleep hours ago!'

'God must have wanted him,' whispered Alice, 'and God knows best.'

They had wept in each other's arms, clinging together for comfort before going to tell the others.

But Davy Brennan, in spite of his unfortunate start, was no such delicate weakling. Milly sighed and smiled wryly as she pulled the blanket to his chin, crossed the tiny space between the two beds and sank down on to her own. The violins were still playing, a mournful, sad sound now, overpowered by men's laughter and occasional coarse interruptions from Bella Pettigrew Lovett. Inside the caravan Alice thrashed from side to side, no doubt in a turmoil of terrible dreams caused by her recent flight and the nightmare place she had left behind her. Should Milly wake her? Reassure her that all was well, and that Bella had informed her they would certainly be moving on in the morning? The more distance they put between themselves and Edward, the safer they would both feel. No, Milly decided to let Alice sleep. If she was dreaming terrible dreams, and no wonder, it was best they come out and be dealt with. It was safer to deal with them in the darkness of sleep than in daylight, safer to murmur your whispering secrets when there was no one about to hear.

# FIFTEEN

It had been dark last night when they arrived at Castle Bellever, Luke Durant's derelict home. Now the sights and sounds of morning were illuminated by shafts of a cold white sunlight, and for the first time Alice Brennan could see the exact nature of her new and unexpected, her cleverly conjured-up world.

Alice rose early. Leaving Milly sound asleep, she dressed and wandered outside. With a gypsy shawl covering her head she followed the circle of caravans, twenty-five in all, and the violently painted conveyances fitted neatly underneath the walls of the castle courtyard. On the lead caravan, in bold, multi-coloured lettering down the sides, and across a wooden banner attached to the roof, was written *LOVETT'S TRAVELLING THEATRE*, and from the loud snores that came from within, Nathaniel Lovett and his fierce wife were still sleeping off the effects of last night's drink.

She was staggered by what her own mind could achieve. She tried not to stare when she passed a family of dwarfs; the women looked like the wooden dolls Edward had ordered, one Christmas, from Germany. There were clogs on their feet, bright cotton headscarves on their hair, and they wore white aprons over their brilliant skirts. The men wore pixie caps and almost all of them were bearded – even here at work they looked like characters out of a pantomime and they seemed to have chosen their dogs for their size, for Alice saw three tiny creatures, well able to hold their own against the pack of gypsy curs that came to sniff a morning greeting.

Past another brightly painted caravan, and a deep bass voice sang snatches of opera between bouts of violent gargling, and every now and then a woman's soprano joined in with the song. Men were leading the horses which had been pastured in the paddock back

135

through the castle gateway and their hooves made a deep clopping sound on the wooden planking. Three tiny children, hardly old enough to walk, balanced on the back of one chestnut cob, and a frisky stallion with wild eyes was being ridden by a sallow man with waist-length hair and a beaded band round his head. He sat on the horse backwards. He looked like a Red Indian. He looked ferocious.

'You're up early. Somehow I didn't imagine you to be an early riser.'

Alice's heart jumped. Could he tell she had been dreaming about him all night? Would he guess that secretly she had been looking for him? And now she had the chance to discover whether he could remember last night, whether he was real enough to remember last night – or was he a new creature, a figment of the next morning? He looked like last night's man, just as handsome, with his tightly curling black hair and his challenging eyes. A red bandanna was round his neck, his sleeves were rolled to his elbows, but over all that a bright blue cape hung loosely round his shoulders. And she knew that he was remembering, too, because of the direct way he looked at her, and he caught her arm with too much familiarity for a man who might have forgotten. How should she respond to him? She lowered her eyes. Last night she had let herself behave like a hussy, allowing him to kiss her, to touch her like that. What must he think of her, a lady, a newly-delivered mother, married, who had been taught that it was wrong even to glance at a stranger. What would he say? Would he refer to her disgraceful behaviour? Did it matter?

'The sun woke me,' she answered his question. 'And I slept all day yesterday. I've had too much sleep.' Alice avoided his eyes.

'And now you want to see your new world.'

'I was interested, yes.'

Luke sent a glance over his shoulder towards her caravan. He said, 'I think that Mrs Toole would be

136

nervous to see us together. She's keen to keep us apart. The old woman doesn't approve of me, she thinks I'm a bad influence. Are you easily influenced, Alice?'

Heat rushed through her because of his tone of voice and the way he leaned down to speak to her so softly. She attempted to keep her voice steady when she answered, 'That depends.'

'Upon what?'

'Last night . . . ' She started in a rush, almost fiercely.

'Yes?'

'I wouldn't like you to think that I always . . . '

'I am just surprised you remembered. It felt as if you weren't there.' And Luke Durant smiled, and as his mouth opened slightly she saw the hard, white shine of his teeth and remembered the way she had made them tug at her lips last night.

Alice opened her eyes very wide and they were fringed with golden lashes. Dragonflies don't dart effortlessly over the water. They beat their desperate wings, unseen, and they die very quickly. If you drew close to Alice you could hear the pounding of those tiny wings. But then she blinked, and her eyes were vacant again. She is so terribly frightened, Luke told himself, so terrified.

But when he took her hand she didn't pull away, she meekly followed as he walked on and explained, 'This isn't just a circus, as the redoubtable Mrs Toole likes to think it is,' and he stopped while Alice stared at the two pacing tigers behind their bars. 'And although we carry animals – see the brown bear over there – they're only part of the entertainment. We are a very versatile company, we have to be because things are changing so fast. We were one of the first to carry our own canvas: we can stage shows on village greens and at fairs if we need to do so. We follow a regular country circuit, but Nathaniel likes to get bookings in variety houses and tavern concert rooms in the towns where the money is more certain and the work more regular.'

137

'You travel all the time?'

Luke nodded. 'Even in the winter we travel. We're one of the most popular companies in theatres and town halls up and down the land.'

'They're such beautiful animals, so wild, I hate to see them caged. But it's the eyes of the tigers that mesmerize me.' Alice watched as a puny little man in a blood-spattered apron pushed a slab of meat through the bars. She stared as the two sleek creatures fell upon it and started to tear it apart. 'What are those eyes full of, Luke? Fear? Hate? Desire? What is it?'

Luke turned to Alice and held her eyes with his own. 'That's the question I'm asking myself,' he said quietly, before pulling her on.

One caravan had its windows completely boarded up, and when Alice asked why, Luke told her, 'That's where we store the props, costumes and scenery. Some of our actresses are exceptionally talented and guarantee us a good following. Just recently some of our competitors have started using the railways for travel, but Nathaniel prefers the old ways and so far they haven't failed us.'

The furthest Alice had travelled in her life was the twenty-mile journey from Winterbourne House to Deale Asylum. Anything she had ever learnt had come from books or the magic slide shows that Edward sometimes arranged for the children on their birthdays. 'Where do we start for today?'

'We arrive at Exeter tonight where we'll stay for three days before moving on. Most of us'll be well occupied. The puppeteers will put up their booth in the city and the main troupe will perform in the theatre. And of course there will be the penny gaffe . . . '

'What is that?'

Luke smiled. 'You've never heard of the penny gaffe?'

'No, I've never heard of anything like that.'

'Well, I suppose it's not the sort of entertainment likely to appeal to a lady. For years the authorities have been trying to close them down.'

Alice stared when a blowzy woman with painted lips called to Luke as they passed her caravan door. She had imagined the inhabitants of this one to be still asleep, for the curtains were drawn tightly across the windows and all was silent inside. The young woman, immodestly dressed, emerged from the doorway with eyes half-closed against the sunshine, frowning. Her long black hair was tangled and uncombed and she wore what seemed to be nothing but a flimsy piece of material, hardly warm enough, and there was a frosty chill to the air. Alice stiffened. At first she imagined her feelings were those of disapproval for a person so obviously immoral, and then, to her shame, she realized that what she was experiencing was a sharp stab of jealousy. For the woman, indecent though she undoubtedly was, and not clean either, was strangely charismatic, and very beautiful. She treated Luke with a bawdy familiarity which seemed to please him, and Alice did not want her in her dream.

'Well now, and aren't you going to introduce me to your new lady friend, my darling? Walking by the varda with your nose in the air as if you don't even know I'm here and waiting.' The woman stretched her hands, flexed the fingers and admired the scarlet nails on the ends. She reminded Alice of the tigers, sensual and impatient.

'Is the coffee boiling yet?' Luke asked her.

The woman tilted her head in the direction of the communal fire. Her voice was husky and deep. 'There's coffee to be had over there, and well you know it. 'Tis a long time since anyone called on me for coffee. I don't make good coffee, 'tis not what I'm good at. I don't cook well either, or sew your stockings, laddie. Trying to impress your new friend with high-falutin' manners, is that what it is, then?' And then she called over her half-naked shoulder, mimicking Luke's voice almost to perfection, 'Oh Jennie, have you got the coffee boiling on the stove yet? Luke is ready for

139

his breakfast.'

There was a curse, another voice laughed, and someone called, 'For God's sake whoever you are, piss off or turn over!'

Alice quickly walked on. She blushed when she heard the laughter and some of the raucous comments that followed. Suddenly, she had to duck, for she was almost strangled by the practice wire. She looked up, alarmed, as she became aware of the tall thin man who balanced in the air above her.

'That's Will Symonds, he works on the high wire. You'll get used to him – you'll quickly become used to all this. It must seem very strange . . . '

'It doesn't matter whether I get used to it or not. But who was that?'

Luke looked confused.

'The woman who refused you coffee. Who were those women?' Alice loathed herself for asking, but she was shaking, shocked by the experience of coming face to face with such lewd behaviour, such foul language. In Deale she had seen many things, she had heard many things she thought she would never hear again, but in the Asylum the patients had an excuse . . . they were sick. But Luke had appeared to accept such behaviour as normal.

'There are many different kinds of people here, all sorts . . . '

'Who was that woman?'

'The woman in the revealing robe is called Unity Heath.' They were approaching the fire now, and the numerous children were holding out bread to toast in the ashes. 'The other five who share that caravan – well, sometimes they perform with the troupe, but they have specialities of their own. They are Gorgios, like us, for the Romanies would never allow their women such freedom . . . but they accept the needs of others and theirs is a most profitable enterprise.'

'The penny gaffes,' said Alice. 'What are they? Secret shows?'

'One day you'll see,' said Luke calmly, lifting the black kettle left by Bella last night, sniffing at it, and unclipping a tin cup from his belt. 'But it's too early to explain everything to you at once. You must take your time, there's so much for you to absorb. And I don't want Mrs Toole to accuse me of being a bad influence . . . not in the morning!' He pointed to a chair. There was dew on the seat. He wiped it and Alice sat down. He poured the thick, black coffee into the mug and offered it to her. She sipped it, warming her hands, wrapping them round the welcome shape. She needed something to do with her hands.

'Pull your chair nearer to the fire,' said Luke. 'You're cold.'

Alice obeyed him, smiling up at him gratefully. But Alice was not cold, she was excited and frightened. For the whole half hour she had spent with Luke she had given not a thought to her fear, to Deale, to Edward or Charlotte. She'd been fascinated by what she'd seen, eager for time to hurry on so she could understand more about these people, see new sights and go to strange places. She must not wake. Not yet. But above all, it was Luke Durant who caused this trembling effect, the shuddering inside. Her breasts felt sore, they were filled with milk, but she did not want her child to suck, she wanted Luke! And the soreness between her legs became a pleasant sensation; she was aware of her body in a way that she had forgotten was even possible.

And Luke wanted her . . . his eyes told her that whenever she caught them. Oh, and she wanted him, not in any demure, ladylike manner, not in the way of the stories she read in her books or even in the magazines which Charlotte so frowned upon, calling them disgraceful and lower-class. She wanted him . . . as an animal wants to mate. She thought of Unity Heath and was horrified by the fascination she'd immediately felt for the woman, that sultry slut with the slanting eyes. She did not know about such people, and yet she had

141

deliberately conjured them up! She realized what she was thinking and some of the coffee slopped out of the mug and Alice shrank into herself, afraid of her clumsiness, terrified of exposing herself, even in dreams, and wishing there was something she could hide behind.

And now, just to see the way the expressions changed on his face, to watch his casual movements, to listen to his enthusiasm for life which came through every time he spoke – just to be near him was enough. This man, this total stranger so despised by Milly, he promised her something . . . something she had always felt was there but had never been able to grasp, hardly able to see. She had tried to reach it once and been punished ever after. She felt she had led her life behind a high wall and now here was someone who was willing to help her over.

She was frightened.

She turned her face away from him. In shame, in case he should know who she was, in case he could see.

# SIXTEEN

As Lovett's Travelling Theatre prepared to leave Castle Bellever, not half a day's ride away Edward Brennan picked at the hot and cold food under silver dishes in his dining room – a few kidneys, a slice of cold game pie, three eggs, a piece of rare steak – and he carefully tested the heat of a warm bread roll in the palm of his hand. Squeezing it.

'I have instructed the children to join us this morning,' said Charlotte, not hungry, and sitting erect at one end of the table with a cup of milkless tea. The silver teaspoon was neatly set in the saucer, she sat with a ruler-straight back, her hands on her lap and not one hair of her head out of place. A dry, mousy beige, it was all swept back off her forehead apart from two tiny curls like the claws of a crab which were set on either side. The bulk of the rest of her hair was plaited into a firm knot at the back of her neck. 'There are matters we should discuss – they must be informed of recent events. They keep asking, especially Nicholas.'

'Where is Nicholas?' Edward was uneasy.

'He has gone for an early ride. I warned him what would happen if he was late to breakfast again.'

Edward, his plate satisfactorily full, pulled up his chair and regarded Charlotte down the long, thin length of white cloth. The tall windows behind her filled the room with a cold winter sunshine. At either side of the table the backs of empty chairs sat in waiting and at breakfast-time, without the displays of flowers and the high piles of fruit, the glasses and the vast arrays of cutlery, this vacant effect was exaggerated.

Edward gave a cursory glance at the newspapers neatly ironed and set beside his place. He took out his fob watch and glanced at the time. 'It is nine o'clock. It looks as though he is going to ignore your warnings as usual,' he said.

'There was no news delivered in the night?' Charlotte's white hands rested, stiff, on her starched napkin.

'There was no news.' Edward broke one of his eggs and watched as the orange spread over the meat. 'Although I half-expected it. If Alice is travelling with Milly Toole they can't have gone far. Neither of them has enough money to take them out of the county. No,' and he buttered his roll before continuing, giving the action the strictest attention, not allowing the slightest smear to touch his fingers because cleanliness was important to him, 'what concerns me most is discovering the identity of the fellow who attacked Myers and his party yesterday. The biggest danger of all,' and Edward put down his knife and placed the salt on the side of his plate with a minute silver spoon, 'is that she has found a protector.'

The clock on the dining-room mantelpiece chimed nine. Edward patted his mouth and glanced at it before he said, 'Myers is coming to see me this morning so that we can discuss our next course of action. We have under a year left in which to get Alice registered as insane. After that, the running of the Asylum comes out of the Board's hands and is taken over by special commissioners. I, as chairman of the local Board of Guardians, will lose what influence I have over Myers and his ilk.'

'Surely Alice cannot fool Myers for much longer. She must be brought back! We should never have allowed her to escape. I was wrong about that, but I overestimated your capabilities. And now, what is being done? Informing the local constabulary is not good enough. Unless Myers will agree with us and state categorically that Alice is dangerous, not much notice of her escape is going to be taken by anyone.'

Edward started to answer, 'I am not a fool. I do realize, Charlotte . . . ' but at that moment there was a tap on the door and Jane, neatly uniformed, announced, 'The young ladies are here, ma'am. Should I bring them in?'

'Yes, Jane, if you would, and you need not stay. I will ring for you when they have finished.'

The faces of the two children, Kate and Laura, were serene and blanked with caution. Their pale blue dresses, the skirts supported by crinolines, reached their calves, and their white stockings disappeard into tightly laced boots. Tiny buttons did up to their necks, and their neat collars were freshly starched. There was nothing to criticize about their appearances. Both held their arms straight by their sides, both stood beside the closed door after Jane had disappeared, and waited to be invited to sit.

It was extraordinary for them to be summoned at breakfast-time. On most days they were excused from taking their meals downstairs, and only saw Charlotte when she came to give them their lessons, between ten in the morning and twelve, but recently even those had ceased. That something had happened was very clear, and the knowledge that it might be connected with their mother made them nervous. Laura, nine, and older than Kate by two years, willed her sister to observe all that Jane had told them, to keep quiet unless spoken to first, not to fidget . . . Laura had hoped that Nicholas might be here. Nicky could sometimes be very funny, and he did funny things, he made them laugh.

'Come and sit down.'

Charlotte's words were clipped and precise. As usual it was not their father who spoke to them first.

'Don't they want anything to eat?'

Charlotte snapped a reply, 'They can have something to eat after we have spoken to them. The food will keep warm for a while longer and we do not want them to linger in here longer than is necessary.'

The two little girls made to sit down beside each other.

'No, not there, Laura. Go round to the other side so that I can see you both better.'

Charlotte observed them carefully. Nothing Jane

could do could remove that baby-doll likeness both of these daughters bore to their mother. Their pale, oval faces resembled hers. Their golden ringlets were natural, their hair did not need curling. And no one had taught them to peer out under their lashes like that . . . unless in their early years they had picked up the mannerism from Alice. Their small shoulders and their long necks gave them that genteel poise, and their elfin chins expressed a certain stubbornness that Charlotte realized they could not correct . . . but even so, it annoyed her.

'Your mother.' Charlotte sat slightly forward. And Laura thought that the subject, smacked down so severely on the table like that was worse than seeing a bowl of steaming spinach, or thin slices of tripe, or an egg custard with skin on. So Laura studied the whitely-swirling patterns on the tablecloth with the utmost attention but the hands on her lap were squeezed tightly together.

'Now then, listen to me carefully. Your mother has recently disappeared from the hospital where she was sent and, what is worse, she has taken your baby brother with her. In spite of searches made by your Papa and a great many of the estate workers, there is no sign of either of them.'

Brother? Laura saw Kate's face turn quickly towards Charlotte. She knew her sister's blue eyes would be wide, avid with interest. No one had told them anything about a brother. Once again Laura willed Kate not to ask questions. They would find out in time, they always did – mostly by accident, when adults would forget they were there and mention things in conversation – but they would find out in the end. To ask directly was never the best way. Across the table, small in the high-backed chair, Kate remained silent. Out of the corner of her eye, Laura saw the question die as her sister's natural interest gave way to the unpleasant memory of earlier mistakes.

'As you have been told, your Mama has never been

well. Your father and I have always had a good deal to put up with in that respect. Your Mama is like a little child, less restrained than you are. Quite beyond control. So, in some ways it was understandable for her to imagine she could leave the place where they were taking care of her and look after a baby in the outside world, without money, with no home to go to.'

Laura bit her lip. She was no longer aware of what Kate was doing and she did not care. Images of Mama, alone and frightened in the dark and with no one to take care of her, came forcefully to mind and Laura feared that her face was about to crumple. It took all the strength she had to hold back her emotions, to stay sitting very still and to listen. She knew that Mama was silly and childish . . . that she liked to laugh a lot, dance and play games. She realized that was not the way an adult should behave. She remembered with pain the way Aunt Charlotte had chastised her, not caring who was about to listen, so that even the servants began to talk to her in that strict way in the end. But Mama never argued back: she either laughed, or cried and fled to her room with her little hands over her face. Sometimes someone would lock the door behind her. But no matter what Edward and Charlotte did they could not change her, because the next day Mama would come to the nursery just the same and lie on the floor and help them with jigsaws, dance to the music of the phonograph, showing them the right dancing steps; she would put on the voices of the different characters when she read them stories, never caring what she sounded like, until Kate and Laura, and Nicholas too, were laughing so hard at Mama's antics that tears rolled down their faces.

If Mama was sick then it was a lovely sickness. She was good to be with, she was fun.

She would sit on tasselled cushions and cover their hair with ribbons, saying, 'Pretty, pretty, oh look at you both you are so terribly pretty . . . ' And Milly would sit back in the rocking chair smiling that big, benign smile of hers and toasting her feet by the fire but watching Mama just the same. Everyone always watched Mama. Sometimes she would sing, but Laura was not sure she liked Mama singing because her voice sounded so sad and there had been times when Laura had noticed Mama staring out of the window into the distance, and then she had seen her crying. She cried when she sang those beautiful songs like that.

But in the end Papa had stopped her coming to the nursery.

'Now Nicholas went to visit your Mama on the day your brother was born,' Charlotte continued. Her voice was not like Mama's, high and clear; Charlotte's voice was controlled, not many highs and not many lows, but it kept to a careful pathway somewhere down the middle. Even when Charlotte was angry she did not raise her voice. At those times her voice went even quieter. Laura watched the way a vein pulsed, close to her hairline, at the top of her shiny forehead. 'And your Papa and I are wondering if Nicholas said anything to you when he came back to the house. We know she was going to Milly Toole's but it seems as though your Mama has other friends, people who are misguided enough to be looking after her, not understanding how ill she is, and how she needs specialist care.'

Having spoken, Charlotte sat back, allowing some space for Edward should he require it. His attitude towards his small daughters was softer, but under Charlotte's gaze they knew he would have to be firm.

'In her head, your mother still lives in those shadow-lands.' He liked to explain it all in that way, thinking it was easier for his children to understand. But they did not understand, and Laura knew that Kate still imagined that the shadowlands was a place, like a fairy-tale castle.

And now, Kate, unable to contain herself any longer, dumped her screwed fists on the table and asked her father: 'But if she is in the shadowlands, and has run away from there, how can she still be in there, Papa? I

148

don't understand. Where is she?'

Charlotte's sigh was a loud one. She raised her thin eyebrows. She stared hard at Kate's hands and Kate removed them – they messed up the neatness of the cloth.

'Sometimes I wonder if there's any point, any point at all,' said Charlotte, pretending to be weary. So Edward tried again.

'The shadowlands is the state of your mother's head; there is no such place, Kate, in reality. But sometimes sick people go there and sometimes they are so sick there is no way out for them. They must be looked after by people who understand about such things . . . '

'Mama loves us. If she has run away from somewhere she will come back here,' said Kate.

'That is enough, Katherine.'

Charlotte's voice was icy cold and her eyes were staring like the eyes of a dead fish.

'Now Nicholas is your brother, and I know that you love him and admire him, but Nicholas can be difficult. He tries to be a man and he is not quite old enough to be one. He is torn between doing the right thing and pleasing his mother. There is a possibility that Nicholas knows more than he is telling us . . . if he is in one of his difficult moods. He might have said something on one of his visits to the nursery and, if he did, then it is your responsibility to inform us, for your mother's sake, for the sake of her safety and her continued well-being.' Edward's voice was slow, he forced tired patience into it.

Neither child answered. The silence was tense. Over their heads Charlotte and Edward looked at each other. Nobody moved. Eventually Charlotte broke it. 'Well, we are waiting,' she said.

'Nicholas did not even tell us we had a brother.' Laura spoke directly to her father, ignoring Charlotte completely. 'Nicholas did not tell us that Mama had left the hospital. He does not talk to us about such things, Papa. And if he had told us anything, we would

149

certainly tell you, because we love Mama and we want her to be made better so she can come home.'

'Is this the truth, Laura?'

Laura faced Charlotte with mute eyes. 'I would not lie.'

And once again Charlotte felt that itch of irritation stinging her hands as she was faced with that same sweet, clear declaration of innocence, those appealing eyes, that unquestionable sincerity, exactly the same as Alice when she was a child. She wanted to get up from the table, push back her chair and slap the child. Oh, it was unfair of her to make these comparisons and Charlotte knew it. Laura and Kate might resemble Alice, but they were not like Alice . . .

There was no knock when Nicholas strode into the room and without so much as a good morning to the rest of his family went to the sideboard and began dishing ridiculous amounts of food on to his plate. Laura looked up, more relaxed than she'd been yet this morning, and was startled to see the questioning look that crossed Charlotte's face, and the answering one on her father's. Something made her think of her mother . . . about the times she had giggled on the wrong occasions. Charlotte and Edward had shared similar glances then, but now it was Nicholas who was behaving badly. Showing off, Jane would call it.

'I said nine o'clock,' said Charlotte grimly. 'It is the height of bad manners to be late when you were expressly asked . . . '

But Nicholas came to sit beside Laura, ignoring Charlotte completely. He arranged the food on his plate to make a laughing face with his bacon, then he moved the mouth and made it sad; the tomatoes appeared to be weeping pure orange tears . . . Laura looked up at him, concerned about the reaction, biting hard on her lip and wishing she was not sitting so near.

'Quiz time, I see,' said Nicholas with his mouth full. 'You have decided to quiz the babies in case I told them more than I told you. Now why would I do that?

What in God's name would motivate me to do that? You are both behaving like people beyond all reason. You call my mother mad but I think you should take a good look at yourselves!' And then he laughed. With his mouth full of food he laughed, and Edward rose up from his chair, tense with terrible anger. He strode over to his son and grabbed his collar between both hands. Edward hauled his son from his chair, and with his knife and fork in his hands Nicholas had no option other than to obey, for Edward was larger and very much stronger.

'Get out of this room!' Edward's face was red, his voice tightly controlled. 'Get out, and only come back when you can behave better than an animal!'

Nicholas threw down his knife and fork, he ruffled Laura's hair and, still laughing, he left the table, striding away casually as if nothing had happened and controlled enough to take his bread with him.

Charlotte rose and moved towards the bell. She tugged it. There was no expression on her face. Kate sat perfectly still, open-mouthed. Laura could hardly breathe. Nobody spoke. Edward remained standing, staring helplessly down at Nicholas' place as if the boy was still there. His napkin was tucked into his waistcoat and Laura could never remember seeing her father look so powerless and small.

When the calm face of Jane appeared at the door, Laura could have wept with relief. But Kate, excited and bewildered by all that had happened, protested, 'We haven't had anything to eat. We have missed our breakfast.'

'Hush, Miss Kate,' and Jane, sensing something was very wrong, hurried the child out before her. 'We'll get you something when we are upstairs.' Laura followed obediently, casting worried glances behind her.

After the children had gone, and the sounds of their feet and Jane's soft comforting words had gone with them, Edward returned to his chair. He pushed his plate away, unable to face the food, unable to face

151

anything. Charlotte's place was as neat as she had left it and when she sat down again it was impossible to see if she had been ruffled at all. She was exactly as she had been before the interruption.

'So . . . ' she hissed, and the only thing that gave her emotions away was the uncharacteristic gesture of touching the end of the teaspoon. She raised it slightly. She lowered it. She repeated the action three times in total silence before sighing gently and returning her hand to her lap.

Charlotte sat very straight; she took a deep breath in order to regain her sensible, down-to-earth attitude. 'We can see why it is equally important that we find both mother and child. It is exactly as we feared. You must be very firm with Doctor Myers when he comes here this morning. You must make sure that you bring him round to your point of view.'

But Edward Brennan said nothing more. He pushed back his chair and he stared bleakly into the fire.

# SEVENTEEN

Luke was more fascinated by this woman who sat by his side as he jigged the reins and the caravan tilted its way down the steep path and between the trees, than he could ever remember being before.

Being together was so easy. Even with last night sitting between them, half-proud and half-ashamed and neither of them knowing quite what to do with it, it was so easy and natural. But she was holding back. There were times when he wanted to wipe that dreamy smile off her face, get hold of her shoulders and shake her . . . She'd been hurt too much. Too much.

As the morning sun dappled the track before them they moved through a million wet puddles of light. The wagons were painted with the colours of the morning and, varnished with dew, they broke through dancing strands of gossamer webs. Luke leaned back in his seat in order to observe her more clearly. She sat beside him hanging on to the sides of the seat because she was not used to this rustic method of transport and she was excited by it, interested in every sight and sound, asking him questions, wanting explanations. She was alive to everything else, but not to him . . . And Milly Toole sat deep in the comfort of the caravan, nursing the baby Davy, trying to listen to their conversation but unable to hear because of the creak of the wooden wheels and the loud birdsong of the morning.

Alice was a good deal older than most of the women who had ever taken Luke's fancy. He knew she was older because she had told him so; she used her age as a defence against him, and her motherhood, and her married state. So he knew, but it was hard to believe this timid beauty was not a young girl fresh from a convent. Her innocence matched the simple golden fall of her hair, the neat whiteness of her teeth, the forget-

153

me-not blue of her childlike eyes. Everything enchanted her and she showed it, viewing the whole world through a veil of perplexity. She was observing – *she was not in it*.

With the artless bewilderment of a child she declared her passion in the way her body moved, in her eyes, in her smiles but she denied all feeling, she denied that anything was really happening, and Luke was fascinated. He breathed a deep gulp of morning air and mused on the quality of desire that so sharpened the senses that nothing was missed: colours were vivid, every single thing around him was pleasing.

Shading her eyes against the puffs of dust that came from the van in front, Alice said, 'I think that poor Seaton was nearly crying when you bade him goodbye just now. He is fond of you.'

'Seaton shared the first sixteen years of my life. We are close as two men can ever be . . . I regard him as family, a little like a grandfather. The only other person in the world I would trust with my life is Nathaniel.'

Alice was alarmed when she first met Nathaniel, when he came to the fire scratching his stomach and rudely demanding why everything was running behind time and why all the horses weren't already harnessed. Only a cup of coffee would mollify him. Luke had introduced her, and he had added, 'I might have found you, but it is Nathaniel to whom you have to feel grateful, for it was he who agreed to accept you into the company with nothing more to go on but my word.'

'I have to thank you then, sir.'

He said, 'My wife has told me about you. She spent some time last night conversing with your nurse, the stolid Mrs Toole. My wife is a duckerer . . . a teller of fortunes . . . but she is equally adept at assessing the present. While you are here you are Luke's guest, and will be treated with the respect that position requires.'

'I don't think I like him,' she'd whispered to Luke after Nathaniel strode away, barking his orders and overseeing the small adjustments being made to some of the wagons. 'He's too big. When he looked at me I felt he was staring right through . . . and where does that beard of his end?'

'While you have him as a friend you're safe,' Luke reassured her. 'But never, ever cross Nathaniel. He's not a man to forgive and forget. He is Romany through and through, and although we often argue, he will never bend his beliefs.'

And now, as they left the castle track and moved out on to the road again, Luke said, 'Yes, Nathaniel is the father who took me in when my own was flung into gaol.'

'You have a father, Luke?'

'I had a father until recently. He was held in gaol so long that his eyes gave up seeing, and his brain gave up bothering to understand. It was a relief to us all when he died.'

'And your mother?' The line of caravans moved slightly faster now, and some women and children were choosing to walk alongside rather than ride. They picked blackberries as they went, chatting and laughing, with wicker baskets on their arms.

'My mother was murdered. They came to the castle and killed her before they ransacked the place, before my father could get back and with all the men riding out with him.'

Alice covered her mouth in horror. 'This doesn't sound like anything that could have happened in England.'

Luke laughed when he reminded her, 'England! Your England!'

With a rushed little movement she laid her hand on his arm. She was watching Luke's hands, the way he guided the horse with just a slight motion of the fingers, a flick of the wrist. She moved her eyes away, but there was nowhere else to put them while they talked. The hedges were too high to see over. Quickly, nervously, she asked him, 'Why wern't the murderers punished? Why did they throw your father in gaol? Why

155

was there no compensation for the terrible things they did? And who did them . . . who were these vicious people?'

Luke leaned down and accepted a handful of blackberries from the raven-haired Unity Heath. There was something secret and suggestive in the small gesture and her hand was brown and quick like a monkey's. Her laughing eyes flashed up at him and Alice frowned. With her was another woman, just as carelessly clad, just as forward, and as she moved past the caravan she lifted her arm and brushed the outside of Luke's thigh.

'I think you should ask Mrs Toole.' Luke turned his head towards the half-open caravan door behind them. 'Mrs Toole knows. And Mrs Toole holds some firm opinions.'

'But she's told me nothing about you,' said Alice truthfully.

'Does she need to speak? Her attitude towards me is surely enough.'

'Why does she dislike you, Luke? I wish Milly was not so quickly condemning in her judgement of people.'

'We spent quite a few hours together at one time, Mrs Toole and I. In the kitchens of your own country home I believe, when you were just a little girl.'

'She never mentioned you to me. She never talked about a child . . .'

'I was hardly a child. A young lad, maybe. I called in once with a message and Mrs Toole was there sitting by the fire with the cook. She was kind to me, we drank tea together, got talking. I took to calling in to see her after that.' Luke mused, he looked down, brushed a twig from his knee. 'I think that afterwards she came to believe I had come there to spy. Then she left Venton Hall and at Winterbourne she always refused to see me. And then I stopped coming. I left the area – too many folks knew me and it became too dangerous.'

'Then you knew her quite well!'

'She was just someone I used to talk to.'

156

'You are hurt, Luke, I can tell – Milly's attitude towards you hurts! Why can't you make things right between you now? I don't know why she distrusts you so but there has to be some mistake. We're travelling with you now as your guests, here at your invitation. The least she could do would be to listen to your explanation . . . '

Luke rested his hand on Alice's arm, his heart melting towards her as he saw the concern on her face. 'She feels deeply about this matter. She is an old woman and set in her ways and beliefs. Any resolution between us will take time. We must wait until she feels able.'

Luke's hand moved from her arm to her knee, and stayed there. Every twig they passed over cracked like a gun, every dart of sunlight spangled like a gem. And she was at one with the earth, damp as it was and as wild. She longed to be alone with him . . . not here . . . but in her own vast bedroom at home with its four-poster bed, and she shivered as she imagined him crossing the room towards her. She would be waiting, watching his movements as he drew back the silk sheet, lifted her nightdress and explored every inch of her trembling body with hands, fingers, eyes, mouth, tongue, until she would call out, twine herself in his arms, wet for him, open for him, happy to lean forward for him, arch backwards for him, kneel for him, and then the moment would come when he would lay her on her back and kneel over her . . . take her . . .

*'Alice! Alice! How long is this child to go without feeding? Have you suddenly abandoned all your responsibilities and decided to act out the part of a gyspy woman who selfishly knows no better than to . . . '*

Luke raised his eyebrows and stared at Alice. He, she thought, would not picture a bedroom. He would probably picture a moonlit grove, with a small stream running through the bottom. He would lay her down in the moonlight and the grass would be wet under her back. He would be big and dark against the sky . . . Oh God, stop me from taking this further. I am no longer a child with no sense, I have learned my lesson. I am a grown-up woman and the mother of four children! Make me stop! Make me stop! Don't let this dream destroy me.

*'Alice! The child is starving here! I have jiggled him and burped him and patted him but now he wants his mother and apart from that I do believe it is time you came inside. Too much fresh air in your weak condition can only cause harm . . . '*

'Fresh air is a natural source of healing, Mrs Toole, and I thought someone with your experience would know that.'

They heard her muttering, 'Such insolence!' quietly to herself, but they only just heard because their eyes were locked and their senses were closed to everyone but each other.

As Alice moved to obey, Luke came close to her ear so his breath was hot there and he whispered, 'How long, Alice? How long are you willing to be treated as a child, to submit like a child, even to flirt with me like a child?'

In surprise she turned towards him. 'I have never . . . '

'You are a woman, Alice.' Oh, that he might put out his hand and touch her again, as he had last night.

But Alice was thinking of Edward. Luke saw her eyes dull again, he watched them freeze over with a veil of pain. 'I have duties. I must feed my child. Milly is right – I have sat here beside you all morning and I have not given him a thought. Only yesterday he was the most important person in my life, the only reason for going on, the only reason for living. He was real. Davy . . . Nicholas, Kate and Laura, but particularly Davy. But now,' she looked away and felt tears sting her eyes. She would have to be punished for this. These thoughts were bad, like dancing was bad, like running across the fields in moonlight was bad, like swinging her children round in her arms was bad, like wanting Edward to love her so much that she ached . . . She

158

had wanted that so terribly. Once.

But that was a long time ago.

Alice searched Luke's eyes for signs of criticism or disgust. In a moment he would turn on her, send her inside and close the door, lock it, perhaps. And she would weep and confide in Milly, and Milly would tell her that she was making things up in her head again, imagining these wanton desires and feelings. They were never really there. Ladies did not have them. There were definite ways of behaving and it was time that she learnt to control her emotions, to deny her heart. To walk with her back straight and her eyes well down, to eat like a bird at the table and to drink just a tiny sip of wine . . . she could pretend, but she must make sure that when Jarvis came round with the decanter she placed her hand over her glass.

'And of course you must not dance, my darling,' that's what Milly used to say. 'And certainly not by yourself, and in that wild fashion. What do you look like, who do you think you are, and what if someone should see you?'

'I must go,' said Alice softly.

'We will stop in a minute beside the road for our lunch. I thought we might stretch our legs and find a quiet place where we can be alone. Will you be finished with your responsibilities by then, Alice? Will you come with me?'

He saw a child, a frightened timid child, overcome by her powerful needs but terrified of being found out. He watched all this cross her face as she steadied herself, and helped herself to rise using one of his shoulders.

'I will see,' she whispered, and her smile was brief.

'You want to come with me,' he said, and his black eyes flashed. There was no pity in them.

'You know that I want to come.'

'Then I will not take no for an answer,' said Luke. 'I will come for you. And, if necessary, I will inform Mrs Toole where we are going.'

Alice's heart sank. This was taking her too close to childhood for comfort. But it's not so easy to control your dreams. It was easy for Luke, he was free. He had always been free, he would not be able to imagine what it was like to live life captive, for ever afraid in case you said the wrong thing, glanced in the wrong direction, missed a lace in your boot or dropped your knife and fork. How could she explain any of this to Luke Durant? How would a man like him even begin to understand? Oh, but she had rebelled against that, she had tried, in all sorts of ways, she had tried. And look what had happened to her in the end – where had she found herself? Shut away in a madhouse by a husband who loathed her and a sister who despised her.

Not a fit mother for her children. Not a fit wife.

That's what happens when you let your feelings go free.

So Alice smiled her little-girl smile for Milly as she gently closed the caravan door. She held out her arms for her baby and undid her buttons.

# EIGHTEEN

No, it would not be easy for Milly to forgive Luke. Her memories of that appalling time were still sharp. Sarah Venton was dead. Her baby son was dead. And Lord Thomas Venton, in spite of the support of his small family and those of his friends who were left, was going fast to the dogs.

No wonder Milly took to spending time in the kitchens with Emma Calder, the cook. Emma was the only person of her own age to whom Milly could safely confide her fears, and gossip was rife in the kitchens. If there was anything untoward going on, then Emma Calder would know about it.

And during those quickly changing times Milly considered it her business to keep in touch.

'These men . . . these creatures who are out for nothing but trouble . . . they consider themselves above their superiors, even Lord Venton himself.' It was a summer evening and the children were upstairs in their beds. Milly had allowed them to read for half an hour before lying down because the night was so light they wouldn't sleep anyway. It was too hot for blankets. She had come down to the kitchens to fetch them some milk, and was now helping Emma to oversee the clearing up after the Harvest Home.

Milly had taken her sweet things along for an hour that afternoon. The grass was dry and long and smelled of hot sap, and clouds of late mosquitoes moved the lazy air. Milly lunged at them with her parasol. They watched the end of the sports, which last year had been organized by Her Ladyship and her friends, but this year had been taken over by the bailiff's wife, Cecily Jenkins. Cecily, in her long white gloves and with her hooped skirt swinging, flapped about a great deal, fan-

161

ning her face with the sports programme and rushing from one event to the other in case she was needed. She was not, since everything was done in the exact same way from one year to the next and the same women did the cooking and the same men carried in the trestle tables and put up the awnings. In one huge tent beef puddings and mugs of ale were provided for the men, while in another the women enjoyed tea, bread and butter and plum cake. And when everyone was satisfied and happy they went outside and sat on benches and rugs in the sunshine to listen to the speeches.

The Rector was a rotund man with a face like a rubber ball and lips that protruded like the spout provided to blow through. His shiny black frockcoat stretched nervously across the circle of his front, held there by one tenuous button. He put his chubby hands behind his back and regarded his humble audience benignly. The Reverend Snaily decided to warm up his little congregation with a joke, for they were not in church now and he had to keep their attention somehow. 'Certain agitators,' he started, rising up on to his toes and squeaking his boots in the process, then smiled broadly and raised his polished eyebrows, 'certain agitators have been seen lately in our district trying to start,' and here he paused and raised his eyebrows even higher, inviting everyone to enjoy themselves with him, 'trying to start an agricultural labourers' union!' He had their attention now and that fact gratified him. There was nothing that people enjoyed more than to be united against a common enemy. They felt safe, thought the Reverend Snaily, to be on the Church's side, to be, for once in their lives, allied with the powerful.

'Now then,' he went on, 'all I can say is that I regret they have not decided to linger here in the sunshine and join us in our merrymaking. I wonder why they are not here! Do you wonder? Do we all wonder? Do we not consider their absence just a little bit strange?'

162

There were small stirrings in the crowd and a few faint chucklings.

'Cowards!' called out the Rector, shuffling his sweating hands. The sun beat down on him mercilessly and he had chosen a position which afforded him no shade. He was sweating profusely. Some more sensible members of his audience had settled themselves around the comfortable roots of the great beech trees. 'Without the courage of their convictions! Men who feel safe only to roam the lanes by night, fearful of the light, of open debate, of censure, and, of course, of failing in their cause. And what, we have to ask ourselves, is their cause?'

The children continued their games, unimpressed. Little girls in pinafores skipped and chanted on the edge of the crowd. The Rector stretched his neck to its full length and frowned across in their direction. They did not notice him but carried on with their game. A small boy standing directly beneath him pulled on the rubber cross of his catapult, twanging rudely.

'Their cause,' proceeded the Reverend Snaily, 'is to disunite, to destroy. Oh yes, I have heard what they are saying. They promise you the millennium. Now I, as a churchman and a believer, have no doubt at all that a millennium is coming, but until that date, and God will decide it, I have to inform you that no earthly one will ever be realized.'

This statement, delivered in short, sweating bursts, was greeted with a smattering of weak applause, the kind of fluttering, summery applause afforded to cricket matches. The Rector went on to confirm what he considered to be obvious. 'From the very beginning God appointed that there should be varying grades of society, high and low, rich and poor, and it is neither for the rich to boast nor for the poor to complain . . . '

'What is he talking about?' asked Alice, pretty as a picture in her frilly blue dress and the straw hat with forget-me-nots on it, as the Rector droned on.

Milly gripped her hand. 'Shush now and listen.'

'He is saying that the people should be grateful with what they've got, and not go round grumbling and being jealous,' said Charlotte. 'Which is quite right.'

Lucinda made off after a butterfly. The Rector looked towards the genteel party from the big house and gave a confidential smile. Milly bowed her head and smiled back. Thomas should have been there to propose the toast and give the final speech on this pastoral occasion, but he was not. He had left for London yesterday, telling Jenkins, who reminded him of his obligations, 'They will get by without me for one year, surely.' But Milly, fond of tradition, felt uncomfortable when his place was taken by the bailiff himself.

Jenkins, a long, sour-faced man with a bad complexion and too low a voice for this performance, raised his glass and touched the Rector's before holding it up to the crowd. The white parting down the centre of his sleek black hair gleamed in the sunshine. 'Raise your glasses,' he called, and some of the women held up their cups, the men looked into their empty mugs but held them up good-heartedly just the same, 'and let's drink to the harvest, to the Venton estates, their future prosperity and the prosperity of all who depend . . . ' but no one could hear him properly.

Suddenly, out of the blue, for no one had seen them coming or heard their approach, rode three horsemen with masks on their faces. There was a scurrying like a small whirlwind as women picked up their skirts and fluttered backwards and forwards, calling. Children stopped their games and stood, fingers to their lips and staring. Men shambled up from their seats and stood with wooden eyes, watching. Milly dragged Alice and Charlotte towards her and frantically searched for Lucinda. She saw her hiding behind a tree and kept her eyes fixed on her, willing the child to stay back with a frantic twirling of her parasol. Because what was this . . . ?

They were not ruffians, and their horses were the sleek, well-bred horses of gentlemen. They wore tailcoats and breeches with buttoned-on boots. They were hatless, but the most distinguishing parts of their dress were the masks – awful, slit-eyed masks in black that gave them the look of savage hunters. The leading horseman leaned forward from his horse and with his whip, flicked off the tablecloth and the silver cups that Jenkins had been about to present. Everyone gasped. Sacrilege! The gaudy prizes tipped tinnily on to the grass and seemed immediately to lose their gloss and look tawdry. Jenkins stood back, quite willing, almost eager to give up his place, but the Reverend Snaily had no such faint heart. He turned like a seal performing tricks on a plinth, revolving to face the group of horsemen as they swirled round him. 'What is going on?' he demanded in his pulpit voice.

'You demean these people.' The leading rider wrestled with his horse to keep it still, but it snorted and pranced in its excitement. His voice rose to cover the sounds of the jangling harness, and his audience was silently receptive. He prodded the vicar's tight stomach with the end of his crop. 'You invite them here, give them plum cake and trinkets, tell them this is the life, reward them for doing well and then you send them back to their pathetic homes to grub about for food where they can, to huddle together for warmth, to send their toddlers to scratch the bare fields, to dispose of their daughters to a sterile life of service, to abandon their sons to the mills . . . and you tell them that this is right . . . that this is all there is . . . '

'How dare you!' exhorted Snaily, pulling out his handkerchief. 'How dare you come here and interrupt a private . . . '

'And when they have given you all they have – their lives, their children, their women – you reward them with the workhouse! You split their families, you take away the last of their pride, and you send them to the bastilles where you remove the last of their humanity from them.' And then the speaker laughed unpleasantly; he flashed his whip in the air and cracked it. 'But

165

not for much longer I think, my fat friend. Your days are numbered! And when the time comes there will be such retribution for the likes of you and your kind you will wish you had never been born!'

'Such threats,' spluttered the Reverend Snaily, patting his forehead. 'Such vicious, mindless threats. And why don't you look around you? This was a gathering of happy, contented people enjoying the day until you came along. Such stories you tell! And look, you are so ashamed of yourselves that you cover your faces with masks. Cowards, afraid . . . '

'Afraid of our friends and supporters being marked down by employers and landowners and churchmen such as yourself, yes. Afraid of them losing what work they have, of watching them thrown from their homes, yes.' And then, suddenly, as if he knew that his words were wasted on such a man, the horseman called out to the people, 'There is a way out of it! If we band together they can do nothing. We handed in a petition and they ignored it. We try to act democratically but that process leans away from us, we lack the power. It is in their hands. But they could not lead the comfortable lives they do if it were not for us . . . the labourers, the factory workers, the navvies and the skivvies.'

Some of the men looked bleary-eyed and blank. Others took down their eyes or looked away, but nobody moved to stop the intruders as they continued to goad the good Rector. They heckled him, they spun him round like a baited bear and he growled back at them, slapping his stomach with his paw-like hands.

'Men of Shilstone, rise up and fight! Things can be changed, change lies in your own hands. Attend our meetings, read our leaflets, listen to our leaders,' and the dark horseman leaned right down and plucked the Rector's glass from his hand. Raising it high in the air he shouted, 'And now – a toast! I drink,' and he threw back his head and gulped down the rest of the dark red wine, 'not to the continuation of the same, not to poverty or to degradation, no, I drink to JUSTICE!' He hurled the drained glass to the ground where it smashed into a thousand pieces.

And then they were gone, as quickly and silently as they had come. And everybody, especially the Rector, was left awkwardly not quite knowing what to do.

'Who were they?'

'Are they local men?'

'Do we know them?'

Lucinda rushed across the grass from her hiding place and buried her face in Milly's skirts. Milly thought it prudent to linger no longer. Without bidding her goodbye, or stopping to thank the nervous Cecily, she hurried her charges across the grass and back up the drive to the house. She rushed them inside and upstairs to the nursery, the place where she felt safest. She lifted her chin to release the ribbon of her straw hat, staring at her flushed face in the mirror, clipping and unclipping her hairpins with a frantic, nervous energy while trying to answer their questions in the best way she could, although not understanding much about it herself.

'They are very wicked men,' she said severely. 'They want everything we know and love to change. They do violent things and they are not kind to their own people. They have burned down barns, they have smashed new machinery. Why only in Buckley, five miles away, they threw a man in the village pond because he did not join with them in their evil schemings . . . and he was a good, respectable man with a family.'

Alice was pale. She said, 'Perhaps there is something in what they say, if there is such terrible poverty . . . if there are children going hungry. I looked, Milly, I looked properly, and I saw tired eyes and pinched faces. And all the children had their pockets stuffed with food. There was nothing left on the plates in the tents. I looked.'

'Don't be ridiculous,' said Milly. 'Lazy ways and indolence, being plain workshy – those are the reasons for hunger and cold. Men won't work unless they fear

167

poverty. They would happily stay at home by their fires and go begging to the parish if they were given the slightest chance. They would turn up their noses at low wages, there would be nobody left to do the hard labour if the workers were not afraid. The workhouse is as basic as it is so they realize they cannot just go there for comfort. Some of these people, you mark my words, would do just that if they were given the slightest opportunity.'

And Charlotte said, 'You are such a fool sometimes, Alice. Don't you know that your strange ideas mean there's something wrong with your head? Of course those men are wicked, you only had to look at them to know. And if Papa had been there they might have hurt him.'

Alice trembled. A sunny afternoon like this, but the child was freezing cold. Milly cuddled her, gently reassuring, and realized she had gone too far. These children, so gentle and protected, must not know about such matters, let alone discuss them. None of this was their concern. She had said too much already. She must say no more, but calm them down instead and get them to bed as soon as possible. Thomas would be furious to know that his daughters had been so dangerously close to such people. If Milly had known what would happen she would never have gone near the harvest gathering. But, for goodness sake, where were you safe any more with such people lurking about?

So, quite naturally, as soon as she possibly could Milly went down to discuss the whole dreadful business with Emma. The boy, Luke Durant, was sitting at the end of the long kitchen table eating an apple noisily and juicily. She was pleased to see him there. She liked him. He reminded her of a young man she had walked out with briefly, many years ago, dark and cheekily arrogant, such a flatterer. And those serious, intense eyes in that young face of his. Milly felt a little bit sorry for him, living what she considered a strange kind of life, so solitary much of the time, with his eccentric father and his frivolous mother in that ancient castle of theirs. The Durant family went back even further than the Ventons. One of the wealthiest families in England, they were certainly of noble blood, but not quite the acceptable kind. Something must have gone wrong somewhere . . . there must have been some in-breeding. They did not mingle with the gentry but stayed a little reclusive, a little aloof, and had dubious friends down from London, mixed with such people as actors and poets . . . Yes, they were a strange lot and consequently here was this rather mysterious, lonely boy, who liked to call in to see her.

'Such a time, Emma, I can't tell you! Such affairs, and here, in this quiet backwater. I mean, you read of such events elsewhere but you never think . . . '

'They are everywhere. They have got themselves everywhere. We shall soon be unsafe in our beds.'

'It is not the likes of you that the Chartists go after,' said Luke, calmly inspecting his apple and licking it greedily before he bit. He flirted with every young maid who went by, and some of the smiles they sent back to him were far too saucy for Milly's liking. Soon he would be a breaker of hearts. He rested his boots on the table and Emma slapped them off with no fussing.

Milly turned to him. 'And what do you know of the Chartists – a boy of your age? You were not there today so you did not see the terror they created, or hear the violence behind their words . . . '

'The state does more violence than the Chartists are ever likely to.'

'Oh, shush with your ignorant interrupting!' Milly silenced Luke as she would have dealt with one of her girls. 'Shush, and let me tell it to Emma.'

'Well,' said Emma before Milly could get happily into her stride again. 'Let me tell you that I have heard that the local landowners have organized a trap. They know where the leaders of this group meet, and they are planning to catch them red-handed.'

'Well!' Milly was relieved to hear that positive action was being taken. Luke sat back, lazy-eyed, filled his cup with more tea and listened.

'The Master's London visit is not just to his gambling dens, oh no, not this time. I have heard, 'twas Joan who heard them talking, that he goes to meet with other men who have suffered at the hands of the mob – local squires with scores to settle. Our masters won't take these threats lying down. This dangerous movement will either die out of its own accord or the masters will stamp it out! We cannot see the country divided; we cannot see all that we have strived for smashed and left to rot in the hands of monsters.'

'And who says these men are monsters?'

Milly turned to face Luke. 'I have seen them,' she swelled importantly. 'And you have not. I have read about their doings, and about what influential, trustworthy people in high places say of them. I am not ignorant on this subject, young man.'

'I think you have no ideas of your own, Mrs Toole. You follow like a bleating sheep.'

Emma laughed. 'Now he's putting you firmly in your place, Milly!'

But Milly gave Luke Durant such a look that she silenced him, and the two women talked and drank tea as they watched the maids unload the wagons of baskets and hampers, empty the tea urns and polish them up, carry trayloads of cups to the pantry as the evening sun streamed warmly through the kitchen door.

Milly was so engrossed in her conversation with Emma, so angry did she feel about what had happened, 'Such a rude intrusion into what should have been a lovely afternoon,' that she went upstairs eventually having forgotten the milk she came down for.

The children were not asleep. Charlotte was tormenting Alice for her peculiar views most cruelly. Quite often Milly sensed a nasty tension in the nursery in those days, a tension that she had never been aware of before.

170

Sisterly quarrels were one thing, but it really was beginning to seem as though Charlotte and Alice hated each other. Milly would have to put a stop to it before it got out of hand.

# NINETEEN

Milly was not at all happy when the caravans rolled to a halt and, leaving Davy sleeping, Alice took off without a by your leave, saying she wanted to walk.

This was hilly countryside. Now and again the travellers were given blinding glimpses of the wet sands and the widening river that winked, dappled by cold sunshine. The heavy barges making for the city looked like fat snails moving in a winding trail of silver slime. They had plodded past mansions and white farmhouses, thatched cottages tucked between yellow woods and fields that sloped and turned to a luscious green as they reached the river. The gypsy children, many of them in gaudy coats of knitted squares, some bare-footed, ventured up the pathways and drives with baskets of watercress, blackberries and fresh field mushrooms. They seemed much older and more reserved than the children who came out to greet them. Whenever they passed a house out came wide-eyed toddlers who let go of their mothers' aprons and ventured dangerously near to the creaking, heavy wheels, screaming in delight and insisting on patting the flat-eared dogs that slunk along beside the procession. Once a dog disappeared with a yelp and returned with a torn, bloody hare in its mouth.

Soon after halting, the horses that were tied to the back of every caravan were staked to the verge for a quick feed, and nosebags were hooked to the harness of the nags that pulled the wagons. Families and friends climbed down and spread themselves comfortably on the grass. Milly moved to the front of the caravan, batting away flies with the same vigour as the horse below her swished its thick tail. She wrinkled her nose. The smell of dung was pungent.

'You don't look too happy, Mrs Toole, but you'll

172

soon get used to the motion as a sailor grows accustomed to the movement of the sea under his ship.'

'It's not that which concerns me. I have had quite a comfortable ride.'

'Oh? And what is it, then?'

Bella lifted her eyes and shaded them, following Milly's gaze towards the field gate over which Luke and Alice had so recently disappeared. She wore her tall hat and the feather in it matched the vivid blue of the sky with little white patches of fluff on it. She handed Milly a wooden bowl in which was a hunk of hard bread and some pieces of chicken. There was ale in the gourd in her other hand, and cold tea in the enamel jug she had hooked round her arm.

Milly sniffed uneasily. 'It is totally unacceptable for my mistress to go tramping the fields in this way. She is not well. She needs care. I have enough on my plate just now without having to contend with the wild influence of men such as that . . . '

'Perhaps Alice craves the kind of freedom of movement and speech that Luke offers her. Perhaps your fears are unfounded, and this kind of life is exactly what she needs after her recent terrible sufferings.'

'I know Alice. I have known her since she was just a little girl. I know what is good for her and what is not. And therefore I would be grateful for your support on this matter, Bella.'

Bella laughed and her face crisscrossed in a thousand dirty old lines. 'Alice is not a Romany girl . . . she is not even a girl. She must find her own path. It seems to me that this might be the first time in her whole life when she's been able to make her own decisions. I'd be downright ashamed of myself if I thought I had any part in taking that right away. Mrs Toole, you must let her go. She is not yours, and she is no longer a child who needs nursing. And that child of hers, that is not yours, either!'

Milly ignored this silliness but gratefully accepted the tea. She saw the ferry boat from Exmouth ploughing its way across the water, very small down there in the dip, a toy filled with tiny wooden people like an ark. She decided there was no further point in discussing her problems with this great ox of a woman who had no more understanding about the niceties of life than the grey-rumped horse that chomped at its lunch and turned its doleful eyes around to regard her every so often. No matter how high she raised herself, even from this elevated position Milly could not quite see over the crest of the field where it dropped into woodland, out of sight. But not out of mind.

Milly sat and Milly remembered and Milly worried.

'Are you sure you're all right? I don't want to tire you.'

Luke was holding her hand. They paused on the slope leading down to the river. Alice breathed in deeply, tasting the salty air and the tang of frost which still touched the grass where the sun hadn't reached it. The air tasted sharp, like bitter wine and she loved it. She felt better than she'd felt for years. Across the river, in the high hilly distance, hounds streamed up a brown ploughed slope, flying streaks of white and tan. Men in pink and women in black flashed after them. The hunt unfurled like a ribbon across the winter fields. The water sparkled with the same lights that filled her own eyes. Magic! All this was quite magic!

Luke, just a few feet below her, looked back and was astonished by the beauty that radiated from this woman who, just yesterday, he had never met. She was smiling that uncertain smile, and her teeth, just showing between her lips, were tiny, neat and a perfect white. The belt which she used to secure her dress had slipped; it sat at an angle across her waist which was small, even so soon after childbirth. In all the excitement one sleeve of the outsized dress had fallen from her shoulder. The skin was white, the bones fragile, and with her head on one side like that her golden hair fell like a glorious shawl upon the smooth whiteness of her naked skin. Luke stepped back towards her, mes-

174

merized, avid to touch this small show of nakedness, to make it real with his fingers.

Entranced by his nearness, and by his touch, she turned her head slightly to watch the movements of his fingers. She let him trace the line of her neck and from there he moved outwards, leaving a pathway of fire behind him. Alice trembled from head to toe and then she closed her eyes.

Luke said, 'Come with me.'

Casting furtive glances over her shoulder in case Milly should be following or in case someone could see, Alice went with Luke towards the queer twilit edge of the copse. Holding his hand she followed him; the dark gloss of his hair shone in the greenish light as they made their way to where the sunshine only flickered occasionally, and the earth was soft under their feet, and the nearby river occasionally winked through a thin pathway of tree trunks. She reminded him of a fawn, a wild, shy creature of the woods as he led her deeper into them.

The resin-scented earth was the first bed they shared, and Luke did not touch her – only her clothes. Alice didn't feel the cold as, slowly, he undressed her, slowly, gently and exquisitely he laid aside her clothes, this dark conjurer who was weaving such magic inside her head.

He unclipped her belt and, kneeling above her, raised her dress over her head, ridding her of the weight of the dark blue, lavishly-trimmed gown with the scrollwork braid. Alice was left in the simple white cotton petticoat of Milly's. His hand moved down to her stockings and her garters. He put his hands underneath her waist to unlace the strings of the petticoat. He slid it off her, and she raised her body to help him. He pulled the material far enough down so that the soft curve of her stomach was showing. Alice felt no urge to cover her nakedness, and she had never felt so naked before. She saw his eyelids lower, she heard his sharp intake of breath.

175

'You are the most beautiful woman that I have ever seen. But I know you so well it is as if I had made you. I know every inch of you.'

She lay perfectly still, as though deep in sleep, her head on her arm and tilted slightly on to her side. Her pale breasts hung, perfectly shaped and full, the nipples dark and tipped towards him. Her waist, her thighs, her slender legs were framed in green light as though she was wrapped in silken sheets of it. She gave a little sighing moan as her body burned and she ached to feel his hands on her but Luke lay beside her quite motionless, content to admire from a distance and quite quiet, so that now she could hear the sounds of the birds in the wood and the faint call of the hunting horn as it fluted and echoed across the water. Luke lay beside her.

'I used to dream of fairy tales, of castles, of romance and of princes. And then as I grew up I realized how far from that real life was. But now, Luke,' and she took up her hand to follow the grooves that ran down the sides of his face to his chin, 'now I wonder if perhaps the stories were real after all. Perhaps there is such a thing as love.'

Dear Lord, she thought, as she spoke, what am I saying to this make-believe stranger and what is really happening to me at this moment? What of tomorrow? They must have ways, they must have terrible ways of waking me up.

Luke said nothing, but after she'd finished speaking he kissed her.

Passion. She gave her nakedness to his eyes and he took her with his eyes alone. He took her with violence and with gentleness . . . both. He did not have to touch her but she was sunk in passion as though caught in one of those tangled thickets, lapped with it, stupefied by it and it smelled of moss and leafmould. In spite of her recent confinement her body ached to take him, but the waiting for that was more sensual than any love-making Alice had ever known.

176

Afterwards – and although nothing had happened it felt as if there was an afterwards because there had been a complete moment – he dressed her with the same gentle concern with which he had removed her clothes. She felt his square, hard hand in hers, pulling her up, pulling her out of the woods towards the light. What time was it? How long had they spent lying together like that? Alice was tempted to rub her eyes, so deeply was she sleeping.

And she suddenly thought of Edward, of the shock of his ice-cold stares, of his actions which displayed such complete indifference to her suffering. Once she had thought she loved Edward Brennan . . . once she had wanted him, not with the same intensity she felt for Luke, for she'd been younger then and more super- ficial, and the situation was quite different. Her love had become disgusting. A travesty of itself, and think- ing of it now made her nauseous.

Edward would call her depraved, he would consider her contemptible if he knew of her feelings now. And maybe she was depraved. Suddenly she laughed out loud. She thought of her old life before Deale. She had called it freedom, but all she could remember of it was the gleam of heavy candelabra, the massive family plate, stiff-backed butlers, stolid footmen, lavender- scented linen cupboards and bunches of keys. Oh yes, keys . . . keys . . . and eyes watching her struggle as she fought against every craving, every hope and every pleasure . . .

Then she saw Deale, the shouts of madwomen, nar- row white beds, jabbering jaws, silent faces and eyes that could not respond.

Oh, let me pretend . . . Alice didn't care. She hoped she would be allowed to pretend like this for ever. What did reality matter? 'I've always been so fright- ened,' she said to Luke as he opened the field gate for her. 'I understand now that the weight I have carried throughout the whole of my life has been fear. But now, just when I ought to feel most afraid, when there

177

are people after me, I have found you and I am without fear. And I feel light as if I've no weight at all. I feel as if I'm not here.'

Laugh if you like, Luke. Laugh!

But right there on the verge, under the exasperated gaze of Milly Toole, Luke Durant took her face in his hands and he smiled when he kissed her.

# TWENTY

The troupe halted to prepare themselves on the outskirts of Exeter. They changed into garish performing
costumes, silvers, turquoises, scarlets, silks and sequins
. . . here was a jester decked with bells and there were
the flounced skirts of the band of drummers, spangled
and feathered. Children swarmed over the caravans,
agile as monkeys, decking them with garlands and flags,
and old handbills advertising previous successes boldly
printed with names – *TIVOLI; PALACE; ALHAMBRA; EM-
PIRE* – were stuck on banners and waved in the air.

A group of bearded Cavaliers and Roundheads in
knickerbockers, ruffs and tights performed a mock
sword-fight. Two grotesquely muscled boxers lunged
and feinted as they tripped along. Bells rang before the
caravan of Jessica Lamont, the most popular actress in
the troupe, and she sat with her head in the air sur-
veying the scene with contemptuous eyes down a thin,
aristocratic nose. The disreputable women Alice scath-
ingly called 'Luke's friends' sat to the front of their
caravan with painted faces, fanning themselves and
blowing kisses, and showing indecent amounts of leg
under their frilly skirts. Unity Heath sat in a dreadful,
manly way, with her legs apart, showing her drawers
and smoking a cheroot through a long, ivory holder.

As they moved towards the city to a loud drumbeat,
firecrackers exploded into the air, thrown by the gaily
dressed children who ran ahead holding out buckets
for coppers.

And Milly Toole, terribly embarrassed to be a part
of all this, put a flat look on her face and retired to the
far recesses of her caravan.

The crowds came to meet them. They roared their
support and approval. Nathaniel and Bella Pettigrew
Lovett made a dramatic picture, standing together in

the lead van. The huge man's beard was thrown over his shoulder and an ancient tin crown replaced his turban which, together with the wild glint in his eye, made his awesome presence more terrible. Bella flashed her jewelled hands; her stream of black hair was decked with ribbons and her weather-beaten face cracked into a permanent, rather awful smile. The dwarfs rode the freshly-groomed horses, as many as six on one mount, and the Indian sent smoke signals into the air straight from his mouth.

There were no gates to this city. The slowly-moving pageant passed along the slanting length of the street, the spires of the Cathedral pierced the sky and among the modern new brick there were fine old timbered houses with richly-carved gables. They passed the Turk's Head Inn, 'The drinking place of the great actor Edmund Kean,' Luke said, as if he expected Alice to know of him. 'It was in the Exeter Theatre that he developed his powers, and Mrs Siddons has played here – there are even stories that Satan himself has played on this stage!'

Alice opened her eyes wider.

It was hard to converse for the noise, the firecrackers, the drums and the occasional fierce blast of trumpets. Alice was enchanted by all of it. Oh, this might be coming from out of her head but this was life! Before this, her existence had been death. On top of it all, as if this exhilaration was not enough, there was Luke beside her. She looked at him, she kept looking at him . . . surely all the women they passed must be staring at him, wanting him as she did? And what could she do if he glanced back . . . if he gave them one of his secret smiles, how could she bear it? He was her creature but could she control him? He'd been full of self-deprecation when he told her how he sometimes took parts in the plays: 'I fill in on occasion in order to oblige.' But now she wondered, and the thought of women looking up at him in admiration filled her with apprehension.

180

Was she in control of all this? She stared about her. Was she?

On and on they went, past winding alleys that led to the river, through the city and out the other side towards the water meadows where they were to make their camp for the next three days.

Since that first childhood meeting with Edward Brennan, the night when she lost Abernathy, in spite, or because of his defiant behaviour, Alice had not been able to help regarding him as something of a 'star'.

In a strange, little-girl way, she supposed she'd fallen in love. Was it love? Had she ever loved? She looked out for him. She asked about him. There had been so much time for dreaming in those years after Mama's death. Thomas Venton was away in London much of the time and when he was home he had little time for his three young daughters. Money, they were constantly being reminded, was short. Milly taught them to knit. They learned to mend their own clothes, to eat little and sensibly, to take their pleasures, as Milly said, 'in the outside air where they are simple, free and available to all'. But after the incident at the Harvest Home, Milly was jumpy, fearing that one of her sweet things might be kidnapped, for ever casting a wary eye around her and preferring to keep within the railings of the park. 'For you never know from which direction the blackguards are coming,' she said. The children grew nervous.

They also grew used to cold rooms. 'You just put more clothes on,' said Milly, 'and don't go drooping about in slithers of silk and moaning.' As if they would – as if they ever had!

But all the time it was imperative that Alice, the firstborn, be brought up so that she would be able to hold her own in the world of society to which, at seventeen, she would be introduced. 'You are a lady,' Milly used to say. 'You hold an important name . . . and that's what your poor mother and your father have always insisted you be brought up to be . . . a perfect lady. Thank God you have the right sort of looks to capture the heart of the wealthiest man. And anything else can be curbed.'

'I do not want just any man,' declared Alice. 'I am in love with Edward Brennan.'

Charlotte, poor little Charlotte with her stunted frame and her mousy hair and her protruding forehead, snorted.

And Milly, disliking Edward intensely, joined in. 'Edward Brennan may be rich, he may be handsome in a dandified kind of a way, but his family have no class. All your father's money and influence will be directed towards launching you properly and I think you will be able to be slightly more selective than that, my darling.'

'And what about us?' asked the sweet Lucinda, so generous and pretty and instantly liked by everyone who met her. 'Won't we be launched, also?'

'Alice, as the heir to Venton, is your father's strongest card so naturally he will concentrate upon her,' Milly replied, instantly regretting her insensitive reference to cards but knowing it was too late to withdraw it. 'If Alice marries well then we'll all be all right now, won't we? But what we all have to do is help bring her out a little, help her to become more confident, chattier, less shy.'

This was easier said than done. Alice did not seem able to understand when to let her feelings show and when to conceal them. And she rarely responded in a ladylike manner. When she did come out of her shell she was too emotional, too demonstrative and landed herself in trouble as a result of it.

It wasn't that Milly didn't tell her. Milly was always telling her, Lucinda was always encouraging her and Charlotte was always laughing at her mistakes.

One Easter weekend, Thomas Venton had a group of friends down from London to make up a hunting party. All sorts of famous people were there: 'Politicians, bankers, even a millionaire from America who has his own racing stables, all from the highest society,' warned Milly, 'and His Lordship has asked that you be there on Saturday evening to join them for dinner and afterwards to listen to the music.'

Alice was dressed very finely. The dressmaker came to the house and Charlotte and Lucinda watched with envious eyes as their sister was placed on a nursery chair and measured, as the rich materials for the new dress were chosen, as her feet were measured for new slippers and her father presented her with a silver chain. 'Your mother's,' he said in a reverent voice, 'the first of many of her jewels which have been kept in trust for you, Alice.'

'Is this a sort of coming out early?' asked Lucinda, fingering the taffeta with deference. The finished dress was hung on a hanger above the nursery fire.

'I suppose you could call it that,' said Milly, her scissors at work on Alice's hair. 'And so it is very important.'

'She'll do something silly again.' Charlotte wore a nasty smile on her face. 'She will, she will, because she won't be able to help it.'

'Nonsense,' reproved Milly. 'Sometimes you can be very unkind you know, Charlotte. You have a quick wit, but you waste it. Such meanness of mind does not become an aspiring young lady.'

'It doesn't seem to matter whether I become a lady or not,' Charlotte pulled a face, 'so why should I care? Why should I bother, or try?'

Lucinda laughed, and that easy laughter removed the tension from the unpleasant conversation.

'Your looks will take you anywhere.' Milly stepped back to admire the finished article . . . Alice, petite, fragile, pretty as a picture in pale blue taffeta and little white slippers. Already a dragonfly.

'You look like a doll,' commented Charlotte. 'There is no expression on your face and you look as if you're made of china.'

183

Alice tried to smile but she was so nervous, so afraid of doing the wrong thing. She knew that the smile was false and probably made her face look worse.

'You look absolutely beautiful,' said Lucinda. 'In fact you make me want to buy you.'

'Well, don't touch her.' Milly stroked the dress. 'You'll crease her all up and it has taken me hours to get that dress perfectly smooth.'

Down the creaking stairs she went, descending to the heart of the house, to its solid, shabby magnificence, knowing there was a crowd at the bottom, her hand getting wetter and wetter as she gripped the banister. Nobody turned in her direction and yet she felt they all had. She went very tiny as she made her way through the twirling finery, the tall, black-legged gentlemen, and who should she talk to now, and where should she go? Thomas, the most handsome man in the house, was engrossed in conversation – he would not welcome an interruption. The only faces she recognized were those of the maids and they, putting on their most formal expressions for this most important occasion, ignored her totally.

She took herself and her distress and went to stand quietly beside the fire.

The meal was no easier. She was placed at the end of the table between two strangers who conversed over the top of her head. She concentrated very hard on her food. She remembered her manners, she used the correct knives and forks, she sipped the wine sparingly, she did not interrupt anybody, and when she was not eating she placed her hands on her lap. Milly, she thought, would be very pleased.

The quartet was boring. They sat for so long on hard-backed chairs in the drawing room that it was difficult to keep awake. But that was all right; she pinched herself occasionally and that served the purpose. It was afterwards, when the musicians had packed up their cases and gone, that the trouble came. She thought that they'd send her to bed, but they did

184

not. Thomas, spying her for the first time, took her small hand in his huge one and led her round, performing gracious introductions. 'This is Alice, my eldest child.'

She offered her hand and gave a small curtsey. She was peered at through lorgnettes, leered at through red eyes, her chin was lifted and her cheeks were pinched.

'A lovely child,' said one grand lady. Alice didn't remember her name. 'Thomas, lucky boy, you have been blessed.'

Alice knew that Thomas did not believe he had been blessed. He had ceased to believe that when Neville died. No, he thought that he had been cursed. Was Alice his curse? Milly said that all he believed in now was the god of luck.

He led her around, he gave her wine and, for something to do with her hands, she drank it.

'How prettily she moves, what natural grace for a child so young. You must not hide her away here deep in the country for too long.' The puce-faced man with the badly-creased stomach bent down and Alice recoiled from his fiery breath.

Some of the party were playing cards; the red and black pips on the white cards winked off the green tables. Some were lolling on the sofas, talking. Every now and then Alice remembered Charlotte's words and put a smile on her face. A woman with an enormous chest and who reeked of perfume got up to play Mama's grand piano. For something to do, for somewhere to go, when Thomas was done with her Alice went to stand beside it. She fitted in nicely behind the palm and she thought that, so far, she had done very well. The night would soon be over and she would be safe in bed with her dreams.

The pianist's eyes were small in her face like tiny currants. Alice watched the fat fingers, moving slowly to start with, and quickening with loud encouragement from the rest of the room, until they began to pound on the piano keys. Faster and faster they went, wizard's fingers making the music; they scrambled like white mice over the keys until Alice could hear the music coming up out of the floor, vibrating off the walls in the room, even seeming to come from the ceiling until it was almost intolerable.

Alice felt very pretty. Suddenly, extraordinarily pretty. And brave. It no longer mattered that she was a girl. The room was full with a thousand tables and chairs and Turkish rugs and china, and the crystal pendants danced in the chandeliers. And Alice was in the centre with the music, seeing herself in a hundred mirrors and she stood up on tiptoe and started dancing. The music made her do it . . . she had no option. She was no longer unhappy or frightened, at least not until the flickering flame of joy went out, the brilliant, noisy room went dark and suddenly Alice, realizing what she was doing, shrank and went cold.

Thomas strode across the floor and clutched her by the arm. He was laughing with the rest of his guests, but his laugh was too high and thin to be real and far more terrible than any expression of disgust. He bent so Alice alone could hear, and she could see the slight twitch of his eye when he said, 'Go straight upstairs, now, this instant. You have disgraced yourself – and your father.' And she felt that tenseness inside him, that stiffness that she thought of as hatred. Tears filled her eyes as she crossed the grand room and, head bent, opened the door.

The fat woman's music, which had stopped, started again as she closed the door softly behind her. But now it only sounded sad; the magic had gone from it.

'She only danced,' said Lucinda the next morning, after the dreadful telling of the thing was over. 'And after all, what's wrong with dancing? She's a little girl, and little girls like to dance.'

Charlotte smiled but said nothing.

Milly eyed Alice frostily over her big, folded arms. She watched helplessly as the child she loved sank deep inside herself once again, and so Milly was overcome

186

and she had to wrap her arms round her.

Alice wept. Her small frame trembled. 'I can't do it. I can't do it. What Charlotte says is true. There is something wrong with me.' And then she whispered, 'Remember my secret.'

'Shush now,' and Milly glowered at the simpering Charlotte. 'You just have some growing up to do, that's all. Your Papa loves you, he depends on you, it's just that sometimes I think he asks too much of you. Everything would be quite different if your mother was still living.' And Milly directed her fierce words at Charlotte.

But Charlotte would not be silenced with a look. 'When will you see the truth, Milly Toole, when are you going to see?' And Charlotte summed up the situation as she saw it as she left the room. 'No one will want her when they know what she does. No gentleman, nobody of quality. And certainly not Edward Brennan,' said Charlotte.

# TWENTY-ONE

The private practice of Dr Joshua Myers was not a flourishing one. For a start the area was underpopulated, and the vast majority of those who lived in it had no money to waste on doctors. But nearer to the truth was the fact that workhouse medical officers were not the sort of doctors those in high places would naturally recommend to their friends, nor would they want them to attend their own children, or come to their houses on social occasions. Myers was in a cleft stick: he needed the parish money to survive but the fact that he took it prevented any kind of natural progress.

But now, much as he detested it, Myers was worried about his job.

Deale had become an asylum by accident, not by design. And certainly Dr Myers would not have wished it that way. Gradually, his intake from the workhouse had ceased to be so much a medical one, but an increasing number of poor wretches who were confused, inadequate and sick in the head. So much so that he could not cope with the other, more respectable side of the work and had to consign them to Dr Trafford, ten miles away. He was left with the lunatics.

From the bedraggled, motley collection of rejects in the workhouse it was often difficult to decide who was mad and who was not. They were all keen to be moved to the Asylum, whining at him to get there, imitating madness and putting on appalling performances, twisting their pinched-up, yellow features into expressions of leering cunning, in order to convince him. The food was better in the hospital half of the workhouse and the patients were not forced to do menial work. Myers was not used to people attempting to prove themselves insane.

Naturally his particular job did not endear him to the

kind of private patients he was trying to attract. Not only was he smeared by the taint of 'workhouse doctor', but the word 'asylum' was even more distasteful. People began to assume that he was not a medical doctor at all . . . that he specialised in the behaviour of imbeciles. They did not want him in their houses.

So Joshua Myers was an embittered man. He blamed his patients for his hopeless predicament, stuck as he was with his miserable career. Constantly he applied for appointments elsewhere, but constantly he was rejected. He would be hard to replace. Now that the medical profession was growing in stature there were not many young doctors fresh from the teaching hospitals who were particularly keen to take such an unpopular position.

Even so, because of Alice Brennan his job was now under threat. Her husband believed her mad, but Myers could not be certain.

At forty years old, still Myers clung to his original social aspirations, lamenting the fact that the only people who ever asked him to supper were the master and matron of Deale workhouse . . . persons whom he recognized as not only his social inferiors, but small-minded and brainless to boot. An unpleasant couple, thought Myers, going along the lane with his long bald head with black fluff on the back of it, his stiff frockcoat and his cane which he waved desultorily in front of him.

Joshua Myers was lonely. He remained unmarried in spite of all his efforts. Even women were afraid of him, fearing, perhaps, that his vaguely blue eyes could recognize madness, that his fat pudgy fingers could poke and pry not only to the secret, dark places of the body, but probe the soul as well. He had a room – there was not much in it, he possessed few personal effects – in the nearby village and nobody called on him there. Now, just before five o'clock, just before real darkness fell, he approached Deale workhouse . . . a sprawling, ugly building . . . you could tell where the workhouse

189

ended and the asylum began because of the bars on the windows. The building took on the grey of the dusk. It beckoned him mockingly with its flickering lights and gaunt chimney-stacks. Lured by the promise of beefsteak pie he passed through the tall, black gates of the detested place, nodded to Corbett inside the gate-house and went round the back to the private wing which was the humble home of his hosts, Mr and Mrs Alfred Flood.

Into the parlour and off with his hat. 'Move, Emily! Fetch the good Doctor a glass of port to stave off the chills of the evening – and be quick about it now!'

Myers was glad to see the lively fire. He was lulled by the bossy, organizing manner of Mrs Flood. Now he was inside he felt better altogether. Here, with these 'lesser' people scuttling around him, he put on an air of knowledgeable dignity and knew they would be impressed.

Mr Flood was already in position in a vast mahogany chair at the end of the deal table with, if you please, his napkin tucked into his waistcoat. The Floods ate early and this annoyed Myers who preferred to sip several drinks beforehand, and talk. Flood was eager to get to the heart of the matter, the food. Above the great oak sideboard, which took up most of the room, hung an engraving of *The Last Supper*. The man was obsessed by food. Myers looked at the workhouse master and thought to himself, once again, what a barbaric, ignorant person this man was.

Labour was not just cheap here, labour cost nothing, so Mrs Flood could relax and oversee while the woman finished off in the kitchen and Emily, the workhouse skivvy, made sure the table looked neat, fiddled with the centrepiece which was an extraordinary silver camel reclining against a tall palm tree with a fern sticking up out of the end of it. She tended to the fire and filled up the scuttle.

'Changes are coming,' said Flood, as Myers ignored his chair at the table and took the one by the fire

190

instead. Flood was referring to the takeover of the country's asylums by the new commissioners. 'Big changes.'

'Changes are usually made much of before the event,' replied his guest, a trifle uneasily, 'but they have little effect on anything in the end. Life tends to go on just the same.'

'You will have to apply to retain your appointment,' said Alfred Flood, a melancholy man who was fiddling now with his knife and fork in his urgency to begin. He was short and comfortably plump with a red, cleanshaven face, but his eyes were like the eyes of a turtle, watchful and sad. He cast them anxiously at his wife, for it was well past five, but she was fussing about the Doctor, placing the table within his reach, dragging the footstool nearer. Flood knew from experience that the man would be impossible to shift once he got too comfortable.

'I don't think there will be any difficulty in retaining that,' said Myers bleakly, very unsure of his own brave words. 'But what I am hoping for is more recognition . . . more money for treatment and some training for my nurses. Getting the necessary funds from the workhouse guardians proves nigh impossible.'

'Stuff and nonsense,' said Mrs Flood, poking the fire which had just been poked by Emily. She crossed to the window and clashed the tapestry curtains closed. 'I don't believe in it. Let the patients look after themselves. Give them something to think about. Idle hands make idle minds.'

This was just the attitude that Myers spent his whole life fighting against and he tightened his lips. 'That is not the case, Mrs Flood,' he said stiffly. 'Lunacy is an illness.'

Mrs Flood regarded him through her shrewd, prominent blue eyes. She flounced down into the chair opposite, wafting the fire accidentally as she did so with her heavy homespun skirt. An acrid billow of grey smoke bulged out from under the chimney breast. It

191

was Mrs Flood who governed the workhouse and it was Mrs Flood who governed Alfred. She wore a fleecy grey shawl and smelled overpoweringly of soap and beeswax.

Her big freckled face drew closer to the Doctor's when she teased him, 'Too soft, you are, always have been too soft.' And then she relaxed into her old argument, 'Now why should the decent, hardworking people of this parish be forced to support those miserable wretches of yours with nothing at all upstairs? 'Tis bad enough that they pay for the ne'er-do-wells on my side of the wall but at least there is some hope of an eventual turnabout . . . though not in many cases, I grant you.'

'Then what are we to do with the mentally ill, my dear Mrs Flood?' Dr Myers held up his glass and eyed her through the rich red glow of the port.

'Pack 'em off. They're no good to man nor beast. Pack the lot of 'em off with the rest of the muck to New South Wales, to somewhere where they won't be so troublesome any more!'

It depressed Myers to be forced to argue his case on this low level, but he was determined to make the conversation last to at least one more drink and Alfred was getting restless. So he humoured his hostess. 'I have to hope that the new asylum commissioners are more sympathetic to my hapless charges than yourself.'

Mrs Flood sat back in her chair, overflowing it. 'There's some, I believe,' and at this she closed one knowing eye, 'who are so eager to avoid your ministrations that they take their cases into their own hands, if you like, and flee the premises as fast as they can, no iffing or butting about it.'

Myers raised his eyebrows. 'You are referring to the recent unfortunate . . . '

'Hah! There were no flies on that one. She knew what she was doing. No flies on her!'

It was distasteful for Myers to hear such ignorant certainties being uttered by a woman with such a limited brain. 'I do have a certain dilemma with that particular patient,' he confessed, sipping his drink to ease his annoyance. 'Her husband is convinced she is quite out of her mind. She came to me so that I could watch her and decide. It is a serious matter declaring a woman of that type insane – not an act to be taken lightly.'

'And?' Mrs Food leaned forward again to enquire. 'What did your professional observations lead you to conclude?'

Myers was forced to shake his head. 'I could not make up my mind,' he admitted. 'From her past history which I learned from her family, there seems little doubt about it – my patient was apparently extremely sick. Yet she gave me no cause to think so during the seven months she spent at Deale, except for the natural reactions of anyone restrained against their will – that, and her extraordinary fear of her husband.'

Flood interrupted. 'Are we going to eat tonight, my dearest, or are we just going to sit and converse?'

'Manners, Alfred, please! It is good for the appetite to spend some time savouring the pleasures to come. I will ring the gong in a moment, when I have re-filled Doctor Myers' glass.'

'What is the point of ringing the gong, my dear, when we are already gathered here and waiting?'

'So that Emily knows, of course,' said Mrs Flood caustically, glaring at her husband. 'Excuse him, Doctor Myers, he has no idea of the finer points of social behaviour.' She gave her husband another furious glance when she added with a snap, 'Never has had.'

'No, well, as I was saying,' said Myers, accepting the second glass gratefully. 'I did not have the necessary time to tell whether the good woman was suffering from a mental ailment or whether, perhaps, she was merely affected by the normal upsets of pregnancy. And now of course, unless she can be found and brought back, nothing can be done.' He did not confess his real concerns to the Floods. He did not discuss the fact that, unless Alice Brennan was brought back and registered quickly and efficiently as insane, there was a chance that he would not be given his job back under the new system, that he would have to go looking for somewhere else without a testimonial. When he'd visited Winterbourne House this morning that fact was made quite clear, not just by Mr Brennan but also by his coldly censorious sister-in-law. For months he had kept them dangling with worries of his uncertainties, of his reticence to certify Alice insane without being sure. But Edward had scoffed at him, 'Surely seven months is time enough? Surely, man, no matter how busy you are, you had the time to observe! And now, Myers, it seems that it is too late, doesn't it?'

Damn the woman, thought Myers angrily, of his missing patient.

The effects of imprisonment in a workhouse asylum on a woman of such gentle breeding must be taken into account. She'd been sad, yes, she'd cried, spent a great deal of time staring out of the windows. He had asked Edward at the time, 'It is normal for families in your position to pay for private nursing. Have you not considered that option? It would be a good deal kinder.' But Edward had insisted that Alice needed much more careful guarding than that. 'And I want her away from the house,' he'd said. 'It is not good for the children to see her when she gets into her terrible states. They've been through enough. God help us, we've all been through enough.'

The tinny twang of the gong in the hall brought Myers back to the present. He cursed the little bit of conscience that had niggled him and caused him to hesitate. Had that been the reason he'd been slow to certify her, or was it the knowledge that he could use Edward Brennan's great need to rid himself of his wife to solidify his position, to demand a higher salary? He took his place at the table. Flood made a great performance of slopping his clear soup. He dunked great wedges of bread in the bowl and sucked the soup off

194

it rudely. Mrs Flood shared a sympathetic glance with the Doctor across the table.

The beefsteak pie was delicious. 'You have excelled yourself once again,' he complimented her, taking another potato. Her face flushed with pleasure. She poured more wine.

Now that Flood was almost satiated he was relieved of the terrible pressures of hunger and could sit back and enjoy the company. He slapped his stomach and burped before hunching himself over his empty plate, waiting for his pudding.

He belched again before he spoke. His coarse, black hair was tight to his head as if painted there. A slick lick of it swept his sweating forehead. 'There was a big fuss made over the incident at Shilstone,' said Flood. 'I believe you were roughly treated by an unexpected little guard of men. If the woman wants to leave Deale it would surely be better to allow it and let her family cope with the problem rather than become so personally involved yourself. Is it worth it, Doctor?' and Flood let his mournful eyes rest on the steaming treacle tart that Emily placed before him and they brightened with eager anticipation.

'Tell us what happened to you, Doctor Myers! Do tell us! Did the villains actually do you harm?'

Myers fingered the sore bit of neck that bulged from his high, white collar. He remembered that terrible night. He had never felt such terror in his life before, had never felt so humiliated in front of so many onlookers. He wondered how the story had been told behind his back, whether everyone at Deale was laughing at him. He tried to read his hosts' expressions but could not. Flood was tucking into his pie and his wife's attitude was one of profound concern.

'I would rather not discuss it,' said Myers, with dignified pain. 'It was not a pleasant incident. Quite uncalled for. It seems to me that the day will soon be here when any Tom, Dick or Harry who feels like it, can take the law of this country into his own hands.

Authority,' and Myers' eyes flicked round the table in search of someone to blame, 'authority is slipping.'

Mrs Flood tutted. 'It was certainly a most strange circumstance . . . nobody knowing who they were and where they came from.'

'Even the constables have drawn a blank,' said Myers morosely. 'It looks as though the culprits will go unpunished.'

Flood's lips were busy sucking up custard when he spoke. 'Corbett is certain it has to be the circus.'

'What circus?' Dr Myers laid down his spoon and forced himself to concentrate upon the moving mouth of the workhouse master.

'There was a circus passing by at the time, Corbett says. He says it could only have been them, because the ruffians were strangers – there were no local men among them.'

'Why did not Corbett report his suspicions to me or to the constables? Why has he remained silent on this matter?'

Flood was scraping pieces of pastry raspingly off his chin. 'Probably because the man is not sure . . . you know how these people talk between themselves and never volunteer anything unless directly asked. Well, it might be a figment of Corbett's imagination, but then again there might be something in it.'

'I fear that Corbett is probably a man of limited imagination,' the Doctor interrupted, 'but if it was men from the circus who attacked us while we went about our lawful business, there remains a certain question of motive.'

'Who knows what drives these types of people,' said Mrs Flood disdainfully. 'We are talking of those who are so far beneath us it would be hard to interpret their actions with any kind of certainty. They will do anything for money, for amusement, or if driven to it by drink. Mr Flood and I have to contend with these types every day of our lives.'

'And if it was them that interfered with you, it might

well be them that has taken the lady and her nurse,' said Flood, with a brightness that was unusual for him.

Joshua Myers could no longer taste his food. What the Floods were telling him was a possibility and one that must be followed up very seriously indeed. He cursed the fact that he had not known about the circus earlier. They could be miles away by now, right out of the county. He was eager to remove himself from this over-hot room, and he detected an underlying amusement in his hosts' interest in his discomfort. He wanted to talk to Corbett, to try and ascertain whether the fellow was certain about the travellers in the village, and he had to find out how close they had passed to the cottage door. The more Myers thought about it, the more likely this theory seemed to be.

Edward Brennan would be generous to the bringer of positive news and Joshua Myers wanted to be that person. He would have no qualms about certifying Alice Brennan now. No matter how much he disliked his job, it was better than penury. He soon made his excuses and left the Floods to their scornful criticisms of him, to their ignorant amusement and their cruel laughter. He would talk to Corbett on his way home and, if convinced, would ride to Winterbourne House first thing in the morning. As the bearer of such hopeful tidings he was sure he would be welcomed there with the greatest of courtesy.

Myers perceived that his grim, somewhat uncertain future, might well be taking on a more hopeful look.

# TWENTY-TWO

Tucked away by her country childhood, cloistered and a virtual prisoner on marriage, Alice had never been to a theatre before, nor had she come anywhere near to a city at night.

She wanted to go. She argued with Milly, 'How can you try and dissuade me? For what possible reason would you rather I stay and spend the night shut away in a few small feet of space no bigger than my cell at Deale? It would be monstrous, Milly. Oh, you can be so very mean sometimes. When you see me enjoying myself you can be so terribly small-minded!'

'I worry about you becoming over-excited my darling, that's all. You are still very weak. By rights you should still be in bed. 'Tis disgusting seeing you up and about so soon after childbirth, no better than a wench in a farm gang with her petticoats tucked between her legs and thick muddy boots like a troll. Alice, my darling,' she wheedled, 'you must remember you are fragile, you need nursing.'

Alice shrugged her shoulders and turned away. 'Oh – and do I look as if I need constant nursing? Do I look as if this new life of ours is draining me dry, wearing me out?'

No, Milly could not use Alice's looks as an argument. She was rapidly improving. In just two days she had come far from the exhausted wraith Luke Durant had carried through Milly's cottage door. Her eyes sparkled, her smile was back and she chattered unceasingly; beguiled by every new sight and sound, her laughter was quick and light-hearted. Worryingly light-hearted. Behind them, while they argued, the immense canvas was going up on the flat, dry grassland. The material billowed whitely in the darkness, illuminated by pots of burning fat which gave out a weird, yellow

198

light and sparked. Smaller booths, like little mushrooms sprouting at the roots of a ghostly oak, shot up out of the grass itself. Shouts of boisterous mirth disturbed the quiet of the countryside. Men banged in enormous wooden stakes and it took three or four to handle each rope.

'I would rather you stayed here with me,' was Milly's doleful conclusion, drawn with a tired breath. 'Davy is only a few days old, and any normal mother would stay in bed for a fortnight – longer, when I think what you have been through. It is certainly too soon for you to go venturing off into disreputable places like theatres. You will be taken for one of the gypsies. You have no respectable clothes – that dress of mine does not fit you and you have no hat.'

Alice tossed her long hair. She refused to pull it back and pin it up in the old style. Luke liked it free and flowing naturally and Alice wanted to be lovely; even in dreams it was good to feel lovely, to feel she was pleasing Luke.

'And how will you get there?' Milly fretted. 'On horseback, I suppose. A freshly-birthed woman on the back of a horse!'

Milly was disgusting about childbirth. Everything she said suggested blood and struggle and pain. Alice couldn't bear any of those words. She wasn't prepared to discuss the matter with Milly any more. 'There is a party of us going and Luke has arranged for a cab.'

'How very convenient.' So Milly lost her argument with a bad grace and a purple face and Alice set off in the first cab with a small party of actresses. The men used horses and rode alongside.

Never mind Milly. Alice's heart was light. This used to be the part of the day she dreaded most – early evening. It was the time when, with the children in bed, she was forced to face those long, terrible, often silent hours downstairs with Edward and Charlotte. If she was good they agreed to play Lotto. Sometimes they would read . . . the three of them, sitting there. How could she follow a story, because whenever Alice looked up there were eyes on her, stony eyes with hard criticism in them. If she moved to get comfortable they would look up, if she cleared her throat they would exchange glances, if she asked a question they would frown.

She remembered Charlotte's question, 'What is it you're reading, Alice?'

'I'm not reading tonight, Charlotte. I have chosen a picture book. It is full of the most wonderful pictures of birds . . . look at the heron about to take flight, look at the power in its wings.'

Edward nodded permission so Charlotte moved towards her swiftly with her hands held out to take the book. How meekly she'd given it up, all the bright colours and the shiny smell of it, and she had sat there for the two hours remaining, mourning her loss of it. Oh yes, there had been so many times like that.

Early evening . . . she used to watch the mantel clock and think it impossible that time could pass so torturously slowly. She used to long for her bed.

Alice couldn't help the shiver, but her fear of Edward was dying. Already that life was nothing but a nightmare. He might even leave her alone; in reality she could be asleep in the churchyard, lying beside the angel with Davy in her arms. Perhaps Edward might be satisfied with the fact that she had disappeared . . . after all, that is what he had always wanted. And the child? Well, why would Edward want the child when he had Nicholas as his heir? No, as every day passed Alice Brennan told herself that in her head she was twenty-four hours safer than she'd been yesterday.

Her dark and terrible memories were fading and she was surprised that she could, so quickly, feel so close to happiness. If it were not for missing her children, she would be completely and genuinely happy. The reason for this was Luke . . . she hated to be away from him . . . she was suddenly gripped by an urgent need for reassurance and she looked for him, peering out of the window. Oh thank God he was there, only yards behind the cab. It was all right. Her confidence returned.

The horse clopped along, their cab rocked gently. The night was dark with unseen whispers which gusted from the backstreets and byways. Such a mysterious darkness was the darkness that belonged to the city. The only lights to disturb the ebony night were the feeble white cab-lamps, the occasional watchman with his lantern and the firefly glows that spluttered outside the public houses. Sometimes a dingy street-lamp spat mournfully. They dropped the performers off at the deserted theatre door and Alice and Betty Groves went into the coffee shop to wait.

They sipped their coffee in a private booth lit by a soft red lamp. Betty Groves took out her knitting. The coffee smell in the shop fought hard and won the battle with tobacco. Betty was obsessed by theatre talk. Her rheumatism had forced her to retire from her job as a dresser and now, when she wasn't pained too much, she was reduced to sewing costumes. She was a mine of fascinating stories, and Alice listened, but wanted to know where Unity Heath and that cab-load of frilly-bonneted women had gone. She had watched their cab – three ahead of them – turn off and disappear down a shabby sidestreet.

'To the room above the tavern . . . but that's not theatre.' Betty compressed her lips and turned up her beaky nose but her eyes were alight with gossipy excitement. 'It is a performance I'll grant you, but you can't call it theatre. Still, each to his own no matter how shameless. I am a firm believer in that and it doesn't pay to be squeamish.'

'Can we go there afterwards?' Her lack of understanding undermined her new feeling of freedom but Betty volunteered nothing more so Alice had to make do with that.

'We certainly will not be going there afterwards.' Betty thrust one knitting-needle under her arm and ran the other through her grey hair. 'And a lady like you

201

shouldn't be asking to visit such places. Now then, 'tis ten to eight and we must get on. There will be a full house tonight and we have to find our places.' Their breaths were frosty in the air, and Alice pulled the workhouse cloak tight round her when they came out into the cold.

A group of scavenging children begged in the gutter and the tattiest smoked a fat cigar. Some wizened women of the night skulked in the shadows and a passing policeman spoke to them severely. A man with an accordion played to the waiting crowd. There was a clutter of carriages and hansoms at the theatre door and everyone was dressed in their finery except for the cabmen keeping warm in their scarves and greatcoats. Alice felt dowdy and plain in her second-hand garb. Piemen plied their wares on the pavement outside, and a man in an apron sold hot potatoes that made her feel hungry.

Out of the cold and inside at last, Alice sat, eyes wide with astonishment. Such splendour! Tier upon tier of faces, the men in their evening dress, canes and whis-kers, the women in their plumed headdresses. The theatre was filled with sounds and scents of expec-tancy, the rustle of silk, the glint of opera glasses and voices shrill with excitement. Soft sounds, muffled by the curtains and the lights and the whispering sense of anticipation.

The orchestra tuned up, deep in the half-lit pit, the great hoop of gas-lights was hoisted aloft, hissing soft-ly, and the front of the stage was a mass of flowers . . . no matter that Betty explained they were only imita-tion, that made no difference to the effects. As the performance began the seething families in the pit, some who had brought their babies, peeled their oran-ges, stopped their fidgetings and quietened down. High in a box and holding her breath, when the heavy cur-tains swished apart Alice saw Luke. Alice saw hardly anything else but Luke throughout the whole of the glorious performance. She saw his graceful demeanour,

202

his highly-polished boots, his costume of silver braid on a royal blue velveteen coat and fear came seeping into her dream. Acting – his voice made him sound big, bigger, much bigger in her head and the laugh that he gave was free and loud, it spread in wide circles up to the ceiling where she couldn't catch it.

Words written by somebody else – right out of her own control.

They reached every corner of the house without effort, bringing gasps from the audience, putting tears in their eyes, hushes and laughter. He was the puppeteer, and the audience were marionettes on strings, bending to his will.

She wished she could stop watching and listening but she could not. Luke glittered there in front of her – hard – she wished he'd go soft and runny and unreal again. Memory whispered. Sitting there stiff as a statue and the dream held her, but now it gripped her in brutal hands.

Her eyes swung from Luke to Jessica Lamont, heavy as that velvet curtain. It was hot; she teetered in and out of reality as the air was pressed in by the walls – hardly enough to breathe. She watched, she couldn't stop herself watching as Luke, so arrogant and swarthy, made love to Jessica Lamont, fragile and pale and so in need of his attentions if she was to survive to the end of the play. Never had a woman looked so tragic, so utterly beautiful. Jessica Lamont cuddled up to the lusty hero, she batted her long eyelashes at him, she sneaked him her coy-eyed glances and Luke appeared truly to fall in love. Right there, in front of Alice's eyes.

All faces stared up at him as he spoke the words which were not hers. Women sighed, they fluttered their fans. Strained and urgent, Alice sat now with her hands gripped between her knees and her eyes staring straight ahead. And Luke had said he was no great actor . . . he had played down this talent of his and no wonder! His performance was deliberately designed to appeal to women's hearts and oh, he was good at it.

203

Revelling in it, flirting outrageously in the looks he sent out to the fascinated crowd. Cool, sensual, the perfect hero.

And she watched his face so urgently it might be the first human face she'd ever seen. I can't have this happen. I can't watch women adoring him – I can't endure it. Why did I invent the pain? Why couldn't I have kept it beautiful?

She wished she had followed Milly's advice and not come.

Was this why he had not married? Was this the reason he continued to travel with the troupe . . . in order to revel in the admiration of women? What reason had he ever needed to pick one and settle down? Luke had the choice of hundreds.

The jealousy began as a tickle in her chest before creeping and leaping along until her limbs were weakened by it, until her heart was leadened by it and her eyes were dry with the harsh reality of it. And still she stared at the man on the stage, with her teeth biting into the perfect shape of her lower lip.

Betty gave a bird-like sideways turn. 'Don't you think he's wonderful?' she asked, still staring at the stage while facing Alice. 'Have you ever seen a man so handsome, a man so masculine and suave?'

'I can't believe it is Luke. I can't believe he can act like that.'

'He was born to it,' Betty replied so matter-of-factly it was chilling to hear. 'And this is nothing. Every woman here is in love with him. He is the reason they come! Even the folks down there in the pit, they stay quiet and behave themselves when Luke is on stage.'

'Oh?'

She wanted to go away with her new-found pain, she wanted to leave this huge, vaulted place and take it to nurse in some dark corner. Or pace backwards and forwards with it, hour after hour to see if it would reduce in intensity the way Milly dealt with Davy's crying. If only she had known about this that first night at the castle, up on that parapet when Luke first kissed her. If she'd known, Alice thought to herself wearily, painfully, if only she'd known she would have pulled back. She would never have allowed her heart to slip, she would somehow have killed off the monster.

There must have been a point when she could have prevented him.

Luke was not within her control. He played other parts. There were dangerous women in her dreams. Did Milly know? Is this what Milly had been suggesting with all her dark warnings? Alice had ignored Milly, thinking her an old-fashioned, strait-laced fool.

She was sliding, scared, along a wall . . . so many walls . . . which wall was this? Oh, why had she let her dream turn around to bite her? And here she was again, she recognized this place with a sinking heart, she quailed when she recognized this ceaseless revolution of thoughts like a terrible carousel that would never stop, would never allow you to get off no matter how sick you became, or how dizzy.

Disordered thoughts. Numbing. Was there no mercy anywhere . . . from sky to sky, was there no pity anywhere in those holes between the stars?

When the audience roared their last applause Alice bowed her head and wondered why there was such a terrible silence in the house.

And when, edgy and impatient, Alice made straight for the caravan, not stopping beside the fire to stay and talk to those gathered here, then Milly took one look at that tortured face, and those wide, pained eyes. She opened her arms as she had opened them so many times, she took Alice into her arms and she said with an awful resignation, 'Oh my poor darling, oh my poor darling.'

205

# TWENTY-THREE

It was to no mean gambling den in the backstreets of London that Thomas Venton went, to play with the last of his pathetic belongings not three years after the death of his wife. It was to the creakingly comfortable, brown-leather respectability of his club.

There he sat in the green baize room adjoining the dining room, as he had sat so many times, but the night he gave his daughter away there was sweat on his upper lip and wet beads of fear on his forehead. He could not get the sight of his wife, Sarah, out of his mind; he could not still the voice he heard in his ears. He closed his eyes, he opened them to stare hard at the flames of the fire, but there she was again with her arms stretched out towards him, beseeching him, crying.

'But you shouldn't have left me,' he called out in the stricken silence. 'You knew I would never survive without you! I loved you, Sarah, and I needed you.'

And her cruel reply came to him through the raw guilt of his own conscience: 'You wanted a son, Thomas. The lovely girls I gave you were not sufficient for you.'

He cursed silently as he laid down his cards.

Around the table were his three opponents . . . Sam Tyndale, Harry Arbuthnot and the boorish Henry Brennan. The latter glowered from under his dark eyebrows as he dealt. Because of his grey, unhealthy countenance, the man looked as if he had never been outside in his life, but had spent every day of it in a darkened room with the curtains drawn against trees and green hills, working out figures, assessing his worth. Every single thing the blighter touched turned into gold. The man had the right connections – dour, gaunt men like himself with their eyes on industry and the political movements of other countries. These men, with money at their finger ends, cared not a jot for their own. They came to live in the country, oh yes, gradually buying up all the great houses and coming down from their city homes to live in country style, but they did not understand it . . . they were not of it. They sold off their farms, they remodelled their houses.

Oh, they did not behave with arrogance, they were not inept or overly ostentatious. They followed the accepted code, sent their sons to the right schools and hunted and shot and fished, though with no great expertise. They were all pathetically eager to be accepted. Thomas sneered at them as he always had because they did not know what to wear on what occasion, how to address whom, how to make morning calls and leave their cards. They were forced to buy books to learn about etiquette; they had to follow manuals.

What they were desperately after was prestige. Thomas had all the prestige he needed – what Thomas wanted, and he despised himself for it – was money.

Thomas had followed advice and searched for the new gold, coal, under his own lands. He had found none. He hadn't really expected to – his luck did not run like that.

People like Henry Brennan changed things . . . they had a morose and miserable sense of morality, and the gentry, so open to criticism because of their lavish lifestyles, were forced to respond, to become, outwardly anyway, more religious, more serious and more responsible. If they changed their ways and adapted they might be allowed to retain some of their old power.

Huh! And the new men brought their own foul brand of competition into the countryside with them. The old landed families were forced to try and keep pace, to do up their houses, to build family chapels – riddled with tracery, stained glass and pious inscriptions, everything suggestive of religion and good taste – gothic! My God, thought Thomas, even our houses have to proclaim their owners as courteous, hospitable and doers of good deeds.

Even Mrs Toole had taken to going around the village in a trap at Christmas with a rug covering good things in baskets. She insisted the girls go with her. 'We are too hidden away upstairs,' Thomas remembered her telling him. 'The girls, especially Alice, should understand something of the world outside.'

'The world outside is a dangerous place these days,' warned Thomas.

'I will take Jasper with me, as guard.' Milly was well aware of dangers from what she called the dark, seething underworld at work among the people. No, Milly did not need reminding. And rightly so.

These unfortunate Christmas visits had led to trouble from a surprising quarter. Alice, normally so timid and silent, came knocking on Thomas' study door quite unexpectedly, uninvited. She had never done that before. With tears in her eyes she told him of some of the conditions she saw on her journeys with Milly. 'Papa, some of those hovels were so dark we could not see the people in the room! They stuff dirty cloths into the thatch to stop the rain coming in and they live so close together they have to climb over one another to get to bed.' She raised her wide eyes to stare at him, searching desperately for the courage she needed to go on before she added, 'The youngest boy of the Whistlers, Papa, I saw that his bare feet were blue in spite of the fact that he crouched by the fire. They are hungry, Papa, and, Papa, they hate us. They pretend that they don't but I saw it, they hate us.'

Attempting to remain reasonable, trying not to show how he despaired of his eldest child, Thomas reassured her. She was far too vulnerable to the whims of emotion . . . even a dog with a limp made her cry. She cried when she should not cry, she laughed when she should not laugh but although Thomas was naturally a sarcastic and autocratic man it was hard to be stern with Alice. Timid, brittle, appealing, at least she was not caustic and sullen like her sister Charlotte. If only Lucinda had been born first, if only Neville had survived. So, trying to be patient Thomas answered his cringing daughter, 'So what would you have me do, Alice? Increase their wages? If I increase their wages they will buy looms and I will have to put up with tired, lazy workers on the farm. Or the man of the house will get himself a cow or a pig and spend all his spare hours attending to that instead of the animals I am paying him to care for. What should I do? Leave them to stay abed in the mornings and employ gangs to do my work instead? Ah yes, and then they would mutter that there was no work to be had. You have too soft a heart, Alice. These people do not see things as we see them, they do not feel as we do. They look to us for firm guidance and leadership and by allowing yourself to be fooled by their whingeings and moanings you do them no service.'

'But they did not whinge or moan, Papa. They held their faces very stiffly and when we gave them their little hampers they curtsied and smiled most politely.'

Why on earth wasn't this fragile little girl content to stay in the nursery with Milly, happily pasting post-cards in scrapbooks, making wax models or pictures with shells? 'Some of them work to undermine us, Alice. They are not good people just because they are poor. Look, if I paid the two and six a day which is what they demand, they would squander it on ale, and that would lead to the men beating their wives and their children, and eventually they would be forced to sell any new objects they bought, bricks, books, kettles, all the stuff that the pedlar brings round.'

William Lovett and his ideas, damn him, and a Cornishman to boot! That villainous man and his radical friends had put their ideas about everywhere. They bullied the weak, forcing them to support their ludicrous cause. The riots had had serious consequences, for a great deal of expensive damage had been done. Thomas, threatened as all landowners were, had organized meetings to deal with the problem. They were foiled in an earlier plan to catch the local ringleaders red-handed in spite of valuable inside information. An army of constables arrived to find the tavern deserted; there was nobody there but the landlord.

There were even rumours that well-known local families were involved in the movement . . . educated people who ought to damn well know better.

And now, seated opposite him at the table, Thomas narrowed his eyes as he studied the face of Henry Brennan. What views did he hold and why had he come here, tonight of all nights? Thomas had only seen him drinking, never seen him playing in here before. His expression gave nothing away. What cards did he hold in his hand? Dare Thomas raise the bet, bearing in mind the straits he was in? Could he fool the man who sat there so inscrutably before him?

He raised the stakes in a firm voice that belied his emotion. Henry Brennan matched him, and raised them again. Sam Tyndale decided to sit this one out, and clicked his fingers to attract the attention of the servant. He ordered more brandy. Harry Arbuthnot, an old friend, an amiable man with a weakness for port, looked closely at Thomas Venton and frowned. He held his cards at arm's length in order to see them more clearly. The clock ticked. The fire crackled. The gaslight spluttered.

'These stakes are too high for me,' Harry declared heartily. 'And the game is no longer a game. It has altogether too serious an air for my liking.' He patted his stomach. 'I am a sportsman, like yourself, Thomas. We stand more chance on the race track than we do with the slant-eyed, feckless, ladies of luck in these packs.'

Breathless with tension, gripped by a frantic desire to win, Thomas dared not adjust his tie and give his feelings away. The stark fact was that he had already gambled with money he did not possess. This time it was all or nothing. He had never been in this dire position before. There had always been something to bail him out, some priceless piece of porcelain, some ancestral picture he could sell. No longer. He willed

210

the only opponent he had left to back down and see his hand. The last time they had played together Thomas had won . . . *fifteen hundred on a son* . . . the debt was paid no matter that the child had not survived. But it was that fatal bet, Thomas considered, that had prompted the premature birth, the death of his wife, and consequently the death of his son. He had won fifteen hundred pounds and lost his whole world that Christmas night.

Agitated almost beyond endurance, Thomas waited for his opponent's decision. Eventually it came, slowly and arrogantly as, with a long sigh, Henry Brennan leaned forward, pulled a pile of banknotes from his wallet and laid them down softly on the table. 'I will raise the stakes by another two thousand,' he said coolly. And then he sat back and waited for Thomas.

Rarely had Thomas Venton been in possession of such a hopeful hand. He had three Kings and two Jacks and the characters seemed to smile at him, willing him on with a kind of coy cardboard smugness. If I back down now, if I leave the game I cannot pay, he told himself over and over again. His only alternative was to persevere. So it did not take him long to cover the bet with a promissory note . . . he was not happy with the nervously-jerked signature on the bottom, it had none of his old flowing style. He congratulated himself on his caution, however: he had not, after all, raised the stakes.

One by one Henry Brennan laid down his cards. Thomas could hear the heavy breathing, slightly snuffly, of Harry Arbuthnot, so close beside him, and Sam Tyndale was sitting back in his chair with his hands together in an attitude of prayer. Thomas wished it was him sitting back like that, observing, uninvolved. One Queen followed another . . . three Queens . . . Thomas felt himself breathe again, felt the knot in his chest loosen. He let his lips come slightly apart, he moistened them with his tongue. And then, with a tantalizing slowness, with a final soft slap of triumph,

211

came the fourth Queen. The last card was a nine of spades . . . why did he notice the last card when it was of such little importance? It seemed it was the only safe place he could rest his eyes. That nine of spades was the only unthreatening thing on the table.

Thomas cleared his throat. At some point he was going to have to look up and hold Henry's brooding eyes. He was going to have to put some expression in his own. But could he choose it? Wouldn't his look be one of sheer hopelessness, of utter despair?

And anyway, did that matter now? Did appearances still matter to a man who had lost everything, and more?

After that it was hard to remember exactly what happened because everything was suffused with the bright pink of shame – being forced to move to the cold ante-room of the club's chairman as if it was a duel Thomas was fighting, with black-coated seconds watching him hard but never quite catching his eye. He had made his terrible confession, confused, stuttering, fingering the large glass paperweight and relishing the feel of its cool solidity in the sticky heat of his hand. 'I have nothing left. My house and lands are mortgaged to the bank, I am already behind with paying my creditors . . .'

'And yet you continued to play the game, knowing this.'

Damn these serious, moral men with their stiff, censorious faces!

So this is what he had always been dreading . . . it was happening . . . it was now. He was a man who could not pay his debts. He was a profligate gambler, a scoundrel. His membership of the club would be withdrawn and his name would no longer be spoken in these tall-windowed, gilded rooms. His signature would be scratched ignobly from the red leather book. It would be as though he had never existed, never raised his glass and murmured a greeting or a joke from that chair by the fire.

Was this what Thomas Venton had always dreaded? Or would it be closer to the truth to say he saw this as the ultimate destination towards which he had always been secretly heading, doomed to arrive at this place of disgrace one day and desiring it to be sooner rather than later?

Sam Tyndale and Harry Arbuthnot withdrew their smiles.

Thomas struggled for speech.

Henry Brennan watched him with cunning in his eyes, and it was at this moment that Thomas realized that Henry had known . . . Henry had made it his business to know about Thomas' financial circumstances before taking part in the game. And before his cab had pulled up at the door this evening, Henry had already decided what form his compensation must take. He'd probably decided years ago. The man was so arrogant he made his claim with his eyes closed.

Thomas shuddered at the cold, unemotional nerve of the man. Again and again he cursed himself for the fool that he was.

'A promise of your eldest daughter, Alice, in marriage, when she reaches the age of eighteen, to my son, Edward.'

'Oh, I say . . .' Harry Arbuthnot gasped in astonishment and his florid cheeks puffed out. 'I say old man, that's definitely not on.' His defeated friend looked like death, and his breaths came with shudders that seemed to shake every bone in his body.

'As a gentleman, the Lord Venton cannot refuse me,' Henry continued in that cold voice of his, quietly mocking, ignoring Harry's futile blusterings.

And so it was that he signed away the future of his fourteen-year-old daughter, and it was just three weeks after that that Thomas, tenth Lord of Venton, went and lay down on his bed. He let his hand search, briefly, hopelessly, on the cold, far, silky side, for his wife, and carefully blew out his brains.

213

# TWENTY-FOUR

'It's all going round and round again. Oh, Milly, help me! Why were we given these feelings if we weren't meant to use them? Where else should we put them? How can I say they're not real when I've never known what to do with them and I'm hurting so much I don't know where to go!'

Milly dropped a quick, motherly kiss on Alice's hair before looking up and gazing bleakly into the distance. How could she say, 'I warned you.' How could she drone, 'I told you so,' when Alice was so tormented? But Milly knew she ought to have been firmer.

She tried to encourage Alice to go to bed but, desperate with her new unhappiness, Alice pushed her away and refused.

'I'm going for a walk,' she sobbed. 'If I go to bed I won't sleep and I'll spend the whole night crying. I don't want to wake Davy up.'

'Is Luke back yet?'

'No, he's not back. I want to wait for him.'

With Alice in this mood there was no comforting her. Milly hung her head when she said, 'Well, what can I say to help you, my darling, save to say that you should have listened to Milly? You know my opinions. For a woman it is not . . .'

'You ought to have told me he was an actor.' Alice's voice sunk to a whisper. 'And pretending. I never guessed because he uses a different name on the bill boards – Robert Melville. How was I to guess that Luke was one of the tallest, boldest names on the boards?'

Milly put on her sensible look. She attempted to wipe the tears from Alice's grief-stricken face. 'You have known Luke Durant for less than forty-eight hours. How can you say you love him, Alice? Now, just you stop your crying for a moment and think about what I'm saying, my pet. This is not love! Love needs time to deepen and flourish . . . my goodness me you hardly know the man.' Her commonsense was making no difference, Alice's shoulders shook all the more. It was late, they were both tired, so Milly changed her tune. 'And just because you've suddenly discovered he's an actor does not necessarily mean that he is not the man you thought he was. That fact does not mean he has been insincere, that he likes you any the less, that he is more likely to cheat you.'

Alice sniffed and stared at her nurse. 'No, Milly, you cannot go back on your earlier words and tell me that now. You are humouring me and I know it. You knew . . . you knew he was a heart-breaker, a man not to be trusted. You knew, but you didn't tell me why. You never gave me your reasons so I let him come into my head and now he is out of my own control.'

Milly sighed. This awkward conversation was taking place at the bottom of the caravan steps. Milly, in her nightdress with only a shawl over her shoulders, wished she could induce Alice to move inside where at least they would be sheltered from curious glances and straining ears. They could talk inside more sensibly, in private, where Alice's foolish behaviour could be concealed. But Alice was determined to remain exactly where she was, talking to Milly, yet all the time she was watching. She was listening and waiting for the return of Luke Durant.

'I knew Luke a very long time ago,' said Milly firmly. 'My conclusions were drawn from that time. He might be a totally different person now . . . '

'I think not, Milly. I think you are deceiving me.'

'Have I ever deceived you, my darling? Would I ever do that?'

'Well, tell me then,' Alice demanded, her face set, her eyes screwed up with pain. 'I want to know. I have

215

to know, for I have gone too far to pull back.'

Milly's response could not be the one she would give to anyone else faced with this same predicament. So she said, 'Stay with me, Alice, stay with me. Come inside, I will make a hot drink and we will talk. Don't go off on your own. Listen to Milly, my darling. Milly only wants the best for you, Milly doesn't want you to go and do something silly.'

'There's no point in me talking to you,' Alice said bitterly, 'for you do not understand . . . not really. You have never understood me. Nobody has.'

'But I can try, dear. I can try.'

But Alice would not be persuaded.

'Tell me about it,' Milly tried once more, but her voice was trembling with the cold. Her face was frozen rigid so it was hard to put the correct expression there. 'Tell me what happened tonight to make you feel so uncertain, to bring on this sort of unhappiness. Was the play no good? Did you enjoy none of it?'

'None of it. No, none of it. Not once I saw the way Luke flirted with Jessica Lamont. Not once I saw the reaction of the women in the audience, and the way he pandered to it . . . revelled in it. Oh Milly, you ought to have seen him.'

'But surely that is the way of an actor, my pet. Surely the part that he played tonight must have demanded it?'

'No.'

'Well, you would do better to talk to Luke about this in the morning. It would be far more beneficial to discuss your concerns rationally and calmly. To confront him like this, Alice, with yourself in one of your states, would be asking for nothing but trouble – because the poor man has done nothing wrong!'

Milly Toole frowned as she thought about her words. How could this possibly be her, standing on those caravan steps defending Luke Durant? How had this odd situation come about? She didn't believe one word she was saying. Shouldn't she be agreeing with Alice,

216

warning her off, joining in with fierce criticism?

But she couldn't. It used to be Alice, Milly wanted to protect, but now there was Davy as well.

That night at Venton, after the brutal death of her father, Alice had gone mysteriously missing. Oh, it had been awful . . . Milly could hardly bear to think of that time even now with all the passage of years between it. Those years should have acted as a buffer. They had not. The memories, for Milly, were sharper than any of last week or even of yesterday.

Everyone else was in shock – well, naturally they were in shock. The terrible news was broken to the children by the chaplain. Alice refused to put down her kaleidoscope and in the end Milly had gently tried to take it, but the tube seemed to be stuck to her fingers. The child would not give it up, she would not take her eyes from it either. Shock, thought Milly, prising the toy away from her. It is her way of protecting herself. She is pretending that nothing has happened and is concentrating on the patterns to dull her emotions.

'What will become of us now?' Charlotte kept asking. 'If Papa has lost all this money, if everything is owed to the bank, where are we going to live? How will we eat?'

Lucinda was pale as a white winter rose. 'Poor Papa,' she wept. 'When Mama died he was lost and lonely. He needed Mama. We ought to have tried to take her place somehow, we ought to have been able to help him.'

'He wouldn't have let you, my darling,' Milly tried to comfort her. 'He was a man who shied away from betraying his emotions. You must not blame yourself in any way at all. Lucinda, you were always the perfect daughter to him and he was terribly fond of you.'

'You wouldn't know it,' said Charlotte sharply. 'The only one he showed any concern for was Alice, and that was because she was his only hope for a better life.'

'Not now, Charlotte.' Milly tried to be gentle. 'I

217

know you are hurt, but wounding others is not the right way of coping with it and I will not allow that sort of talk, not at this terrible time.'

Normally Milly did not look in once her sweet things were safely in bed. No, she liked to go to her own room, enjoy a quiet cup of tea, undress and get herself comfortable. But this night she prepared to remain by the nursery fire and pop in on the hour every hour. She was alert to the sounds of weeping, of unhappy little feet trailing across the floor, of whisperings, of nightmares. It was after eleven when she discovered that Alice's bed was empty. She searched the nursery, she even opened all the cupboards, but Alice seemed to be missing.

Extraordinary! And horribly worrying, given the circumstances.

Eventually she was forced to wake Charlotte. Sleepily Charlotte muttered, as casually as you like as though Milly ought to have known, 'She'll be in the stables, Milly. That's where she always goes for comfort.'

'With the horses?' Milly was surprised. After the tragic demise of Abernathy Alice had shown little interest in animals. And she was nervous of horses, although, at Thomas' insistence, forcing her on, making her ride in spite of her trembling protests, she had overcome the worst of her fears. Milly imagined Alice cuddled up in the straw in her long white nightgown, the hooves of some great beast coming dangerously near to her darling's drooped head. Milly was overcome with emotion. Poor child, what a sad little picture, going off alone to the stables for comfort, unable to find it elsewhere.

'No, silly, not with the horses,' said Charlotte, turning over dismissively. 'With Garth the groom.'

The groom? Milly was stunned into silence. Had she heard correctly? What sort of accusation was this coming out of this thirteen-year-old's mouth? What did she know about things like this? Then Milly said, 'Charlotte! Sit up this instant! What on earth are you telling me? Repeat what you said so that I can see if you're telling more of your lies or not. Turn round! Sit up!' And Milly lifted the candle high so it rested on the child's plain face. 'Charlotte! Wake yourself up properly!'

'With Garth the groom.' Charlotte, obeying, repeated her words in the same dispassionate style.

'I was asking about Alice, dear. Are you sure you are properly awake?'

'Alice,' Charlotte spoke impatiently now. 'Alice is in the stables with Garth the groom. That's where she goes during the day when she tells you she's picking flowers to dry. She doesn't go into the rose garden at all. She goes straight to the stables where she knows Garth is waiting. She loves him,' said Charlotte simply. 'Like in Cherry's books.'

Milly, sensing a terrible tasteless joke, or some cruel vindictive trick, tried to smile. 'I'm quite serious, Charlotte. Look, Alice's bed is empty. I am worried about her. She's probably gone off somewhere terribly upset, to cry by herself. And I need to know, quite seriously now, where she has gone.'

Charlotte's mousy hair was as dry as the skin on her sleepy face. The vein on her forehead pulsed. She drew her thin lips together and there was pleasure in the telling when she said, 'There is no point in pretending any more.' And Lucinda stirred in the bed next to her. Milly looked round anxiously. She did not want Lucinda to hear this, joke or not. This was no subject for such innocent ears. But it seemed that Charlotte was determined to explain, whether Lucinda was listening or not. 'She is walking out with Garth, Milly. And that is the truth of it, believe me or not, that's up to you. You asked me, and I have told you. Now, will you allow me to go back to sleep?'

Confused, bewildered, Milly wandered away from the bed. She went to the window and held up her candle. Foolish, useless – there was no view of the courtyard from here. What on earth was she to do?

Surely there could be no truth in Charlotte's vile accusation? She thought about Alice, sweet, demure, chaste, pretty, obedient little Alice. The very thought of anything like that was absurd. She thought about Charlotte with her mean ways and her vicious lies and she realized that yes, this was just another of her little barbs. Although what a time for it . . . the night of her father's tragic death . . . and what a subject! The unpleasant child had certainly excelled herself this time.

But the question remained: where was Alice? If she wasn't in the stables, then where was she? Ought Milly to alert the household and instigate a search? Of course she should. She should act immediately. She should wake everyone up. One of the rioters might have got in through the window and kidnapped the child . . . anything was possible.

Milly Toole paced the floor, there and back and there again. Her large strutting figure cast tall shadows over the nursery walls. But wait . . . a warning voice said . . . a little voice deep in her subconscious. Wait, Milly, hold for a while. Think for a while before you act impulsively.

Because if there were any truth, any slight smattering of truth in Charlotte's dreadful story, and if the whole household were alerted, then everyone would know. And what would that do for the future of the Venton household, motherless, fatherless, totally dependent on Alice's good marriage? A fourteen-year-old girl cavorting in the stables with one of the humblest servants – it was unthinkable! The rumour would spread like wildfire until nothing could put it out, until it was established as fact and Alice's reputation, her whole future was totally ruined.

Milly, worn out with it all, eased herself down in the fireside rocker. She leaned forward and held out her hands to the fire. They were workworn hands. Hands red and raw from the caring for children – these children, her children. And they were wholly her responsibility now. Nobody else knew them. Nobody else loved them.

Should she go back and question Charlotte again? Maybe she'd been talking in her sleep. The child was clearly disturbed and who wouldn't be after the day's terrible, dark events?

Milly Toole was thrashing about in her head, her thoughts taking her this way and that when the nursery door opened and Alice tiptoed in. She jumped when she saw Milly sitting there in the semi-darkness.

'Oh,' she fluttered, 'I didn't expect anyone to be up.'

Milly rocked, trying to calm herself when she asked, 'Alice, for goodness sake, I have been worried half out of my wits. And where on earth have you been with just your nightdress and your shawl?'

'I have been for a walk.' And Alice's demeanour was all innocence. How could Milly possibly question it? How could she put Charlotte's filthy accusations to this sweet child? But Milly was het-up and worried. Milly was not her calm self. And apart from that there was damp straw on the hem of Alice's nightdress.

'Charlotte has told me you often go to the stables when you go off by yourself.' Milly's voice was hesitant, but at least she had started. She eyed Alice carefully.

The child had been crying but that was understandable. She had a great deal to cry about. They all did.

'I have been talking to a friend,' said Alice, with a sob in her voice.

'Oh? And who is this friend of yours? You have not mentioned a friend to me before.'

'I did not mention him because I knew you would not approve. His name is Garth and he works in Papa's stables. And I think I am in love with him.' And it was then that Alice burst into tears. Terrible, awful tears that seemed unstaunchable, that appeared to take her over and render her senseless to any outside reation.

'But . . . really . . . how . . . Alice. How can you think that you are in love? My darling, you are fourteen years old and how could you possibly be in love with a groom?' Milly was utterly astounded. She'd never heard of anything like it. 'Heavens above, you can't even know the meaning of the word!'

'I knew that would be your attitude!' Alice's tears turned fiercer. They ran hotly down her face and she screwed up her fists so the knuckles went white. 'Garth is a human being! Just because he has a lowly job, just because you consider him beneath your contempt, just because he is not well-born, that does not mean he is an animal, Milly!'

'Well, no, Alice, and I was not meaning to suggest that he was an animal. What I was trying to say was . . . '

But Milly never got to explain what it was she was trying to say, because Alice collapsed on the rug in front of the nursery fire and howled, 'And it doesn't matter anyway because he does not love me! He said that he did! He said he would love me always and never anyone else. But now he won't see me. All his sweet-talking was lies. I have tried all ways to be on my own with him, but he won't. He won't even let me talk to him . . . '

What was this? This was so appalling it didn't have a name, or if there was one Milly couldn't think of it. She felt herself slipping way out of her depth. She was dizzy, close to faintness, but not now! Oh Lord, not now! 'Does anyone else know of this?' she asked. 'Does everyone know except me?'

Alice could hardly be bothered to answer. 'I wish I was dead,' she wept. 'I would do anything in the world to make Garth love me. I would cross to the other side of the world with him if he asked me. I would tramp the streets like a beggar. I would dance naked on a stage if he asked me . . . and no, nobody else knows except Charlotte.'

Milly could hardly speak. She croaked, 'And all the other servants, I shouldn't wonder . . . '

'How can you care about things like that when you

can see that my heart is broken?'

Milly's voice turned severe. 'Alice! Today your father took his own life!'

'I do not care about that! Can't you see? Can't you understand? Nothing else in my life is important to me but my love for Garth. It is all that I live for. He is all that I want . . . he is big and safe, like a giant tree, he protects me. And now it's all over and . . . '

'How far has this . . . this love of yours gone? Alice! Alice, answer me!'

Milly knelt on the rug beside the weeping child. She gripped her wrists tightly. She had to get some sense out of her.

'What do you mean, how far?'

'What have you allowed this . . . person to do to you, Alice?'

Alice's eyes were wide with bright blue innocence. She allowed herself to be pulled into a kneeling position. Her golden hair was wet, it stuck to the sides of her face with passionate tears. 'Why, I gave him all I had, which was me,' she said simply.

Did the child understand what she was saying? Milly had to clear this up for once and for all. 'You mean he touched you? Did he, Alice? Did you let him do anything to you, down there in the stables? This Garth, did he . . . did he . . . it's not possible that he . . . '

'He loved me,' cried Alice, letting her hair fall over her face. 'I asked him to, and he loved me.' The pretty little doll was suddenly gone, and the figure that replaced it was dejected and hopeless. 'Yes, if that's what you want to know, Milly, he loved me. He kissed me. He touched me. He looked at me all over and I was without my clothes. And it was wonderful. Shall I tell you how he loved me?'

Milly got up with difficulty. She looked down at the child on the floor at her feet. She was lost for thoughts, let alone words. Alice peered up through her hair to locate her. She wrapped her small, childish arms round Milly's fat ankles as she continued to weep. 'Oh help me, Milly, please help me. For I know I cannot bear it!'

Something cracked. Something drove Milly, something so deep and so instinctive it couldn't be fought. She set her face and her heart so they were cold and hard as granite. The hands that gripped Alice's wrists were cruel, the love gone from them. Her voice had never sounded like this before. 'Listen to me now, Alice.' And then she shook her, silencing the sobs. 'You have never been down to the stables to visit this Garth! You have never visited the stables in your entire life, save to collect your horse. Nobody has ever touched you . . . '

'But Milly . . . '

The child wept. Milly thrust her face forward. She clutched her more firmly. She shook the child hard, she was limp as a doll. 'You have never heard the name Garth in your life. If he walked past you you would not know him!'

'But the things he said to me . . . '

'The things he said to you were contrived in your own dizzy head. He said nothing! He meant nothing! He does not exist. You have always loved to fantasize, you read too many books . . . '

'Milly, my heart feels as if it is shattered inside me.'

And then Milly let go her grip and slapped Alice's face. Hard. First one side, then the other. There was no holding back, but oh how it pained her to do something like that. The child reeled and fell to the floor, gasping. 'You are fourteen years old! You cannot have such feelings about anything, certainly not a man! You have imagined everything that happened, Alice, it's all there, inside you. Nothing real. Nothing but your own infantile yearnings, the wicked thoughts and feelings of a child allowed too much freedom to read and to think . . . '

'He touched me. He lay on top of me! He put . . . '

Another hard slap. Then another. Until Alice cowered and wept on the floor, protecting her face from the blows. 'And I am waiting for you to repeat these words after me, correctly, with no mistakes. "I have never been down to the stables and I know nobody by the name of Garth" . . . '

There were hours of sobbing and weeping then. Hours of remonstrations. And once, out of the hot, heavy, hopeless atmosphere, 'Is my father really dead?'

'Yes, your father is dead. But you know nobody by the name of Garth and you have never . . . '

'What is going on?' Charlotte, still half-asleep, wandered into the day nursery.

'Go straight back to bed this minute, Charlotte. This is nothing to do with you.'

'But I thought I heard someone crying.'

Milly was fierce. 'That is still nothing whatsoever to do with you.'

And Charlotte went creeping away, slyly peering back over her shoulder.

Eventually, when it was almost over, when the child was white-faced and subdued, Milly hugged her tightly and said, 'We will call it a second secret, Alice. I have kept yours over all these years and now you keep this one for me. You must forget this night. Deny it. Put it somewhere far out of reach and never think of it again. You do not have these feelings, you have never had these evil thoughts and you read all that happened, you read the story from a book!'

'But I hurt deep inside me.' She looked like a ghost.

'No! You do not hurt – you imagine you hurt. Nothing has happened to you, Alice, nothing. You have made it all up in your head. Now say it again so I can hear you . . . ' And away they went, round and round, all over again.

You can only do your best. You can only do what you believe to be right. 'Don't go off on your own, dear. Stay with me. Let us talk.' The night was freezing cold now, and quite black. Everyone else had gone to their beds. There was nobody round the dying fire.

'Go to bed now, Milly, and leave me to work this out on my own. I have to be on my own. I have to see Luke. You can't help me. I know that you want to try, but you can't help me, you never could, could you? I'll be all right. I won't do anything foolish. After all, I have Davy to think about now. Luke will come, and who knows, maybe I can change it.'

Change it? Heavily Milly Toole mounted the caravan steps. She didn't bother to look behind her. She doubted that anything would now be all right. In her experience things like this never were. And she knew Luke Durant. She knew him, not so well as she knew Alice, but oh yes, she knew him.

Milly sighed deeply and drew her shawl firmly round her after she had closed the caravan door. She went to sit on her small, firm bed. She did not lie down. She fingered her crucifix and she closed her eyes most wearily.

# TWENTY-FIVE

It must have been well after midnight when Milly heard
Luke's return. She peered out of the caravan door but
there was no sign at all of Alice.

She heard him bid his companions goodnight. She
heard them peg down their horses. She heard a group
of them make for the wagon of that disgraceful woman,
Unity Heath and her cronies. She heard soft voices, and
laughter. Luke had not accompanied them. Preferring
solitude, he had obviously gone straight to bed.

Milly waited. She hesitated. Davy was sound asleep,
snuffling softly there in the corner under his fringed
crimson quilt. Should she interfere? After all, what
Bella Pettigrew Lovett had said was perfectly true –
Alice was a woman and should not need looking after.
Milly should leave her to her own devices. Ah, but it
was not quite as simple as that, not when you'd spent
a lifetime caring. Not when you'd been through so
much.

She stabbed at her hair fiercely with her pins. If only
she'd been listened to. If only Alice would take notice
. . . and then the apprehension was too much for Milly.
She creaked open her caravan door and made her
heavy way down the steps, heading towards Luke's
caravan. She paused at the bottom, between the shafts.
There was no sound from inside but a candle burned.
Milly called softly, 'Luke, Luke?' The last thing she
wanted was to wake everyone up or draw attention to
herself as she stood there, feeling like an interfering old
fool in her nightdress and with her slippers on.

In Unity Heath's caravan there was drinking going
on.

Luke's head came questioningly over the top of his
door. 'What on earth . . .' he started. He recognised
Mrs Toole and he smiled. 'It's late to be visiting, and

227

you look cold down there. Come up.' He opened the door and gestured invitingly. 'Come in. Make yourself at home.'

Stiffly she climbed the steps, cursing her need to do so and still wondering about the good sense of her actions.

She didn't return his broad smile but looked about her nervously. It was neat and tidy in here, clean she supposed, although she resisted the temptation to test the surfaces with her finger – a bad habit of hers, she knew, but one that stemmed from being in charge of servants. And then she asked him, 'Have you seen Alice?'

Immediately the smile left his face, leaving an expression of frowning concern. He answered quickly, 'She came back before me. She travelled with Betty Groves – she ought to have been home a good hour ago.'

'She's home.' Milly chose a place to sit down among the cushions where she did not have to squeeze herself under a fancily-carved cupboard. 'She's home, but she's very upset, terribly upset. She said she was going for a walk but I don't doubt that eventually she'll come and find you.'

Luke sat down opposite Milly, his elbows resting on his knees as he leaned forward to give her his full attention. She noted the rings on his fingers. His face was still streaked with half-wiped greasepaint and his eyebrows looked very dark. He said, 'What has upset her so? I hoped she would enjoy tonight. I thought it would help to take her out of herself, help her to forget.'

Milly sighed and sucked in her cheeks. She fingered her crucifix, lifting the weight of it, letting the cool chain drip in her hand. This was going to be difficult. The starting was the worst part. She hoped that once she had started the explanation would come easily and that it would sound reasonable. What was she here to explain? Quite unaware she was doing so, she rocked backwards and forwards gently as she started to speak. She said: 'You have to remember that Alice has been through a terrible ordeal . . .'

'Well of course I realize that. I would be a damn fool if I didn't.'

'No.' Milly couldn't abide interruptions. She knew what she wanted to say and interruptions only made the whole effort harder. 'I don't just mean lately. I'm not merely talking about Deale, the birth of the child, her terrifying escape, her exhaustion.' Milly stopped for a moment to think. She started rocking slightly more quickly. 'I'm talking about her life before that, her marriage to Edward, her life at Winterbourne. I think I am going back further than that even, to her childhood. You know that her father took his own life?'

'I had heard that, yes, at the time I think I heard that.'

'Well, that's not easy for a child to deal with at such an impressionable age. A girl in particular, one without a mother to comfort her and show her the way. Everything was left to me. I had the huge burden of bringing up those three children, virtually on my own, having to answer to Henry Brennan who took on the responsibility of Venton Hall and everyone in it. He bought his way in,' Milly tutted. 'He paid off the debts and he bought his way into our lives.'

'I'm more concerned about Alice now. You say she went out? Where can she have gone? Will she be able to find her way back?' Luke's presence, his calm, sensible voice as he made his enquiry, was comforting.

'Oh, she'll come back,' said Milly, pushing that problem to one side for a moment. 'She'll want to see you.'

'Perhaps she won't want to disturb me at this time of night.' Luke's voice was all concern.

Milly dismissed this question. She couldn't be bothered to give it an answer. 'For a girl to have to cope with the aftermath of her father's suicide and later, to be informed that she is promised in marriage to a man

229

who has been chosen for her, that she has been lost in a hand of cards, that is something quite hard for anyone to come to terms with.'

Luke was astonished. He shook his head and the dark centres of his eyes were angry. 'I did not know about that . . .'

Milly smiled bleakly. 'There are not many who know about it. So I am telling you the various reasons why Alice tends to behave a little oddly sometimes . . . out of character, one might call it . . . childishly, without thought. Her temperament is changeable. She gets upset very easily. She does not give her trust lightly.'

'Mrs Toole.' Luke sat back and regarded the agitated woman before him with exaggerated patience. 'This is all very interesting, and I'm sure these are things that I need to know, but what has any of this to do with the present situation? What upset Alice tonight, and what part in it all did I, unwittingly, play?'

'She saw the way other women admired you.' Milly decided to leap straight into the thick of it. There did not seem to be any alternative with Luke sitting there demanding to know. She could not beat about the bush any longer. At least she had managed to give him some warning. 'I'm afraid it's as simple as that. And she saw the way you acted with Jessica Lamont. The theatre is a new experience for Alice – all that atmosphere, playing parts, clever acting. She is fond of you, Luke. She has known you two days and yet she is . . . she is . . . extremely fond of you.'

'Are you trying to tell me that Alice saw my performance tonight and was jealous?'

How could she put it more accurately? Milly decided to agree with Luke. 'Yes, she was jealous, but more than that, she felt, rightly or wrongly, that you had been leading her on and that what she feared had come true. That whatever has passed between you was insincere, that you did not mean what you said. She thinks you should have warned her. She would rather you had told her about your stage name, explained, a little more clearly perhaps, how it was going to be . . .'

'But that is utterly ridiculous! How can she possibly see me on stage and draw such extraordinary conclusions? What sort of man does she think I am that I can pretend to care for her one minute and turn from her the next?' And then he sat back and sent Milly Toole a suspicious look when he asked her, 'Is this to do with you, woman? Is this to do with something you might have said to her?'

Milly shook her head quickly and the miserable concern on her face convinced him. She had no real need to explain. 'I said nothing to her at all. And if I had said anything, you can be sure that Alice would not have listened. Not that I didn't have reason. I wonder if I should have told her all I knew . . .'

'But you didn't,' Luke interrupted again. 'So it was not your vicious tongue that gave her crazy ideas.'

Milly was not going to have this. She had spent some considerable time this evening defending this insolent man who now sat there so glibly accusing her. This was not fair. 'My vicious tongue, as you call it, has every reason to be vicious when it comes to matters of that sort, Luke, and don't you forget it.'

'You only know half of the story.' Luke's voice was measured, his eyes careful.

'I knew Lorna Drewe and I know what happened to her!'

'Do you think that I liked what happened to her? Do you think I condoned it, or that I wouldn't have tried to help if I'd known?'

'But where were you, Luke? Where were you when that poor young girl needed you? And there were others, Luke, oh yes, I remember. All the young maids were after you then. First you chose one, then another, but it was Lorna Drewe who reaped the bitterest harvest. They flung her out on to the streets, along with the child. Oh yes, she never said who the father was, but I knew. They wouldn't give her a reference or anything else and then one day she threw herself and

231

her child under the wheels of a passing dray . . . she was sixteen, Luke, just sixteen years old at the time when she died.'

Luke closed his eyes. 'You are suggesting that I knew she was with child and did nothing about it?'

Milly put on her high-principled look. 'I am suggesting nothing. I am merely stating the facts of the case as they were at the time.'

'I see there is nothing I can say that will change your opinion of me, Mrs Toole. Your mind is made up. You drew your conclusions years ago and you are not prepared to listen to the other side of the story.'

So flustered was she that Milly persevered. 'I can just about forgive you for your wicked behaviour. I can understand how, at the age you were, you were influenced by your family in political matters and that it was hard for you to refuse to ride with them, to carry their messages, to come into our house and spy out the lie of the land.'

Luke attempted to interrupt but Milly would not let him. She waved an excited hand in the air to dismiss whatever he was about to say. 'But what I will never forgive you for is the death of that poor little maid. That a man can be so insensitive . . . can take his pleasure with such wanton indiscrimination, such little care for the consequences . . . can ride off into the blue leaving that sort of tragedy behind him. Well, well . . . ' and Milly puffed herself up as she spluttered. She ended on a high-handed note, with her chin in the air, 'That I can never forgive.'

'So be it.'

Milly was startled. She had expected an argument. Nonplussed, she said, 'I trusted you, Luke. That was the trouble. I trusted you, and I liked you. I hate to admit this, but at one point, back then, I almost saw you as the son I never had myself. And then . . .'

'And then it all changed, didn't it, Mrs Toole? Suddenly, and with violence, everything changed.'

'You brought it upon yourself,' said Milly. 'You and

your wild family. And you were too cowardly to come back and face the music.'

'I did not hear the music. Nobody told me that Lorna had a child. I was far away from Venton at the time trying to cope with difficulties of my own. I never knew . . .'

'Oh?' and Milly wore a look which said she did not believe him.

'Mrs Toole, you must feel relieved, at last, to rid all this from your system, but it isn't helping us with our present problems.' He was cool and calm and this annoyed Milly. She had right on her side and yet she felt she had lost. She had come over here in order to warn him. Alice was highly-strung and Milly hoped Luke might now be prepared for hysterics. Perhaps she'd been wrong, perhaps there would be none.

'Will you sleep?' Luke asked her.

'I doubt it.'

'Will you sleep if I promise you I will stay up all night, searching for Alice? Would it help you to know, Mrs Toole, that whatever you might think of me I am sincere in my feelings for Alice? The last thing I could ever do would be to hurt her. I know she has been hurt. I understand that you came here tonight to tell me that she has been hurt, badly. Trust me, Mrs Toole. It would make everything so much easier if you could bring yourself to trust me!'

How could she possibly trust him? Milly could not mistake the truth in his voice. But he is an actor, she reminded herself as she descended the steps and came down on to the wet, dewy grass, feeling it soak through her slippers. He is a professional deceiver. What am I to think? How am I to feel? There are so many reasons why Luke Durant might want to play games with Alice.

But Milly did sleep that night, if a little restlessly. She was, after all, not young any more. And she was exhausted.

# TWENTY-SIX

Luke found her. Forlorn and alone she sat in the centre of a ring of sawdust while the great canvas billowed foamily around her. He stood at the side entrance for a while, quite still, letting his eyes adjust because the light was poor – muted moonlight, strange, and not of this world. It matched with the troubled, lonely woman at the perfect centre of it.

It was almost quiet, save for the occasional sleepy roar of a tiger. A baby cried and a dog barked, but inside the marquee these sounds came from a very great distance. The party at Unity Heath's was over, the revellers had returned to their own caravans or were staying the night according to inclination. Alice played with the sawdust as a child would play with sand, raising it up into little mounds and patting it, swirling circles, running tramlines into it with her fingers, her head on one side, admiring her work. And gradually, as he watched, he saw how her body shuddered sometimes, exhausted with crying.

Not until, quick with relief, he crossed the surround of grass and went to stand beside her, did Alice seem to notice him at all.

'Oh Alice! You had poor Milly quite beside herself. The old woman had got all sorts of strange notions into her head.'

He stood before her, feeling helpless, wanting to get nearer but not knowing how. For she did not raise her head but continued to play with the sawdust, more slowly, more deliberately. And then she said in a tearful voice, 'And you, Luke? Were you worried? What were your thoughts, I wonder?'

Now he knelt down beside her, trying to see her face, but it was impossible because of the cascade of golden hair.

234

'Of course I was worried. Surely you knew that I'd be worried. And I couldn't understand the reasons for all this distress. Milly tried to explain something of it to me . . .'

'Milly! She has been saying bad things about me!' It was almost a snarl, as if she hated her nurse and Luke, startled by her so sudden anger, saw how she hitched one tress of hair behind her ear and glanced nervously at him out of the corners of her eyes. She did not raise her head but her teeth tugged on her lip as if she instantly regretted her outburst.

And Luke thought: she's just like a child. A child who has been denied candy, who has been sent to bed too early and now she resents it and has decided to come to her father!

'Milly has your welfare at heart, Alice. She has said nothing to me but good, but she did tell me you were upset by my performance as Robert Melville. That was the reason she gave me for your sudden disappearance, and I take it that same reason is causing this behaviour now.'

'You think that I was jealous?' This time Alice shook back her hair and raised her head, and Luke could see how violently, and for how long she had been crying.

He didn't touch her but he continued to smile, fondly, gently, as he told her, 'That's what Milly said. Are you going to tell me for yourself?'

Her lips trembled slightly. She continued to play with the sawdust. She sat, cross-legged, and her black cloak hem made a perfect circle around her. She was beautiful. As she sat there like that, sad, pale, her face a picture of misery, he thought that he had never seen such perfection before in the face of any woman. And yet she was tense as an animal as she sat there. And Luke realized that he had adjusted his manner to accommodate this, speaking gently, moving slowly . . . he must not frighten her.

'You didn't tell me,' was all she said.

'What was there to tell? That I could act? That I

could put on a performance? That I could have some fleeting effect upon an audience . . . as could any actor worthy of the name – or what is he doing on the stage? Alice! Oh Alice! How could you translate that to mean that I wasn't the man who had kissed you? How could you possibly forget the man underneath the paint?' And he held out a hand and touched her hair, very gently, very slowly. 'You must have been terribly hurt by someone . . . you must be very afraid to trust . . .'

And then she smiled. But it was a smile that had been learned, worn like a mask to conceal any real emotion, not touching her eyes. They stayed quite blank as if an opaque veil had been drawn down over them. 'Jessica Lamont. You were most convincing when you played opposite Jessica Lamont. You must see that she is very beautiful. You must be affected by that husky voice of hers, her doe-like eyes, her voluptuous body. Have you seen her naked, Luke? Have you made love to her? Because while I watched that play tonight I could not convince myself that you had not.'

Luke stopped smiling. He said: 'Such compliments! I was not aware of the strength of the performance we gave. No, Alice,' he continued to stroke her hair reassuringly and she did not pull her head away. 'In answer to your strange question, I have never seen her naked, nor have I made love to her. But I have loved other women in my life . . . can you feel jealous of them, people from the past who are like most memories, pushed to the back and almost forgotten?'

'There was someone special. I know these things – I find them out. There was a girl called Lorna Drewe. She had your child, didn't she, Luke? You gave her a baby!'

As she spoke she screwed herself up into a terrible knot with her suffering face at the centre of it. She pulled in her arms and wrapped them around her. Expressionless now, Luke said, 'Mrs Toole told you?'

'I listened,' said Alice, quite without shame, but accusingly from the hollow she had made of herself.

236

'I listened to everything that she said. I was hiding in the shadows beside the caravan.'

'Then you also heard what happened to her.'

'I heard that you would have gone back. If you'd known about her you would have gone back. And what would you have done then, Luke? Married her? And how many more were there like that? How many that perhaps Milly does not know about?'

'I wasn't twenty years old. I was no different from any other young lad at the time. Those things happened years ago, Alice. So long ago I find it quite hard to remember. You sound like your nurse . . . are you, like she, unable to judge a man as he is? Do past relationships have to be so important?'

'Did you love that girl? That girl who died? Lorna Drewe? Tell me, the truth, tell me!' And Luke was startled by her sudden movement. She pulled at his cloak, she tugged it towards her with both hands.

'I don't think that I loved her, Alice. I was fond of her, of course. I would have married her, yes, if there'd been no other way of helping her. Certainly I would not have knowingly abandoned her to her fate, as Mrs Toole is so fond of suggesting.'

'So.' All the breath went out of Alice in one long hiss. 'So, you admit it. You would have married her!'

'I did not say that I loved her! I would have married her if marriage would have helped her.'

'And the child?'

'Nor would I have abandoned the child. What sort of man have you turned me into? What sort of creature do you see in your head? Have you lost all sight of me, Alice? Look at me!' And he leaned forward and took her face in his hands, holding it firmly so she was forced to face him. But her eyes would not hold his. 'Look at me! We talked of love only yesterday. We went walking together. You showed me yourself. You allowed me to kiss you.'

'Nothing happened – nothing! Whatever happened took place inside my own head.'

237

'Sometimes, Alice, it's impossible to understand what you mean. Whatever you are trying to say, we were close, and for some reason of your own, after your visit to the theatre tonight, you feel that we are strangers again. Why are you lying to me, Alice? I know you do not honestly believe that. What do I have to do to prove that I care?'

'You hate me now, don't you? Seeing me like this . . . you hate me now.'

'Alice, why would I hate you?' And then he asked gently, 'Is that what you're trying to make me do? Well, I can tell you now that you won't succeed; whatever you do you will fail.'

Luke Durant wished he could walk away. That was what he ought to have done and he knew it. But it was the very vulnerability of Alice Brennan that attracted him to her; she was still in pain and he loved her. He could not explain it, not even to himself, but he loved her. She needed him, he knew that. To walk away from her now would be to destroy her.

Was she a cause? An honest man, Luke had to ask himself this . . . was she just another cause, and was he putting himself forward as her knight just in order to fight the dragons? Because he sensed those dragons all around her, oh yes he certainly did. They breathed their fire all over her, they clawed at her skirts. Was it the dragons that made her so beautiful? She was the damsel in distress and he was her saviour. An unlikely knight – dispossessed, hunted like she was and haunted by the past. Games! Fantasy! Theatre! And he'd been brought up on causes, fighting for right no matter what the consequences might be, taking the side of the defeated and the downtrodden. Was Alice an embodiment of all this . . . all wrapped up in the lustrous, fragile shell of a lovely, helpless woman?

Why wouldn't she look at him? Why did she keep closing her eyes?

He released her and she let her head fall as if he had dropped it. Her chin drooped on her chest. He said:

'I could accuse you in the same kind of way. You are a married woman. You are married to Edward . . .'

'You know the circumstances of that. Milly told you.'

'But did you not love him at all, not ever? Did you always hate him?'

He could hardly hear her when she answered, but her whisper was vehement. 'Any love that I felt was made up. I loathed him.'

'But you stayed with him.' Luke was patient.

'There was no alternative for me. And I had Nicholas . . . the children. Where could I have gone?'

'You fled in the end. You fled from Deale. Was it not possible for you and Milly to leave before, if everything was so terrible?'

'I was afraid.' There was a sob in her voice and her chest shuddered again.

'You are afraid now. I can see no difference.'

'Perhaps I ran out of hope,' she said.

'You hoped that your life might change? That things might be different? Is that the reason that you stayed? And yet you tell me that you hated him.' Luke wanted to understand.

She lifted her head defiantly. 'Why are you attacking me?'

'I am asking you for the truth. I was not aware that I was attacking you. I'm sorry if it sounded so. I didn't mean it to sound like that.'

'It felt like that!'

'All I'm trying to do is to understand you. All I want to do is to love you and protect you.'

Alice sighed, and for the first time she allowed her eyes to meet his, allowing that he was a real presence and not just a doll she might be making up conversations with. She was trying to tell him something but it was an effort. 'I can't say why I stayed. It's too difficult for me to think back and work it all out. I was young . . . I was different . . . there were reasons why I could not just get up and throw everything off me, duty, responsibility, in order to follow my own heart. I was always taught that that was wrong. That I should put myself last. That family came first. Edward came first.'

'And you were an obedient child?'

'Now you are laughing at me, Luke.' But Luke was heartened to see that Alice was trying not to smile.

He wanted to fold her in his arms and cover her face with kisses, but he forced himself to talk. He sensed that she was not ready. Somehow he must break through this strange detachment of hers – wake her up. 'None of that really matters, Alice, does it? I can see that, and I just wish you could see it, too. We are here, together, now, there is nothing else,' and his eyes took in the massive tent which furled and flapped with the gusting wind.

Had she listened to a word he had said? It was impossible to tell; it was hard to interpret her expression. It was certainly softer, more open to him. A sense of protectiveness and strength made him certain when he stood up, lifted her and held her against him. She let herself lie softly against his chest. 'I want you to come to bed now. I want you to lie next to me for the rest of the night. I want to warm you, reassure you, hold you, touch you. And soon . . . soon . . . when you are quite better . . . one night soon I want to make love to you.'

She didn't answer. Nor did she resist as he picked her up in his arms, and he felt he was half-taking part in a play – half-real, half-make believe – so strange was the light and the sound of the flapping canvas and the fresh smell of sawdust. He crossed the short stretch of grass, mounted the steps with ease, kicked open his door and laid her down on his bed.

'And now,' he said, as he began to undress her, as he undid the buttons at her neck and continued down, 'I want you to tell me that you trust me. That your earlier confusions are all forgotten. That we are as we were before and that you are as certain as I.'

She fingered his face before lifting up her arms and

placing them round his neck. In a quiet voice she started, 'I wish . . .'

He had to prompt her. 'What do you wish?'

She thought before she spoke, shifting her body beside him. 'I wish I did not think that I loved you.'

He arranged her head on the pillow, her hair spread gold on the white surround and he thought of gold on an altar. His kiss seemed to give her life. He could feel the warmth surge through her. Having pushed down the loose neckline of her shift, he circled her nipple with his finger, considering her words, the perfection of her skin, the full swell of her breasts. He brought his mouth down on her nakedness and she touched the dark curls at his neck with timid fingers.

Luke got up, crossed the room and lit a candle. He returned to sit beside her, and gently eased her arms from her dress, slipped it down her body and off at the foot of the bed. He laid it there, folded it. He returned for the shift and that light cotton garment followed easily, softly as any caress. He removed her under-clothes, revealing her belly, honey-smooth thighs and legs and the golden, closed triangle, licked by the flame of the candlelight. None of her suffering had robbed her body of its wonder. He moved his mouth back to her breasts, he left them hard behind him, the nipples taut and tilted as he traced a line of fire with his tongue down her body, circling, tasting, until he rested between her legs and placed a kiss on the golden down.

He almost felt despair, so desperately did he want to give her pleasure, but it was too early. He felt despair, but one that was touched with joy. For Luke sensed that somehow, for some reason he could not understand, he had almost lost her. He had found her again; he had pulled her back to him just in time.

# TWENTY-SEVEN

Charlotte Venton, pale, tense and nervous, awoke soon after dawn, sat up in bed and looked across at Edward as he lay sleeping beside her. She tightened her lips before she put out an arm to wake him.

'It's time, Edward. Soon Myers and his people will be here. Mrs Webber has organized an early breakfast, and I have packed you a small trunk . . . '

Edward opened his eyes and they warmed immediately at the sight of Charlotte. Then he thought about the prospect before him and groaned. With cool fingers she leaned across and stroked his forehead. As if she read his thoughts she told him, 'Perhaps this will be the last time. Perhaps at dear last we are nearing the end of all this.'

Edward would have liked to believe her. He would love to return to her tonight with his quest completed. He would give almost anything he had to bring her that perfect gift, to lay it at her feet along with himself, to watch her eyes brighten as she accepted it, to see that slow smile start until it touched the whole of her sad face, lit it up and made it beautiful.

'Yes, perhaps . . . '

'You lack confidence. That is part of the whole trouble, Edward. You go forward without the conviction you need, and that makes the task so much harder.'

He raised himself on one arm, pushing the covers down to his waist. He was hot, nervously hot and the thick, embroidered canopy, the gold-crested curtains, made the atmosphere airless and thick to breathe. He made his excuses as he so often did. 'I have learned this attitude from experience and you know that, Charlotte. For how many times have we hoped that this would be the last struggle? How many times have we

242

told each other stories, tried to convince each other that we are near the end? I've lost count. And I've almost run out of hope. You cannot blame me for that.' But, looking up at her where she sat in bed beside him, Edward knew that she did blame him.

'If Myers' conclusions prove true – if Alice *is* with the circus and you have discovered they stay at Exeter for the next two days, there should be little difficulty in bringing her back to Deale and concluding the matter quite simply. At last that dratted doctor has decided on his diagnosis. At last he has promised to certify my sister. Once she's back in Deale there'll be no more escapes . . . and nothing will matter, anyway, for this time she will be registered insane.'

'When you talk about it you make it seem so absurdly simple.'

'And it would be simple, if she was alone with Mrs Toole. The only unknown factor now would appear to be her new protector.'

'Some ruffian she has snared with her pitiful tales and her provocative stares . . . ' Edward pushed off the covers, drew back the curtains and let himself down on to the floor. Rumpling his hair he crossed the soft carpet of the room and opened his dressing-room door. Before he stepped off into the cold of the unlit room, he paused, and turned back to the bedroom. A small lamp burned beside Charlotte as she sat there with the curtains drawn back around her, but the lamplight did not illuminate her face, it fell on the bedside table, on the book she had left there.

In that grey light the room looked false, and so did everything in it. Edward walked into his dressing room and started to select his warmest travelling clothes. His closet smelled of mothballs. His clothes did not smell of himself, but of treatment against destruction.

'Don't fall into the trap of underestimating Alice's powers again,' Charlotte called to him from the bed. 'We have done that too many times in the past. Remember!'

243

Yes, he could remember. Like the fog he could see seeping and banking towards the house, bearing the morning with it, Edward Brennan's memories were foggy and grey; shadowy episodes, a troubled sleep feverish with nightmares. But if he could accomplish his task, if he could finally, irreversibly, put an end to Alice, life might turn beautiful again.

Charlotte was enchanting but, even to Edward's eyes, she was not beautiful. Charlotte was strong, Charlotte was sincere, Charlotte was safety, like his sensible mother . . . and Edward craved strength and safety. He shied away from butterflies, he cringed from beauty, now – he was even a little afraid of his own daughters, happy to leave them to Charlotte – beauty, the butterflies, turned into snakes and bit him. Edward felt very cold as he stood there, a mass of white flesh and alone. He thought, as he drew on his hose and buttoned his riding breeches, how he could divide up his life into sections. There was boyhood, safe, sensible: he had been sent to school, he had worked hard, enjoyed the holidays, pleased his parents – Henry, a big, silent man, ambitious for his son; Florence, a powerful, large-boned, formidable woman. They had wanted the best for him. They had fought for the best for him, almost seeming to sacrifice happiness themselves to promote the fortunes of their only son. He had been, he supposed, an arrogant, clever child, vain, fed by his father's great ambition, constantly told the world was his oyster, that his father had paved the way and that it would be up to him to carry on. A cold, unimaginative couple, they had taught him how to make the best of a bad business, how to play for safety in a crisis, how to skate on thin ice, how to win the approval of men, yes, about goodness and badness, loyalty and treachery . . . they had brought him up on high, sensible principles.

Little about happiness.

Nothing about love.

Through hard work and applying himself seriously

he would find happiness. Money was something you could depend on. Pleasurable sensations were ephemeral. He had feared God and the Devil. He feared his parents and obeyed them dutifully.

And then Thomas Venton had killed himself. Henry Brennan had ridden to Venton Hall and Edward had accompanied him.

It was only the second time he had been there. The first was several years ago, one Christmas – he hardly remembered any of it except that he had been expected to spend the night with the three small Venton girls in the nursery and their dominating nurse, a dragon called Toole. After they had gone to bed Edward had returned downstairs. Finding a fire in the deserted study, he had spent the night on the chaise beside it. And then there had been the drama of Sarah Venton's illness, the premature birth. Everyone had left . . . the Brennans had left.

They returned at Easter-time. Henry had gone on a tour of inspection leaving Edward to walk in the gardens, savouring the sunshine, not quite knowing why he'd been expected to accompany his father that day but he'd enjoyed the ride and they were to stay for dinner.

The child's voice was soft, fresh as the morning air, keenly sweet as a bird's note. Edward, embarrassed to find himself a listener to someone who did not know he was there, coughed loudly to declare himself and walked round the box hedge into the rose garden to excuse his presence and introduce himself.

She could be no older than twelve but he had never seen anything so close to utter perfection. Her face went crimson when she saw him. Her eyes were a very dark blue.

'I know who you are, you don't need to tell me. You're Edward Brennan and you were very rude when you spent one night staying with us. I remember, you refused to go to bed, and you upset Milly. You were cruel. Horrid.' She'd been enticing a tortoise to come out from the undergrowth. She'd been holding out a piece of lettuce in her hand. Now it fell limply at her side as she stared back at him, as if she was reading his thoughts.

'He's gone,' she told him, throwing him a wide look of appeal.

'Who's gone?'

'My tortoise. I put him to sleep in a box last year. But he's not in it. He's gone.'

Edward had knelt down on the ground beside her then, helping in the search for the elusive creature. But it had felt as if he were breaking through a dream. He wanted to hold out his hands to touch her. Her arms, legs, wrists and ankles were so slender and dainty. The golden curls at the nape of her neck were enchanting, he found them enticing. Her baby blue eyes and her rosebud mouth made her look like a nymph in a picture book.

He was disturbed by her accusation. He couldn't get it out of his mind, he considered it unjustified. Cruel? No, he'd only been determined to win. Should he explain to her? No, it was unimportant. Her gaze was deep, clear and unswervingly true. But she was just a child. A fairy child in a dress of the palest green and silk slippers just showing under the hem of her skirt. And he felt ugly and old and wicked to be thinking about her in this way, here in the softly-scented fresh air beside the sundial . . . dark anguish filled him. He felt guilty and unclean. Never had he experienced these feelings before . . . he'd been warned about sexual matters in a dour, roundabout way by his father. He'd listened, shifting uneasily in the leather chair in Henry's study keeping his eyes to the floor. Because he had not understood what he was talking about. Until then. Until the child came.

He was trapped inside some terrible iron machine. Not at all the tall, thin brown-faced boy who stood there before her, with scratches on his legs from so recently climbing trees and going after birds' nests through brambles. Secret things. Games he would have

246

been ashamed to tell the boys at school that he still played. Games that now, he was ashamed to admit to himself that he still played.

And now, thinking about the moment he fell in love, the fog rolled back from his mind and Edward Brennan remembered the stillness of it, the glow of it, the magical mirage effect of it . . . no grumble of distant thunder . . . nothing dark or grey or evil to disturb it. Except for the fear which had existed in his own mind as he saw himself as no longer a jolly, hard-working, healthy boy but a sneak, a deviant and a man.

And after spending the rest of the afternoon acting as secretary to his father, taking a careful inventory of what valuable items were left in the house, they had returned home with Henry telling his son, 'Most of it is gone, gambled away and lost to the family for ever. It is a tragedy. To see the state of that house, it is a tragedy.' But the spicy tang of success – of spite – was at the back of his mouth and in his words.

Edward had sat at the table that evening next to his father, heavy and coarse, a powerful, shrewd man, one of the richest mine owners in the south of England. And Edward had suddenly wondered if his father was a lonely man, and if the task he had set himself . . . success at any cost . . . afforded him any rest or relief. There was no romance in it, nothing holy about his Holy Grail. And his mother, there in her frumpish dress, seemed brutal and congested behind the cold mask of her features. Could they tell? Did they know, as they sat on their secure chairs at their solid table, about the disgusting, filthy desires of their burning-eyed, secret-thinking son?

How frightened he'd been then – gripped in the clutches of a kind of insane terror. Because he'd fallen in love with a child . . . but surely, he was little more than a child himself? Or was it, more likely, because he'd felt the first stirrings of sexuality? Edward still didn't know which.

247

Myers might know. Edward patted his mouth with his napkin and concealed a small, sad smile.

Across the breakfast table Myers solemnly ate his food. Charlotte rang for more tea. The men whom Myers had brought with him were eating in the kitchens with the servants.

'As I said before, I hope I'm not leading you up the wrong path,' fretted Myers. 'It is only a rumour . . . '

'It is the only possible lead we have,' said Charlotte. It was too early for her to eat so she sipped tea instead. Early morning, and yet there was not one hair out of place, one button left undone. 'And it does sound plausible. From where else would a posse of strangers have come? From whom else would such an unlikely pair of travellers been given a ride without questions being asked?'

'Well, I'm merely trying to warn you not to get your hopes up,' said Myers with anxious emphasis.

Edward was simply grateful, grateful in a dull sort of way for having been given some course to follow instead of having to sit about the house waiting, listening to Charlotte berate him for being a fool, listening to the children bemoaning the loss of their mother, and to Nicholas' insults.

'If all goes well we will be back this evening,' he said to Charlotte.

There was a rapid step in the hall and the thud of an angry hand on the door before it was flung open. Nicholas entered the room with a rush like a bull. He did not stop until he reached his father at the far end of the table. He stood there, shoulders hanging forward, head down, wild blue eyes very bright under lowering brows. There were dangerous sparks in them, and there were sparks in his words when he spoke, ringing with accusation.

'Where are you going?'

Charlotte answered. 'We think we might have found your mother.'

'Yes, so I heard.' He ignored her and took his furious

face down further towards his father. 'And what do you intend to do when you find her? Capture her, as if she is some kind of common criminal? Capture her and take her back to that foul place?'

Edward flung down his napkin. He stood up. They faced each other and Nicholas gripped the table, his face pale and frightened.

In a voice full of quiet reason, Edward asked, 'What alternative do you suggest, Nicholas?'

His son spoke quickly, biting off his words. 'I wish I had not told you about her plans. I wish I had kept that information to myself. She trusted me . . . she trusted me and yet I, unknowing, never suspecting the truth of the matter, came to you with her plans, hoping that you might prevent her from harming herself and you . . . '

'Nicholas . . . ' He barely breathed the word. 'We have to find her. We have to bring back the child. It is essential, you must understand . . . '

'To replace me! You want the child to replace me! I've seen you!' And he nodded towards Charlotte. 'You and your whore. I've seen the way she looks at me as if she thinks . . . '

'Get out! Get out, I tell you! Do you hear me?'

Nicholas hesitated. His face went crimson. Then he looked at Charlotte and stiffened. The colour drained from his face but he stood his ground. He held his head high; he seemed to exercise an enormous effort of self-control when he spoke in a voice that was clear and steady, the tremble in it hardly detectable: 'Father, you should not be doing this.'

They faced each other and for a moment Edward looked into the eyes of his son. Everything seemed to hang, for a moment, in the balance. All the heaviness that was in them both seemed to hang there, between them, put there by the words of the boy.

Something snapped. Edward said, 'Damn you, Nicholas! Get out!' And Nicholas dropped his eyes, turned on his heel and left the room.

Half an hour later the small party left Winterbourne House, clopping at a steady pace down the drive. Edward and Dr Myers travelled in the carriage while Corbett, Duffy and a third man called Callow, wearing the three-pointed, uniform hats of Deale Asylum, followed behind on horseback.

# TWENTY-EIGHT

Milly grumbled to the baby as she handed him over to Alice to feed, tutting under her breath and giving dark glances beneath storm-cloud eyebrows. 'And it would have been considerate for somebody to have told me. How was I to know you were back? I have not slept a wink all night.'

'You were asleep when I came in,' said Alice sweetly. 'I had to wake you.'

'Well, then, I must have dropped off just twenty minutes ago.' Milly would not give in. And Alice sat down with the child on her lap, crooning to him as she fed him.

It was a very different Alice who sat on the narrow bed while the sun streamed in from the half-door, darkening the lights in her hair, from the one who had disappeared, desperate and hysterical, into the darkness of last night. Her face had lost all its earlier tension. It was softly full, gently composed, and her eyes, when they did not look at the child, were far away. Dreamy eyes, thought Milly impatiently. And when she spoke she knew that Alice, nodding politely, did not really hear her.

'I love him,' said Alice, addressing her immediate surroundings more than her concerned nurse. And then she said it again, 'I love him.'

'And what about all last night's nonsense, then? Where does that fit in?'

'That was a misunderstanding,' said Alice, pushing back her hair, drawing a tress of it, first, from Davy's tiny fist before twirling it round her own finger. 'I think he loves me, Milly. Truly, extraordinarily, I really think he does. I think that for the first time in my life I have found someone who cares about me.'

'I doubt that very much. How can a man love a

251

woman who's willing to throw herself at him? What sort of love do you call that?'

Alice's breath left her chest in one long gust. 'I find it strange, sometimes, Milly, the way you always have to spoil everything. You have to cast your dark clouds on to the brightest of days. You are so full of forebodings . . . so convinced that nothing will ever turn out for the good. I could almost say it is your miserable countenance that causes the grief that has so dogged my footsteps . . . '

'You are imagining things again, Alice.' So familiar with this conversation was Milly Toole that she continued to twist the baby's clean nappies over the miniature basin, holding them aloft as the drops dripped out, her great hands red from all the pummelling, the muscles on her arms under her pushed-up sleeves bulging happily, free from constriction. With pegs between her teeth she slopped in her slippers to the string above the opened door and pegged out each strip of material so that she formed a line of perfectly neat little squares.

When her mouth was free she said, 'You make up the people around you, you put ideas into their heads in order to fit with your own convenience. You always have.'

'And I don't think you should talk to me like this,' said Alice.

'Someone has to, Alice,' chided Milly. 'None of your feelings can ever be trusted.'

Alice moved the child to the breast which was full, dabbing the first one dry. She loved him, oh yes, she loved him. Look at him, he was perfect, and beautiful, and he was forward; his eyes were already beginning to focus. When he stared up at her he was losing that newborn confusion and his look was a direct one. If it was not for the fear of Edward and the low, dull pain of missing her other children, she'd at last have made up her own heaven. Nothing could be more pleasant than this. She remembered Luke's love-making last night. Bad fantasies – oh God, she had wanted him . . . even in the state she was in, still bleeding, she had wanted him. She knew that a woman so freshly birthed – (Milly's expression, Alice couldn't bear to see it like that) should not have those feelings. Yes, she was aware of that. But Luke knew, Luke, the man of her own creation was not disgusted, Luke did not appear to mind, not at all. She recalled then some of the things he had said – that was easy – his words were swimming around and around in her head so there was not really room for anything else, certainly not for Milly's boring repetition. Alice felt sorry for Milly. Look at her now, only concerned with getting the washing done, making sure the caravan was spick and span, shaking out the bedding and replacing it neatly on the bed, hanging up all the cups, stacking the plates. Why? For what reason? Nobody was going to come in and inspect it, award points for cleanliness or for order. Poor Milly was stuck in a groove, dragged along through life like an old plough scraping a straight furrow. And even when freedom stared her in the face she could not grasp it. She did not know what to do with it.

So many people were like that, thought Alice, smiling. They lived without dreams and they stayed safe.

Through a couple of wooden clothes pegs Milly mumbled tightly, 'And don't try and tell me that this time it's going to be different.'

'I would not try to explain anything to you,' Alice replied placidly. 'For it's not worth the bother.' She held the small body out between two hands at arms' length, congratulating herself as if for a miracle, regarding Davy fondly before bundling him over her shoulder to burp him. She patted his back lovingly. He snuffled at her neck, and she flushed as she remembered Luke's lips last night, the words Luke had whispered, the promises he had made.

She laid the real child down on the bed beside her and Milly swooped. She took over Alice's part without being conscious that she did so. Her large, comforting body strode the five steps from one end of the caravan to the other, patting the warm, floppy back of the child. Crooning softly.

Comfort. That was the reason, Milly had decided, long ago, that sent Alice about what Milly referred to as her 'unfortunate escapade'. The poor child was desperately searching for a replacement for her father's love, and for a mother's care. A loving child, shy, eager to give, she was insecure and she yearned for security. And who could wonder at it? It was just extremely unfortunate that she sought it in the arms of a man. It was just rather distressing that her craving for love . . . for comfort . . . was so strong that she had no thought for decorum, no care for caution, and absolutely no understanding that what she did was wrong. Appalling. Disgusting. And quite the wrong way for any woman to behave, let alone one of Alice's standing.

Charlotte was scathing in her attacks on Alice's behaviour. Lucinda ignored it all, not seeming quite to understand . . . and that was a blessing. And Milly, well, once she had put a stop to the matter, denying it so strongly that she almost managed to persuade Alice to deny it had happened herself, thought it was best forgotten. Milly knows best, oh certainly, but for a year after the incident Alice went into a long decline . . . hardly eating, refusing to be touched, taking no care of herself or her looks, refusing, sometimes, to get out of bed in the mornings. Oh, that awful year when Alice was secretive and peculiar, hiding herself away. Crying.

'Nothing happened!' Milly used to snap a reminder. 'It's no good you giving me that pained look of yours because you know as well as I do that nothing happened!' And Milly would tap her forehead, accusing Alice of a mental weakness, as Charlotte so often did.

Milly looked at Alice now, sitting there pretending not to be listening to all the outside sounds, pretending not to be listening or looking for Luke.

'I'm going to sit on the step for a while. It's stuffy in here.'

254

Milly fingered her crucifix. She'd have thought, by now, that Alice would have grown out of this sort of nonsense. Heavens, she had her children, she had the dire reminder of the results of her behaviour spread out threateningly behind her. All the recent past happenings were, in a roundabout way, a consequence of it. And yet she still had not learned! Milly had never imagined anything like that ghastly business would all start up again. But one look at Luke Durant as he carried the exhausted mother into her cottage three days ago had been sufficient warning. Here was someone strong, someone to protect her, someone to give herself away to. The inevitability of it was quite awful.

She remembered hearing Alice scream, 'If my feelings aren't real then what is real? Milly, what is there to trust?'

Those sort of feelings – huh! If everyone followed those sorts of feelings where would we all be? Perhaps Milly should have been more frank with Luke last night. Perhaps she might have been able to explain, to warn him. No . . . this disloyal thought brought Milly to an abrupt halt. She could have been back in the Venton nursery; she wore her starched, white pinafore. Her pattings were fierce on Davy's back. He brought up wind and he gave a milky, smiley dribble. She could never do that. Her role was the same as it had always been . . . she must protect Alice at any cost . . . and how did she honestly know, in spite of all she was saying, that this might not be different? That this might well be true love at last? Well, she didn't know. And she had no right to interfere. What would the knowledge of that do to Alice? The very idea appalled her. It did not bear thinking about. But not once during all that terrible time had Milly considered leaving Venton, abandoning her sweet things.

Well, how could she? If she went there was nobody else.

'They have brought the bear out,' called Alice from the step. 'Come and look, Milly. They have put a hat

255

and coat on him, and he is waving a walking stick in his hand! And people are beginning to arrive for the first performance. The booths are opening. D'you think I should go to Bella's tent and get my fortune read?'

You see! Everything was suddenly perfectly all right! There was not a cloud in the sky. Alice was in love and the whole world had to be viewed through rose-coloured spectacles. She seemed to have completely forgotten about last night. Luckily, all thanks to Luke, it had worked out satisfactorily . . . but there would be a time when it wouldn't. Alice herself would make sure of that – making so free with a man. And how else could Milly respond but to take it hour by hour? She couldn't prevent it, could she? She never had been able to prevent it. Only deny it.

'I'll just settle Davy and I'll come outside and join you, my darling.'

'Hurry Milly, hurry, it's all happening! I have never seen such bustle and excitement and you're going to miss it. Bring Davy out with you and put him to sleep outside. This rich air will do him good. But hurry Milly, before it all quietens down.'

'It has only just begun,' said Milly, with a slight dourness that was missed by the enchanted Alice. It would seem that Alice had even managed to forget, for a while, about Edward and any likelihood of pursuit. Milly considered it would be unsafe to bring the baby outside. Anyway, it was too cold, he was far too young. He would be better inside and wrapped up. Milly would not lower her guard. No matter what was going on out there she would not leave the step.

Milly had been the first to be told about Alice's engagement to Edward Brennan. She'd been told by Mr Philpott, Thomas' solicitor. The news, so directly delivered, had caused her to fall back in her chair, almost in a dead faint. The long, thin man had had to revive her with salts. She'd asked him again and

256

again but he had not changed his words. 'There is no alternative but for the agreement to be carried out,' he said in that melancholy, monotonous voice of his, as if the sky had fallen down and Milly's head ached so intolerably that it felt as if it had.

'I cannot believe it. I cannot believe that men, in their games, could do such vile things.'

'The marriage would have been an arranged one anyway, Mrs Toole, because of Alice's position. Apart from the slightly doubtful circumstances, the outcome, if you'd be so good as to consider the matter sensibly, would more than likely have been the same.'

'That is not the point.' Milly, knowing he saw her as a hysterical woman without any sense in her giddy head, and despising him for that, fanned herself with the papers he had passed across the desk for her to peruse. 'She is just fourteen years old, Mr Philpott. She has no understanding . . . '

'There is no suggestion that the girl be informed of this matter yet. Henry Brennan has not yet told his own son. I am of the opinion that it would be more suitable, under the circumstances, if the two young people were informed of the decision together, nearer the time. Mr Brennan has been appointed guardian for the Ventons' three minor children until they come of age. He is the trustee of the estate and he has agreed, out of the goodness of his heart, to keep the children on here, and to deal with the finances of it until such time as they come into his care when Alice reaches the age of eighteen.'

Milly shook her head, confused. 'So everything is decided. It seems that all this has happened so quickly. Just a few months ago Lord Thomas was alive . . . life was difficult, but it all seemed normal. Now, suddenly, we are almost prisoners, not just for now but for always. It feels quite an intolerable situation and I am sure . . . '

Mr Philpott sourly interrupted Milly's splutterings. 'Mr Brennan has left the internal running of the household in your hands, Mrs Toole. As the person most concerned with the upbringing of the children he decided that would be most appropriate.'

So . . . there was no way out of it. It seemed that a trap had snapped shut.

And more and more frequently Edward Brennan, the arrogant young boy Milly so despised, took to coming to visit but, because of the circumstances there was little that Milly could do to prevent it. This new Edward Brennan was an improvement on the snooty adolescent she remembered from his Christmas visit. His manners were charming and he seemed to have all the time in the world for her charges. Sometimes she experienced relief when he called in the trap to take them out for a while.

'Be careful. Mind for the rioters!'

'Oh, the rioters are no match for me!' he shouted back. All the girls were flattered by his attentions. They played up to him, even Alice, and deep in her surly depression, even poor Charlotte. You could see she adored him, insisted on curling her hair when she knew he was coming, even rubbed her cheeks – Milly had caught her in front of the mirror – and bit so hard on those thin little lips of hers. It was quite pathetic.

And you could see that Alice was taken by him. This was the worrying part. It was encumbent upon Milly to make sure that Alice's disgraceful behaviour was not repeated or discovered by this young man who was to be her future husband . . . if there was any suspicion of it then the marriage would surely be off. No bad thing? Oh dear, that was hard to say. Because if the marriage were called off then the whole of society would want to know why. The secret would be out. There would be no suitable match for Alice anywhere. Charlotte and Lucinda, without dowries, would be homeless, because certainly the shrewd Henry Brennan would not agree to pay the bills or keep up his neighbour's household unless his future daughter-in-law was an agreed and acceptable part of the plan.

No, Milly was put in an extremely difficult position,

and unable to say anything about the engagement until the appointed time. But, to Milly's relief – and she watched carefully – Edward did not seem to be affected by Alice's frail beauty. He would surely discourage any brazen behaviour caused by her inability to control her primitive feelings. No, Milly would have said that Edward was far more interested in little Lucinda, still so much the child of the three but growing up quickly as they all were. Frighteningly quickly.

And this was the most unfortunate part . . . Lucinda appeared to feel the same way about Edward. The two of them, despite Lucinda's tender years, were becoming inseparable – in an innocent, acceptable, pleasant way.

Puppy love, thought Milly, not overly concerned at so early a stage in the proceedings.

'Milly! Milly!' Alice's excited call interrupted her musings. 'The Punch and Judy show has begun! The field is filling with people! What on earth are you doing in there that is important enough to merit missing all this! Imagine, Milly, just imagine the looks on their faces if Kate and Laura were here to see this. How they would love it! Do come outside. And Bella is here to see you. She wants to know if you would like to go to the show this afternoon.'

So Milly Toole puffed as she reached around to untie her apron. She was never certain about whether she ought to wear her hat . . . on the steps she would be half outside and half in, and she was not sure of the etiquette of this matter. She decided to leave it off, although she knew that Bella Pettigrew Lovett, no lady, would be certain to be wearing hers.

Milly sat down. Alice, a look of bliss on her face, put her arms round her. 'At last,' she said. 'See! Look at it all!'

Milly shaded her eyes with her hand. It was quite remarkable. A steady stream of people . . . both high and low, were queuing to pay their twopence at the gate. Bearing brilliantly coloured balloons and paper flowers they made their way to the booths or sat on the grass, ignoring the cold, with the picnics they had brought. Some of the performers were warming up behind the Big Top . . . a man balanced fifteen glasses of ale on the end of his tobacco pipe, two clowns tumbled, some horses were being decked with bells . . .

'Isn't it all magic? Isn't it all wonderful? Did you ever see such excitement, such splendour?'

Milly's heart melted. Alice was still such a child. She had never grown up, that's all. Perhaps she was right, perhaps Luke Durant was the man she had always been waiting for. Perhaps Milly was just being sour-faced about everything and she should stop looking on the black side.

She forced a smile on to her face. She smiled at Bella and bade her good morning. She agreed she would go to the circus . . . 'If Alice agrees to mind Davy.' She even allowed herself to smile at the stupid antics of Mr Punch and cringe when she saw the crocodile.

'This is a new life, Milly,' Alice leaned towards her and whispered, her eyes very bright and her voice quick and breathless. 'A new start for all of us. Once we find somewhere to settle we will fight for the return of my children. Luke and I might even be wed. I am so sure, this morning, so wonderfully confident, so certain! Laugh with me, Milly! Live it all with me in all the colours there are. I am seeing them, now, for the very first time. It's so strong, Milly, so strong, it could even be real!'

Oh Lord, listen to her!

And then the little crowd around the puppet booth fell silent as the baby was thrown out of the booth and the crocodile went to gobble him up. The audience drew in their breaths. They hushed.

But Alice's silver laugh tinkled out on to the morning and Milly heard herself say, 'Shush, Alice, my darling. Not now. Control yourself!'

260

# TWENTY-NINE

Shortly after their arrival at the Old Bell Inn, bulging and beamed and tucked underneath the shadow of Exeter Cathedral, Edward Brennan sent Dr Myers off to organize an official riding party.

'It is absolutely essential that this be done right,' he told the flabby doctor, who was tired after the journey and would have preferred to settle himself and have a short lie-down.

'Why can't we rest tonight and move in the morning?' asked a mutinous Myers. 'Corbett, Duffy and Callow will be fresher after a good night's rest. The circus will still be here, and apart from that, it would be far simpler to retrieve Mrs Brennan and her child and return instantly to Deale. If we take her this evening she'll have to spend the night with us here. That situation could well prove difficult.'

Edward would not be dissuaded. 'I'd rather strike while the iron's hot. The authorities must be involved and we must attempt to locate my wife today.' Quite naturally, Edward was eager to be through with this miserable ordeal. The sooner it was all over, the better.

Myers could see that Edward was nervous. When you were used to dealing with overwrought people it was easy to spot the signs. There was an unhealthy waxiness about his face, a sheen on his forehead and he cleared his throat too many times for totally rational behaviour. There was a strained look about the eyes of the man and an artificial steadiness in his voice. This man is under pressure, thought Myers. This man will stop at nothing to attain his ends.

'And all will be made much easier,' said Edward, bending to peer through the diamond-paned window, pulling apart the small curtains, 'now that you have, at last, agreed to put a signature on the bottom of the page.'

261

'I'm still not convinced of her madness,' said Myers uneasily, comparing the room which Edward had taken with his own smaller, darker one at the top of the house. He pulled the canvas jacket from his stiff, brown case and adjusted the leather straps before laying it down on the thin bedspread. Edward should see what this was going to involve. This performance was not going to be pleasant and Brennan should realize that.

Corbett, Duffy and Callow were sharing a room in the attics. The inn was full, and Edward had had to pay the landlord over the odds to force the man to find them the kind of accommodation they required. 'If we're successful this evening it's going to be necessary, Myers, for you to spend the night in here with Alice and myself. She's not going to submit to her enforced return submissively. I'm going to need your help.'

Was it malice or desperation? The spare flesh under the doctor's eyes pushed up and creased them into slit consternation. Myers wondered, yet again, what force was driving this man, what catastrophe had pushed him into the arms of that cold, unbending woman who waited for him at his home. Whatever the reason, Myers was compelled, by his personal circumstances, to play his part in the capture and return of that unhappy woman, Alice Brennan. And he wondered if Edward, so single-minded in his quest, had thought out the consequences of a night spent holding his wife prisoner. Her limbs would be bound, but not her mouth. And people had eyes – they could and would see. The journey home would be difficult enough.

But although Myers was forced to comply with the plan, that did not mean he approved of it. And there was another thing . . . he would have been happier to strike in daylight rather than accomplish the deed under cover of darkness.

Nevertheless, in under two hours, with much use of the signed, official certification, Myers convinced the local police superintendent of the necessity for swift and positive action, and, having retrieved their own three burly assistants from the taproom downstairs, the peculiar party set out.

The overcast day brought darkness early. The streets were deserted save for a few young bloods who had started their revelling early, and they went purposefully about their business. In two or three hours' time they would be rather less certain of their own direction.

Edward, holding the reins and following the mounted party of constables – his own men rode behind – felt shabby and mean, as if he was a creature of the night about some nefarious business. He felt more in tune with the cloaked figures of the women he saw skulking in the passages or lit in silhouette at tavern doorways. He wondered how they could linger there so long in the cold. He identified with the small groups of ragged men who blew on their fingers as they gathered on street corners under the gas-light, discussing, no doubt, dubious affairs. He pulled his scarf across his mouth and this gesture highlighted his feeling of dark conspiracy, although it was more to do with keeping the damp night air from his throat. There was a sour unpleasantness about it . . . he imagined it must come up from the river. He knew he ought not to feel this way, but there was no avoiding it.

He wondered if Myers was experiencing these same unpleasant feelings but thought not. Perhaps Myers, by the nature of his work, was resigned to it. He knew those rough and simple creatures Corbett, Duffy and Callow, warmed by an excess of ale, no doubt, and with little between their ears, would be feeling nothing but eagerness for the chase. But it was he, Edward Brennan, who had turned his wife into this hunted creature . . .

Edward fixed his eyes stolidly on the carriage lamp, thought about Charlotte waiting for news, and hardened his heart. How she would despise him if she could read his thoughts, sense his weakness. How he needed her for strength and courage. How totally dependent upon her he had become. What would he be without her?

They left the outskirts of the city behind and then there was the wider, cooler, fresher feel of the countryside. Even the hoofbeats sounded different, not ringing but echoing off space instead of stone buildings. Not far to go now. In spite of his determination to remain calm, Edward felt himself tensing. He flicked his whip, and his hands gripped the reins which felt slippery between them. In spaces between the tall hedges, over the five-barred gates they caught fleeting glimpes of light down below in the water meadows as they approached the circus. The huge white canvas appeared to send its own light out around it. People on foot, hurrying in the same direction, called out to them goodnaturedly as they passed. A few drunks who had failed to reach their destination had been positioned safely on the widest parts of the verges. There they lay with their bottles hugged to their chests, precious, like babies.

The little procession, with the carriage sandwiched between the six leading constables and the three Deale assistants following close behind, clattered down the last hill and now they were able to hear the music. Hurdy-gurdies, drums, a tuneless trumpet, the wild squeals of children, a crack in the air from a firework lit up the night with its own fiery song. Edward wiped his forehead with his sleeve and glanced across the box at his companion. Myers was sitting inscrutably beside him staring owlishly off into the distance.

'This is it,' murmured Edward, in need of reassurance now. He knew their approach would be seen. They had picked up quite a little army of stragglers, attracted to their carriage lights, and some of them even tried to hitch quick, perilous rides on the mounting step.

They ducked to avoid a low-hanging branch as they entered the circus field. At the gate, impatience filled Edward with blind desperation as they paused. The wait seemed interminable as the leading constable bent

264

down to speak to the group of gypsies who huddled there collecting the entrance money. 'What the hell does the man think he's doing?' Edward's voice rasped into the darkness. 'Announcing our business to all and sundry? My God, is the man a raving idiot? If my wife is here she will soon know of our presence. Press on!' he shouted. 'Keep going. There's no need to stand there and discuss the situation as if it was a country fair we were here to enjoy!'

Dr Myers rested a calming hand on Edward's arm. 'It was you who insisted that this matter be conducted in a proper manner.'

'There is nothing proper about this.' Edward's voice was shrill. 'This is crass stupidity.'

Giving over the reins to Myers, Edward leapt from the carriage and blundered across the ground, making for the circle of caravans he could just see down a slight slope in the field, nearer to the river. If Alice was here surely that is where she would be – in bed and resting with the child beside her. The convoy of men from Deale pushed past the hold up and followed him on horseback. Occasionally, Edward stopped to make terse enquiries, emphasized by wide gestures of distress. 'It is my wife . . . ' he called to the bewildered fair-goers. 'I am searching for my wife. Have you seen her?' And he began to give a description. Everyone shook their heads and stared after him as he floundered on in the same direction.

A whip crack. In the gloom and the solitude of this shady side of the field the sound was loud as a gunshot. Edward paused in his rushings. The horses pulled up behind him. He looked up to face the man on the stallion. Was this some performer, perfecting his act? No, there'd been a violence about the action that was sharp as the sound itself. Edward frowned. It was hard to define the man's features in the poor light but it was the voice, when he spoke, that bewildered Edward. Hadn't he heard that voice once before, a long time ago?

'Where do you think you are going?'

And then Edward realized that the man was masked.

'Stand aside. I am here on official business to find my wife. The police are not far behind me. You cannot prevent me . . . I have the documents.' Could this be the man who had attacked Myers and his party at Milly's cottage? Every time Edward tried to pass by, the blackguard nudged his horse with his knee and that black animal moved in his pathway to block him. Damn this absurd game of hide and seek. Where was Myers? Where were the constables? If they didn't hurry it would be too late!

The whip cracked a second time. 'Go back,' said the voice. 'There is nothing for you here.'

'Who are you to dare to speak to me in this way? This is not your business. By what right do you interfere with the proper functionings of the law? By God the constables will have your name and you will have to answer for this . . . '

Precious time was passing and still Edward could not get by and it was useless for the three outriders to continue on their own. They were reluctant to do so. The masked rider was not playing games: he filled the night with his threatening bulk. Corbett, fortified by drink, tried to lunge his horse at him, but the masked man brought down his whip so hard on the horse's flank that Corbett's white cob put down its ears and threatened to bolt. Corbett struggled with the reins and hung on for all his worth before retreating behind the others.

Desperate though he was to get by, Edward could not force back the sights and sounds of another night, another violence done nearly twenty years ago. The trap. The trap set by his father, the shed full of machinery that was not machinery but just great brown boxes of packaging. They had put the word about that new machinery was being introduced to the Winterbourne estates. They had known that the rioters would come.

The square wooden barn was ringed by members of the local police force and government men who had to be paid for. This was an army equipped with sophisticated weapons. As Henry Brennan so rightly said, 'This has to be stopped, and now, before it gets further out of hand.'

Edward remembered the perfect stillness of that dark night. The crescent moon gave out no light, it could have been carved upon the sky its arc was so perfect and it smiled. He could smell the man who waited beside him, the sweat of anticipation, the stench of fear mixed with the desire to kill. He'd been hardly a man, just seventeen and keen to ride at his father's side. It was good to see his father out among men and not sitting morosely calculating in his study, or visiting the mines . . . the indoor life of a man of money . . . so grimly and proudly bequeathed to Edward. Yes, Edward had felt proud of his father that fatal night. Proud to see him leading men in such a valiant battle for right against those who plotted in darkness.

They heard the scufflings, the whispering approaches. Those waiting tensed, lifted their batons, the whites of their eyes were all that showed and the barn smelled cleanly and sweetly of fresh oak and an owl hooted from somewhere under the eaves.

An explosion, then, of sensation and sound. Caught like rats in a trap. And those with right on their side followed the example of Henry Brennan, baptized themselves with the blood of the wicked as they cut and thrusted, beat and bludgeoned, shot and pounded the ragged assembly of peasant rioters. The latter had no chance. They were foolish men who acted from emotion, not cool and calculating and calm . . .

And Edward himself was not the coward he feared he might be. Delirious with it all, frenzied to find himself quite without fear, he had beat and rent and torn into flesh along with the others until he was worn out, gorged by it all. Exhilaration was in his eyes, a kind of ecstasy in his heart, but then he saw the boy bending over his wounded father, Mathew Durant.

The boy was his own age . . . dark, tall, defiant, his quick eyes darting wildly. Henry cried, 'Catch him! Hold him! We can have some games with that insolent braggart . . . take him alive, godammit!'

But Edward's new-found power ebbed away as he faced the lad, as their eyes met, brilliant, staring, terrified eyes, both sets of them; Edward's brown and the boy's pure black, Edward with his gun already loaded and cocked, and yet as hopeless and helpless as he had ever been. The fear was back, his knees were buckling. The only difference between them was that the boy's face and hands were crimson with his father's blood while Edward's father roared from behind him, 'Seize the bastard or shoot him, one or the other . . . '

Slowly the boy had risen to his full height, only briefly unlocking his gaze to glance at Mr Brennan. Edward smelled hay then, newly-gathered; it mixed with the wood and oil in the barn, it mixed with the blood. Henry Brennan fired and the moment was gone. The boy fled and Brennan's curses filled the empty space. The hay smell was gone and only the acrid smell of burning, shot and blood was left – a slimy, slippery smell . . . the stench of Hell.

After the bloodbath, when they returned to the house and were congratulating themselves, slapping each other's backs and sharing a flagon of wine in the courtyard, then Edward remembered the words the boy had spoken and the low voice he had used. 'I will never forget who did this. Not to my dying day. And I will hold you responsible for the fate of my father . . . personally responsible. Never forget. Never forget the threat of my curse.'

But his own father was laughing. 'The unholy Durants – they will not ride again, I'll warrant. Nor will they linger to haunt the county with their revolutionary ideas and their wild ways. Their home has been ransacked tonight, razed to the ground. And I'd not be in the shoes of anyone in it when Pete Caswell has fin-

268

ished with that little lot.'

Applause. Loud applause and more self-congratulation. 'My boy,' said Henry, 'tonight I was proud of you. Tonight you became a man.'

Edward Brennan already knew he was a man. Every night in his bed, dreaming of little Lucinda, he knew in what way he was a man. Coarse, immoral, with irreligious thoughts that took him into dark, terrifying places. And now the killings . . . a strange kind of man then, who could feel such hot, sticky lust and who was yet unable to kill a boy when it was demanded of him.

Was it the fireworks that scorched the air, that reminded Edward of that time as he almost retched at the powerlessness of his present situation? This same feeling of helplessness again, of failing to be the man he so desired to be? Or was there something about that voice? For whatever reason, even in his tortured desperation Edward recalled that time, the coming of his manhood and the curse of the boy Durant. And Edward strained his eyes in the darkness but the man remained a silhouette, a dark effigy against the sky.

# THIRTY

A damp night mist hung on the darkness and clung, wraithlike, to the awnings and stalls, dripping off the trees, turning the ground soggy and muting all footsteps.

By the time Dr Myers and the official party caught up with him, Edward was standing in the middle of the circus field beside the main entrance to the marquee. There he was confronted by the stern-faced proprietor who had discarded his turban and crown and instead wore a tall top hat which afforded his already massive frame still extra height and made him appear giant-like. The shadow he cast on the canvas beside him loomed up it and over it like a monster out of some black deep.

'And I am assuring you, sir,' Nathaniel Pettigrew Lovett was saying in a deep, growling voice, 'that I have never set eyes on such a person, that we have no room for passengers in our troupe and that we only carry those who can contribute in some way to our livelihoods. I am not running a charity here, or a sanctuary for the insane, Mr Brennan.'

Edward fidgeted under Lovett's impolite stare, gazing around him all the time, staring at every passer-by, convinced that the man was lying but frustrated by his inability to accuse such a person. He rubbed his frozen hands. He stamped his feet. Myers, coming to stand beside him was no help, and the superintendent of police seemed more intent on finding out what was going on under the Big Top. Two constables remained at the gate with the horses, and Corbett, Duffy and Callow dismounted and gathered round, barely-concealed boredom on their bovine faces.

'Nevertheless, we have to instigate a search,' said Edward haughtily, mustering his dignity, for even now, with all these people milling about, with all the confu-

270

sion of fireworks, cantering horses, half-naked tumblers, saddled tigers with jewelled bits between their jaws, even now, if they moved swiftly, it might not be too late.

'Certainly,' said Nathaniel, scrutinizing Edward down his crag-like nose and bringing a pipe from the depths of his extraordinary beard. His huge fur coat was settled like a kingly robe around him. With shock, Edward noticed the size of his hands. 'And I shall be delighted to conduct you.'

'That will not be necessary.' The superintendent went stiff, rigid as his moustache.

'It might not be necessary but I feel obliged to do so,' said Nathaniel.

Edward's eyes sharpened in the dim light and missed nothing. Damn this delay! There was no sign, now, of the trouble-maker on horseback. After escorting Edward, much against his will, into the presence of Nathaniel the masked horseman had disappeared. There were only a few people wandering around outside because the main performance had started and those with tickets had abandoned the booths and the food stalls and gone inside. Those without, mostly children, with a few drunks and beggars among them, had loosened the pegs and were peering under the skirt of the canvas. A row of bare feet and tattered boots formed an untidy, petal pattern on the grass.

Nathaniel passed by, looked down in a patriarchal manner, and ignored them. He led the group of men straight towards the caravans. A dark, swarthy woman, just as peculiar and formidable as the circus owner himself, introduced herself as his wife. She appeared to have been sitting beside the fire minding a group of small children, and as she walked towards them she called out behind her to a slatternly gypsy, 'Your chavvy is bawling, Mika. He's been bawling for hours. For Gawd's sake do something about it.' And Mika, a disreputable woman, rose with a muttered curse and crossed the grass to the caravan, answering the reedy call of a baby's cry. She did not remain inside, but appeared not five seconds later bearing a filthy child in her arms. Unconcerned by the pitiful wailings, she returned to her place by the fire where she rocked it.

In spite of Edward's growing impatience Nathaniel religiously knocked on every door with the gold knob of his cane, starting at the lead caravan and moving around the ring, even though it was obvious that most of them were deserted. Into each van went three members of the small police force. There was no reason to remain long inside, for it was apparent that neither Alice, Milly nor the child was hiding in any of these. At all times Edward's eyes moved about the field, searching for signs of panic, of a figure darting away into the shadows, of suspicious, frightened eyes. But none of the eyes of the people who opened their doors were frightened; on the contrary, they were cold, hard and accusing, resentful of the disturbance and not, it would seem, slightly interested to discover the reason for it.

'Is she dangerous, this person you seek so avidly, this woman who you go to such lengths to secure?'

Dr Myers, breathless for the ground was uneven and the cold was attacking his chest and he was excited, answered Nathaniel's question for it had been directed at him. Nathaniel noticed, with interest, how he first looked to Edward for permission to speak. 'She is dangerous to herself. She is a victim of her own wild impulses. She has been known to act with violence . . . '

'She has violated the law in some way?' Nathaniel's eyes were quite black. They held a discomfiting force although his voice was politely attentive.

Edward coughed before interrupting. He was the kind of man who walked with a slight stoop and kept his hands behind his back. He was the kind of man who used words and position in order to get his way. Now his words were tinged with bitterness when he said, 'She is my wife, sir, and I do not consider it proper to discuss her condition with strangers.'

They moved on to the next caravan. Nathaniel knocked before opening the door and standing back to let the search-party in. 'I think we ought to be told, in case we should come across her and her companion some time in the future. We must know how to handle her, before passing her over to the law.'

'Her illness does not immediately reveal itself,' said Joshua Myers with caution. They moved slowly on. There were no lights in the next caravan but even so Nathaniel, heavily dignified and determined to make his point, mounted the tiny steps. 'It is deeply buried,' the Doctor went on. 'It tends to erupt in times of crisis.'

'Ah yes. I see.' And Nathaniel Pettigrew Lovett gave an unpleasant smile.

His wife, Bella, although uninvited, accompanied them, trailed along beside them, not speaking, but an enormous, uneasy presence in the way she stared at Edward, her eyes dark and unfathomable between those snaking swathes of wild hair.

There was a sudden gale of laughter and they were forced to move over as a carriage drawn by two plumed horses came threateningly near to the group on its way towards the gate.

'Stop that vehicle!' shouted the superintendent with his hand in the air.

'All the departing vehicles are being stopped and searched at the gate by two of your own people,' Nathaniel reminded him.

'Never mind that. I want that vehicle stopped. It is being driven dangerously.'

'We are in a field,' said Nathaniel, 'not the public highway. And my people have to practise their acts.'

'Nevertheless there are members of the public about and this is no place for a chariot race.' Determination was on the thin face of the superintendent and his uniform buttons glinted in the flaring rush-lights. He was tired of trailing around, plodding up steps and down them again when it was quite obvious to him that nobody was going to be found. And he resented being called out tonight on what he considered quite accurately to be private business. It was cold, it was dark and his wife would have a fine fire going at home and she would be sitting beside it, hogging all of it, and as far as he could see no law had been broken.

Nathaniel boomed out an order. His voice was so loud that every single person in the vast space about him tensed and looked up. The laughter from the closed carriage ceased abruptly and, with extraordinary skill, the carriage was brought to a halt.

Regally Nathaniel approached the carriage, his cloak tugging along the grass behind him. The driver, in a glittering livery of silver blue which was more suitable for a palace than a circus, stepped down.

'You want to see inside?' Nathaniel asked the superintendent with forced deference.

'If you would be so kind.'

Nathaniel gestured to the driver who gave a small bow on opening the door. Edward pushed past the superintendent. He narrowed his eyes and peered inside. Perfume and sweet-scented soap assailed him. The atmosphere whispered of an aroma of expensive oils, of crimped hair and tumbling curls, of pleasant, sweetish perspiration, of lingerie, luxury and silk. He opened his eyes wide and stepped back from the breeze of feather fans, searching the superintendent's face for his reaction. The man thrust his moustached face through the door and withdrew it speedily. His eyebrows came out arched. He stiffened his back. He clicked his heels.

'Ladies,' said Nathaniel with a smile so sudden that his beard jerked. 'Ladies, on their way to a soirée, I believe.'

'A soirée?'

'I believe that is what men such as yourselves prefer to call it.'

'What would you call it, sir?' asked the policeman warily, wondering if this was something he ought to step in and stop.

274

'Just another performance, similar to many others. We are in this business to please the public and the public have varying tastes.'

Edward, recovering from his surprise, stepped up and took a second look. He wanted to scrutinize the faces of every one of these women. This would be such a simple way for Alice to escape, and goodness knows she was capable of anything . . .

'You don't just have to view the goodies, darling,' a coarse voice assailed him and he could feel the woman's breath hot on his cheeks. She winked at him crudely before stretching out her arm and letting it rest lightly on the side of his neck, tickling him there. Her perfume was fierce, he considered it almost violent. 'Come on, get in, there's room if we all push up. Lottie'll sit on your knee, won't you, sweetheart? She's the one with no drawers on. She doesn't like drawers, do you, Lottie? Come on . . . move up, let this punter in.' And they did, giggling, although the velvet interior was packed and even the floor was piled with costumes, hat-boxes, bulging cases and a pile of shoes.

Edward, flushing, feeling the hot sweat of shame trickling down his back in spite of the cold, forced himself to continue his search. But the faces were like those of dolls . . . such paint . . . such glitter . . . one had a cloud of butterflies down her arm, another's bare cleavage was dotted with sequins, another woman's eyes were violet between the slits in her gold mask. He closed his ears to their lewd taunts, his mouth to the fetid atmosphere. Some, if not all, wore decorated wigs. One was a milkmaid with plaits. So difficult was it to see, such was his confusion, that it was almost impossible to count their number, let alone to differentiate one from another. Alice could not be in here. Even Alice would not put herself among their number.

Frustrated and angry, he withdrew.

'Are you certain you are quite satisfied? I'm sure the young ladies would not refuse to get out one by one and parade in front of you. I think they are probably quite used to that although I personally do not make a habit of attending their performances.'

'Let them go,' said Edward limply, and the superintendent lifted his arm once again, and that was generally taken as a signal for the driver to mount the box once again, for the incredible party to carry on. Their laughter could still be heard as they moved off, passed through the gate, and took the left-hand turning towards the city.

At the fire, Edward let his eyes rest on every baby and there were a surprising number. Didn't these people know that these children should be safely inside? Hadn't they heard of the dangers inherent in the night air? It would seem not. Some were being listlessly suckled by mothers who had no shame for they made no attempt to cover themselves as the male party approached. Some of the infants were lying about in baskets and boxes, roughly tucked up beside the fire. Wasn't anyone afraid that the fire might spit at them, that burning embers might fall on them? No, it seemed more important for these mothers that they huddle together at night for a chat, for the drinking of their home-made wines, for the communal minding of these unfortunate offspring while they scratched themselves and laughed their dirty laughter. What a disgraceful example of womankind. They were, with their sparkling earrings, their common gestures – one was wiggling at her ear in this public place, another seemed to be having something removed from her lank, greasy hair – they were the poorest examples of motherhood Edward had ever seen. They took no notice of Edward, of the constables, of the three henchmen, Corbett, Duffy and Callow, although those lumpish cads eyed the alcohol with unseemly interest. Of the dangers that Edward could see all around him, these simple women took no notice. His child could not possibly be here. Alice, no matter how low she had sunk, would never allow it. And if she did, there was always Milly. However misguided she might be, however fooled by her cunning mistress, Milly would never allow any child to be out in the open at night like this . . . and with such an appalling set of people. Such influences!

'There is only one place left to explore and that is the circus itself.' The superintendent was tired, his moustache drooped mournfully. The quest was turning into a failure. They should never have attempted it. He had an uneasy feeling they were being made fools of and he did not like that at all. He licked his fingers and twiddled the ends of his moustache so it stood more stiffly.

Dr Myers' three outriders were unwilling to leave the warmth of the fire and the hopes of a warming nip from one of those seemingly communal jars. Corbett was feeling belligerent. He would have liked to have taken a look inside that carriage. 'There must be an audience of several hundred people in there. How on earth will we be able to find two among that number?'

'We must stand still and watch and wait,' said Myers gravely, 'which is what you are being paid to do.'

'We don't know the women,' argued Corbett. 'There's no point in us searching further.'

'You will accompany us if you please,' Myers tersely declared. 'The woman, Alice Brennan, is so striking it would be difficult for even you to miss her, Corbett. There would be very little she could do to cover her looks. And the rest of you must remember the descriptions you were given. Mrs Toole is a large, grey-haired, elderly woman, quite fierce, and she will more than likely have the baby with her. Now remember your instructions . . . we will give the signal and you will observe. You will follow close on her heels until she is away from the crowds and then you will take her, quickly and without attracting too much attention. You will carry her to the carriage where Mr Brennan and I will be waiting.'

With a grumbling coming from behind, the party strode across the untidy grass, edged their way through the entrance flaps and, taking their places at one side with their backs against the canvas wall, they stood and they watched the audience as avidly as they viewed the performance.

Some of them watched with casual interest, others stared more intently. Edward, tight-lipped, took his eyes carefully round, fixing them on every face before moving on to the next. The prancing horses that passed across his line of vision maddened him. The strain of trying to hold his sham expression of casual interest told in his face. Dismayed, he suspected that this whole journey had been a complete waste of time. He still believed . . . perhaps because he had no alternative and he couldn't go home without hope . . . perhaps it was something to do with the memories the masked man had recalled to him . . . for either reason he still believed that Alice was somewhere here. She had to be. And he had to find her. Patience must be his watchword. Tonight was not all the time he had. She might fool him tonight . . . she might outwit him once again as she had after her escape . . . but she could not fool him for ever. He held himself rigid. There was cold fury in his eyes. Happiness had been snatched from him by a cruel trick of fate. He would not have his happiness denied him for ever!

At the point at which they entered, the audience was silent with astonishment. They had the freaks in the ring and the clown judge with the red woolly hair was giving his verdict. Edward sighed . . . the tastes of the common people. My God, it seemed there was nothing so low, so pathetic that would not interest them. It was nauseous to see. He would not demean himself by watching.

Myers watched. Myers observed more from professional interest than anything else. Vaguely he wondered what such a life, displaying your grotesque malformations for a living, would do to a person. What sort of opinion must you have of yourself? Even worse than an amused or a disgusted reaction must be the pity. But these poor wretches were luckier than some, for at least they were earning money. It was not so long ago that people deliberately mutilated themselves in order to become freaks . . . not only themselves, but their children, too.

What a world, thought Myers, what a world. He, too, was eager to find Alice Brennan for his own very sensible, practical reasons. But he had always doubted the worth of conducting the search tonight. The element of surprise would have been more valuable in the morning when there were fewer people about and fewer activities going on. But there was still time. If they did not succeed tonight there was always tomorrow and the day after that. It was not essential that Myers return to Deale in a hurry. He glanced across at Edward Brennan and saw the determined look on his face. This man is tortured, thought Myers before returning his gaze to the misshapen creatures in the circus ring. He is not just keen to find his wife, which is understandable in the circumstances, no, he is driven by some inner desperation. He is fired by it, driven to distraction by it, and if he fails to find her this time the desire might well become an obsession.

In their own ways, and for their own different reasons, they watched and they waited.

# THIRTY-ONE

Milly Toole thought she would collapse from the shame of it all. She could hardly believe what was happening. She'd been sitting there in the audience, persuaded to come to the show – she hadn't honestly been that keen – when all of a sudden she'd been grabbed from behind and hauled out of her seat. She'd been sitting there quietly, admiring the horsemen's skill, cringing from the ferocity of the tigers, clapping politely, when someone had gripped her so hard and so suddenly she hadn't even been able to protest.

Kidnap! But at my time of life? Milly knew there were places in London to which defenceless women were taken prior to being shipped abroad to unspeakable people and pagan palaces. And, with a terrifying flash, she considered this uncouth, barbaric place was a most suitable venue for such traders to procure their living wares! She had no inkling as to what could be happening. She had feared the worst. She hadn't the strength to plead for mercy.

In the small, busy tent at the back, right beside the performers' entrance, they had dragged her down, stuffed things immodestly up her dress, pulled a wig down on her head, disturbing her hair most terribly, forced her feet into great clumping boots and then she'd been pushed into line with a terse command to, 'Hold your tongue and do what everyone else does, or you'll be letting everyone down!'

'Why are you doing this? Leave me alone! Don't touch me!'

'He is here. The man in the dark hat is here.'

'The man in the dark hat! What dark hat? What has a hat to do with it?'

The whole world was mad. And now here she was, standing in front of a thousand leering faces and looking like goodness knows what. The excitements and exhaustions of the last few days, and now the sudden burst of activity, these bright lights and strange faces almost overwhelmed her. The huge circle of canvas began to swirl dizzily and her stomach to churn. She closed her eyes and stood rigid for a moment, waiting for recovery.

She looked to the right of her and found that her eyes were directly in line with somebody's waist. She took her head up, and up, even further, until, with astonishment, she saw the little head balanced way up there on top. The man was so thin it was pitiful, but how was it possible to fill that frame . . . he must have been eight foot high . . . with any normal kind of shape? And, what was worse, this living skeleton was dressed as a leopard tamer, with skins draped around him so that a great deal of his naked body showed. Why, Milly was sure she could smell him! An unpleasant skinny wet smell, a tiny bit salty.

She turned away.

Hesitantly she let her head take her to her left-hand side and nearly lost her mind because for just one terrible moment she thought she stood next to the bear. The woman, but was it a woman, was covered in hair! Thick, matted, reddish-brown hair that sprouted from every single inch of her skin. Her fierce little eyes were forced to peer through two partings in her head. And this was almost the worst part . . . all she wore was a pair of breeches cut off at the knee, and the skimpy top of a shift. The rest of her was quite naked, but not quite naked, because of the hair.

Milly stiffened.

She leaned forward slightly and glanced anxiously along the line. Such a pitiful gathering of humanity. And horribly shocking. For the bloated hulk of a woman who sat in the throne- like chair on wheels, well how could a person of that size walk, what sort of bed could she sleep in and how did those little arms reach that mouth to put the food in? The person with no

281

arms and legs rested quite straight and dignified where
he had been put. You could not read his expression or
guess at his age. There was no suggestion of eyes on
the face of the girl with no eyes, just smooth, blank,
empty spaces of skin, scooped there, in the shape of a
spoon. The little girl with the angelic face and the
golden curls, who had flippers instead of feet, was
smiling. And the tall boy with the build of a man but
the muzzle of a dog, well, you could not tell whether
he was smiling or not. But he wore a lead round his
neck . . . as a kind of joke then, Milly supposed.

But nobody in the audience was actually laughing. It
was hard to gauge their reactions. Some of the women
held handkerchiefs in front of their faces. Some of the
children pointed.

A slave? The black man was dressed as a slave, with
shackles on his ankles and chains at his wrist. All that
covered his shining torso was a strip of pure white
leather. There was a ball and chain in his arms. He
appeared to have forgotten that he had no need to carry
it. He could put it on the ground if he wanted. Now
and then he revolved on the spot to show his back to
the crowd. They gasped. And Milly saw that it was
criss-crossed by deep welts, as if he'd been badly
slashed . . . in some dreadful accident, perhaps, in his
youth.

The smallest dwarf, whom Milly knew to be called
Georgio, stood there with his arms crossed and a grin
on his face. He did not reach her knees, but at least he
was dressed correctly. She knew that he was renowned
for his healing powers, that he was considered quite a
wise man within the troupe. He did not look like a wise
man now, was not even pretending to be so, apparently
perfectly happy to look, to be thought of as, a moron.

Well! And Milly herself? Her heart still pounded
from the shock of her crude manhandling. She thought
her arms would be bruised where the ruffians had
gripped her. She looked down at her feet. Why would
anyone wear such ridiculous, long, clown-like boots,

red at the tips with blue pom-poms on? She lifted her arms and felt the huge hairy thing they had forced on her head. Horrible! She could feel that hideous tufts of hair went off it, pointing in all directions. Ridiculous hair. She could hardly move for the stuffing which itched next to her skin; it forced her actions to be clumsy and awkward. They had covered her dress with sacks . . . just ordinary, animal-food sacks, not dyed or treated or anything so pleasant as that. So what was missing from this tragic array of humanity? She could see the dwarf, the fattest lady, the hairy woman, the tallest man, and a selection of terrible others. What was she meant to be? And why?

'Move, for God's sake,' muttered the tallest man, and his voice reached her on a gaunt, hollow echo from his great height. He stooped, but he still did not reach her ear. 'Act the part! You're supposed to be mad! You look daft as a brush, now prove it!'

It was then, just as she was about to storm from the arena in terribly angry self-righteousness, that she saw Edward. And understood about the dark hat. And froze. And whisked her frightened eyes away, although she could still see him in a frame in her brain, just like a treasured and much stared-at photograph: tall, arrogant, terribly correctly-dressed, quite out of place here as he stood with his back to the canvas, scowling. His dark eyes were searching around, his head hardly moving, so slowly did he take his eyes from one face and on to the next. The men beside him she did not know, although she assumed that the neatly-dressed, flabby man with the domed head must be the Asylum doctor, and the other three his henchmen. And he had the police with him, too. For the first time Milly understood that they were not merely fleeing from Edward, but from the law itself.

Then she felt fear, terrible fear, like a dagger in her chest. There was a wound there, hurting. Breathing was hard, so was calm. Panic rose like a cold wave that gushed from her throat and into her stomach, churning around down there with her last meal. Her knees were already jerking without her help. She could be made out of rubber, in danger of deflating completely and falling down. Drawing immediate attention to herself.

No matter how terrible this was, for Alice's sake, for Davy's sake she must do this right!

For a few moments she stood there trembling with futile fury, tears smarting behind her eyes. It was years since she'd felt as helpless, as manipulated as this. Disconcerted, she began to pull funny faces while her cheeks burned and flushed scarlet with mortification. She expected everyone to laugh and jeer but nobody did. She raised her shoulders and let them fall. She let her elbows go out then in. She wrinkled up her nose. She let her legs jerk in the way they obviously wanted to. The awful part was that it all began to feel quite natural. She tried to think of a puppet being jerked. She tried to concentrate on that and not let in anything else. She mustn't overdo it, she realized that. She did not want to attract all the attention. She only had to convince them that she was not quite right, not all there. She dreaded to think what she must look like. What colour was the wig they had used? And what sort of powder had they daubed on her face?

Somwhere very deep inside she thought to herself – I will never forgive Alice for this. Never. Never. And this thought, the self-pity that this thought induced almost reduced her to tears. For the first time Milly experienced an instant when she regretted Alice's escape from Deale and her involvement in this. For the first time she wondered if it might have been better if Edward had caught her and taken her back. She thought of her cosy cottage, of her chair by the fire, of the quilt on her bed. She even thought of the bag of oats in the kitchen cupboard, and of how it would go stale before she could get to use it. Soon it would be Christmas, one of Milly's favourite times. She'd been looking forward . . . yes . . . even on her own . . . There would be no little tree this year . . . no point in it. And where would she be? On the road, she supposed, travelling onwards to God knew where with Alice, getting all tangled up in Alice's problems. The terrible round appeared to be starting again.

Edward. His presence so near was terrible. She imagined she could feel his breath at her heels. She imagined she was a fox and he the leading hound, coming deadly near, slobbering and baying.

Where was Alice? What had they done with Alice? And Davy! Milly's hand flew to her lips. She had left Alice in charge of Davy. Alice had sworn not to leave him . . . no matter what happened. Not even if Luke came by and tried to tempt her away. Even now perhaps they had taken Alice; while Milly had been calmly watching the show they had crept up and taken her . . .

No! No! Milly forced herself to think clearly. If they had Alice they would not be here now, searching so intently. They would not bother with Milly Toole if they had Alice and Davy. Alice must have escaped them, too. Ah! This thought came piercingly sweetly into her head, giving Milly courage. Luke must have hidden her somewhere. Poor Alice. Perhaps Alice was, even at this moment, going through some ghastly experience similar to her own.

Between them they had been through so much. Surely, now, they deserved some peace? She thought of the years of bitterness and struggle, she tried to remember the happier times. But all she could recall was Charlotte's voice saying scornfully, 'When will you see, Milly, when will you see?' – always the worm in the darkness feeding on beauty, gentleness and grace, all the attributes she so sadly lacked. And there was little Lucinda, golden and innocent, proclaiming, 'But I love him, Milly, I love him! And he loves me! We are determined to wed and it doesn't matter what anyone says.' Only Alice had nothing to say. Only Alice remained awkwardly silent.

What could she do? What could anyone have done? She tried to forget where she was and what was happening. How long could this ordeal go on? Milly stood in the circus ring and she jerked and she twitched as if she always behaved like this, giving the performance of her life and knowing in her heart of hearts that this was a humiliation she would never, ever, no matter how long she lived, get over.

Suddenly she sat on the floor, hid her face in her hands and wept.

She convinced them all.

# THIRTY-TWO

*It's only a dream it's only a dream it's only a dream . . .*
She wanted to scream it.

It didn't matter how many times Unity Heath told her she was safe now, that Edward would not realize his mistake and follow, Alice's face was white like a ghost's.

And she felt sick. The rocking motion of the confined carriage, the clammy heat within it, the perfumes and oils and the close proximity of so many bodies was nauseating. Her unlikely companions reassured her, but as she told them again and again, her voice rising hysterically, 'None of you know him. You don't realize his determination. You have no idea what he's like once he's set his heart on something.' But her voice was like a voice in a nightmare, she could not make it reach its listeners.

'I thought he was quite a sweetheart,' giggled Angela, whose arm was covered with butterflies, 'with those broody brown eyes, nice firm skin and lovely hands!'

How could they jest at such a time and on such a subject? But then, how could they possibly know the cruel, scheming man that lurked beneath Edward's polished pose? It didn't show. He was a most credible, persuasive man, that was the trouble. When he thrust his head into the carriage just ten minutes ago Alice had jumped back, horrified, comparing his smooth head and his glassy eyes to those of a striking viper. She'd imagined he stared straight into her eyes; she was certain she had been recognized. For hadn't she stared back equally intensely? But while his eyes were fascinated, hers were held by terror – he would see the rise and fall of her chest, the dryness of her lips, the pulse at her throat, the trembling of her hands.

Would someone tell Milly? Would someone explain

287

to Milly that she hadn't deliberately abandoned Davy, that she'd had no choice in the matter at all? She'd been doing exactly as she was told. She'd not even been outside on the step. She'd been inside the caravan with the child in her arms, crooning over him, enjoying the feeling of having him all to herself again, when Bella Pettigrew Lovett stormed inside without knocking. She made her announcement without preamble and with no thought to its consequences.

'Your husband has arrived with his troops. Luke is holding him back, but we haven't got long.'

No feeling . . . numb . . . like being dead or a doll made of stuffing. Slack-jawed, vacant-eyed and imbecile. She must have Davy with her but Bella wouldn't listen. Bella had to move her because Alice could not move herself. Her arms and her legs had gone dead; they were heavy, immobile.

Propelled by Bella she'd gone down the steps and across the short distance to Unity Heath's caravan. Once inside, still helpless to move or ask questions, her clothes had been stripped off her completely, she'd been daubed with a transparent, sticky resin, they'd showered her with a jar of glitter and buckled undergarments on her the like of which she had never seen before. They had scooped up her hair and covered it with a jet-black wigful of ringlets. They'd pulled a fussy, frothy material over her head. It was totally lacking in substance, filmy like gauze, like foam on the top of a wave: crimson and netting and straps of ribbon.

They laid her back on the bed. She closed her eyes and managed to whisper, 'Where's Davy?' as they attacked her face with a paint-brush.

'Shush. Never mind Davy. He's taken care of. Mika has him beside the fire. She has covered his head with charcoal. He looks like a Romany now . . . brown like a little nutmeg and he's howling lustily. Davy is fine.'

'But Milly! Edward will find Milly. He will force her to speak. She pretends, but she is as frightened of him as I am.'

'As long as Mrs Toole keeps her head she will be as safe as you are.' The woman doing the painting licked her lips with a shiny triangle of tongue, pushing her concentration around her mouth as she worked. Her starry eyelashes crinkled, long like tiny spiders' legs. She was little and dark and spoke with a foreign accent. 'When I have finished with you not even your own mother will know you.' And her dark eyes sparkled, her body moved with a restless vivacity.

'Edward will know me.' Just the sound of his name, just the word in her mouth brought the tears to her eyes.

'I doubt it,' was the firm answer.

Alice lay there quite at their mercy, all willpower gone, all ability to make a decision for herself torn off her and thrown away as simply as the gown they had stripped from her body. Naked both outside and in. Nothing there. Nothing but fear and terrible, trembling trepidation. She waited for his voice. Her limbs were tensed, ready to jump at the sound of it. She wanted Luke. If she could only run and find him, hide her face in his coat, shiver in his arms . . . Milly's words rang in her head: 'He said nothing! Well look, he doesn't want you, does he? He's told you he doesn't! A figment of your imagination, all going on in your own head, child, do you understand? Do you understand?' But not Luke, oh no, not Luke. Alice pushed the words away. She would feel safe again if Luke were here. Where was he? What was he doing with Edward? Perhaps Edward was talking to Luke even now, telling his lies, turning him against her. Oh no, please, please God, no.

'Lie still! I've nearly finished.'

The five women in the caravan crowded round to judge the finished result. They were smiling. 'You'll have to look to your laurels, Unity, for I'd say that this one almost outshines you!'

Unity arched her painted eyebrows. She was dressed in taffeta, dark colours, black, purple and a watery turquoise. Her voice was husky like a caress and she narrowed her luminous eyes. 'Too demure . . . too dainty . . . she lacks the style.'

'It's never too late to learn.'

Alice looked miserably back at them. She had a part to play, but what part? What was expected of her now? The danger was such that she had no choice and nor did she care. She would do anything to escape Edward – to avoid waking up – anything which would enable her to stay here with Luke. She cast nervous eyes around her. In a heady rush, quite dizzily, she saw that this caravan was softly furnished, pungently perfumed, draped with stockings and bonnets, littered untidily with half-opened jars, sweet-scented crystals, gaudy jewellery and sticky lipstick. Although it was crammed to the roof with bangles and beads, strewn with scarves and furs, it seemed larger than her own because of the mirrors. Carved and ornate, they were everywhere. In an alcove at the back the cushioned bed was fringed and draped with voluminous curtains held back by hefty tassels. This bed dominated the rest of the comparatively small space. Everything seemed to be secondary to the bed as though just a backdrop for it. This effect turned the bed into a kind of throne. In spite of her terror, Alice was horribly fascinated by the bed, by the women who fluttered around her, by the way they laughed and giggled together; no subject, it seemed, defeated them.

'But I can't leave,' she sobbed. 'I can't leave here without knowing what has happened to Davy and Milly.'

They ushered her out, ignoring her protests, and she felt the night air chill on her half-clothed body as they pushed her into the carriage. She hated to be out, feeling so vulnerable now with all the space about her and knowing that Edward was somewhere in it. 'We would be safer inside,' she protested. 'We won't get by him. He'll find me!'

'If you'd managed to get a look at yourself before you

came out you'd cease your worrying,' said Unity. 'You should not be so craven! We are a match for any man! Do you consider for one moment that if he recognized you we would let him take you?'

Alice was astonished at the woman's courage. She had never heard a woman so confident before . . . and look how she presented herself! She wore her feathers proudly and walked with her head high, striding as she climbed up the steps and into the carriage, no sign of shame at her immodest exposure . . . no coyness there, but proud, even regal, as she lowered her lashes and signalled for Alice to follow.

Had Unity Heath never been taught, as Alice had, that her own body was disgusting? Apparently not. Apparently this lesson had never been learned by any of her companions. They flaunted themselves as they settled down into the comfort of the carriage like travelling queens, not caring about an indecently low cleavage, or the revelation of too much ankle, or an immodest number of bracelets pushed high up a naked arm.

Alice shivered. Sex. They stank of it. She closed her eyes. It was hard for her even to dream about the word. In the whole of her life she'd never said it. And now here it was, settled down all around her in the slant of an eye, the angle of a neck, the crossing of one ankle over another. Alice shrank nervously into one corner of the carriage. She clung to the leather strap. She felt threatened by it . . . almost as strongly as she now felt threatened by Edward. Which was the most violent of the monsters? Was it out there stalking the night, waiting to claim her? Or was it in here, posing as smiling friendship, inviting her to lay down her defences and trust it?

'We should go round the edge of the field,' she leaned forward and whispered, her eyes startled, wide. The carriage lurched and rolled across the uneven ground. She steadied herself by the strap. 'We should not be cantering across the middle like this. We'll attract attention to ourselves and Edward is bound to find us.'

'You'll not influence Absalom. Once he's got the reins in his hands he's a madman. We will deal with Edward, my dear, don't worry.' And so certain was Unity Heath that, for a second, Alice believed her.

And then came the shout. And then the carriage drew up. And then Edward's head . . . his terrible face . . . his stare . . . reality loomed. She could smell the Asylum.

It was soon over. The short experience, long as a lifetime, was soon over. They were amused when they saw Alice's terror, and yet they were profuse in their comfortings. 'He's gone. He's gone! Relax now and enjoy yourself.'

'We should have stayed in the caravan. We should not have left the circus. We are vulnerable and alone now . . . with no protection.'

'You mean we have no men!' Unity's voice was hard – amused, but hard.

'I would feel better if Luke . . . '

Unity smiled. Her feathers fluttered regally as the carriage rocked along. One jewelled hand was cooling itself out of the half-opened window. 'It will be good for you to deal with this without Luke.'

'For what reason?' Alice was confused. She needed Luke. She needed his firmness by her side.

'Because it will be good for you to learn to look after yourself,' said the make-up woman with the foreign voice and the fluttery movements. 'I think you have been brainwashed for too long, Alice. It is time you got a look at the outside world.'

'Milly would not agree with you. My nurse would tell you I have had too much to do with the outside world,' Alice volunteered, made brave by the faces and voices around her.

Unity Heath withdrew her hand, leaned forward, held Alice's chin lightly, and her face and eyes lit up with a brilliant smile. 'We'll see,' she said. 'Your baby is safe. Your nurse is safe. And look at yourself . . . you are safe . . . '

'For now,' said Alice. 'But what of tomorrow?'

Unity tossed her curls and leaned back into the seat again. Her bangles jangled. Her eyes sparkled. 'Ah, tomorrow must take care of itself.'

Alice could not believe that any man would not be in love with Unity Heath. And if this was so, what about Luke? What man could ignore her, with her green eyes, her glossy black hair which cascaded round her shoulders. Her skin was dark, her golden earrings sparked off it, and those eyes of hers held such a wicked look, such a challenging look, cynical, aloof, as if she held herself above all that she saw and was disdainfully laughing at everything.

Sitting directly opposite her like this Alice was nothing but a pastel wraith, a nothing, even her voice beside Unity's sounded reedy and weak. All the colours they had decked her in tonight did nothing to contradict the image she saw of herself. Neither did her fear of Edward help her. She wondered what Unity must think of her, whether she despised her, so vulnerable like this and in need of help. How would Unity Heath have coped with Edward and the Brennans if circumstances had been different? Would she have triumphed over all of it . . . screwed down her heel on the lot of them with one of her throaty laughs? Would she still look as she did now, in control of the whole world, loving herself and amused by it all, if she had suffered as Alice had?

It was impossible to tell.

Earlier, Alice's jealousy had been directed towards Jessica Lamont the actress. Last night and on into the morning Luke had assured her she had been totally wrong. Their performance last night had been one of a thousand others. None of the signs he had sent her, none of the words he had spoken, none of those soft embraces had meant anything. And Alice believed him. Alice did not want her jealousy to turn on Unity. And she knew, if she asked her about Luke, that Unity

293

would not lie. Alice did not want to ask her. She did
not want Unity to think her needy like that. She was
afraid of this woman who knew so much, and she
wanted to be liked by her. She wanted to copy her . . .
to look like her, to *be* her. She wanted people to look
at her and feel the same way they must feel when they
looked at Unity Heath.

Was she dreaming her because – secretly, awfully –
this was the kind of woman Alice would like to have
been. These thoughts made Alice feel pathetic, second-
rate and uninteresting. She was not good enough for
Luke. Not real enough. And she had wicked thoughts,
she was immoral. Her body was ugly and dirty . . .
everyone had always told her so. Laughing was wrong.
Dancing was wrong. Flaunting your body and your
feelings – wrong, wrong, wrong. Luke could not possibly love her. These thoughts, they made her feel angry
towards the woman she so admired and wanted to be.

She listened for Edward. She waited for the sharp
command of Absalom to the horses. Any moment now
she expected the carriage to pull to a sudden halt. Then,
no matter what Unity said, the door would be opened
and she would be dragged down the steps. No one but
Luke could do anything to prevent it. They would gag
her. She would hear the cruelty in Edward's voice as he
issued his vicious commands. Her limbs would be
strapped and she would be bundled, terrified, into Edward's conveyance and taken back to Deale. She realized that, yes, they could do that, even in the middle of
the dream. They could take it from her and control it
if she let them. This time they would make sure she was
given no opportunity to escape. This time there would
be no more hope . . . she would never again feel the rain
on her face or the wind in her hair . . .

The women were gossiping, conversing about
people and places she did not know. Alice was not one
of them and never would be. She was from a different
world . . . they were lower than she, they knew no
better, 'worse than animals, women like that', Milly

would say. Yes, if she closed her eyes and concentrated hard, Alice could hear her nurse's voice. And Charlotte's. 'Alice! Pull yourself together! Remember who you are!'

Edward's eyes – disgust.

Unity saw the tears that, no matter how hard she tried to prevent them, started from Alice's eyes and hung there, waiting, bulging on the lashes. All the shimmering hues of the shocking woman moved forward with her. She put her hand on Alice's knee, and it was cool and gentle as she whispered, 'You are a very lovely woman, Alice. And you have one, firm, very precious thing to hold on to. Luke Durant is in love with you, my dear. I have known him a long time, so I know. But before you give your own love back, find your own strength, Alice. He deserves that. He is a good man. He does not give his love easily.'

'I love him already,' Alice protested, feeling silly and childish and strangely angry. 'I loved him almost from the start.'

Unity Heath leaned back in her seat and stared at her hard.

# THIRTY-THREE

She never forgot that night, so frightening, so terrible, when she was forced out of the carriage and up the dimmed staircase to the room above the tavern in Cannon Lane. There was no alternative for her; there was nowhere she could have waited outside and the bar downstairs was as alien to her as the heated room above it, full of hard-drinking men, thin grey dogs and forbidden to women.

It was not just frightening and terrible to Alice because of what she saw, and that was bad enough. The effects of the lurid eroticisms on her own imagination were much, much worse. She worried and wondered about herself, she was confused by her own immodest fascination for the women who did it and the men who watched it. The atmosphere soaked her through to her underwear as if the room was wet, as if all the eyes gave out a kind of steamy perspiration, eyes like windows, dripping and all fugged up. Surely she should not react like this! Had she been made wrong? Had she been flawed somewhere deep inside before birth? For there must be some element that made her different from other women who would have felt faint and disgusted by the things that went on in that upstairs room.

Oh, naturally she was shocked at first to see bodies flaunted, to see sexuality so brazenly wielded for pleasurable purposes. But she was not disgusted – quite the opposite. She was exhilarated by all of it, embarrassed at first, yes, but eventually the things she saw seemed far more natural and delightful to her than the veiled sort of sexuality that went on in the real world. All the games, all the pretence, thought Alice, went on in the fussy drawing rooms and cold bedrooms of well-bred people. Here, in these dimly-lit rooms of her head, life exploded into reality . . . everything was on display and

296

open to real enjoyment and nobody seemed even slightly ashamed or repelled by any of it.

Meanwhile Milly, overly upset by her brief performance in the circus ring, and tired and fed up by the travelling, relaxed her control a little. 'Three days is such little time to rest. Must we be travelling on already?'

Since undergoing that dreadful experience she took to visiting her fellow 'competitors'. At first, she was drawn to them by pity and concern, but then gradually she began to enjoy their company. They were not unhappy people, made miserable or mean by their cruel accidents of birth, but among the merriest and most friendly of all the travellers. The freaks travelled together and Milly sometimes chose to ride with them. She refused to dress up as a freak again, 'No, not even to save my life,' she protested. Instead she agreed to have her hair dyed red, to wear a scarf and an earring and to cover her shoulders and her head with shawls. And she needed little persuasion to come to the conclusion that Davy would be less conspicuous if he spent more time with the gypsy, Mika, and her large family group.

After the three days camping outside Exeter, with no further interference from Edward, the troupe moved on, stopping briefly at small towns along the route. They travelled ponderously through a changing landscape. Fuming chimneys broke smooth skylines, and mills and waterwheels crouched beside rivers and streams. The nearer they grew to the towns, the closer the brick chimneys clustered together and the darker was the sky. They passed smouldering lime kilns and coke ovens, crimson furnaces and clanking forges which belched out cinders and brick dust. Sometimes you had to hold your nose against the stench of the bone mills and gasworks.

There were many vagrants on the road – men, women and children, ragged-looking and weary – journeying away from the country to find unskilled work in the towns and cities. There were groups of rough-looking, frightening men they called navvies, with picks and shovels over their shoulders who worked in the railway gangs. The countryside was riddled with their work – cuttings and viaducts and tunnels – and the first time Milly saw a train she cowered, her hair on end at the sight and sound of the monstrous roaring thing. Were these gangs of people the same who had gone to wreak havoc brandishing their torches at night? Milly watched and wondered. She had never travelled so far or seen such sights before. There was no way of turning away from it. It was there, all around you, wherever you looked you saw it; this was a very far cry from Shilstone Village and her comfortable cottage, from the kind of life she was used to. Milly grew more and more unsettled. She had never for one moment imagined that human beings lived their lives in the conditions she was seeing around her. Oh yes, she had known that some were richer than others, and some more respectable, and some more worthy and hard-working. But now, as she looked around her, she felt that the bottom was falling out of the world she had so blindly lived in, for there was starvation, cruelty and filth – and over all this there was hopelessness. She brooded over these new revelations as the procession of caravans followed the canal, grey and dismal in the rain and the barges shone blackly with their smooth lines, their backs humped by coal.

Alice looked round, waved to Milly and smiled. Dressed as a Romany and eating chicken between her fingers like that, her old nurse was hardly recognizable. Alice travelled with Luke, alert at all times for the sudden arrival of Edward. But the stallion was roped to a ring at the side of the box, saddled and harnessed, ready for flight, and Luke carried a pair of revolvers on his belt.

'He cannot pursue us for ever.' Luke was more hopeful than Alice. 'The more time passes the better. His obsession will die. He will be forced to return home.

298

And not every county will oblige him by providing extra forces. His three men, and Myers, must be grumbling by now.'

'You don't know him.' Alice stroked Luke's hand and glanced anxiously behind her. She could not shrug off the knowledge that Edward was near.

'I know that he is a weak, ineffectual man.'

'The worst kind,' moaned Alice. 'For they cannot stand to be beaten. And he has Charlotte's strength behind him.'

Whenever they stopped on the road Alice fed the baby and Milly went to inspect him, making sure all was well. 'If I'd ever thought I'd allow one of my little ones to be left all day long in the hands of a gypsy!'

'These are not ordinary circumstances,' Alice reminded her. 'Nobody could have foreseen that this would happen to us. You'll get him back in the end. He'll be yours again one day.'

'How and when and where?' Alice could be so annoying! For goodness' sake, when was she going to face the future? Couldn't she see that life could not go on for ever like this?

As it was, she should not be fraternizing with that immodest Unity Heath. She should not be going about with those shocking women, calling on them in their caravan, sitting beside the fire with them and borrowing their clothes.

'They are not the sort of people we want to talk to,' said Milly. 'They have the morals of animals. They pander to the basest instincts of men, willing to do anything for money.'

'I think they do it because they enjoy it. I was there, I watched them, and I don't think they are pandering to the men . . . while they are pleasuring the men they are also pleasuring themselves.'

'That's worse then,' said Milly. 'That is unforgivable. Women ought not to have feelings like that as you well know. I cannot bear to think about it and I would rather we closed the subject. But keep away from them,

Alice. You know how easily you are influenced in matters about which you know nothing.'

If Milly even began to suspect what went on up those ill-lit staircases at night she would insist they left the troupe altogether. She would look at Alice in that pitying way, she would accuse her of sinking to the lowest depths, she would certainly forbid any friendship. And Milly would be right! Alice knew that. But Alice enjoyed dreaming about them. She was bewitched by the sensuous excitements she witnessed, for they echoed the darker, wilder side of herself that, up until now, she'd secretly believed was her madness.

Unity Heath didn't see it as mad. Unity Heath saw it as quite healthy and natural. So did the others who gathered there, as they went from town to town, from one penny gaffe to another.

There was fear in these thoughts for Alice, as though she had hauled up an anchor and was now drifting in a small canoe closer and closer to a raging waterfall. She sensed the danger, and yet she liked the rocking motion. She liked the speed and the fear and the feeling of being so wildly alive. Was this madness?

They had called it madness.

And she had come to believe them.

The upstairs room was crowded. It had a peculiar hot smell about it that was quite different from any other, compounded of cigar smoke, exotic perfumes, hops and sulphur. Down three sides were alcoves in the walls where four or five people sat with a bottle on a table before them. Along the fourth wall was a solid wooden bar and both men and women sat along it on stools. Alice had gone to sit at the bar with the others, gazing around her with nervous interest, realizing what she must look like and what sort of woman she would likely be taken for. When she was spoken to she smiled hesitantly, hiding behind her fan. She sipped her drink politely. The bright lights of the place were reflected off mirrors in the walls. The men at the bar treated their visitors like queens, and Unity, Angela and the others slid off their feather stoles and drank copiously, flirted outrageously, laughed charmingly and gave every impression of thoroughly enjoying themselves. Even the conversation that fell and swelled around them was full of excited anticipation, a little like the theatre, but nearer, closer, hotter somehow. This was life! This might be a dark underworld place where gentle people ought not to go, but there was a throbbing energy about it which Alice had never found anywhere else . . . no, nothing even close to it. Unity Heath watched her with unconcealed amusement.

The lights were dimmed.

It was all right. It was perfectly all right. Alice wasn't really there.

Dancers – is that what they were, then? On the small stage in the centre of the room Unity Heath ran her hands boldly over her own body, showing no embarrassment at all at the close scrutiny of the avid audience, the eager eyes that watched her. The light from the street-lamp outside slanted through the curtains and painted a silver line on the floor. Her cheeks were delicately flushed and her lips were wet, a shiny red. Her full-tilted breasts pushed against the tight bodice of her dress, she moved with an easy grace and she held her head with poise. Her black curls tumbled around her and her eyelids drooped sensually over her flashing green eyes.

Alice looked round. Everyone who watched the dancer had a breathlessness about them; they were no longer stretching down for their glasses and their conversations had ceased. All stared at the dancing woman who held them in the grip of her gaze. She was an enchantress, bewitching every one of them as she moved, not in time to the music, but several lazy beats behind it. But her steady gaze was neither friendly nor unfriendly, it asked for nothing and it gave nothing away . . . it was honest. She was proud of herself, pleasuring herself as much as those who observed her, secure and confident within her own body. This was a dance of love as exotic birds dance in paradise, and there was no shame in it.

Alice also held her breath, guiltily, slyly, stopping herself from giving quick looks round to see who would come in and pounce and punish them all for this secret wickedness. How did she dare . . . how did they all dare to assume that this was all right?

One by one the other girls joined her and the stage became frothy with lace and petticoats, olive-smooth thighs and arms, modest and coy, brazen and wanton, they each had their own styles of dancing. The languid air was heavily moist, aromatic like a Turkish bath would be. Slowly they stripped off their gowns and unlaced each other's stays, they lifted their shifts over their heads, they handed a glove, a garter, a suspender to the watchers in the audience, and they continued to reveal themselves until their breasts were naked, round, firm and swelling from the narrow waists as, tall and slim, they swayed to the music. No one, any longer, had a name or an identity, for all were under the same enchantment. There was no offensive, ribald behaviour, just exclamations of admiration, sighs, flattery as the women drifted languidly into the crowd and allowed their breasts to be fondled, their necks to be kissed, their skin to be stroked by exploring fingers, warm, magnetic and animal, as both performers and audience pleasured themselves without the slightest tinge of shame. And afterwards, Unity told her, the women would choose a partner for the evening, or several partners depending on her mood – someone to take her to dinner later, and maybe to bed.

The sights and the sounds intoxicated Alice. She felt a fever in her body. She wanted Luke.

How could Luke possibly love her? Who was she? What was she?

She was the woman who, after her wedding night, had moved silently across the room to the bathroom as if in sleep; she was the one who had picked up Edward's razor and opened it before returning to the canopied bed. He'd woken up to discover her standing there, not knowing where she was or what she was doing, or where she'd got the razor from.

'What are you doing, Alice?' he asked her coldly. 'Don't you feel well? I'll fetch Charlotte.'

'No, no, please, don't bring Charlotte. There's no need for that.'

But there'd been no mention of the way he had scorned her, no explanation for the reason he had spurned her so cruelly that first night.

And then, after she'd watched the show, Luke came for her, still in his costume with greasepaint in dark circles round his eyes. She buried her head against his chest; she tried to hide in the depths of his cloak.

He eased her off him before he asked, 'What is it? What's wrong?'

But Alice didn't answer. He lifted her into the four-wheeled trap. He urged the two chestnut horses to gallop as they came to the open countryside. 'I am sorry you had to endure that ordeal. There was no other way. We had to get you away from Edward . . . I am sorry. I wish it had not happened,' he shouted above the wind.

How could she explain her reaction in a way that would not shock him? 'I like their company,' she shouted back. 'They are good fun, they laugh a lot. And what they do is quite harmless.'

'Certainly it is.'

'Why?' she asked quickly. 'Have you seen them?'

'Of course I have seen them.'

Alice was silent for a while, pondering and brooding. The cold wind froze her face. Her hair blew out of her cloak hood and she had to hold the thick material tightly round her. She was wrapping her feelings up, too, hiding them again, so fearful of what they might do if she let them go free. While they cantered like that Alice turned aside and whispered into the wind, 'Luke,

303

I love you, I love you, don't leave me. Don't let anything I might do or say make you leave me.'

He could not hear her.

Luke slowed the horses down as he came to the
narrow country lanes. She thought once more about
Unity Heath. How could Luke fail to want her? Perhaps she had refused him . . . although that, for Alice,
was hard to understand.

She loved him so much. She could not bear to think
that, because of her own dark desires, because of her
madness, he might turn his back and walk out of the
dream.

# THIRTY-FOUR

The weather grew colder as they travelled on; the sky bulged with snow, days melted into each other. The fields became filled with the silence of winter. Time had never passed so fast for Milly.

Milly travelled with a tot of rum in the flask at her belt. She wrapped her feet in rugs and her hands were thrust deep into fur gloves. She raised the neck of the flask to her lips and glanced round in case someone saw her. What must she look like, with her flaming red hair and her tangle of shawls and her one fiery earring? She'd be accepting one of Bella's evil-smelling cigars next. She was losing all pride in herself; she was slowly turning into a gypsy.

And she should not, surely, enjoy the company so much. She should not be the first, when the troupe halted in the evenings, to haul up her chair to the fire, eagerly waiting for the others. Her laughter should not have that coarse edge to it, rising higher than anyone else's. She should not be so keen to encourage the women to tell their stories, to sing along to the songs of the men. She should not be so full of admiration for Bella Pettigrew Lovett, looking forward to seeing that eccentric figure with the flowing sleeves and the feathered hat, disappointed if she was not there. There was nothing to admire about such a creature. She should not go so happily into the caravan full of freaks, always with a gift to make her visit acceptable – a baked cake, oatmeal biscuits, or even a raffia mat she had made on the journey during the day, so much did she enjoy their friendship and their company.

She watched the extraordinary closeness of Alice and Luke with growing concern. Where would it end? He encouraged her in her wild ways, oh yes, she had seen them go dancing off over the fields at the last full moon. He was as reckless as she, and neither of them knew any better. To Milly, who suspected he was using Alice for his own purposes, their heady plans were ludicrous. And Alice was in a peculiar mood, elated one minute, the next frail and subdued. Milly remembered the year of her illness, the time after that terrible business with Garth, when she had been . . . very strange. Perhaps there was someone in whom Milly could confide? Perhaps there was someone, at last, to whom Milly could tell the truth which was settled like such a great weight on her chest. But to what end? What difference would that make? All that would happen was that Luke would turn away, leave Alice, let her down. Destroy her. And how could Milly possibly be the cause of that, she who had defended Alice for so long? Milly looked at Bella Pettigrew Lovett; she spent long hours with her, she had never before had such a friend. And Nathaniel, although a terrifying man with a roaring temper, was as wise as his wife when you got him alone to talk to. Milly grappled with her worries as she had always grappled, quite worn out by all of it, but fortified by the fun and the new company she kept, and warmed by her love of the baby, Davy, who slept in the arms of his mother at night and flourished by day in Mika's loving care.

What a different, extraordinary world she had found herself in. So different, it made that other one seem like a play and the people in it performers coming out from curtains promptly on cue, reading their lines mechanically, trapped in their parts, prisoners of fate, with no destiny of their own, their futures already mapped out for them.

Venton Hall, in spite of Henry Brennan's intervention, was quickly going to seed. With Thomas and Sarah gone there was no core in it . . . even the billiard-table smoothness of the parks and lawns took on an old man's tufted look. The outbuildings, badly in need of repair, were straggled with the wild white trumpets of bellbine, dog roses, and whiskers of twitch grass poked through the unkempt pathways. Even the fountain basins were cracked and dry like old skin stretched over hollowing bones.

It was impossible to get the servants to behave with the same respect when there was no resident master or mistress in the house. Milly tried her best, but they were a tight-lipped, surly lot, more likely to move on to loftier positions than to stay and serve the same family for a lifetime under the circumstances. They knew, they all realized that once Alice was eighteen she would marry and the family, such as it was, would move away. No, there was no longer any sense of loyalty, no longer a sense of pulling together, of belonging.

And every month Milly had to account to Henry Brennan for the outgoings. Although she delegated and divided the responsibilities between the cook and the housekeeper – each ruled their own domain – it was Milly who had to explain any discrepancies that might arise. These meetings were formal and unpleasant. The man had the memory of an elephant and the watchful eyes of an alligator. And he was mean . . . far meaner than Lord Thomas who had no money to speak of at all and yet sprayed it around like water. 'Careful', Mr Brennan called his own attitude. 'The pennies are important, Mrs Toole. Do not be frivolous with the pennies . . .'

As if Milly had been frivolous in any way in the whole of her life! He never raised the subject of Alice's engagement to his son, Edward, and Milly did not like to introduce the subject because there was something unseemly about it, something a bit nasty and she did not want to talk about it with this dry, withered man.

He was unpopular; he had no charisma, he was tall, grey-faced and humourless. Rumours of the poor conditions in his mines and factories abounded, he paid his house servants as little as he could, but he was grudgingly admired for the way he had, single-handed-ly it was told, stopped the rioters. It was said that he'd been quite unscrupulous in his dealings with the prisoners he took . . . and they were the lucky ones, for most had been killed. The local justices, influenced by their own needs and landed positions, dealt out long sentences – and quite rightly. There were no uprisings any more, no more nonsense like that. The people were quiet, resigned to their lot and Luke Durant was a wanted man; he did not call any more.

Milly felt betrayed by that boy on a personal level. And a fool, for trusting him. Who would have believed that his family, so ancient and noble, would have played a leading role in that violent business? And there she'd been like a feeble-minded fool, sitting sipping tea with the lad, gossiping away about this and that with her wagging tongue loose in her head like an empty-headed scullerymaid, and she remembered the time he'd sat there and listened while Emma the cook informed them of an earlier plot. No wonder the barn-burning wretches had got away that time. No wonder the government troops had returned, red-faced, on finding the tavern deserted. Luke Durant must have pricked up his ears and ridden off, hotfoot, with that little piece of information!

Snake in the grass! Spy!

Yes, Henry Brennan had ruthlessly put a stop to all that. Luke's father, Mathew Durant, had been thrown into gaol, his lands and estates confiscated. It was most unfortunate that the soldiers had wreaked such a cruel revenge on the women and servants they found at Castle Bellever. Milly didn't see why they should have suffered – they would not have had anything to do with it. It was awful. Luke's mother had been shot in the head . . . trying to defend the place, they said. And only some yardboys and one old servant survived. 'Shame,' said Emma. 'I'd heard it were a lovely place . . . surrounded by trees, covered with roses, and that glossy old moat winding like a silver ribbon around it, like something out of a dream.'

'It was nothing but a nest of vipers! The whole place and all who were in it had to be completely destroyed if the countryside was ever to find peace again,' – that is what Henry Brennan was saying to excuse his excessive behaviour.

Henry's son Edward was slightly more appealing. He called whenever he could, whenever his father agreed to release him for a few hours from business matters. Although Milly never forgot his rude behaviour that long-ago Christmas and, although he still had that stubborn, proud insolence about him, he had mellowed over the years, had become quite a presentable young man with none of his father's insensitivity about him. He was fun-loving, greatly influenced, of course, by the sweet-natured Lucinda, with whom the boy was quite besotted.

Watching their obvious fondness for each other proved a great worry for Milly, knowing what she knew, knowing that it was a relationship which could not be allowed to continue. She considered the boy should be told of his engagement to Alice before his courtship grew too intense. But Milly consoled herself that Lucinda was still very much a child. Their involvement with each other was not likely to last.

And Alice, thank the Lord, was getting better.

'What's the matter with her?' Charlotte would ask. 'Why isn't she coming down to join us for supper again?'

'She is not speaking today. She wants to be alone. She is growing up, Charlotte, that's what's the matter with Alice, and it is proving a most painful business.'

'Is she ill?'

'Not ill exactly, but . . . '

'It's her head, isn't it? She's not right in the head. And you are protecting her.'

'Her head, Charlotte! What on earth are you talking about?' Milly was needled beyond endurance by Charlotte's malicious suggestions.

Her fury with Luke was increased by the tragedy of

Lorna Drewe, a wicked, pretty little strumpet who came to work in the Venton laundry. This event settled over the house like a blanket of sorrow not six months after the stamping out of the riots. All the girls had been after Luke. Milly should have been firmer, but the kitchens were Emma's domain and she hadn't liked to interfere.

When they discovered that Lorna had contrived to carry her child for nine months without detection, when that little matter came into the open – the naughty girl – it was Milly who had to go begging to Master Brennan; it was she who had to plead the girl's cause. She'd discussed the situation with Emma. 'She'll not say who the father was,' said Emma. 'She is a stubborn, silly creature who does not seem to realize the trouble she has landed herself in!'

'You must make her say,' said Milly. 'He will have to take the responsibility. Men! They cannot be allowed to get away with this, time after time.'

'It's no good, Milly, she's tight-lipped about it. There's no budging her, the little hussy.'

'She doesn't need to say,' sniffed Milly. 'To anyone with any intelligence at all it is obvious. But where is he now, that's what I'd like to know! Where are they when they're needed?'

They dared not keep quiet about the matter because Henry Brennan stressed the importance of knowing what was going on. 'I might not be master of this house, I might not live in it, but I expect the everyday events to be brought to my attention immediately. If this is not done you will find yourself, no matter how indispensable you are to me, having to look for another position I'm afraid, Mrs Toole.'

'But is this that sort of event?' asked Emma, wheedling, for she was fond of Lorna. They all were, and shocked that she had kept her secret for so long. 'Isn't this a domestic matter that we could sort out ourselves?'

Milly was inclined to agree but, in spite of her dislike

of Henry Brennan, she'd never imagined his reaction would be anything other than one of stern sympathy. After all, what was it to do with him? So, confidently Milly told Emma, 'He will tell us to deal with this ourselves. He will quite likely chide me for bringing it up. After all, it is a delicate matter, and women's business when all's said and done.'

So, waiting for a convenient time, and carefully assessing his mood, she told him.

She was quite unprepared for his angry reaction. 'Why is this girl still in my employ? And how is it you failed to detect her condition earlier? I think you did know! I think you both knew . . . yourself and the cook! And yet you harboured this immoral creature within the house, kept her room and her place at the table. I cannot believe it! What sort of morals do you deal in, Mrs Toole, and in what sort of way are you bringing up the Venton girls? This . . . this strumpet,' and his face grew thin with disgust as he spoke, unable, it would seem, to repeat Lorna's name, 'this strumpet should have been thrown out immediately! Chastity is essential, Mrs Toole, unless the whole atmosphere of a place be tainted by immorality.'

'But I'm sure, Mr Brennan, sir, that this was an accident, a foolish, silly adventure . . . '

'Be quiet, Mrs Toole! I want to hear no more about it! I want the girl gone before tomorrow night.'

'But where? There is nowhere for her to go. Now she has the child to care for . . . '

'That is not my business, and since when has it been yours? I employ you to ensure the smooth running of this household, to bring up the Venton girls as correct, modest young ladies, not to go round concerning yourself with the immoral animal acts of those who skulk in the lower kitchens . . . Now, if you consider you have not enough to occupy yourself without taking the part of those who have no rights to be supported, then I would be grateful if you would inform me, now, of that fact.'

311

Yes, it had been as bad as that. There was nothing further Milly could say and there was no way anyone could help the afflicted child. She packed up her bundle and tearfully left, still saying nothing. She loved that baby like a doll, always a fool over chickens and kittens and puppies. She'd looked after her own mother's babies before she came into service and she was pathetically obsessed with her own – not all that bright, but good-hearted. And it was one week later that they heard of her pitiable, violent end, under the wheels of Morrison's dray. She had gone to the back doors of various houses begging for a position, but one look at the baby and she'd been turned away. The workhouse, Milly supposed, held too many terrors for her. She had decided to end it.

Terrible! Tragic! That poor girl's face as she left – Milly would see the bewildered expression on it for as long as she lived. She was such a little scrap of a thing. 'I'll not be parted from her, Mrs Toole, not for nothing or nobody, I won't.' Luke Durant ought not to spend so much time putting right the wrongs of the world, but should look closer to home, taking proper responsibility for his own reckless behaviour! Milly was bitter . . . she wondered if her anger was caused by her earlier sense of betrayal, by her own inability to plead for the girl. If she had approached the subject more cautiously, behaved a little more abjectly, or even, better still, if she and Emma had decided to deal with the matter themselves, they would have found a way. Oh . . . it had been awful . . . the self-recriminations, the nights she'd spent unable to sleep, dreaming about that poor child and her baby.

It was all Luke's fault! And where was he? Couldn't he have risked his own skin and returned to help Lorna out? The fact that Luke did not know never crossed Milly's tortured mind.

Time heals. Time went by. Alice grew more beautiful by the day. And better – still dreamy, still inside her own head a lot – but she was looking better. The

Brennans could not criticize Milly there. Alice was growing into a demure and beautiful young lady, and the sad part of it was she would have been able to attract any man . . . the highest in the land. She could have had her pick. Men were drawn to her and she . . . she laughed and she danced and she flittered from feeling to feeling like a candle flame, shy, unsure of herself, fading and flaring as her moods took her. The only man that did not seem instantly enamoured of her was Edward Brennan. Edward, who preferred Lucinda.

Soon after Alice's seventeenth birthday the invitations started coming in and Mr Brennan was carefully selective. He liked to choose what company the Venton girls kept and he was most strict about it. His future daughter-in-law must be perfect, her social life untainted. Image was all-important. Milly quailed inside herself, imagining the calamity that would befall them all if a whisper got out of Alice's disgraceful affair, her foolish, unnatural behaviour.

Now it was truly over Milly dared think about it. Where had it come from? My God, was it some ghastly trait, inherited? It was whispered that there had been madness in the family, generations ago, and that it had manifested itself in all sorts of terrible ways. Could it have lain dormant for so many years only to raise its ugly head again in Alice? Surely not! God would not be so cruel, hadn't He done enough to this little family? And why Alice? Why now, at this most important time? Milly dismissed her dark musings as the silly hysteria of a middle-aged woman. Just as long as she could keep the covers pulled over Alice's darker leanings, she might grow out of it, and certainly once she was married she would calm down and all would be well.

It was Charlotte who loathed to accept invitations, who whined and pleaded to be allowed to stay at home, who did not want to go.

'There are enough servants at home to look after me here. I could even manage to look after myself! You and Alice and Lucinda would have a far better time

313

without me. And I should be much happier left at Venton by myself sitting by the fire and reading. Surely you can see that, Milly?'

'Charlotte, your sisters need me as a chaperone, and quite apart from that it would be seen as an insult if you dropped out. I do not ask you to attend every ball although I cannot rest knowing you are here alone, so every now and again you must come with us.'

Charlotte kept trying. She feigned illness at the last minute. Milly would go upstairs to find her, her thin face crumpled, red-eyed from crying, pale-cheeked and curled up in bed. 'You are beginning to build it up into something far worse than it really is. This party is one night out of your whole life, that's all. And when it is over you can pretend it was just a dream.'

'A nightmare,' choked Charlotte. 'And a nightmare I know I will live and re-live a hundred thousand times.'

'Maybe so. Maybe so,' said Milly. But she insisted.

Over the years poor Charlotte's looks had not improved. The girl was too thin, with the waxen complexion of the sickly. There was no colour about her, just that same scorched-earth look, and she stooped around the house with that sullen look on her face, mean and accusing. It didn't matter what clothes she wore, Milly was always encouraging her into bright dresses, but in the end she stuck to greys and blacks and occasionally a sombre navy blue. Sixteen – it ought to have been the time of her life, but Charlotte looked ten years older. Luckily for her, she would never be put on the marriage market. Balls and parties were anathema to her. Men shied away from her caustic tongue and sharp looks, and would-be girl friends were put off by her unkindness.

'What is the matter with me, Milly? How did I come to be so plain and ugly – why couldn't I look like the others? Listen to them getting ready next door. Listen to them giggling, choosing their dresses, curling their hair. They are full of excitement while I am cold with dread already.'

314

'Your mother never really enjoyed social occasions. She was always a rather retiring soul, forced into company by her position. But she did not enjoy it, Charlotte. She made herself do what was right.'

'My mother was beautiful,' said Charlotte.

And there was no answer to that. It might have comforted Charlotte to know that this was the last time her presence would be required at such a painful event, that tonight, the engagement between Alice and Edward would be formally announced. Then, mercifully for Charlotte, the balls and parties would cease . . . they would move to Winterbourne House and Charlotte could be as retiring as she liked. Milly bled for the child. Her attitude was quite understandable. Balls and parties were no place to be when you were plain as poor Charlotte. But what could Milly do? Henry Brennan insisted they all go . . . Milly did not feel like going to plead on Charlotte's behalf, and Charlotte was being silly. She need not be alone with her awkwardness. If she wanted to she could find a quiet place where there were others like herself, shy and retiring. If she forced herself to have patience, to be just a little bit less hostile, she could sit and sip wine with friends, enjoy the music and make pleasant conversation. It was not essential, after all, to find a man!

But she'd said these things so many times before it was a waste of breath to say them again. No, Charlotte would stand there, po-faced and angry, making herself quite unapproachable.

Ah yes, the night the engagement was announced. Milly remembered it now as she rocked along, looking about her secretively before taking a nip of warming rum. The Venton party, fanning themselves and sticky with the heat that stuffed the airless carriage, had arrived at Winterbourne House that hot summer afternoon with Charlotte still complaining. But Milly had felt light-headed with relief. The worrying, watchful years would soon be over. Soon Alice would be married, settled, a mother perhaps and Milly would have done her job well.

Milly took another nip from the flask. They would stop in a minute, on the outskirts of London. She'd be glad of it. They were staying in the capital for more than a month and Milly looked forward to the rest. Tomorrow she might stay inside her caravan, tidying it up, making it cosy, making it into a proper home.

She frowned as she looked on the strange world about her, remembering that other one.

How wrong, how terribly, dangerously wrong she had been.

# THIRTY-FIVE

Edward was biding his time. They had been on the road for three weeks now, and he could not afford a second mistake. This time, when he struck, the operation must be successful.

This strange way of life made Edward feel cut off from the world. He was certain that Alice travelled with the circus. He scarcely noticed the towns they passed through or the inns they slept in. There was nothing, other than Charlotte, to tempt him home. Of his children he preferred not to think, especially Nicholas, and he had been so proud, so full of hope for his son. But now, suddenly, everything was different. Lately, Charlotte had started to point out all sorts of small incidents, odd behaviour . . . 'It is true, Edward! Nicholas has inherited Alice's sickness and some time, soon, you are going to have to face it. You have no heir! One of your daughters will have to suffice if you cannot retrieve your new son.' And certainly Nicholas was being very difficult at the moment. The prospect of what might be happening to his eldest son was too awful to contemplate.

Edward had no friends. Henry had always discouraged him, saying, 'Friends drag you back, pull you down. There is nobody in this world worthy of trust. No, my boy, leave other people well alone. Trust in yourself if you can – if not, trust no one at all.'

Myers was growing more difficult by the day and Corbett, Duffy and Callow had always been surly and truculent. Now, as Christmas approached, they wanted to know when they could go home; they wanted to return to their families.

But Edward dared not return, not without Alice and the child. As far as his business interests were concerned, well, they could be left in the hands of his

317

managers, carefully-chosen men who were as astute, and probably more single-minded, than he.

The five men discussed the problems facing them as they sat in an ante-room at the Queen's Arms, beside the fire, waiting for a supper of roasted wild duck. Every one of the party was tired and drawn. Edward Brennan's long legs, tight in black trousers, were stretched straight out under the table in a posture of false relaxation, for the man was stiff as a bone. He was tense, nervous, and his half-sleepy eyes never lost their watchful air.

A cold wind gusted down the chimney and rain, or was it snow, spattered and hissed on the logs. Myers said, 'The trouble is that the blighters close ranks. Corbett and Duffy have tried to extract information from the stragglers . . . men in taverns and women hawking their wares to the shops. They have tried persuasion and bribery to no avail. So we're in the hopeless position of not knowing for certain whether the women are travelling with the troupe, or not. We could have come all this way only to find ourselves up a blind alley.' A man who enjoyed what comforts he had, this travelling life did not suit the doctor. He was gloomy and unenthusiastic. Not for one moment had he expected to be away so long. 'All of us,' he said, looking morosely up at the others for support, 'are for ending this as soon as possible. I have my work to do, and the men have families waiting at home. We started out in good faith,' he added as a reminder, 'but now we have had enough.'

Corbett, in spite of the fact that he was eager to explore the fleshpots he'd heard about in London, agreed with him. 'There's a kind of madness about what we are doing, and we can't trail these people for ever. They're not blind or stupid, they know we're here . . . they can't not know. If they don't see us lagging behind on the road in the daytime, they meet us in the taverns later. They share out their information, so every member of that troupe knows exactly where we

318

are. Every single one of them is involved. On the days when the circus is performing they keep watch, and on other days, without the rest of the public about, we stand out like sore thumbs if we get anywhere near the camp.' And Corbett, red-faced from the fire and the beer, finished angrily, 'And my job is not peering over hedges!' He drained his glass and banged it down on the table to let everyone know he was ready for another.

'One more week, that's all I'm asking.' Edward wiped his eyes as the fire belched smoke; they were red-rimmed from the cold and from the travelling. The lantern-light which flickered over him from the mantelpiece above cast gaunt, yellow shadows on his face. He flapped the handbill he had shown them earlier. His tone was quietly contemptuous, but underneath that was an undisguised tension. He sat forward in order to encourage them. 'Listen to me: the troupe stays here for a month. During the journey the've been on their guard, but now we must convince them that there's no further danger. I chose this tavern with a purpose. There is a performance in the upstairs room tonight . . . a disgraceful, lewd affair put on by a group of circus whores and I've decided that tonight both Myers and I will attend. We'll mix with the filthy vermin, mimic the drunks among them, and let it be known during the evening that I have decided to give up the chase and return home tomorrow.' Edward paused briefly on noticing Corbett's glowering, envious expression. 'It's an event only patronized by gentlemen, Corbett. There are similar diversions for the lower classes and I'm certain you will have no difficulty at all in seeking them out for yourself – all three of you. And then, in the morning, we will make a great play of packing our bags and leaving. Only then, when we've convinced them they're no longer in danger, will we be likely to succeed.'

There was a small, uneasy silence. 'You still believe that your wife travels with them?' Joshua Myers wrapped his pudgy hands round his glass, annoying Edward by the lack of conviction in his tired gesture and tone. It was clear that the physician no longer believed they would find Alice with the circus, that he was demoralized by the whole business, distrustful of Edward, concerned that they were all being swept up in the whims of an obsessed man.

'I think it is not only likely, but certain. There are other factors involved in this, the details of which it's not necessary for you to know.'

'It is only fair, given the circumstances, that we should be put fully in the picture,' objected Myers. 'To what other factors do you refer?'

Edward shook his head. 'No matter. They are between the person concerned and myself. Just let me reassure you that the most important issue, now, is to take them off-guard. And then I think I can safely guarantee that next time we will be given all the police aid that we could possibly require for our purpose.'

'You sound very certain.' Myers was unhappy with this new sense of secrecy and uncertain about his role in the events promised for later this evening. How much further was this man prepared to go, and for how much longer was Myers prepared to humour him for the sake of his own security? There had to be a limit, and Myers felt they had almost reached it. After all, poorly placed or not, and stuck in a job unworthy of his talents, he was still a professional man with a reputation to protect. For Edward the circumstances were different. Gentlemen were expected to sow their wild oats every so often. And Myers glanced anxiously at Edward, at the eyes burned up with fatigue, at the desperation he saw there.

Edward turned away and let his tired eyes rest on the fire. A small smile tightened his face. Luke Durant! How ironical this was proving to be! It had not taken him long to remember after that first confusing and unexpected meeting with the dark rider in the circus field. For some hours Edward was unable to place the voice, but then, in a startling flash, it came to him. There could be no mistaking the voice of the boy on the night they had routed the rioters, lured them into the trap before wreaking a dreadful revenge. How could Edward forget the wild look in that boy's eyes or the words he had spoken? He ought to have killed him then, he ought to have followed Henry's orders, because the spectre of that moment had haunted him ever after. Guilt . . . guilt and the sudden, awful question that what they were doing might be wrong, that there might be some right in the Chartists' cause, that the law was the place to sort out these questions and that what they had taken part in with such gleeful abandon was nothing but cold-blooded slaughter.

Oh yes, driven by this same uncomfortable feeling of guilt, Edward had intervened, preventing Henry, with some difficulty, from killing Mathew Durant, Luke's father. But the length of the gaol sentence afterwards, the lack of mercy that was shown to the man, the killing of his wife and family and the ransacking of his home had not eased Edward's sense of shame. And he had never, honestly, been able to get rid of it.

Once the terror and horror had left him there had been the fear. He hated and feared Luke Durant. Then, as a boy, and now as a man, he feared his enemy's revenge. Edward would feel far happier, would sleep more easily at night with the knowledge that the blackguard was safely under lock and key. He rubbed his hands. They remained cold in spite of the warmth from the fire. Fate was, at last, proving kind. Alice had been taken under the wing of a wanted man . . . the same man, most surely, who must have interfered with the doctor's party when they called at Mrs Toole's cottage. Luke Durant . . . getting his own back now in a clever way by defending his enemy's wife, travelling with a circus and performing under the name of Robert Melville! And Alice, of course, would fall for it. Alice would believe the man wanted her for herself – she'd play straight into that ruffian's hands. Edward smiled as he reluctantly admired the nerve of the man. Once Edward had recognized him it was easy to find out the rest, a simple matter to make enquiries. The authorities would have to act on this new information. It was a larger matter now, no longer the small, personal quest of a man searching for his insane wife. Quite a different affair.

But even with this hopeful new light thrown on the matter, Edward was terrified that something might still go wrong. The authorities might channel all their efforts into seizing the villain, Durant, and Alice, forgotten in the fraces, might manage to stay free. Myers and his men were not prepared to remain much longer. They had no stomach for the chase, they were not driven by personal motives. No, Edward would have to think carefully, plot cunningly, in order to make quite sure that, in all the ensuing excitement, Alice and her child were not forgotten.

Every other day he penned a letter to Charlotte, telling her he was getting closer, assuring her the ordeal would soon end. He must make it happen. He must!

He pulled the fingers of each hand, slowly, meticulously, and cracked the bones.

# THIRTY-SIX

This was becoming a troubled dream – feverish, with periods of nightmare and moments of ecstasy. So much of it was out of her own control, but then, dreams are. How many years had she spent hugging shadows in her sleep?

London shocked and excited Alice. From an early life among the serenity of the trees and the silence of the hills, London was a terrifying place. Gone were the controlled voices of childhood, demure movements – running was never permitted – contrived, polite conversations, averted eyes and hours of silent sewing and reading. Instead, there were strange wet twilights, lamps reflected in mud puddles and lights flaring above the doorways of public houses. And sound. And the sense of beautiful romance in the streets. How different . . .

Before the invitations started arriving life at home had been static; before the balls began and without either parent, with Milly the only adult company for months at a time, Venton in those in-between years was very dull. Not for them a life of flitting between Mayfair and the country, shooting parties in Scotland or visits to Baden Baden, Pau or Menton, like some of their neighbours. Most of it had been so monotonous that it was difficult to know how to pass the time. They depended on newspapers for their news and that was dominated by the social scene in the capital . . . news of Lady Bloomsbury's cold . . . the standard of cooking in the Duchess of Sutherland's household, and much of their conversation was reduced to the level of the weather or some scandal from the gossip pages.

How had she come to love Edward? How had she dared to love for a second time? By so completely blanking out the first it did not exist – anywhere – not even in memory?

'He said nothing! You did not go to him! You knew no one called Garth!'

The days when Edward came to visit, to take them out for a ride in the trap with a picnic up on the box beside him, were good days. And when he came for tea they found his conversation witty and exciting. It was flavoured by reality, by real people and real events. They played games of cricket on the lawn, and he taught them how to play tennis. Yes, they looked forward to those days. They all grew fond of Edward, even Milly in a defensive, suspicious kind of way.

Henry Brennan, their new protector, did not favour education for girls, and while Milly tried as best she could, all the books that were sent to the house concentrated on morals and spiritual values. Every single thing they read told them that proper young ladies were not capable of learning, or of self-discipline, that it was manners that mattered, and looking after men. Lucinda took to sneaking down to the servants' quarters and bringing back piles of romances which they hid under their beds, and which she and Alice read by candlelight.

Charlotte preferred educational books, and spent hours trying to teach herself Latin. 'We should have a governess,' she moaned. 'Even the local children go to the village school while we sit here all day long, moping and learning nothing.'

'I've asked Mr Brennan but it's no good, he's violently opposed to it.' But secretly, Milly was as worried about their lack of education as they were.

Yes, they were buried away before the balls started. Like forgotten people.

Anyone who was anyone went to London in May and June, but it was important to be seen to leave it by August. So when the hunting season began Milly would let them follow the hounds on foot, wrapped up warmly, with, and yet certainly not quite mixing with, the local farmhands and labourers. They came home

324

red-faced, cold and excited, but Charlotte groaned in despairing fury, 'We should be riding out with them like other girls of our age. We should not be having to stagger through the mud, climbing the gates with the frock-coated peasants with their filthy boots. Those boorish creatures.'

'With the money they get they could hardly dress otherwise,' said Alice quietly.

'Be patient, Charlotte. You will be asked, when you are a little older. You will all be asked when Mr Brennan considers the time is appropriate.'

'Why has that man taken over our lives like this? What made him decide he wanted to own Venton and how is it possible he has such control over our lives? Can Edward say nothing to influence him?'

'He paid your father's debts for him,' said Milly, 'and now let's not talk about that any more.'

'But will it be for ever? Have we no say at all? And what does he get out of it except for a country house which he rarely visits and extra land when he already has thousands of acres of his own?' Charlotte ignored her and would have gone arguing on and on if Milly had allowed it.

It never used to be like that. Alice could just remember the days when the house was filled with guests. Those who wished to hunt would be provided with a hunter and the ones who made up the shooting party would go off in the brake to shoot down the pheasants that streaked in gold across the cold winter sky. Her mother might stay at home and play croquet on the lawn with her friends if the sun came out, and in the evening there would be music and cards and billiards. She remembered the servants in liveries of blue, white and gold. She remembered the dinner table loaded with silver. She remembered learning to ride, and hating it – but she must do it, she was forced to do it, in order to overcome her fear – being forced to gallop round the gravel walks of the house by Masters, the chief groom. And all the time Thomas must have been running up debts he knew he could not pay.

Then she remembered the gloom and the sorrow that filled the house after Sarah's death, and when Thomas took his life not three years later, that sorrow settled on the house like a spreading black stain that would not rub off. All the bad luck seemed to have started on the night she swore on the life of her unborn brother, the night she gave Abernathy away, and the following day when they discovered the strangled cat.

Their days were spent in waiting. They were prisoners to the long, cold winters when most of the heat from the fires was sucked up the chimneys and Alice, Charlotte and Lucinda spent long hours cuddled up beside them, or went early to bed, the only places they were sure to be warm. Meals were not lingered over, for the dining room was icy. The food was plain and often cold by the time it arrived from the kitchens. There were some days when they sat in the dining room, formally dressed as required, but with rugs round their legs. Charlotte asked Milly, 'Well, when will Alice be going to London? She's never going to catch a husband in the country. She'll never meet the right sort of man here and then where will we all be? Lucinda and I have no chance. Lucinda and I have no marriageable qualities.'

'I'm not worried about that,' Lucinda chipped in. 'I have already promised myself to Edward Brennan.'

Milly looked up quickly, but did not reply.

'There is no prestige in that. His father is in trade. He is vulgar, untitled, the owner of a few dirty old coalmines,' said Charlotte. 'Most young men have to marry for money, but that one is going to have to find some noble blood. I know his kind. He peers longingly at high society. He is eager to find a way in.'

'I don't care what his father is, and however much you protest, I can tell that you like him, too, Charlotte. You like him a lot! Why, you even preen yourself and rub colour into your cheeks when you know he's coming. You flirt with him. You make sure he's given the biggest piece of cake and that he sits closest to the fire. You enjoy his conversations . . . you can be clever together and you revel in trying to outwit him. So don't be so cruel and two-faced. I love him. And I am still a lady, Charlotte. We might not have Alice's chances but we are both titled ladies.'

'That doesn't count for much.' Charlotte's reply was biting.

'Mr Brennan is a very rich man, and thoroughly respectable,' said Milly.

'You've changed your tune,' snorted Charlotte.

Was it that dull, dreary life, the scandalous books, the never-ending hours, that gave her the need to love Edward?

And then, gradually, as Alice's eighteenth birthday drew nearer, life began to improve. There were new wardrobes for all of them and Henry Brennan gave orders for Sarah's old barouche to be renovated. It was a beautiful affair with dark crimson panels, and even the spokes of the wheels were striped in crimson, black and yellow. The heavy silver harness was decorated with huge rosettes of dark blue and white. And Jasper's livery was new. He looked as he'd looked in the olden days . . . in the good days . . . perched high up on the box in his breeches and silk stockings with a superior smile on his face.

'Will I be going to London?' Alice asked Milly, not sure whether she wanted to go or not. She felt pathetically inadequate for a sudden launching into a society she knew so little about.

'That won't be necessary,' said Milly. And Alice frowned, and didn't understand. And every Sunday they went to church and sat apart from everyone else, behind curtains, in the family pew.

It did not matter. The invitations began to arrive and Milly began to accept them with Henry Brennan's permission. They went to the parties and balls at the local great houses. And at every one, Alice excelled. Alice was queen. She had no need to do anything – Milly said that just the sight of her was enough. She is quite better, thought Milly. The sickness has gone. There was a radiance and gaiety about her and her eyes sparkled, her skin flushed, her golden hair glittered beneath the fabulous lights. Free from restriction, she let herself move to the music and felt happier than she remembered feeling in the whole of her life. It was not the flattery or the handsome young men who queued up to dance with her and became quite savage with each other in the excitement of all of it. It was the feeling of freedom, the fun and the energy and that came from herself.

Men made fools of themseves, proposing on the spot. They gave her flowers, they queued up for dances, they promised her loyalty for lifetimes and sometimes even after death but her eyes rested on no one. They stared far into the distance. She would have liked Edward Brennan to dance with her more often, for she danced well with him and he held her firmly, but Edward's eyes were all for Lucinda . . . and anyway, Alice mustn't . . .

Lucinda, still only fifteen years old, was sometimes allowed to spend a short time downstairs. Edward used to argue with Milly, insisting that she stayed longer. Charlotte, abandoned and all by herself – she even refused to sit beside Milly – glowered, moaned and detested every single minute of it. Milly sat at the side of the room, under the palms, and watched, stiff as a board in corsets and black taffeta and with her eyes fixed on Alice. She need not have worried. Alice had learned her lesson. She dared not give her love again and get punished, like the last time.

All this Alice explained to Luke as they walked through the lively bustle of the London streets. Life swarmed around them . . . children with cold, polished faces, drunken men fighting, a woman scuttling home with a penny loaf under muslin.

Were they real to everyone else or was everyone else, behind their eyes, dreaming their own dreams? Did everyone know they were in love? Could they see it in their faces as they passed by? Alice thought so. She wore a cloak trimmed with swansdown which Luke had bought her and a fur muff to keep out the cold. Luke's collar, shirt-front and cuffs gleamed white, his black and silver cravat was fastened by a large pearl pin and his boots were varnished – his dark, rugged looks caught women's eyes.

She felt safe holding his hand as they went by the luxurious shops that lined Regent Street. The cabs and horse-drawn trams moved at a reckless pace, driven with fury. It was a chaos of cracking whips, hooves, grinding wheels and axles, and the acrid animal odour of horse-sweat, leather and dung. They stopped to linger in a stately square, listening to the beggar on his accordion before moving on and staring up at the houses that stretched in such stuccoed dignity north and south of Oxford Street.

Luke said, 'You should have arrived in a fashionable carriage and put up in one of those great houses behind the railings like that one over there.'

'So should you, if life had treated you differently. Yet I wouldn't have it otherwise. I can't imagine a more romantic way to see London than this.'

Her first sight of London had been from afar; it was half-buried under a pall of smoke which had already blackened the outsides of many of the buildings. So much ancient magnificence mixed with so much squalid poverty . . . it was hard to make sense of it. Lovett's Travelling Theatre put up their canvas at Greenwich, beside the river, alongside the trees which were sprinkled with lanterns and when the wind shifted at night the tiny lights looked like misty glow-worms.

Luke was performing tomorrow night in Drury Lane, starring opposite the haughty Jessica Lamont. No amount of persuasion from Luke could make Alice change her mind; she could not go and watch him. 'I know that to you this makes no sense. I know you cannot understand it. But for me, to watch you is too much to bear.'

'Alice, you can't go on feeling so threatened by situations that exist only in your mind. I've told you, I'm quite unaffected by the words I am forced to say and the embraces we exchange.'

'But the audience?' Alice cuddled up closer. She looked forward to the return journey, safe in the cab and close to Luke in a world of their own – he had tried to persuade her but she had refused to travel on the river. She looked forward to tonight when he would be at the camp all evening and she would share his bed, with Davy in the basket beside them. She wished he did not feel that he had to work, for surely Nathaniel Pettigrew Lovett could find another actor. 'All those women who, by the end of the evening, are in love with you – what about them?'

'How many more times must I tell you? That's not love and I'm not looking for that sort of affair. By the time they step out of the foyer to their carriages in the cold night air, any effect I might have had on them has gone. Surely you see that?'

'I doubt it.' Alice tried to smile but shrugged instead. 'I can't see it your way. I can't abide it!'

'Sooner or later you are going to have to trust me, or this jealousy of yours is going to spoil what we have.'

'Ah!' Alice's eyes blazed with the abruptness of pain. 'You accuse me! Can't you understand that my feelings are proof of my love? Wouldn't you feel threatened and insecure if the circumstances were the other way round? Wouldn't you be begging me to stop?'

'No. It wouldn't matter to me if you spent your day surrounded by men who worshipped you because I trust you.'

Alice turned away. She stared into a dark shop window; the leaded panes were dusty and made the goods for sale tatty and second-hand. And one day would their love turn into that . . . if she didn't respond to him properly, if she didn't behave as she ought? How, she asked herself with a desperation she tried hard to

330

conceal: how must I behave and what must I be, in order to keep Luke's love?

# THIRTY-SEVEN

'It felt as if it was going to thunder. It was hot, sticky and the air was heavy.'

That night, safe in Luke's arms, she tried to complete the story.

'It was before the ball began, before anyone else arrived. We'd spent the afternoon unpacking, we were bathed and dressed and excited. Up until then I had not taken much notice of Florence and Henry Brennan . . . oh, I knew he'd taken over my father's responsibilities and that he was our legal guardian, but all the communication had taken place through Milly. He rarely came near the nursery. He'd never even introduced himself or talked to any of us about our futures. So many things were happening which we didn't understand that his sudden presence in our lives was taken for granted. When he visited he generally stayed in my father's study and saw the servants in there. It was Edward we saw more of.'

Luke lay beside her and stroked her arm. His presence was warm and comforting as she ventured into the darkest of memories where the shadowy past turned fluid.

'If only things had been different,' he said, and nuzzled her neck and made her draw up her shoulders against him, shivering all over. 'We would probably have met, fallen in love and married . . . '

'It couldn't have been like that. I was already promised. Nothing could have broken that legal paper which Henry Brennan had drawn up and which my father had signed.'

Alice pictured it vividly. She distinctly remembered the thin rustle of her voluminous dress as she came down the stairs at Winterbourne followed by Lucinda who wore a delicate, ice-cool blue gown. Lucinda was sweetly cherubic, like a Christmas angel. Charlotte would stay in her room until the last possible moment. Milly had remained behind to be with her, 'Because if I leave her alone for a moment she'll take off her dress and get back into bed and then there'll be all sorts of fussing and I don't know what else to get her up again.'

Milly was edgy tonight; it was probably the thundery weather.

Alice could understand Charlotte's feelings. She had seen her on previous occasions, skulking in corners with that tight-lipped look on her face, repelling all friendship, hostile to every well-meaning approach. Alice would have been happy to help her, to stay at her side for a little while but when she'd done that in the past Charlotte's reaction had been so bitter . . .

'Don't patronize me, Alice. Don't feel sorry for me, either. One day you'll come to realize that all that you are is a pretty woman wrapped in gift paper, a woman with no education, no mind of her own, offering herself as a permanent comfort in some man's bed. And some of us know how well-experienced you already are at that!'

'Charlotte, how can you be so cruel? As if I have a choice in the matter! We will all benefit if I make a good marriage . . . we will all have the chance of a better life. I have a choice to make, too, and I would never agree to spend the rest of my life with a man if he did not attract me . . . if I did not want to find myself in his bed, as you put it!'

Charlotte narrowed her eyes. Her face grew thinner and shrewish. She brandished her words like weapons and they were sharp, lethal and kept well-polished. 'That is not a matter you should be considering at all! Those are feelings you should not have. You do not function correctly as a woman . . . look at your past behaviour – you are nothing but a bold-faced whore underneath all that delicate charm! Oh, if they only knew! If all those young men who swarm around you only knew what went on inside that pretty head of yours! Underneath all that

333

gaiety you are uglier than I am. My ugliness shows
while yours does not. You are lucky, Alice, very lucky.
And no one dares say anything because we are all afraid
of spoiling your blameless reputation. All of us, even
Milly, we all depend on you!'

So Alice left Charlotte alone.

At the bottom of the stairs was a huddle of people.
There was Edward and Henry, Florence, formidable in
an unflattering kind of dark, ivy-leaf green, and a lean,
grey man in a business suit whom she recognized
vaguely and who was introduced to her as Mr Philpott,
the Venton family solicitor. 'And we would be most
grateful if you would accompany us, my dear, into the
study in order to finalize a most important matter.'
Henry rarely addressed her directly like that.

Alice raised her eyebrows at Edward but he just
frowned in reply, as ignorant about all this as she.

The study of Henry Brennan was a brown, dry room
that smelled of ink and leather, nothing like the room
her own father had used as his den. At Venton the light
shone in and there was generally a dog on one of the
sofas and, terrified as Alice had always been at being
summoned down to it, at least the room felt loved and
lived in.

They assembled to a contrived kind of calm and
order, and the men's attitudes matched with the fact
that every single book on the shelves was in place.
Henry and Mr Philpott took the more comfortable
chairs behind the square desk while Alice, Florence
and Edward sat upright before it. What was happening? Did Milly not know about this? Why hadn't Milly
warned her?

'Now.' It was Mr Philpott who spoke first, lowering
his head to stare across the space, spindly spectacles
balanced on an even thinner nose. There were flakes
of skin on his head between the wispy strands of grey
hair. 'On March the twenty second, in the year 1846,
a very important document was drawn up between
Lord Thomas Venton, since demised, and Mr Henry

Brennan at the premises of 28 Carrington Street, May-fair, the Gladwin Club.'

Nobody spoke. Florence's large hands were motionless on her lap. The skin on her fingers overlapped her rings; they took the sheen off the green she wore. Edward shifted and cleared his throat and kept his eyes fixed on the brass inkwell. Henry gazed across the desk, staring at a place on the top of Alice's head and the solicitor rustled the papers. Alice wanted to laugh. She felt a giggle rise in her throat and feared there was nothing she could do to control it. In a minute it would burst from her mouth in a dismaying froth of unforgivable behaviour. She dug her nails so hard into her hands they almost cut through the skin. With enormous difficulty she fought for control and managed to keep it. This could not last long. When it was over she could run into the hall which was decorated with streamers and flowers – she'd already been to peep – and explode behind a curtain.

'In this document,' Mr Philpott went on gravely, and the corners of his mouth were wet while the rest of it was flaky dry, 'which I now lay on the desk before you, a certain arrangement was made. In full reparation for the debts he had accrued and owed, in final payment Lord Thomas Venton, the second party, promised the hand of his eldest daughter, Alice, on attaining the age of eighteen, in marriage to the son of the first party, the aforesaid Henry Brennan of Winterbourne House in the country of Devonshire.' And Mr Philpott let his hands slide over the document in a gesture of final release before sitting back and regarding his audience, pushing up his slipping spectacles as he did so with a rigid index finger.

Florence sighed and looked up suddenly, taking her eyes to her son who was ashen white. He seemed to have failed quite to understand.

'Tell me,' he started. 'Tell me properly what you are trying to say. As I understand it you have arranged my marriage without my knowledge . . . '

335

'As so many marriages are arranged these days my boy, for the convenience of both parties,' explained Mr Philpott, seemingly unaware of the young man's revulsion. 'It is nothing out of the ordinary.'

'And did it not occur to you that it might have been slightly more considerate to inform me of this earlier? I am twenty-two years old! And yet you did not consider it necessary to let me in on this . . . this plot.'

'Don't be silly, Edward,' said Florence, in the tired, monotonous tones that said all argument was futile.

'And what if I refuse?' Edward stuttered. He was up from his chair and leaning across the desk, gripping the edges and staring angrily down at his father. 'What if I absolutely refuse to have any part in this? Am I expected to have no say at all? Don't feelings come into it anywhere?'

'No, Edward, I am afraid they do not,' said Henry, and his gaze was coolly calculating compared to all the heated frenzy of his son. 'Feelings change, position does not . . . if it's guarded wisely. You will carry out my wishes in this just as you have carried out my wishes in other aspects of your life, understanding that I am older and wiser than you and care for nothing else but your welfare and advancement.'

And then Edward Brennan drew himself up to his full height. He made his announcement in a voice that was completely devoid of all feeling. 'This is quite intolerable! I am already in love, Father. I am already promised to someone else. And I would like the opportunity of discussing this with you before we proceed any further.'

'You refer, of course, to your childish infatuation with the youngest Venton girl.' Henry's voice was as calm and matter-of-fact as before. 'Yes, I know all about that, there is no need for discussion because any such liaison is out of the question and I want to make that point quite clear to you now.'

'But . . . Lucinda is of the same family . . . '

'That is not the point. That is not in the agreement.

336

I hold the estates in trust for Alice, and when she attains the age of eighteen, and marries into this family, they will come to you. They do not follow Lucinda. Quite apart from the fact that no such alternative was agreed, this is a legal document, Edward, and cannot possibly be contested.'

'And if I refuse?'

Henry Brennan raised his thin eyebrows and gazed off into the distance. 'If you refuse I shall have no option but to disinherit you.'

'But all you have worked for, Father, your ambitions, your achievements, have been so that they could be built up and carried on! You have made a point of telling me that . . . '

'I am a man of my word, Edward. My honour is more important to me than personal ambition. I would be sorry if you chose to disobey me and followed the road to disaster, who would not be sorry? You are a fine young man. Your mother and I are both proud of you. But this matter is not one of choice, and there is no question of changing it. You will marry Alice Brennan when she reaches the age of eighteen and there are no alternatives.'

Alice no longer wanted to laugh. She could not lift up her head. It had taken her longer than Edward to understand exactly what was happening and the consequences of it, for her, were far more painful because the bargain Thomas had made . . . the use he had made of the daughter he only ever professed to love, tossing her away like that . . . was nothing to do with the protection of the family, their future security and happiness, no, nothing so noble as that. It had been done *in order to satisfy a debt he could not have otherwise paid*. A gambling debt! It was the outrageous behaviour of a profligate wastrel and a fop!

If Neville had lived Thomas would never have been driven to such wild extremes, to such totally irresponsible behaviour. It was because he was left with such an unsatisfactory lot . . . a girl. He had lost his wife and his son and all he had in his house to return to was daughters! How easy it must have been for him to give the eldest away so that he could die, free of debt, and with honour!

Honour?

And then, sitting there being haggled over like that as if she were a piece of wet fish in the market, how was that expected to make her feel? She was fond of Edward . . . as a child she had thought she'd loved Edward in a childish kind of way. What was love? What did she feel towards this good-looking young man who stood there protesting so furiously before her?

And Lucinda? What about Lucinda? Sweet, guileless Lucinda would be broken-hearted. She would expect Edward to behave like a knight in shining armour, to mount his horse and carry her off so they could live happily ever after, but real life was not like that. It was nothing like that. Alice knew, Alice had seen what real life was like. Without his father's wealth Edward would have nothing. The fact that he had welshed on a promise . . . never mind that it was not his own . . . would be quickly reported and he would be frowned upon wherever he went. He had no wealth of his own and how long would their love last if they were forced into a life of poverty? Lucinda's love was strong, but she had not the slightest idea of the harshness of life in the outside world. She could hardly cook . . . she had never cleaned a room in her life. She was without education. There was no way Lucinda could earn her own living.

Oh yes, Alice saw quite plainly how it would be. It was not only herself who was involved in this . . . it was all of them. Even Milly! Had Milly known about this all along and yet said nothing?

Lucinda would have to let Edward go. No matter how much she loved him, she would have to release him. The only way the four of them could secure any kind of future for themselves would be if Alice married Edward as arranged. Henry was right, that stolid man with the unhealthy complexion and the greedy, money eyes, was absolutely right, there was no alternative. Alice had been signed away . . . the Venton estates and the house were owed to Henry Brennan who had taken over all Thomas' debts and was now waiting for his lawful repayment. Without his backing there was no chance that Alice could ever find another man . . . there would be no more balls or parties. She doubted if there would even be food on their plates for many more days! If she refused they would be turned out of house and home. Venton would be sold . . . there would be nothing left.

'So that is how I was told.' She turned to Luke and smiled emptily. The candle flickered in the corner of the caravan, softening the world, even managing to soften her memories. Outside there was silence; just the river whispered, and the breeze in the trees, for the last of the fair-goers had left the park and gone home. 'And that is how Edward came to marry a woman he did not love. But it wasn't as simple as that. After-wards, events happened very quickly and it was all so tragic it is hard for me to remember, let alone talk about.'

Their fingertips touched first. Her head rested on his shoulder while he stroked her face and neck. She kept her eyes closed and her lips were lightly smiling and when he felt for her breast she moaned, 'No, Luke, no, you will think me too willing and I am so afraid of these feelings.'

He pushed down the bedclothes and let his eyes wander slowly over her body before he gently persisted. And when she gasped his name he could tell that she loved his touch and yet feared it, wanted him and yet was afraid. Why? Why did she love him so passively, why was she so afraid? She stroked his hair in a dreamy way and allowed his hands to explore her nakedness.

He whispered, 'I will be very tender,' as he covered her with kisses, and she felt her body stirring almost beyond her control. She savoured the firmness of his limbs, the strength of his chest and the hard muscles in his arms. She tried to squirm away, fearing her own abandonment when she felt his lips move from the wet points of her nipples to the warm, soft place between her thighs, soaked with her own moisture, afraid of what he would think if she allowed herself to let go. She locked her legs together and fought to keep them closed – she did not want him to taste the extent of her own passion – but he parted them with his hands. The restraint she craved was not possible. She moaned in fear and delight, opening herself wide underneath him and laying her arms above her head, stretched out, glowing all over, spread on the pillow like a sacrifice. There were tears in her eyes and when she breathed it was in great draughts of pleasure. She must not stray into these dark realms . . . she pulled him up towards her passionately, abruptly, and drew his mouth down on hers.

To dare to love again . . . and then, still at sea in a wild confusion of agony and ecstasy mixed, she welcomed him inside her. She clung to him with her legs and her arms and cried out when she felt the force of his love which he thrust so deeply into her. As if he was touching her very soul, as if there was no place left which she could deny him. Even in dreams.

# THIRTY-EIGHT

So this was his punishment for his wicked feelings. This was his just reward for falling in love with a woman who was still a child.

Lucinda's reaction to the news of Edward's and Alice's engagement was terrible. And, what was worse, she refused to understand his dilemma; she seemed quite incapable of realizing how impossible it would be for them to live without Henry's patronage. Tearfully, between bouts of desperate sobbing, she begged him, 'And how could I come to live in your house after your marriage to Alice? How could I see you every day, sharing the little, ordinary events – meal-times, walks, picnics – knowing that you belonged to somebody else and that I could never love again? Drying up over the years, turning bitter and ugly like Charlotte, a miserable spinster only fit to read to your children or stitch the lace for your pillowcase? How could I do that, Edward? For me that would be a fate worse than death and now you seem to be saying that that is the future decreed for me. I believed you when you said you loved me, Edward! I thought your meaning of love was my meaning, that we would spend the rest of our lives together, holding hands and supporting each other through the bad times as well as the good. I thought that, for you, it would be impossible to give yourself to anyone else.'

'Lucinda, you are breaking my heart . . .'

She was small like a little bird. Her head hardly reached his shoulder. She clawed at him. The depths of her desolation frightened him, he who found it so hard to show his own feelings because he had been taught very strictly not to. But deep inside he felt just as despairing. She raved on, 'Me – breaking your heart!

Mine is already broken and thrown away, tarnished and worthless. I hear the words you are speaking and yet I cannot believe it is your mouth which forms them. Let me touch you, Edward. Come closer. Hold out your arm, let me feel it so that I know this is really you and not some monster come to me in a nightmare. Tell me this is a dream from which I am going to wake in a minute, crying with relief! Tell me, Edward! Tell me, or go away, leave me alone and let me die!'

Punishment, yes. After that awful time – and the consequences – punishment was all that Edward Brennan craved and punishment was what Charlotte had so astutely given him. Even in bed . . . she doled out an almost total feast of pleasure followed by punishment.

Yes, Edward Brennan felt himself drawing so close to Alice now – Alice, and all the misery she had caused him – that the memories came flooding in. This afternoon he had gone, brandishing his cane, pushing and pressing his way past all-comers, passing through slums of wretched, tumbled houses, ignoring the beggars who tried to waylay him with their insolent eyes, hollow cheeks and infected, matted hair. Ignoring them all and intent on his mission he found the police station and spent an hour there, discussing his plans. He came away satisfied, reassured that it was not only Luke Durant who was going to be apprehended at last, but Alice also, and the baby. Soon it would all be over and he could return home with his newborn son and report his total success. He did not much care about Mrs Toole . . . she would learn a lesson from this. She would learn what happened to employees who were disloyal to their masters, who bit the hand that fed them. Oh yes, Edward would make sure she lost her cottage in the Winterbourne grounds. She would have nowhere to go, but it did not much matter to him where the old woman ended up.

Now Edward and Myers were sitting, stiffly erect and

342

a little apart from everyone else, in a corner of the stuffy upstairs room at the Queen's Arms in Bayswater. Corbett, Duffy and Callow had gone off to explore, no doubt, the seamiest parts of London with a loutish man they had met in the bar who promised them sights that would 'make their eyes pop out of their heads on stalks'.

'It's not my eyes I'm worried about,' replied that coarse man, Corbett, thickening his words with a dirty leer.

Now Edward watched the display before him with guarded eyes. He could not imagine anything more revolting than this. Something about these dissolute women reminded him of Alice. They wanted pleasure from their own bodies. They craved it like the whores that they were – no, they demanded it! And their eyes were proud and brooding as if they enjoyed every moment of their shameful activities.

It was boiling hot in the room and sweat poured unpleasantly off him. Why did nobody think to open one of the windows? He shuddered and looked at Myers, interested to see the doctor's reaction. Myers was not uncomfortable like Edward. That balding, domed-headed man, although he pretended the opposite, appeared to be enjoying himself. Indeed, he was tapping his foot to the sleazy music and his quick little eyes missed nothing. He patted his speckled forehead freely.

Edward leaned forward. 'Riddled with disease, of course,' he muttered.

'Sure to be,' said Myers, not moving his eyes from the leading dancer, a sultry gypsy who rubbed her breasts and pulled at the dark-tipped nipples with awful abandon, gyrating her scantily-clad hips obscenely so that once again Edward shuddered.

And then, if you please, the women began to make love to each other, to caress each other in the most intimate fashion, lovingly and lewdly. Modesty was a word these creatures would never begin to understand. What should be done with such people, thought Edward, as he watched a woman wearing nothing more than a veil and wisp of thin material between her legs, kneel on the floor with her great breasts swaying, her back to the audience – nothing more than a beast, or a cow to be serviced – while another, near-naked, mounted and rode her like a stallion! Her buttocks were rounded and firm, the lips of her sex red and swollen. Had they been painted? Surely not! Edward could hardly bear it. He looked away. No wonder she wanted to cover her face!

These creatures were a world away from Edward's idea of a perfect woman.

Lucinda, pure, sweet and modest, was a gentle dream child, a fairy girl to Edward. More of a little girl than a woman, needy of his protection against the slings and arrows of the wicked world. And yet with one cruel blow she had been taken away from him and he had been presented with the far more alarming figure of Alice . . . she with the knowing eyes and the wildness underneath that the young man feared and did not understand. It was in her eyes, it was in her walk, and it was there, veiled in modesty, beneath those demure glances. Afraid of her in a complicated way, he had always stayed slightly aloof from Alice. He was friendly, of course, polite – but he kept his distance. As for Charlotte, he had felt sorry for her! Edward smiled when he thought about that, but quickly wiped the smile off his face when he saw Myers looking at him. Yes, he frowned, at least poor Charlotte had been no threat to him in that way.

That night, when the ball was over, Lucinda had come to him. Her feet were bare and she wore a simple white cotton nightgown . . . she looked just the same as he remembered her when she was almost eight years old on that first Christmas, there in the nursery with that dragon woman, Mrs Toole. Over the years Edward had watched her grow with satisfaction, for she had never really changed. Her eyes were the same innocent blue, clear as a summer sky, and her lips were the full-budded lips of a child, her smile a sweet and natural one. Her hair was curly and she did not bother with sophisticated styles. She was still young . . . only fifteen, and their romance had been one of secret whisperings, the giving of a rose, the exchanging of locks of hair, the shy holding of hands in the garden.

After being told the devastating news, after her initial outcry, Lucinda had fled upstairs and had not attended the ball. All evening Edward had worried, wondering whether to go in search of her, or would it be kinder to leave her for a while to weep on her own? He was thrust by expectations into the arms of Alice, the most popular, sought-after partner in the ballroom. And Alice? She had never appeared to care about any particular dancing partner. She was happy just so long as she could dance, just so long as she was allowed to move to the music. There was a sadness about her tonight, though. She felt limp, as distressed as he. They talked as they danced, about Lucinda.

'In the end she must get over it,' said Edward. It was a statement and yet he was wanting Alice's opinion.

'I don't think she will.'

'She is very young . . .'

Alice answered, and her dress shimmered with gold lights as it swung backwards and forwards about her ankles, 'She is young, but she loves you, Edward.'

'What are we to do?' Edward's eyes were pleading. 'How can we help her?'

'There is nothing we can do. We have to obey them – what other way is there?'

'You think that I should have flown in the face of my father and refused, outright, to our match?'

'No, I don't see how you could have done that. Even for Lucinda, eventually that decision would have been

345

the most unkind.'

'Then what can I say to her? How can we heal her?'

'They say that time does that, but in Lucinda's case I don't know . . .' and Alice's words trailed off into the sadness of the music.

'And you?' Edward asked her. He looked very fine in his dark evening dress, his brown wavy hair just a fraction too long, his eyes sad and brooding. 'Is it too cruel to ask how you feel about this? Is it too soon?'

'I have been brought up never to question why, to submit, to be obedient, to honour the wishes of my parents . . .'

She was making a valiant attempt to cover her misery. When she smiled up at him there were no lights in her eyes. He said, 'I want to know the truth of this, Alice. If we are to be wed and I am to follow my father's directives, I have to know whether you are as reluctant as I.'

And then he was able to watch the mask drop over her face as she replied, 'There is nothing else we can do but obey them. You do not repel me, Edward, quite the contrary. I have always felt an attraction for you, since the very first time we met. Our marriage would not be, for me, the end of my world. I would be prepared to act as a good wife, to obey all my vows.' She looked him straight in the eye. 'And I think I could grow to love you.'

Edward was shocked. Her directness and her willingness to adjust to the situation so meekly frightened him. What answer had he wanted? Had he hoped she might refuse to comply so that he could go to his father in all honesty and tell him the arrangement could not be fulfilled, not because of his own stubborn nature, but because of hers? Had he hoped she might not be astute enough to know there were no alternatives? He looked down at her; for the first time he allowed the sensations of touching her to come through and reach him. She was perfection in his arms, beautiful, warm,

346

sensuous, responsive to his own body and she smelled sweetly of roses. But the thought of having to do to her what he would have to do if she was his wife . . . this thought not only terrified him, it repelled him!

But his voice was calm and even when he said, 'So we are going to have to convince Lucinda that the marriage will take place in spite of her pleadings.'

Once again Alice lifted her head and looked at him directly, and there was pain in her eyes when she answered, 'I am afraid that we are.'

Was he so weak that he had hoped to find an ally? Had he hoped that between them, if they were strong enough, they might have been able to fight the decision he did not feel able to fight on his own? Whatever, if this was Alice's attitude there was no chance of that now.

Full of tortured despair, and with these thoughts gnawing unpleasantly in his head he bowed out of the next dance – there was no shortage of young men to take his place – and found himself standing next to Charlotte. He would have ignored her . . . he wanted a chance to be by himself and think for a while before he went to find Lucinda, but that small, thin woman dressed in grey rose from the little sofa and came to stand beside the marble pillar that Edward was half-hiding behind. He feared Charlotte. He feared her caustic tongue. Her opinion was the last one in the world that he wanted to hear and yet it would seem, by her direct approach and the stern look on her face that she was determined to give it.

'They are to make the formal announcement in a minute,' said Charlotte unnecessarily.

Edward passed his hand across his eyes. He could endure no more of this. He knew about the announcement. He and Alice would have to stand together in front of the hundreds of guests here tonight and feign great pleasure. He did not know if he was up to it. He did not answer Charlotte's observation but nodded his head and continued to lean limply against the pillar.

'So Alice, at last, has got her way.'

Had he heard correctly? Edward frowned. He searched the girl's face for lies but her expression was quite open; her comment had not been viciously spoken, just terribly soft and sincere.

'Alice has been forced to accept the situation out of necessity, as I have,' he replied, carefully making sure nobody else could hear. 'It is unwelcome for both of us.'

'Lucinda will not give you up.'

Edward sighed heavily. 'Lucinda will have no choice. She is in the same unpleasant position as we all are.'

'It will not be like that. Lucinda might look like a child, speak like a child, even act like a child, but Lucinda has the feelings of a woman. She will never let you go.'

'Then she does not know the grim determination of my father. She cannot know how appalling the alternatives are. She cannot have realized that, unless this marriage takes place, she . . . all three of you, will be destitute. What sort of love would mine be if I allowed these things to happen to her? What sort of protection would I be giving to Lucinda, then? Alice understands that as well as I do. This is no easier for me, Charlotte, than it is for Lucinda. I feel the same agony inside . . . but I recognize the bleak facts. However emotional we might feel, however much we know that our lives have been shattered and will never be the same again . . . it is not possible to deny the truths of this matter. It would be foolish of us, cruelly irresponsible to do so. Neither of us have the weapons with which to fight against it.'

'And yet Alice is meekly compliant . . . she feels for poor Lucinda and yet she is prepared to do the decent thing. Is that what she was confiding to you so sweetly just a moment ago when she danced in your arms?'

Something in Charlotte's tone made him glance at

her sharply. What did she mean, what was she trying to say?

There was no time for further conversation for at that moment the orchestra paused, Henry Brennan took the floor, closely followed by his wife and, amidst all the flowers and the streamers the awesome announcement was proudly made. The guests clapped and smiled, said what a wonderful couple they made in a hundred different, indulgent ways. Edward stood stiffly beside Alice. Both of them tried to smile but his face felt tight as a death mask and he wondered if this was as hard for Alice – but when he looked down she gave nothing away. With his eyes he searched for Charlotte but she was no longer there behind the pillar in that same corner. And he thought that she must have retired from the room and gone upstairs to be with Lucinda.

Later Edward had gone to search for Lucinda. Mrs Toole guarded her bedroom door and told him she would not see him. He argued. She would not give way. Desolate, he retired to his room, ready to face a sleepless night and it was just one hour later that Lucinda came to his door. He let her in, with no knowledge of how he would comfort her but determined to try. He wanted comforting, too. He was as needy as she, after all, Lucinda was his life and a future without her was almost more than he could bear. But Edward, being a man, was forced to be brave.

'I have thought it all out,' she told him as she slipped into the room before him and went to stand in front of the curtain like a bewildered little ghost all in white. There was a look of bright determination on her face as if she was relaying a speech she had been rehearsing all evening. This firm voice did not sound like Lucinda's and he feared the threatened hysteria under the steeliness of her tone. 'Milly has finally convinced me. She has spent all night trying to comfort me and I am forced to face the facts. However,' and she stood very straight, her eyes red from crying and her face as white as her gown, 'I have decided that, when you are mar-

349

ried and I come to live in this house with my sisters, I will give you my body at nights so that you are not forced to take your pleasures with a woman you cannot love. I will be available for you . . . we will be lovers, Edward, in the true sense of the word. You might belong to another woman on paper, but your body and your soul will belong to me.'

He strode across the room and gripped her by the arms, shocked beyond belief by her words. 'Your body?' And he spat the words with accusation, as if she had slapped his face, or assaulted him so savagely she had to be restrained. He gripped her arms so hard he hurt her and, staggering back, she tried to throw him off.

'What do you mean . . . your body?' She was his little girl, pure, innocent . . .

She thrust out her small chest, balanced herself sturdily on her bare feet when he released her so suddenly. 'I am a woman. I have much to offer you, my darling. And tonight I am prepared to show you all that I am and all that I have so you can make the decision which will take the pain out of most of this. I will never be able to bear your children openly, I will never be able to walk by your side. But at night, when it's dark, when the curtains are drawn and the wind is blowing outside, at night we will belong to each other . . . our love will be a wonderful, secret thing of the night.'

He watched with awful fascination as she began to peel the gown from her shoulders. As she let it fall to the floor, the grey light of the window rested on her nakedness. He saw her breasts, fully formed . . . neat, tilted towards him like two rounded hills. Reluctantly, flushing with shame, he let his eyes follow the shape of her down past the narrow circle of her waist, down round the smoothness of her spreading hips to the small, golden triangle between her legs. Right there, before his eyes, she stepped out of the small pool of white cotton like a nymph rising from a white linen waterfall and she walked towards the bed. She drew back the curtains. She climbed upon it. The small lantern above flickered wickedly over her wantonness as she arrayed herself languidly there, legs apart, arms stretched out, and on her face was the shameless smile of the harlot, the wanton smirk of the whore.

What was this? Where was the precious innocence he had so ardently loved? What had happened to his little girl, to his special child? Edward wanted to scream. He wanted to throw back his head and roar like a wild beast in his anguish. He no longer had a care for her feelings, for her pain . . . for if pain could drive a woman to this . . . then he had never known her. He had been in love with an image and now that image was dead. It was futile. Everything he had ever done, everything he could ever be, was futile. Hopeless.

'Get out!' He threw his words back at her, over his shoulder, because he could no longer face her.

'Edward!' she pleaded in a voice that was back to her own . . . a childish voice, full of need, wanting reassurance.

He would not give it. She was vile! He said again, very coldly, 'Get out, before I move over there and throw you out.'

She pleaded, 'You cannot do this to me. This is the cruellest thing . . .'

He could hear her nervous approach. He could hear the rise and fall of the breath in her chest. He turned away. He crossed his arms against her. He closed his eyes against the sight and the sound and the smell of her.

She gave a little sob, pleading, 'You are doing this deliberately in order to make it easier for me, aren't you, Edward? In your mind you believe you are being cruel in order to be kind. Tell me this is so. Tell me. You have no need to deny your desire for me . . . perhaps I was a little too hasty, perhaps I assumed too much. My dear . . . won't you look at me?'

And he knew she was covering her body again, hastily, while she spoke.

351

'Get out. I never want to have you in my sight again.'

'Edward, we must talk. We cannot part like this. I thought I had borne all that there was to bear, but this is too hard for me. I am not strong enough for this. Please! Please!'

'You ought to have thought about that before you came here tonight with your vile suggestions . . .'

She hesitated, stammered slightly when she replied very softly, 'I did not think the offer of my body would strike you as vile.'

The pathos of her own twisted thoughts sickened him. To think that he had considered her sweet and pure . . . the perfect woman . . . to think that he could have been so fooled by this cheating, deceitful creature all garbed in white. Nausea rose in his throat. The palms of his hands were soaked in sweat.

'Go! Now! Before I turn round and catch sight of you. I warn you, Lucinda, I would not be responsible for my own actions.'

Without another word, softly she went. He felt the draught at his ankles, he heard the quiet closing of the door. And it was a good ten minutes before Edward Brennan felt loose enough to unlock his tight body and turn round. And then he strode to the bed and ripped off the coverlet, making sure he folded it inwards and got no taint of her on his hands. He wept as he went about his work, tears of fury and helplessness. And everything was red in his head, red and raw and bleeding inside, in the crazy place behind his eyes.

And then, when he had screwed up the cover and thrust it into the bottom of his wardrobe he flung himself down on his clean bed and wept as he had not wept since he was a child and six years old. The time when Florence had caught him touching his own body in the sweet, warm darkness, and had come like a shadow with a knife to inflict the wound, she warned him, 'Will put a stop to this nasty, disgusting habit of yours before you drive yourself pocked and blind and everyone in the world will know of your filthy, bestial habit.'

She had not returned with the knife. But he'd dreamed she had. And every night after that he had lain awake for hours, expecting it, feeling the cold, cruel cut of it, weeping from the terror of it.

# THIRTY-NINE

Punishment. Oh yes. Vile. And now the gypsy women were mingling with the audience and nothing was decent, nothing was good. But they were here with their parts to play and Myers reminded him of it.

'Are you ill, Mr Brennan? Would you rather retire and leave the rest of this unpleasant business to me?'

'No, no,' he assured the doctor, pulling himself together. 'Somehow we must begin a conversation with one of these women, inform them of who we are and of our intentions to depart from London tomorrow.'

Myers cast wary eyes about him. 'I don't think many folks here are interested in conversations just now,' he muttered. 'It seems to be a time for action . . . '

'Offer one of the women a drink,' said Edward harshly. 'I know their sort. They'd never turn down a free drink.'

Myers was out of his depth. Nevertheless, the next time the little blonde Frenchwoman, all but naked, passed the place where they sat, her bright eyes very alive and interested, he beckoned her over politely. 'My friend and I wondered if you would care to join us.' And Myers pulled up a chair.

'Are you two not enjoying the performance?' she asked playfully, having introduced herself as Lottie, having watched, with great interest, Edward wince. She was like an expensive, exotic kitten, with her eyes very round and blue staring out from the honey-blonde hair that fringed her face. There was a tiny blue bow fastened to the top of it. Myers called for a glass and poured the ruby red wine. He noticed his hand was trembling. He concentrated on steadying it while he listened to her. 'Is there something you would have preferred? I am sure there is one of us who could surely accommodate you. After all, my companions and I, we do not like to leave unsatisfied customers.'

'It was all very nice, very pleasurable, my dear,' said Myers a little aloofly as he sat back and pressed his glass to his lips.

Lottie shook her head and leaned towards them coyly. 'Surely this is not all you require.' Myers felt her body coming closer . . . if he raised his hand but a few inches it would stroke her skin.

'We are here only briefly, for tomorrow we have a long journey to make.'

'Oh?' The French girl began to lose interest. She started staring around in the smoky gloom, eager to find a group of more ardent customers.

'Just to spend some time with you, just to have you sitting so close, that is enough to satisfy me,' said Myers, lying through his teeth and wishing that Edward Brennan was not here, cursing the fact that he had not been sent to carry out this mission on his own. There was, after all, no reason why they shouldn't carry out their plan and enjoy themselves at the same time. And this girl would be more than happy to oblige them. Myers could see that . . . it was plain in the hot glow that came off her skin, in the teasing sparkle in her eye. At the other tables the customers were doing far better. They each shared a woman or two, or three, passing her round from one knee to another after taking the time to savour her charms, to argue over her best points, to point out and comment and display . . . and all the while the wine flowed and the musicians played on and the atmosphere grew warmer and Myers grew more uncomfortable. Damn his companion and his high-handed, lofty sense of morality, his stupid games. Blast him! Was fun a word he had never heard of ?

'We have been travelling for three weeks,' moaned Edward, suddenly deciding he had better take part or the one girl they had managed to attract would desert them. 'We have failed in our quest and now, defeated, we have decided to give up.'

'Quest?' The girl let her eyes open wide. She licked

her lips. 'That sounds interesting. There are not so many men romantic enough to journey on quests these days. Was it a romantic one? Do tell me!'

Her accent made her voice attractive. She purred, although she was still looking round. She was playing this conversation game in order to be polite and Myers, sensing this and growing more and more frustrated as the minutes went by, hurried on. 'Our quest, I'm afraid, has been a sad one with little romance about it. My friend has been searching for his wife who is ill and needs attention. I am her physician. And, unfortunately, we were given false information. We believed that the lady in question had been taken in by a group of travelling players. We have followed the troupe all the way from Devonshire only to find we were mistaken.'

'Oh? That is surely very sad.' Lottie curled up her body and pouted. Edward stared at her hard but there was no way of knowing what she knew. She sipped her wine and fluttered her long eyelashes at her captive audience. 'But in that case, under these terrible circumstances, why do you not seek comfort by making the most of the pleasures offered here tonight. What a cold, lonely journey home. Oh, I can hardly bear to think of it. To me it seems sadder still to think that you cannot even allow yourselves to forget for a while, comforted by a little too much red wine perhaps and succoured in the arms of a pretty woman.' And without saying another word the woman got up and arranged herself on Myers' knee with a comfortable, cat-like motion, circling his neck with one arm while she held her glass in her free hand. She crossed her legs and allowed her feet to rest on Edward's knee. 'There,' she crooned, bringing her painted lips to Myers' ear, 'that feels better already, doesn't it, my little fat man?'

Myers, puce-faced, was not able to argue, nor did he want to. He did not know what to do with his hands. If he moved them even slightly to one side or the other they brushed some part of the lady that it was unseemly to brush. Edward's eyes were fixed firmly on him. My

God, thought Myers to himself, trying to cope with an uncomfortable erection, I cannot stand much more of this.

And then, like a miracle, Edward got up, and so violently abrupt was his action he almost tipped up his chair. He held his head high and his eyes were cold when he said to Myers, 'I must go. I can stay here no longer. I can see that you, Myers, are quite happy to remain, but I need my bed. It is far too hot in here and I have to go and find some fresh air.'

Guiltily Myers began to rise, but the French girl clung like a limpet and anyway, why shouldn't he stay? They had done what they had set out to do, they had put across the false message. There was no doubt that it had been received and understood. And just because the fine Mr Brennan was satisfied with that, it did not mean to say that Myers had to follow him out. My God . . . Myers might be dependent on the man but he wasn't owned by him, was he? So Myers allowed himself to sink back into pure enjoyment, and, such was the Doctor's great need that he managed to watch Edward's erect back as he stalked from the room with absolutely no sense of shame.

Edward went to his room, flung open the window and his lungs gasped for air. It was not good air but city air, mixed with horse-sweat and animal dung, flecked with the grit of ironworks and sooty chimneys. And yet he stood there and gulped it down as if breathing normally would choke him, revelling in the fact that at last he was alone.

Were all women the same . . . basically, underneath the modest blushes, were they all the same? No, he knew that was not true. For he had found one who was not like that, who had no desires of her own other than to accommodate his. Charlotte was always disapproving of his needs and yet, for his sake, because she loved him, she allowed him. But after that, always after that, the punishment would follow, and that, dear God,

357

made everything all right.

He couldn't have borne any of it without her, without her strength and her comfort when they had come to tell him in the early morning, 'Lucinda, my dear boy, Lucinda has been found drowned in the lake. You must not blame yourself, Edward . . . ' His mother was speaking, his mother had come to tell him the terrible news and he remembered how he had studied her face with such meticulous care, how every detail of the room he was in suddenly had seemed so important, even the way the second hand moved on the clock, hardly at all . . . and the light coming in through the window that, such a short time ago, Lucinda had stood before. Warm. Alive. His.

'Now, Edward, I know how much of a shock this must be to you,' Florence went on, easing her large body down on the edge of his bed so that the covers slipped towards her. 'And I know that, if you decide to be foolish about this, you are going to tell yourself all sorts of silly things. But a girl who would do a thing like that was never going to be any good to you . . . to anyone. Someone as weak and feeble-minded . . . '

'Stop a moment, Mother. A thing like this? You said that she did "a thing like this". What does that mean, Mother? What did Lucinda do?'

'My darling, Mrs Toole hadn't seen her all night. She must have decided to wreak her revenge on all of us . . . because remember, Edward, suicide is a very vengeful thing for anyone to do . . . and she must have walked out into the water until, quite simply, it closed over the top of her head.'

Oh, dear God, no! Oh, oh . . . someone take the pain away. Oh God, don't let me hear any more, he screamed silently as the tedious voice of his mother droned on.

He threw off his covers, pushing Florence Brennan off the bed so that she half-slipped down on to the floor and he rushed out, clad only in his nightshirt, down to the shore of the lake. Lucinda wasn't there. They must

358

have wrapped her up and taken her indoors. But her spirit . . . it was still there, in the willowy cool of the morning, in the sweep of the still, silver surface that looked so thick you thought you could walk on it without it giving way. The bull-rushes stood like soft sentinels, gazing at what he had done and nodding in judgement and the wisp of mist that covered the water was like a tired eye closing on pain.

He stretched out his arms, wanting to follow his love and yet knowing he was unworthy. The lake was too pure to take him. The water lilies trembled on the surface making their own lisping sounds, and the punt he had used as a child was broken up – a little wooden shape crouched beside the boat-house – still held there by a thin coil of rope, unable to escape from childhood as he was.

He knelt there, wrapped for comfort in his own arms. But there was no strength in them now. His tears flowed – too late. Blame himself . . . blame himself . . . *of course he must blame himself* . . . who the hell else was there to blame? He cried out to God in his agony. Surely Lucinda was not so far away already that she could not hear him?

And then . . . Charlotte. What was she doing there? Had she been watching for him? Had she known that he would come? He was hardly aware of her presence . . . until she spoke. And it did not seem that she was speaking to him, but her voice just went very naturally out into the cool of the morning, as untouched by all this, as unmoved as all this nature was.

'May God forgive her,' she said.

Slowly Edward turned, too tortured to reply but he must defend Lucinda; if they were the last and only words he would ever speak in his life he must speak them.

'May God forgive me,' he sobbed to himself. 'Lucinda is not to blame for the extent of her despair.'

'I was not referring to Lucinda,' said Charlotte shortly. 'May God forgive Alice, is perhaps what I ought to have said.'

'Alice?' Who was Alice? What had anyone else to do with this? Everything around him was blurred by tears. The sky mixed with the water and the earth shimmered like an endless sea, on and on towards a horizon which no longer existed. The world had lost all sense.

'This is Alice's work, my dear Edward, and nothing to do with you. Nothing you said or did could have prevented it. You either believe me or you do not. I care not a jot either way. But I will always be here for you, to hold you, to comfort you, or just to listen to you if you want me. And I am easy to find.'

And with that, no emotion, no grief, no blame, Charlotte had taken one long, last look at the sombre lake of death, and then, with her head held high, she had turned and walked away.

# FORTY

With his trunk packed on the bed behind him, Edward sat beside the window at the small desk and wrote his last letter to Charlotte. It was not a letter which explored feelings or emotions, it was a factual letter accounting for his actions, his whereabouts, telling about the reaction of the police and the plans he had made at the police station. Naturally he did not mention the evening's unsettling events in the back room of the tavern, or Myers' disgraceful behaviour. The important part was that the trap had been laid. The adversaries' guard would be lowered. He and Myers had achieved that much tonight.

'*So tomorrow morning we leave this tavern and put up in the suburbs, and the day after that I will be bringing the child home,*' he wrote, and his writing was neat and clear. '*And this time, Charlotte my dear, I cannot see what can possibly go wrong. Give my love to Kate and Laura . . .* ' and his hand hovered above the paper when he thought about Nicholas. He could not think what to put, or even if he ought to refer to the boy at all.

He lifted his head and stared tiredly out into the darkness of the London night and pictured Charlotte receiving the letter. She would slit the envelope neatly with a thin paper-knife. She would hold one hand to her brow, smoothing it slightly while she scanned his words with quick eyes. He needed to write to her. He needed, always, in some way to be joined to her.

Charlotte had offered him healing. A balm for a wound so painful that Edward could not endure it. For this wound was so steeped in the pus of guilt, so flooded by the sour blood of shame that, for some time after

Lucinda's death, he could not be on his own with it. And his mother, Florence, set her firm face determinedly against him, and his father smoothed over the whole event as easily and as superficially as that cold, wet surface had closed over the deed itself.

Milly, normally so available for comfort, was closed against everyone, smothered by her own grief and struggling to deal with her own share of the blame. 'I knew poor Lucinda would be badly upset. I knew it would take her time to recover. But never, dear God never, not in my wildest dreams did I ever imagine she would go this far!' she wailed. She walked around the house shaking her head and exchanging one soaked handkerchief for another. Her wide face was contorted with agony, she aged ten years overnight and, for the first time in her life, she lost control of her hair. To see that thick, lustrous mass which was now streaked with threads of grey, straggling down in untidy hanks, still with its pins scattered in it, was more telling than any expression her ravaged face could ever wear. 'She was not that kind of person! Lucinda was such a hopeful, happy child! She would never do a thing like that.' She repeated her words over and over again as if by doing so she could bring Lucinda back to life, and round and round she went in the circle of her own tortured thoughts, unable to escape from the disbelief of it all. 'I blame myself,' concluded Milly.

Alice's reaction was harder to define. She was very quiet and pale but her eyes were dry and her face was set . . . into something resembling a sad smile. But when Edward asked her, her reactions were similar to Milly's. She told him, 'Edward, it isn't your fault. It's nobody's fault. I can't understand how anyone like Lucinda . . . you can't have these feelings, you see . . . you mustn't have them and this is the kind of thing that happens when . . . ' And then, with enormous effort she breathed deeply and said, 'You never know someone. You only think you know them but you don't. I wish I

362

had known, oh dear God I wish I had known, because I might have been able to do something.'

'Yes. We could have done something,' said Edward, tortured beyond all endurance.

'It does feel like that,' said Alice quietly. 'But if anyone could have said anything to help it would have been Milly, and Lucinda spent the whole evening with Milly. Milly says she thinks she felt better before she left her room, saying that she was going for a walk. And it's just incredible to think that my sister must have known, even then, what she was going to do.'

'I don't know how to bear this,' sobbed Edward, passing his hand across his eyes. 'I just don't know how to . . . I loved her, you know. I truly loved her.'

Alice did not answer, but nodded as she turned away, drawn, suffering. She did not heal him. No amount of talking could heal him or take away the memories of those dark moments when, he was convinced, his cruel rejection had sent Lucinda to her death.

The only real succour to be found came from Charlotte and her cold commonsense. She, it would seem, was coping with her own grief and was consequently able to stretch out and help him heal his, unlike his mother who seemed annoyed by the depths of his reaction as if she thought he was merely pretending and could pull himself out of it, pull himself together somehow and get on with the business of life.

'I am always here when you need me,' Charlotte repeated. And, astonishingly, she was. He began to wonder why he had thought of her as cold. He brooded over the matter and came to his conclusion quite easily. She was not cold, just shy, and used to being ignored because of her homeliness and her unease in company. And she was not the ugly woman he had so glibly assumed her to be. How cruel men can be to plain women, he thought to himself.

Edward took to walking, to flinging himself out of the front door and setting off down the drive with his coat half-off, half-on, to where he did not know or care. But, no matter how fast he walked, alone with his thoughts, all he found was self-torture. Often he would pass the lake and pause there, and stare at it, imagining the sweet girl he knew standing there on the edge, imagining himself there, in time to save her. The lake was deep. The slippery sides dropped away suddenly. There was a small island in the middle of it to which he had once encouraged Lucinda to swim; it was a favourite swimming place where guests had been swimming earlier on the night . . . so she knew the depths of the lake. Her death could have been no accident. And Lucinda was a good swimmer. She'd had no need to die.

He sat glumly beside it to think, allowing the thousand things he would like to say to Lucinda to burst through his head . . . passionate, heroic things . . . like in the old days when he had believed they could always be children together sharing an innocent dream . . . not clouded, not besmirched with unclean thoughts and the sour taint of sex.

He was glad when he felt Charlotte come to sit beside him. For a long while they said nothing, but he knew she was there for him, and he felt absurdly grateful for that. Something in the way she looked at him gave him the strangest feeling that she alone might understand what had passed between them that last night, and that she alone would not criticize or hold him to blame for his feelings. Plain, unfeminine Charlotte, so totally uninterested in men, while not sharing his unnatural attitudes, might understand them.

Staring hard at his hands he said, 'Charlotte, I don't know what I'd have done during these past weeks if I hadn't had you beside me for support. I value that. I might find it hard to show, I do find it difficult to express my feelings and that was part of the problem . . . I value your help and support more than I can say. You've been a great comfort to me at a time when I

364

have never felt so utterly desolate and alone.'

And then she started accompanying him on his walks. They went miles, sometimes speaking, sometimes not, but he was always so totally comfortable in her presence, knowing that she wouldn't expect him to flirt with her, or gratify her with little compliments, or use the nonsense conversation he had always associated with women. And slowly he began to think how much easier it would be if she, Charlotte, was the eldest Venton girl, that it was she he must marry . . . not the terrifying, puzzling confusion that was the beautiful, fragile Alice, who would take so much appeasing and satisfying and who would be the object of every other man's eye, the object of envy, the symbol of success, the woman every man, *the woman every normal man wanted*.

They sat on a high hill and down below them was a long strip of green meadow which cooled the eye and rested the mind. For as far as he could see, right off into the far distance, this land belonged to his father and would be his one day and yet he had done nothing, nothing at all to merit it. The cackle of rooks came from the copse above them. A light breeze blew and ruffled his hair like fingers running through the locks of a child. He shivered, and then, with an enormous sense of relief mixed with a terrible shame, he found that he could not staunch the tears. He turned as if to get up and leave but she caught hold of his hand. And then he buried his face in her skirts and sobbed like a child, 'Sometimes . . . sometimes, Charlotte, I feel I am not a man . . . and it was that that caused Lucinda's death.' She stroked his hair with a cool hand and she smelled of safety, like his mother. She smelled of Parma violets.

Eventually she said, 'But Edward, you are going to have to be very, very strong.'

'Charlotte, I don't understand.'

She smiled away into the distance. 'I think you do,

Edward. I think you understand much more than you have ever allowed yourself to consciously recognize.'

He felt like a fool, and he didn't want to destroy the newly- found image that this serious, delicate, wise person had bestowed on him, she who was always so sparing with her compliments. So he kept quiet, but joined her in her stare instead, feeling better than he'd felt since before the terrible tragedy of Lucinda had occurred. From high up here, with Charlotte so stoic beside him, he could pretend that the horror was merely a dream and he and she, so close together like this, more like twin gods looking down on it . . . not part of it . . . not involved in it . . . certainly not *the cause of it.*

Charlotte said, 'Soon you must marry Alice.'

Edward shifted, disconcerted to hear Charlotte pursuing the subject he was so unhappy with. She should have known to keep off it. Didn't she sense his unease? He felt a momentary pang of disappointment, as though suddenly, her wisdom had failed him. But then she went on and his attention was gripped by her words. 'There are very important reasons why you must marry Alice. To refuse would be to invite the biggest scandal that society has seen for years. A scandal in which the reputations of both our families would be ruined.'

'Charlotte, I'm sorry, but I don't understand.'

'Then you're not the man I thought you were and I don't know how to tell you.'

He was deeply distressed that Charlotte should be looking at him with that veiled contempt in her eyes. They had been so close just a moment ago. He felt he had never been so close to a human being before – to a woman. Charlotte's voice was so soft he was in danger of missing the words when she went on to say, 'Alice is very sick, Edward. She is smitten with a sickness that ran in our family many generations ago and has returned with no mercy to afflict her, as the first-born of the Ventons.'

'What kind of sickness?' But he felt ridiculous asking.

'Edward, I have to tell you that Alice is insane.'

He started to smile. He shook his head. He stared hard at Charlotte letting his mouth drop open. This could not be a joke, for she was the last woman on earth to joke on any subject . . . let alone one of this nature. He withdrew his hand from hers and took it nervously to his ear, tugging stupidly at it, and then he put his head down and ran his hands through his hair. He looked up and smiled vacantly at her again.

'Are you seriously telling me that you have not recognized any of the signs?' she asked him.

He shook his head, miserably unable to answer and gazed off into the distance again. And then he asked her, 'Who knows about this?'

'I think that my mother knew. And my father. I think that that was the awful revenge that he wreaked upon yours.'

'But I always believed . . . '

'Marriage to his daughter . . . yes, position, acceptance, noble blood, but along with that attractive package came madness. Hidden. Unseen. Oh yes, but it's there and my father, he knew. And he made a fool of your own father in the process.'

'And Mrs Toole?'

'Mrs Toole is a simple soul and chooses to deny it, but she knows. Oh yes, she knows. She has set herself up as Alice's protector. I can remember the countless times that the truth would have come out except for the devious protection granted to Alice by the misguided Mrs Toole. Time after time, as children, Lucinda and I were blamed and punished for childish crimes we had not committed, hauled before our father for behaviour which was blamed on us. Even he, knowing what he knew, preferred to pretend otherwise. You were there, Edward, when she gave away Abernathy her cat. But you were not there in the morning when he was found dead, strangled in the night, nor did you

367

see her almost total lack of reaction to the event while Lucinda and I were broken-hearted. She can't bear to lose love you see, my dear, or anything or anyone whom she thinks she loves. And when Neville was born Mrs Toole was too confident. She lowered her guard for an instant and the child was smothered with its own pillow . . . '

Edward, his heart pounding now, and breathless, tried to interrupt. 'Surely you can't be suggesting! Now wait just a minute, Charlotte!'

But Charlotte's smile was cool and resigned. 'Oh, it was covered up. It wouldn't do, would it, for the truth to be known? After all, we were quite dependent on Alice's future for our own. How could a family such as ours possibly admit to madness? Think of the shame! Think of the scandal! And is it any wonder that my father, after that terrible event, gave away his daughter so effortlessly and was even glad to take his own life, *knowing what he knew*. How could he, a man of honour, do otherwise?'

Pounding away in Edward's brain, pulsing there in his head like a thing alive was only one question. He asked it hoarsely. 'Lucinda?'

Charlotte nodded. 'So you see, you had nothing at all to blame yourself for, my dear. Which is exactly what I have been trying to tell you all this time.'

'But how could she have done that?'

'Very simply, I assure you. There is enormous strength when madness strikes, Edward. She would have been offering company and comfort. She would have been suggesting ways to help ease the pain. It was a hot summer night, almost airless if I remember. What more natural suggestion could she make than a swim in the lake? Others had been swimming only moments before. And Lucinda, so innocent, so wounded, so needing diversions of any kind, would have happily obliged.'

'They swam out together?'

'They were probably making for the island when Alice decided to act. She has always secretly loved you, Edward, and not only you, oh no, there have been others. And Lucinda was telling her, was blithely telling everyone, that she wouldn't let you go. No matter what happened, she wouldn't let you go. Alice had to make sure. That's all.'

Edward slapped his forehead with the palm of his hand. He reeled with confusion. 'Alice has killed three times! I find this incredibly hard to take in, Charlotte. She has killed three times and yet no one has found out?'

'Oh, she's cunning.' Charlotte could be discussing the weather so casual was her conversation. 'On every occasion it was easy to blame someone else, or to put the reason down to other causes. How easily everyone believed that Lucinda had taken her own life. It seemed the only reasonable explanation, didn't it? And Neville was ailing.' Charlotte stared at Edward blankly. 'The baby would probably have died anyway. And the cat . . . well . . . it was easy for Alice to blame that on me.'

'But she had given you the cat! She had chosen to give you the cat! I heard, I was there at the time!' The terrible truth battered against Edward's dulled consciousness and yet, along with the horror there was this tremendous sense of relief that someone else could be blamed for what he'd considered was his crime.

'She had given me the cat, yes, but she couldn't bear the possibility that it might cease to love her and transfer its affections to me. In exactly the same way that she couldn't bear to think of her father loving his son more than he loved his daughter. She has not only killed, Edward, but she has manipulated the world to suit her own ends. The moment she became a woman she needed men to love her, and she went out to get them without giving a thought to principles of decency . . . and when her love failed to give her what she wanted, then she ranted and raved, her madness

369

came to the fore and would have been on display for the whole world to see had not Milly decided to protect her. For a whole year she rarely went out. Milly told everyone she was frail and ill, but I heard her screams. I heard the madness in the crying. It was Milly who covered up for her, it was Milly who protected her, and it is Milly Toole, because of her foolish behaviour, who is the only person who can fairly be blamed for Lucinda's death. We can't really blame Alice, you see, because she can't be held responsible for her behaviour.'

'And yet you're suggesting that I marry this . . . this . . . crazed creature? Only a moment ago you told me the marriage should take place! How can you possibly believe that I could carry out such an arrangement, knowing what I know? I will refuse! My father must be told of this. If he is told, and Alice is removed to a place of safety, then the engagement will surely be cancelled . . . '

'My dear Edward, stop to think for a moment. There would be a trial. There would be such dreadful publicity. Everything would come out into the open, including your relationship with poor Lucinda. *Everything that happened between you would come out.* And Mrs Toole would take Alice's side, as she always has. There would be such a scandal. Both our families would be disgraced . . . your father for being so deluded to suggest such a bet and my father for agreeing to it. Your father would never consent to your marriage with the sister of a madwoman and a killer. This sort of stain spreads to everything around it. No, keeping these terrible matters a secret, that is where our strength lies, Edward. I can cope with Alice. I know her better than anyone else. I understand her. I have watched her.'

'But could she kill again? If we ever had children . . . How would we ever know? How could we ever feel safe?' Edward, waiting for comment, glanced at Charlotte's averted face and saw the small flush that touched her cheekbones.

'If you refuse to marry Alice your father will disinherit you. Bear that in mind, my dear. And remember what the scandal would do to you personally; remember your part in the events of that night and think how it would sound spoken coldly in a courtroom. Together, Edward, we can carry the burden of Alice. We will watch her. We will control her.'

Edward sobbed. 'I must have some time. I must have time to consider the implications of all this.'

Charlotte tightened her lips with conviction. 'You must understand why I had to tell you these things, Edward. I had to relieve you of your guilt over Lucinda's death. I could see how much you were blaming yourself, torturing yourself, believing you had driven her to suicide. Lucinda could never have committed suicide, my dear, no matter what you said to her. No matter how you hurt and rejected her. She was not that kind. And I consider you too good a man to deceive.'

'Oh, Charlotte.' Edward was weeping openly now. She had such strength. She had such courage. 'How could I live without you? How could I have survived these past black weeks without you? How you must have suffered over the years and yet you are my strength . . . and now you release me from the worst horror of all and yet I wonder if I would rather have believed it was otherwise.' But Edward lied. He knew that he lied. He knew that, no matter how terrible the truth, he would far rather believe that it was not he, but Alice who had killed Lucinda.

'We draw strength from each other. And, if we are wise, we always will.'

'And we say nothing to Alice? Do we let her know that we are aware . . . ?'

'Never! Never let Alice know what I've told you or what you suspect. And never confide in Milly, either. Now that you know you will notice all sorts of little things, things that are almost too small for anyone else

371

to recognize. She has to be treated almost like a child, pampered, indulged, but strictly controlled. Watch Mrs Toole, my dear Edward. Watch Mrs Toole. She deals with Alice with a perfect touch. She has a lifetime of experience to call on.'

'The wedding.' Edward covered his face with his hands. He whispered, 'It has to go ahead, doesn't it? There is no way out of this now?'

The rooks tossed like cinders in the sky, fluttering shadows on the grass when Charlotte answered, watching him narrowly, 'You must be very strong and very self-controlled. You must convince Alice that you are eager for the match. You must reassure her that you are recovering from Lucinda's death, and that you are as happy as possible with the original arrangement. Alice will do anything for love! You must do this, Edward, for your own sake. If you fail, we all fall. The scandal would ruin us all.'

'And I need you, Charlotte.' Edward raised his head mournfully.

'Yes, my dear. You do need me. We need each other.'

Edward paused before sealing the envelope. Was Myers back in his room yet or was he still revelling in the debauched orgy at the back of the house? Ah yes, it was always so hard to find a person who was totally dependable. Who would have thought that the Doctor . . . he had been so lucky to find Charlotte at such a desperately miserable time of his life. It was a miracle, really, and one for which he never ceased thanking God.

After Lucinda's death Henry insisted that Alice, Charlotte and Mrs Toole remain at Winterbourne. 'I see no reason to delay the wedding,' he told Edward stiffly. 'Nothing that has happened is relevant to it, nothing about the situation has changed.' And was he surprised when Edward did not argue? Was he surprised with the new-found assurance he saw in his son? It was impossible to tell, for Henry Brennan did not show his feelings. And for Henry and Florence that was a busy time, putting Venton Hall up for sale and preparing for the wedding.

For Edward, after Charlotte's astonishing announcement, following her advice had been hard. Still reeling from the effects of Lucinda's death, yet he was forced to play his part. If he wanted to keep Charlotte near him, if he wanted her strength to support him – and he did want that, didn't he? – then he would have to go ahead and marry Alice. Charlotte was right; she had summed up the situation very well – there were really no satisfactory alternatives.

So he tried very hard to overcome his natural revulsion and, with Charlotte's help, he succeeded. He convinced Alice of his fondness for her and, just as Charlotte predicted she would, Alice responded. The more compliments he gave out, the more she smiled at him; the more he flattered her and held her hand, the closer she drew to him. Charlotte was right, Alice would do anything for love . . . for what she perceived to be love. It was almost embarrassing, it was pathetic to observe the simple speed of her growing trust in him.

'We've both been so wounded,' Alice smiled up at him when they walked together in the garden, past the place where Edward had first seen Lucinda all those years ago, just a little girl with all that sweet hope in her face. 'We both need to love and be loved in order to recover from such terrible pain.'

Edward smiled down on Alice. She was cunning, oh yes, you would never guess. And it was easy to see how, in the past, it had been so impossible for anyone to blame her, with those wide blue eyes and that innocent stare, so full of trust and so loving. Just like a delicate china doll. She often talked about Lucinda, and sometimes her eyes even shone with tears as she recounted some childhood memory and shared it with him, squeezing his hand as she did so, so that Edward was tempted to shake her off as he would shake off a clinging snake. Poisonous! *Alice was poisonous.*

The ceremony itself was probably the worst time. Edward might have backed out at that stage if he had not spent the entire night before it with Charlotte, who encouraged him to go through with it all. She had needed all her talents for persuasion, all her clever arguments. He had stalked backwards and forwards across the floor in her bedroom, chanting the words, like a mantra, 'There must be some other way. There must be some other way.'

Eventually Charlotte lost patience. She grew angry. She accused him, and in his miserable bewilderment he wondered how she knew so much. 'Remember, Edward, what happened on that last night between you and Lucinda! How sincerely, how misguidedly the poor child offered herself to you and how you rejected her!'

'How do you know that? Did she talk to you?'

'Nobody needed to tell me,' Charlotte scoffed at him. 'Knowing you as I do, and knowing Lucinda, it is quite obvious to me what happened. You do not need a sharp brain to work that scene out. Why else would she have gone rushing off into the night to find herself at Alice's mercy? Why else would she . . .'

'Stop! Stop! Enough.' Edward could not bear to return to those memories again, they were much too raw. He collapsed on the bed. 'We are making promises that are to last a lifetime, Charlotte. I am binding myself to a madwoman for the rest of my natural life. And what if anything should happen to you? What if I should be left alone with this?'

'Trust me, Edward. You must trust me. A time will come when it will be prudent to rid yourself of Alice . . .'

'To rid myself?'

Charlotte came to sit down beside him. She nodded.

She took his hand and he noticed how cold and firm hers was. It made his feel flabby and huge inside it, clumsy and ill-formed, stupid and uncoordinated. Yes, that was often the effect she had on him, and his need of her cool assurance grew. 'One day, when all this is behind us, when we have had time to settle into our new lives, there will come an appropriate time. But we must be sensible and watch carefully. Henry is not a young man, and Florence can be overruled. When the time is right we can declare Alice's madness openly . . . between us we can make sure it is revealed for all the world to see.'

'The fact that she has killed?' Edward's mouth fell open.

'No, not that, my dear. Never that. No, I was referring to her everyday behaviour. People will be able to watch her. People will soon know and Mrs Toole will no longer be in the defensive position she once occupied. Without her nurse's constant protection Alice will give the unsoundness of her mind away.'

Edward said, 'It's hard to see how. She's excitable, a little dizzy, governed by her emotions, but that is a long way away from madness.'

Charlotte smiled. 'You do not know her, Edward. You have not lived with her yet.'

And that comment, made in such freezing tones, didn't help Edward's anxious state of mind. He said, 'You are asking a great deal of me, Charlotte.'

She withdrew her hand and the space beside him felt very large when she got up and moved towards the window. Her back was towards him when she spoke. 'I had hoped you were doing this for yourself, for your own reasons, Edward, not for mine.'

She was angry and cold; she was closed against him. He felt her withdrawing her love and the feeling was as real and as violent as having the blankets pulled off his warm body on an icy morning. He was desperate to appease her, to feel himself warm and safe and secure once again. He said, 'I am sorry, Charlotte. The thought of tomorrow has weakened me. I am looking for someone to blame for my own predicament. I should not have blamed you. Never you. Please, I beg you, forgive me.'

She did not move from the window. 'How do I know that you will not turn round and blame me for any future difficulties that are bound to occur? You must remember that you are doing this for your own sake, Edward, that I am merely here to help and to guide you, that it matters not a jot to me what happens, for myself. My only concern is for you.'

'I know that. I know it. Come back to me, Charlotte. Come back and say you forgive me.'

She turned and approached the bed. 'You are tired,' she told him, 'and no wonder. You must get some sleep if you are to perform well tomorrow.'

'I can't go back to my own room. I can't bear to be by myself tonight.' And he felt ridiculous. Like a child.

'Very well,' she said coolly, looking down on him mockingly. 'Get into my bed and I'll sleep beside you.'

Like a child he obeyed her, so relieved to feel her in control once again. Naked he crawled under the covers, and waited while she modestly changed into her nightclothes and got in beside him. He turned to her, wanting comfort, wanting to feel the strength of her arms. With loathing he felt the start of his passion and he turned away, sickened by it. But Charlotte forgave him. Charlotte understood. Charlotte recognized his needs and quickly and sensibly satisfied them. But afterwards came the punishment he craved and the cold words, 'You are a man, you cannot help these feelings. But they have to be dealt with severely and never indulged without penance.'

And she was right, oh so right. Charlotte understood. The night before his wedding, in bed with Charlotte, and he never forgot it, he never knew another moment when he was not in need of her. Every night after that he knew that Charlotte would be waiting, severe and yet patient, just and unwavering in the nightly doses of punishment she meted out.

So that when, the following day, in the cold grey silence of Shilstone Church he exchanged his vows with Alice, he found he could gaze as directly into her eyes as she gazed into his. He made his promises knowing exactly what he was doing and why he was doing it. And he was doing it because he wanted to, not for Charlotte, not for his father, but purely and simply to gratify his own needs.

Edward Brennan had to keep Charlotte beside him and there was no other way than this. He could not face life without her.

# FORTY-ONE

In the morning, while everyone else clustered round listening to Unity, Angela and Lottie tell their story, Alice returned to her own caravan and attempted to liven up the tiny wood-burning stove with vicious little stabs, feeling defeated and sick. Edward was always one step ahead of her. He had always been one step ahead of her with his schemes and his plans.

They would believe it! None of these people knew Edward, realized the lengths to which he would go to achieve his aims. Somehow she would have to convince Luke that his intentions to leave London and give up the chase were just part of his plot . . .

'Don't worry. Nobody's going to lower their guard on the strength of such an obvious ploy.' So sunk in her misery was Alice that she had not noticed the opening door. Luke came up behind her and wrapped her in his arms. Immediately Alice felt safe; they were intimate again. It was incredible to her how easily this intimacy flowed between them without the need for speech. She listened when Luke went on, 'This is all part of his plan and this little trick means he is going to strike again quite soon. We are always watching.'

'Oh Luke, when is he going to give up? What are we going to do? How long can we go on living like this, forever having to watch over our shoulders?'

Luke tightened his arms around her, he warmed her. 'Your husband's determination is quite extraordinary. I imagined that long before now he would have given up this ludicrous chase and gone home. But it now appears the opposite is true and he has no intentions of releasing you. I am having his movements watched. He is leaving the Queen's Arms this morning as promised, and he can be certain of an unexpected visit

378

from me as soon as he reaches his new destination.'

'Oh no, Luke . . . don't go near him. He would turn you against me!'

Luke looked down at Alice with tenderness in his eyes. He wanted to sweep aside all difficulties and shield her from life. He was a very long way from the man whom Edward perceived him to be – the rogue, the fighter, the wild man with the notorious reputation that Edward, through fear, had never allowed to die. And nothing about his attitude this morning suggested the great extent of his concern. As usual he displayed a sense of healthy relaxation with his sparkling eyes and his quick smile, and even the way he held his head with the blue felt hat tilted jauntily on the back of it gave the impression that he was confident and happy.

He would have to talk to Edward whether Alice liked it or not. This absurd state of affairs could not go on for much longer.

Luke did not tell her that when last night's performance had finished he had gone to the Queen's Arms expressly to confront Edward Brennan only to find him, with a red-faced Dr Myers beside him, sitting in a corner watching the show. Luke considered calling him out but decided against it. There would be other, more convenient occasions and he was interested to know for what reason the man was patronizing such an event. Luke was not certain if he had been recognized the night Edward and his party swooped on the camp in Exeter, on the night he held them back so that Alice and Davy and Milly had time to be hidden. But he was fairly sure he had been recognized . . . and that made the situation a far more perilous one. It would not ease Alice's anxiety to know of that early encounter between two young men both out of their depth, half out of their minds with fear and revulsion as they confronted each other across all that bloodshed so many years ago.

As soon as he heard her name Luke had known who Alice was. It made no difference to him. Both he and

379

Edward had been hardly older than children; certainly neither of them could have influenced those events. And Edward had done as he'd been bid . . . he had managed to save Mathew Durant's life . . . it was not his fault that Luke's father had been thrown into gaol under such a cruel sentence. Luke harboured no particular grudge against the boy he had encountered on that terrible, unforgettable day. If anyone was to blame it was Henry Brennan, his father, and that man was dead . . . life had moved on . . . the world had moved on. There was no room for such old hostilities in Luke Durant's life, and if Luke despised Edward it was purely because of the cruelties he had inflicted on Alice. However, there was no getting away from the fact that if Edward had recognized him, the danger of his position was highly increased, and Alice and the child were in greater peril because of it.

Now he weighed up his words very carefully when he told Alice, 'There is only one sensible way to settle this madness, and that is by talking to each other. Edward wants you out of his life. He wants to divorce you . . . for reasons that I do not understand he seems to want to be rid of you. There is no need for him to take the extraordinary step of locking you away in an asylum . . . you would happily agree to go with me and I would happily agree to take you. Somewhere in that there must be some ground upon which the two sides can meet.'

'He doesn't just want me shut away!' Alice's voice rose as she protested, wanting to silence his strong, deep voice. 'I do not like to hear you talk like this . . . as if Edward is an approachable man, a man to be trusted! He wants Davy also. And he has my other three children! And if he gets the chance to accuse me of adultery I will be forced to give Davy to him and I will never see my children again. He is not a man to talk reasonably on any matter at all and he will not compromise! To think otherwise is to underestimate

Edward . . . I have fallen into that same trap so many times. I beg you, Luke, I plead with you . . . *do not go near him!*'

Luke's face was grave. He had to tell her this. 'There is no way, Alice, in this day and age, that you are going to be able to get your children back. The law is on Edward's side.'

'If I could prove what he had done, if I could show the terrible cruelties he has committed against me then, surely, someone would show me mercy! I was never mad, Luke, and yet my husband tried to shut me away. He shares a bed with my own sister!'

'The man has a certificate signed by the doctor in Deale. That may be difficult to counter.' She had to know the problems that faced them.

'Then Edward must have some hold over Myers. He must have signed the document since I left Deale because I know that the doctor had not come to a decision while I was there. There are other physicians, Luke. There are specialists who are above bribery, if we could find them. There must be a way for me to stay with you and get my children back.'

The rain pelted down on the caravan roof; it slicked the small windows and tickled the fire. It was easy to believe this small world was a real one . . . the only one . . . if they could only shut their eyes to reality for ever, and simply pull the curtains, hitch up the horse and travel on.

But Luke said, 'Yesterday I spoke to my lawyers about this matter and they are looking into it. For now we must concentrate on preventing Edward from acting foolishly and taking you back before an agreement can be reached. I have to go and see him, Alice. Before we leave London this matter must be resolved.'

Alice turned away. She gave her head a series of small shakes. She huddled beside the fire, picking up a cushion and hugging it against her chest, plucking at the fringes with her fingers. She said, 'He will say things about me. Dreadful things . . .'

Luke knelt down beside her and repeated the words he had spoken before. 'And you think that anything Edward Brennan said would influence me?'

She did not look at him. She stayed very still but the long jet earrings she wore were still trembling after her last plea. The shawl of golden hair tumbled in curls on to her back and that stiff, resolute expression she wore threatened to make her seem stronger than she was. She continued to gaze into the stove, watching the red melt the ashes to white, watching the shapes fold and shimmer, feeling the heat of it on her own eyes so hard and so long did she stare. Her voice was expressionless when she said, 'He has influenced everyone else . . .'

'Not Mrs Toole.'

Suddenly Alice's resolution crumpled and she buried her face in the cushion. Her words were muffled. 'I do not honestly know. Milly pretends, she is very loyal, but sometimes I have wondered. You see, Luke, Milly could never understand about . . .'

Luke waited patiently for her to finish her sentence. He saw fear in her eyes and her lip trembled. Softly he said, 'Alice, please don't underestimate me. I want to understand – I feel there is so much about you that I do not truly understand.'

'You are a man,' she said. 'I am a woman. You will condemn me.'

He straightened himself. He picked up Milly Toole's large rush chair and placed it beside Alice's smaller one. He sat down in it and he waited. 'We have to be absolutely honest with each other. That is a risk we have to take if we're to defeat the monsters ranged against us.'

But how could she be honest . . . totally honest? 'Well,' Alice pulled on her lip, the crackling fire filled the short silence and Luke could see her make the decision to trust him. 'There are no excuses for what I did . . . no reasons to give you. But I had these feelings and nowhere to put them. I fell in love, Luke. When I was fourteen years old.' She kept her eyes on his face. 'Or I thought it was love. It was not, of course. Those wicked feelings are nothing to do with love, I know that and yet . . . I could be free with Garth. I could be myself. I was free of the enormous effort of concealing my feelings . . . all my feelings. Luke,' and she stared up at him intently, 'outside I was sweet and pretty, smiling a lot, oh yes, smiling, but inside I felt like a savage. Do you understand me? Even the wind, Luke, it called me insistently from a wild world outside life. I wanted to throw precious things and break them. I feared that once I let myself cry I might never stop. I had to stop reading poems. If anyone scratched my face I knew they would see what was underneath it . . . a girl with glaring eyes, blinded by rage, sometimes, thrashing about inside my white cage like a wild cat! So I smiled a great deal. I wanted to give my love and yet there was nobody there to return it. And the new emotions that were growing inside me, wild, bad, wicked feelings, well, I did fall in love. It must have been love. It hurt like love does. It tore me in pieces, it ripped me in half. I was mad.'

Luke watched Alice and listened, longing to hold her and reassure her but knowing she must tell him in her own way.

She spoke very quickly as if she was eager to get this over. 'I loved the way Garth looked at me. I saw how his eyes lit up when he saw me and there was a reflection of my own wildness there. And I began to realize that I did have something honest to give . . . and if I gave it he might give me back what I wanted. So I gave myself to the man who said he loved me, I let him. I was not happy with an hour, or two hours of warmth and closeness. I wanted him to love me, properly to love me as I wanted to be loved, as I loved him, with all my heart and soul. But he didn't. He couldn't. It was all unreal, Milly said. It didn't really happen. Oh

Luke . . .' and Alice managed a brief, sad smile when she went on, 'Oh Luke, poor Milly! How appalled she was with it all! And Charlotte told me these disgraceful feelings of mine were madness. Yes, that's when they first began to talk about madness. And so I looked around and yes, I realized that others were not like me. Others were not driven wild by deep, impossible yearnings so they wanted to go out and dance in the moonlight or get themselves soaked in thunderstorms or run and run until they dropped, until all their wildness was used up and worn out of them. No, I seemed to be alone with all that. And nobody understood it. They looked at me strangely. They thought me vile – that I could give myself to my lover like that at the age that I was, not caring about anything as long as he gave me his love. No, just not caring.' Alice looked away and was silent before she turned dully to face him. 'And now, Luke, what are you thinking? What is going on in your head underneath that quiet smile?'

'I am thinking that whatever I say you will not believe me. You are so convinced of your own wickedness that you're not going to listen to anyone who tells you it is all right. Of course you loved him – whatever love is. You should not have been made to deny it. It had nothing to do with madness. Sadness, yes, because Garth could not make you happy or give you the love that you craved. I understand all those feelings of yours and I also see how, in the world in which you were brought up, it was extraordinary enough for someone to call it madness.'

Alice's words were slightly less forlorn when she continued: 'So I believed there was something wrong with me long before I married Edward. And so did Milly. I was furious with Milly for not telling me about Papa's arrangement. She knew all the time . . . and yet she kept it quiet from us all, because that's what she'd been told to do, she said. But surely she realized the effects it would have on Lucinda? She ought to have done

384

something to prevent that! But Milly denies those sorts of feelings, she disapproves of them so much she thinks that they cannot exist. Lucinda was only fifteen which is a child in Milly's eyes. Milly was as shocked as everyone else when Lucinda drowned herself. Nobody could have foreseen that. Oh Luke, if you had only known her, you would have believed, as we all did, that she was just not the type of person to do that! She was not intense about life, like me. She was not sour and mean like Charlotte. She was placid and sweet and good-natured; she would have recovered, she would have been happy again. She was full of happiness. Life could never be the same after Lucinda died like that.'

'But whatever had happened, the "arrangement" still had to be adhered to?' There was a sourness in Luke's tone and Alice looked at him sharply.

'Yes,' she said. 'There was never any doubt about that. It was the only future we were ever likely to have. We were little more than paupers, and everything was already owed to Henry Brennan anyway. There was this awful feeling of betraying Lucinda . . . that it had all been my fault again . . . all that guilt. Should I have refused to marry Edward whatever the consequences? Hadn't there been something Edward or I could have done? And those feelings, they lasted a long, long time.' Alice looked at the floor. She crossed one foot over another and she wiped her hands on the cushion as if to clean them of something invisible there. 'I still feel some of it now. I will never be without that . . . because of what she did. And nobody realized the depths of her misery, and she didn't feel able to tell us. Milly must have told her she was making it up in her head!'

'And Edward told you he cared for you?'

'Oh yes. That was the ironical part. He was very loving and caring, and I began to feel that maybe here was someone, at last, whom I could love without punishment. It was hard to dare to do it again, after the first time, but I had always admired him . . . all of us felt that way about Edward. And his sincerity seemed to be genuine. He courted me, Luke. Yes, even though the marriage was arranged, even though the tragedy had so recently occurred, he courted me.'

'So you stayed at Winterbourne House, and you were married to Edward?'

'The wedding was very sad because all we could think of was Lucinda. But I was reassured by Edward's attitude . . . so sensible, so safe, so certain that what we were doing was right. I wanted to believe him, Luke. I wanted to believe that we could start our lives again . . . we seemed to have spent so long in waiting, my sisters and Milly and I. Milly said I must never let him know I was not a virgin. That I must mimic virginity on my first night in his bed. That if he or Henry or Florence knew about my wicked behaviour they would never forgive either of us. I was unhappy with the deceit but I saw that I had to do it. And when I think how concerned I was about that small thing I have to smile . . . because it really didn't matter after that. Nothing mattered after that.'

And then Luke did get up and hold her, because it was quite clear that Alice could not go on alone. Until now she had controlled her emotions and told him the truth simply and honestly, hesitating in places, searching his face for reassurance, but she had managed to describe how it was. Now those memories were getting darker. 'But it was all pretend again. It was all in my head. Milly was right, there was nothing there. I had made it up and it wasn't really happening. And I hate him,' she cried. 'I hate his voice and his face and his memory. And I hate the thought of my wedding night so intensely that I've almost wiped it out of my mind. But now I can see the bed itself so clearly, and myself, lying there, knowing that I must pretend to be pure but waiting for him eagerly, waiting for his advances and knowing how important this was going to be . . . not a game any more, although my body was still part of somebody else's bargain.'

And it took time for Alice to explain to Luke how roughly Edward had taken her so that her cries were perfectly truthful and she did not have to pretend. It took time to describe the hatred she felt being spent upon her, and the way she had tried to respond, with love, as she thought she ought to, as she wanted to. And then his reaction to the feel of her arms and the touch of her hand. The way Edward had recoiled from that, the look of disgust that covered his face when he looked at her naked body, the way he had flung himself from the bed and crossed to the basin to wash his hands. And then had disappeared for most of the night, leaving Alice hopelessly weeping. Only to return in the morning as dawn began to creep through the window turning the room into a cold, pale cave with no love in it.

'I got up,' she told Luke, simply, with no expression on her face and her voice was steady but cold as ice. 'I don't know, even now, if I was asleep or awake. I crossed the room and went into the bathroom and I picked up Edward's razor. Then I walked back to the bed. He was sleeping. I stared at him. He had pretended to love me . . . he had promised me something and yet he had rejected me. There was hatred all wrapped up in his love and I was bound to him for the rest of my life. I stood for a while beside the bed feeling so cold, so despairing, studying the face of the man whom I had chosen to trust. And then he suddenly opened his eyes and they were wide and staring and I realized just what I must look like. What I was doing! So I dropped the razor and he asked me if I was feeling well. He looked at me in that special way that Charlotte sometimes used. He said he would call her. I didn't want that. I didn't want him telling Charlotte about what I had done. But I couldn't stop him. He pulled on his dressing gown, pushed me aside and went to fetch her.' Alice sighed. She was trembling all over and frozen stiff in spite of the nearness of the tiny stove. Luke could ask no more of her. He held her. He kissed her hair. He stroked her and murmured words of comfort.

And then he said, 'So that's when it all began. That's when they started their game. But why? What was behind it? Why did Edward turn on you like that and where does Charlotte fit in?'

Alice shook her head and her golden curls tumbled around her. She wore the expression of a hurt child when she told him, 'Charlotte must have told him about my wanton behaviour. They were close, by then, Charlotte and Edward. She helped him with his grief. They spent hours together and they must have decided that his marriage to me was the only course they could take. Henry would not have accepted his marriage to Charlotte. So Charlotte must have told him and explained it away as my madness. But I didn't know! I thought that what they were whispering together was true. By merely wanting Edward to love me I had made myself disgusting again. There was something wrong with me and I was different from all other women. The looks on their faces told me all I needed to know, and not just then. It went on and on and on, Luke. At the breakfast table. While we sat together in the evenings. When guests were present. And their attitude soon spread itself so that everyone seemed to take the same attitude . . . people started to watch me! Even the servants. And it is only since coming here and spending time with Unity Heath, listening to her and watching her that I came to understand that you did not have to be mad to enjoy your own feelings. It is only since I came here and met you . . . and was loved by you.'

'You bore this monster four children?'

Alice shuddered. 'There were occasions when he seemed to want to punish me like that. After that first night we slept apart but there were rare occasions when Edward would come to my room, take me no matter how strongly I protested, spitting insults into my ears while he raped me, ravaged me, telling me that I was his wife, like it or not and that he was entitled to use me as he liked. And so the children were conceived . . . every one of them born out of hatred, Luke, even little Davy. Every one.'

'You gave your body to me. You trusted me.' Luke continued to stroke her, to try and staunch the weeping which seemed to come from somewhere so deep that the grief was unreachable.

'But this isn't real either, Luke. I am safe because this isn't real. The only part of this which feels real is all the jealousy, all the mistrust! I cannot bear you to look at another woman for fear you will reject me! And when I see women with the beauty and poise of Jessica Lamont, with the natural, sensual qualities of Unity Heath, I wonder how you chose me, dream or no dream, and I think there is some reason for which you are using me and I do not know it yet. I haven't grasped it. There must be some reason you are using me and yet I don't understand.' And then she sank into silence again, and it was much more than a silence, it was a kind of resigned stupor as if her words were so old and worn she was sorry she'd had to recount them like that, off by heart.

Luke sighed heavily. 'Then it is only time that will reassure you,' he told her. 'Time, and my love, and the knowledge that you are a beautiful woman and worthy of the deepest love. That your body is beautiful and your feelings are beautiful, not to be hidden away and ashamed of. Good God, Alice, you have been abused and used all your life. And all I can say is thank God that I found you, that I was in time.'

'Do not go to him,' Alice pleaded. 'Do not go and attempt to reason with Edward!'

And Luke, unable to see another way, held her tight and rocked her gently in his arms.

389

# FORTY-TWO

Late morning, a white, after-rain light, and the every-day, ordinary life of the troupe went on. Under the dripping trees animals were led out and exercised, the drawfs practised a tumbling routine, the curtains of Unity Heath's caravan were drawn, two swordsmen were clashing their blades and Luke left Alice in order to meet Nathaniel and sort out last night's takings. The watchers took note of the strangers loitering beside the park railings in the distance. They saw the unmarked vehicles down the side street. The last violent burst of rain had given the troupe a great deal to be getting on with . . . buckets were positioned under drips and the heavy puddles of water that rested on, and threatened, the great central awning were being swilled off by gyp-sies brandishing long-handled brooms.

But the sentinels saw the trap closing. Luke was warned: he was making his preparations. In a little while he would take Alice, Davy and Milly out. The tension in the air was wrapped in a winter stillness.

'Milly knows best.'

Yes, and Milly had always known best, right back to the departure of the gin-swigging, sour-smelling Aga-tha, and there had been such comfort for Alice in those three words because they were said with such certainty and they took away so much confusion.

'Milly knows best.' The safest words in the world.

Even when Alice's children were born and those words were not spoken any more, they were still there, hovering in the air around Milly, unspoken but every bit as certain. So that when Nicholas cried Alice had automatically handed him over to Milly. When Kate had a chill it was best that Milly took charge of her . . .

for Milly had experience of such things while Alice was
. . . Alice was . . . *what was Alice?*

She had never resented Milly's intrusions – far from
it. Relief was what Alice experienced whenever Milly's
big, solid frame came into the nursery, releasing her
from responsibilities which she felt inadequate to
undertake and allowing her to enjoy the best parts of
childhood – the story-telling, bedtime-kissing, clothes-
choosing, game-playing parts. Oh, and she had loved
the children, resenting the evenings when the nursery
lamps were lit and the room was folded up into such a
flickering cosiness, when it was time for them to go to
bed and for Alice to leave the security of the Winterbourne nursery and go downstairs again to the freezing
cold atmospheres, the dark stares and the ill-concealed
criticisms that made up the vastness of Winterbourne
House. The nursery was the only place in that house
where Alice felt loved.

She'd been such a fool, she thought now as she
watched Milly bring Davy into the caravan to change
him. Then Alice fed him and loved him a while before
handing him back to be cared for – for his sake – by
somebody else.

She'd been so blind, because a ridiculous length of
time went by before she became aware of Edward's
infatuation for Charlotte, and even then, when it was
so obvious it couldn't be avoided, Alice had found it
hard to believe.

She thought she could understand it. After all, Edward made it quite clear in every word and gesture that
Alice was no company for him; Alice was wilful and
excitable and in need of constant watching, constant
control. He treated his wife like a petulant child – she,
who had always been so biddable, so afraid of misbe-
having, so keen for love and approval. But it made no
difference what she did or how hard she tried to please
them. Edward and Charlotte together were too much
for her. How easy it was, she thought, for them to make

faces over the most innocent utterances so that they sounded ridiculous and inane – even a comment on the weather would be greeted with raised eyebrows as if there was more to it, or it had been unnecessary, or she had broken some silence which, until she entered the room with her silly remark, had been precious.

How easy it had all been, because of her overriding sense of guilt. And she knew full well that they discussed her behind her back.

And throughout that time Milly had been busy protecting her! 'You are imagining things,' she told her. 'You know you have always had the wildest imagination. And Edward and Charlotte are quieter people, drawn to each other because of their interests. I know that Charlotte is one year younger than you, dear, but even to me she always seemed ten years older. And Edward is probably still fretting over Lucinda. You must be patient, my dear, you must be patient and uncomplaining. You are a wife and a mother now, not a little girl who must always be pampered and in the limelight.'

'I was never pampered and in any limelight, Milly. And I am not imagining this. And I know you have noticed it too . . . how could anyone not?'

'Well, Henry Brennan has grown very fond of you and you cannot complain about that.'

'And Florence?'

'Florence looks to me as if she has always disapproved of anyone who is capable of smiling and enjoying themselves. Your mother-in-law spends most of her time in her room with the curtains drawn and smelling salts to her nose, afraid that dirt, or life might touch her. Be grateful for that, Alice. Florence does not interfere. She has never once come into the nursery.'

It was true that Henry Brennan liked her – much to Charlotte's annoyance and consternation – and that fact made a great deal of difference to Alice. Gradually she had come to return the compliment, choosing a

chair beside him, reading to him in the evenings, purely because the atmosphere changed when he was
around. The old man was safety. It was not so easy, at
those times, for Edward and Charlotte to club together
so closely or to be so openly critical. But his was an
uncomfortable patronage. Henry was a cold, crusty old
man who hardly cracked his face into a smile. His face
was as grey as his hair, the shade of worn-out old iron.
His conversation was grating and invariably boring and
he spoke very slowly and carefully as if he was afraid
of letting out some great truth. He patted his mouth
with his napkin at the table, almost between every
word, ensuring that nobody interrupted or took advantage of his strenuous pauses. He was not remotely
interested in personal conversations about life at home,
the children or the servants. He detested gossip. All he
was truly interested in was the expansion and the continuing success of his companies. If she'd confided in
him, Alice knew that her unhappiness would not particularly concern him. He approved of her . . . that was
all. He thought her dainty and pretty and ornamental
to have beside the decanter – a lady, the last of his
ambitions for his son fulfilled. But his lofty manner and
his authoritative attitude at least put a curb on Charlotte's tongue.

Of course Alice had tried to tackle Charlotte . . .
right at the beginning when it all started. 'You must
know that things are wrong between us, Edward and
I. It is difficult for me to understand. I do not know
what to do in order to right it.'

'Do you wonder at it?' Charlotte, ramrod-straight in
her mottled blue satin, continued to arrange the
flowers in the jade vase in the pink drawing room. The
sun flooded in but brought no warmth to the long, thin
room. Alice had nothing else to stare at but Charlotte's
shoulders and they were slim with a neat row of material buttons tightly hooked up her back and stopping
at the frill that capped them. Hard, ungiving shoulders,

just a support for that small, rigid head, just a thin cross for that body to hold to. 'Do you honestly wonder at it, Alice, bearing in mind the truth of the matter? Edward is no fool. After your wedding night he would have known how slyly you tried to deceive him . . .' The stems went into the vase one by one, thrust into the water by two mean fingers.

'You have told him all about me, Charlotte, haven't you?'

She stopped arranging the flowers but she did not turn round and Alice was glad of it. She did not want to see the expression on Charlotte's face. She knew what it would be, she had no need to see it. 'I had to tell him. It was my duty to tell him.'

'Ah, but I would have liked to hear the way you told it, how you interpreted it and what else you made of it.'

'There is nothing to be "made of it", Alice. It is there, a plain fact in need of no interpretation from anyone. You are an abnormal woman. You have obviously inherited the instability that runs in our family. Our father had it . . . he gambled his life away as a result of it. Edward is a good man. He went through with the marriage in order to satisfy his father . . .'

'To satisfy you, Charlotte! You were always so afraid of poverty. You feared for your future if the wedding did not take place – why don't you admit that? And you used Edward's grief to influence him and gain his favour.'

Charlotte turned round then and confronted Alice with her chin held high. She was holding a flower, a pale, limpid thing, in one hand. Its head drooped on its stem. Charlotte's expression took the last of her resistance from Alice. A trapdoor of hatred had opened and the horrible contents were suddenly spewed out before her. Alice opened her mouth to speak but was unable to utter a word. She listened to Charlotte because she was forced to. Face to face with the venom she saw in her sister's look, she could find no strength to leave the room.

'You! You have the gall to accuse me!' Charlotte hissed and her lips drew back to reveal her teeth. 'You, who have never known what it's like to be worst, to be last, to be lowest . . . the forgotten one! But oh no, Alice, all is not what it seems. I had no need to use Edward's grief to snare him! He would have come to love me in the end . . . even if I had said nothing, he would have recognized the truth. A man needs a dependable woman, strong, moral, forthright and determined, not a weak, dizzy creature with no more stamina about her than a wisp of straw! You might be beautiful, Alice, but underneath all that you are nothing but a whore and it is beginning to show my dear, oh yes, it shows. You crave love! You are disgusting! But Edward has the measure of you now . . .'

On and on Charlotte went, spitting out her hatred until it soured the air, making it difficult to breathe, difficult to open your eyes without them stinging. Alice refused to hear any more. She continued to stare at Charlotte but she ceased to see or hear her.

When it was over she ran to Milly for comfort. Milly said, 'Charlotte has always been jealous of you, Alice, and is it any wonder! Take no notice of her cruel jibes, she has always suffered from these unseemly displays of hostility. It was cruel of her to tell Edward about that terrible blot on your past and it is natural that he should resent that. What husband would not? I prayed none of that would ever come out, underestimating the viciousness of your sister. But you must see this as all part of the punishment, you know, Alice. You cannot behave like you did and not suffer later on. No, Edward might enjoy her company sometimes for Charlotte has a quick wit and can be charming when she tries. But you are reading too much into this, there is no conspiracy against you. Just concentrate on being a good wife and mother and all will come well in the end. You have always expected too much from other people.

There are many married couples, my dear, who share the same house and yet are not in love. Love only happens in stories; in real life it is a rare thing. Just be satisfied with your lot, as I am.'

And then those same words had rung again in Alice's ears: 'Milly knows best.'

Alice finished feeding Davy. She wrapped him up, preparing to hand him back to Milly. 'He is growing fast,' she said fondly. 'He is going to be a fine boy, just like Nicholas.'

Milly smacked her lips in satisfaction. 'That's what comes of having the loving care of experienced hands,' she sniffed, and nodded pointedly towards Alice, 'in spite of the wild longings of his beautiful, silly mother!'

# FORTY-THREE

So when Milly turned round and said, 'This has gone
far enough. I have blamed myself in the past for not
being firm and heaven knows we have all suffered on
account of it,' – when she turned round and said that
Alice sat down and stared.

Milly continued with hardly a pause for breath.
'Well, not this time, Alice. This time I am going to
follow my instincts because our situation is precarious
enough as it is without you sinking into one of your
destructive depressions . . .'

The words tumbled out of Milly's mouth as if she'd
been holding them in for too long like a deep breath.
She rushed up and down the small space cradling Davy
in her arms as she talked, filling the caravan as she
went, overflowing it and spilling over.

'I have watched you, Alice,' she said, mouthing distaste at her own unpleasantness but unable, now she'd
started, to stop. 'I have watched you and worried and
spent sleepless nights agonizing over where this unsuitable affair of yours is taking you. Once again, in spite
of all my warnings, you have fallen in love, you have
allowed your emotions to control you . . . and look at
us! Just look! A pathetic little family of three, homeless,
vulnerable, penniless. Quite dependent on others for
our daily bread. Well, Alice, I have to tell you that I
can no longer cope with the inevitable consequences of
it. I feel that you have abandoned Davy and me and
allowed yourself to escape into this fantasy place just
as you did before. No, no . . . don't interrupt me. I
have been wanting to say this for days now, and you
can't deny that it is a fantasy place because Luke is all
but a stranger. You know nothing about his past and
even less about his future . . .'

'But I do know!' Alice protested. 'I know about his lawless escapades, so long ago now it is hardly relevant. I know all about Lorna Drewe, the girl who killed herself. I know that he is a wanted man and is doing all in his power to right that . . .'

'Oh yes! Little Miss Clever, is it now? So you know all that about him, do you? And I'm sure he made quite certain he smoothed that all over and made his mis- demeanours acceptable in your eyes. Well, he would, wouldn't he . . .'

'He would, Milly, yes, because he loves me and I love him.'

Milly would have covered her ears if she wasn't carrying Davy. 'That's enough, Alice, that's quite enough. Don't you think I have heard those words from you often enough in the past to know how meaningless they are? Do you give me no credit for having any intelligence at all, Alice? Oh, I know what you take me for . . . I know the impression I give . . . nothing but a bumbling old good-hearted fool with not the commonsense of a peapod. Good old Milly who can always be relied upon.

'I don't think of you in that way! I have never taken you for granted. I have always appreciated your love and loyalty and I do not know how I would have got by without it . . .'

'A damn sight better, most probably,' said Milly, still rushing up and down in a fevered attempt to reach the end of her discourse before her courage failed her. 'If I had not been around to rely on perhaps you would have taken on more responsibility for your own wild behaviour, maybe you would have curbed it!'

Alice said, 'You are going a long way back, Milly. Twenty years – and I am not the person I was then. I am not the girl who went searching for love . . .'

'Oh? Is that so?' Milly stuttered. She came to a halt opposite Alice. She looked down on her golden hair, on her bewildered face, so pretty, so vulnerable, so

398

easily wounded. 'So you are now telling me you are different! And how am I to believe that? The situations look remarkably alike to me. Here you are again, literally throwing yourself at a man when you feel frightened and you want security. Have you learned nothing from the past, absolutely nothing at all? Don't you see that most of the misery and misfortune that has befallen you ... and me ... and your children ... dates back to those days? How else could Charlotte have convinced Edward of your madness? She had to base it on something, and what could be more appropriate than that?'

Alice sank wearily back on the bed. There was no defence against this. There never had been. 'I can't explain that behaviour to you, Milly. I know it was wrong. It was just a phase in my life when I craved comfort.'

'But it was not love!' Seeing Alice's obvious distress, Milly subsided a little. 'And can't you see that exactly the same thing is happening to you now? You saw Luke Durant and that was enough. You needed a protector and he, well he has always had his own motives. So within the space of a few hours you flung yourself at him, body and soul. And me? What was I doing? Well, I was doing exactly as I had always done, looking at you with that old fondness, thinking to myself – well, my sweet Alice is a woman with love to give and nowhere to put it, there is nothing I can do when she is gripped by these wild emotions so I will wait and watch and support her and pick up the pieces afterwards.' Milly turned violently round and continued marching so suddenly that Davy cried out and shot out his arms in protest. 'But I am older and weaker and the situation is more perilous now than it ever was,' she went on, holding the sob in her voice at bay as she came to the end of her frantic tirade. 'Luke Durant doesn't want you, Alice! He has no need of anyone. He is a rogue and a wanderer ... always has been, always will be.'

'You are saying that this is nothing again, nothing but something I've conjured up? That I must deny it? I must pretend again?' Alice's face displayed all the emotions she felt inside. She sat and listened to Milly as if her body was being assailed by the most violent blows. She sat as if she knew there was no point in a struggle because this adversary was stronger and crueller than any she had ever known. 'You are saying he is a figment of my own imagination, just like Garth was?'

'No!' Milly's voice sank so that the sounds of outside came in. Children calling dogs to heel. The regular thud of a horse's hooves as it ran round in a ring. The mournful hoot of a barge on the river. 'No, Alice, I am not even saying that. I am telling you – and believe me, this is as painful for me as it is for you – I am telling you that what Luke wants is revenge. Revenge against Edward Brennan who was the indirect cause of his father's imprisonment and miserable death and his own disenfranchisement. Your husband, Edward, whose father suppressed the rioters and who ordered the killing of Luke's mother! He has not told you this, Alice, has he? No, don't bother to answer. I can see by the look on your face that he has not. Nor has he told you that it was Edward's father who caused the death of Lorna Drewe by ordering the poor child from the house without a position, without hope. They are old adversaries, Alice. They met many years ago, and confronted each other then as they confront each other now! Only now the position is different – Luke has the winning hand. Oh my dear, don't you see? What other reason can there possibly be for his great interest in you?'

'For myself?' Alice whispered.

'Bah!' said Milly, continuing on. 'This romantic nonsense – when will you get it all out of your head? You are no longer a little girl. I ought to have told you before – I ought to have put a stop to this before it all started. I knew it! I knew it! But I hoped it would not come to this. As usual, I was afraid to interfere and I

400

suppose I half-hoped . . . And now look at you!'

'What made you change your mind? What made you decide to tell me this now?' Alice was pleading.

'Because I fear there might be violence and loss of life,' said Milly. 'Because I fear that Edward is getting nearer and that the trap is closing. Because, knowing him, I suspect that Edward is even more determined, hoping to kill two birds with one stone, to revenge himself upon Luke Durant at last and capture you and Davy at the same time.'

'What do you think I should do?'

Milly paused, a little overcome by her own daring, uncertain now, how to proceed. 'I think we should leave the troupe and try and make it on our own,' she said. 'It is not an option that appeals to me but it is time we faced reality. We can no longer sit back and allow things to happen to us, hoping for the best. We did that for fifteen years at Winterbourne House, and look what came of that. It's time we took our futures into our own hands. Goodness, Alice, this is no way of life! Edward is not going to give up and we cannot drift like this for ever. It might be all right for the gypsies, but not for the likes of us. Davy needs a home. We could hide ourselves in London and maybe earn a living. I can sew, launder, clean, cook . . . I might, even at my age, be able to get work in the kitchens and support you both. There might possibly be a respect-able way for you to earn money, Alice, a way for us to make a home here and settle down in safety, without the constant fear of recapture. You cannot depend upon Luke, can't you see that? You cannot always turn to a man and use your body for barter.'

'I did not think it was anything like that.'

'No! That's the trouble, you never did. And now I am going to give Davy to Mika so that we can sit down quietly and talk about this. There are plans to be made, Alice, and you are going to have to help me make them. The Pettigrew Lovetts might help us. They might have connections in this barbarous city. They might even lend us some money to enable us to make a fresh start. There are all kinds of possibilities, my dear, and when you have recovered from this . . . as you will recover . . . you will see them as clearly as I do.'

Milly bustled out and made her way across the grass to Mika's crowded caravan. She breathed in gustily. She noticed that her legs and arms were trembling. Had she done right? Or had she been too cruel? She couldn't be certain that her suspicions were true . . . well, how could you see into somebody else's head, how could you read their thinking? Milly's decision was based on the one fact she clung to: she knew, better than she knew anything else, that she could not live through another of Alice's traumas. She just didn't have the stamina. She wouldn't survive it, and she doubted if Alice would this time, either.

And even a fool could see that they should not be sitting back doing nothing, waiting for the inevitable capture. No one believed Edward's tale that he was leaving London. Even those that didn't know him could see through that. And Milly knew her employer well enough to understand that he'd have to act soon in order to satisfy Charlotte.

And Milly had never trusted Luke. What was he doing about all this? An actor and a wanderer, a drifter and a rogue . . . Luke had served his purpose. He had got them away safely. But Milly did not consider Luke remotely capable, neither sensible or responsible enough, to take proper care of Alice.

Action was eminently better than passivity – any action. They should have acted years ago, Milly knew that now. They both knew that now. They should never have submitted to life in that house. The situation there had gone from bad to worse, but barely noticeably, very gradually. It was hard to say at what precise point Alice's life had become intolerable. And

402

in those days, Milly recalled guiltily, it had been she who had urged Alice to accept it. 'You cannot abandon your children. You are a wife and mother. You cannot follow your own desires . . . look what happened the last time you did that!'

And Milly remembered Alice's answer. 'This is quite different. Why can't you leave my past alone? I was young – only fourteen years old. Why must everything always be blamed on that?'

'Because that's what has brought all this down on you as I always feared it would,' Milly used to answer.

'But they are calling me mad! Oh, they never come right out and say it, but that's what they're meaning. They hide things from me, Milly. They tell me things and then say I have made them up. They watch me all the time . . . and now some of the servants have started to watch me, too.'

'Tut! What a wild imagination you do have, Alice!'

Was it right what they said, that Milly Toole had always been blind? Had she always preferred to see things her way rather than face the unpleasantness of reality? She'd been accused of it often enough.

While Henry Brennan lived Alice enjoyed some small protection. Florence had retired completely and was seldom out of her room. Even her meals were taken to her on a tray. But there was a new mistress of Winterbourne House, and that person was unquestionably Charlotte. How that had happened was hard to define. Milly spent most of her days in the nursery with Nicholas . . . and then Laura and Kate were born. Milly was happy to be in the nursery, ecstatic to care for small children again, much preferring their easy company to the unnatural life downstairs, and she couldn't be bothered with dressing up in the evenings and all that fussy nonsense.

But she had been concerned about Alice.

Her young mistress grew pale and nervous. She took to spending nearly all her time in the nursery . . . when

Charlotte allowed it. Only there did she seem to be happy, playing with the children and singing them songs. Milly had to work quite hard to keep her authority in it and to stop Alice from bathing them or dressing them or feeding them every time . . . what sort of nurse would allow a mother to do that? It was bad for the children. They would lose respect. They would come to regard their mother in a most unnatural way. Oh yes, Milly had had to fight her corner in those early days.

But the situation got worse.

The atmosphere in the house was terrible. Milly asked for – and got – a cottage in the grounds. She took to spending more and more time there, and was encouraged to do so by Edward who was always most generous and polite. They promoted the nurserymaid, Jane, who gradually began to take over. And Milly had to admit that she'd been relieved. Well, she wasn't getting any younger and her rheumatics were playing her up very painfully.

She took to spending more time downstairs at the express wish of Alice. 'They are slowly driving me mad, Milly, please believe me! I need you there for support. Sometimes I don't know if it's me or them, I'm so confused and nervous, but I can't really be getting everything wrong! They hate me, Milly. Charlotte has told lies about me and has encouraged Edward to hate me.'

At first Milly had not believed her stories, for why would Charlotte and Edward conspire to do that? There was nothing to hate about Alice. And then – and Milly disliked admitting this, even to herself – she had started asking herself if it could be true. *Was* Alice unbalanced? There had certainly been a kind of madness in that early, immoral behaviour of hers and the awful year that followed. And these days she was always forgetting things, misplacing things, and she was a little hysterical when she came to the nursery. All that wild energy – sometimes it took hours to settle the children down when she'd gone. The staring at herself in the mirror and the sad songs she sang. Wistful, yearning songs. 'Stop that,' Milly used to say. 'Look, you're upsetting the children.'

'I am so unhappy, Milly. I want someone to love me so badly.'

'Your children love you,' said Milly sternly. 'I love you! Surely that is enough.'

'I want more than that,' replied Alice.

'Well we all have to learn to live with what we've got and make the best of it,' said Milly flatly.

And Alice asked her, 'Didn't you ever yearn to hold someone's hand in the moonlight, and ride off in the rain to a secret meeting, to kiss beside a silver lake? Oh, why were we given these feelings if we weren't meant to use them?'

'Good heavens above, Alice. What will you think of next?'

Yes, there was a time when Milly wondered . . .

But she had sat and observed and had gradually realized that there was something going on downstairs which was not merely a figment of Alice's imagination. And it was only because Milly took the time to listen and watch that she noticed how Edward and Charlotte set little traps. And how easily Alice fell in them. She noticed, too, how they looked at each other over the top of Alice's head. She saw how they never quite left her alone . . . someone was always watching her, criticizing her, chastising her. And Alice accepted it meekly, just as though she was still a child and had never really been allowed to grow up.

Oh yes, Milly watched and she saw how it was and how subtle it was. But why? Why?

And then they even took to locking Alice up in her room.

Milly moved in then. Ferociously.

'Charlotte,' she said, 'this is quite unforgivable! What do you think you are doing locking Alice in her

405

room as if she was a naughty child? What on earth has Alice done to merit this! She tries to please you. She never answers you back. She is obedient and willing and desperate to do the right thing.'

'You never could see, could you?' was how Charlotte answered, so prim and severe in black like that. 'We all suffered because of your rather convenient habit of burying your head in the sand. For years we suffered, me and Lucinda.'

'I really don't understand what you're talking about.'

'Alice is sick, Milly! Alice is deranged and needs to be dealt with in the only way that it's possible to deal with people like that.'

'I am going at once to see Mr Henry. He should be told of this. He would not be happy to know this was going on in his house right under his own nose!'

'Go and see him if you like,' Charlotte sniffed, putting the key to Alice's room deep down in her pinafore pocket. 'But he probably won't even recognize you. Alice is not the only one in this house who is losing her mind.'

'As you well know, Charlotte, Alice has always been perfectly sane in her mind. Probably saner than you or I.'

And Charlotte had looked at Milly sharply. And Milly had let her eyes fall. 'Was it sanity that drove her out to the stables all those years ago? Answer me, Milly. Was it sanity that led her to give herself to that disgraceful groom? Was that sanity, when she ranted and raved afterwards, sobbing as if her heart would break? I really don't think so, Milly. No, I don't think so at all. And you never did satisfactorily explain the death of that cat!'

'You can't be suggesting . . .'

But Charlotte had turned on her heel and left.

So Milly had gone to find Edward. 'It looks as if all the stories that Alice has been coming to tell me are true. Why are you treating your wife like this? It is outrageous behaviour! What are you leading up to?

406

Have you no shame, Mr Brennan? I mistrusted you once, many years ago, when I had to take care of you for a few unpleasant hours one Christmas. But over the years I have come to respect you . . . not like you, perhaps, but respect you. And now I demand to know what is going on in this house.'

Edward's reply was sad. 'Charlotte warned me that it was no good confiding in you, Mrs Toole,' he said. 'Your loyalty to Alice is admirable, remarkable even, but not necessarily the kindest way to deal with her. I think you have much to answer for if you bothered to examine your own mind and separate your emotions from the facts.'

'What are you saying?'

'The tragedies that have beset us – the dreadful, unforgettable tragedies. Do you think they were all natural events? Do you honestly still believe that?'

'What tragedies? What on earth are you talking about? It is you and Charlotte who have lost your minds . . . in fact I am quickly coming to the conclusion that I am the only sane person in this house.' Milly had stood her ground, staunch and bulky like an English bulldog prepared for a fight to the death. But Edward had not allowed that. He had looked at her sadly and left.

And then it was that Milly realized, a little belatedly but better than never at all, that Edward and Charlotte were lovers. Should she tell Alice? Did Alice know?

Milly had not known what to do. And so she had done nothing.

When Florence Brennan died hardly anyone noticed. The old woman had not visited the downstairs of the house for years. The only way you knew she was still living was if you watched the procession of trays, the odd coal-bucket making its way along the landing to her room and the thin fume of camphor that sometimes trailed, like a lingering memory, from under her door. Kate and Laura were four and five years old when

407

Henry died and Milly managed to prevent them being dragged along to the funeral.

'No,' she said. 'Never! Over my dead body. I'll never forget the looks on the faces of my sweet things when they had to be present at their father's and mother's funerals. And this relative is once removed . . . they hardly knew their grandfather. They should not go to that.'

She could get her way over little things, but never the big ones. The children had not gone to the old man's funeral, but Alice went. She was the only member of the family who wept, and no wonder.

Alice took to coming to Milly's cottage in the grounds, bringing the children if she was allowed. They had some happy times there. Alice said, 'If only we could all live here together. If only we could be free.'

And Milly had not known what to do. So had done nothing once more. Had busied herself over tiny things from which she still managed to take pleasure like baking her own bread and making jam.

And then they had stopped allowing Alice to bring the children.

And then they had refused to allow Alice to visit at all.

Oh yes, they had a great deal to talk about. There were plans to be made. Never again was Milly Toole going to be driven into a corner like that. Never again would she allow herself to behave so feebly. Any action was better than no action. She could see the signs . . . bad signs . . . and she was determined to take counter-action . . . and fast!

Milly had been forced to tell Alice about Luke. She'd been forced to make her face things clearly. There had really been no other option.

She handed Davy over to the gentle Mika. Who would have thought there would ever come a day when she trusted a gypsy with one of her children. She corrected herself . . . *Alice's child*. But then Alice had

408

never been a real mother – only playing at it when Milly let her.

Milly turned and walked heavily back to her own caravan, prepared for the worst, prepared for a flood of emotional tears, for high drama, for turmoil of the very worst kind. Look how Alice had reacted after she'd watched Luke in the play! Yes, she was unstable in her relationships, in these silly love affairs of hers, but sane as you or I about anything else. Once she was over this Alice would see that Milly was right. It might take time . . . but in the end Alice would see that Milly, over most things, still knew best.

Milly was slightly less certain about her second decision of the morning. In fact she knew that some people would call her wicked for what she'd done, because she had told lies . . . had gone to Bella Pettigrew Lovett and explained why Edward and the doctor were after Alice and why they considered her mad. She'd repeated all those foul insinuations in front of Bella, and she'd even been quite impressed by the conviction she'd heard in her own voice. Lying was easy. Perhaps it was easier for someone who never told lies. Yes, Milly had told Bella everything – working her way through Charlotte's evil accusations from the cat, to Garth, to the baby Neville and then she had, almost sobbing, told her about poor Lucinda – the worst, the most ludicrous thing of all, not least in view of Alice's so tightly-guarded secret. 'Alice,' concluded Milly, 'poor, confused, lonely little Alice.'

And when Bella asked if it might have been better for Alice to remain in Deale, Milly was quick with her answers. 'Oh no, she had no need to be in that place. Alice needs to be with me . . . I am the only one who can control and understand her.'

Milly had not said exactly *that she believed the stories* . . . but she had allowed herself to be forced to confess that, yes, all those suspicions were probably true. She thought she'd done it quite well. Well, what else should she have done? She'd said what she had for the best. It was essential that this affair be finished and she didn't want Luke undoing all the good she had done, coming after Alice and changing her mind. They would soon be off on their own, just a little family of three, fending for themselves which is how it ought to be – a proper way to live. Luke Durant would soon fade out of Alice's life.

It was for the best.

But that knowledge didn't make Milly feel any better. She felt uncomfortable about the things she had said. She did not like telling lies and, if possible, she would not tell them again. Bella, sad and distressed, had undertaken to pass the truth on to Luke. Milly couldn't have done that.

Back where she started, Milly opened the caravan door. She stepped inside and peered anxiously about her as her eyes adjusted to the gentler light. 'Alice?' Where was she hiding herself now? More silly games!

Milly adjusted the pins in her hair as she stuck her head outside once more and searched around. 'Alice!' she called. 'Alice!'

Milly went cold all over. Alice was being silly again – she had gone! Milly ought not to have left her. Oh no, not more dramas, not more hysterics! Milly rolled her eyes to the ceiling and clutched at her crucifix. Please God relieve us from this! She'd thought Alice might have matured . . . that this time it would be easier, but no. Milly ought to have known better. It didn't look as if this situation was going to turn out at all as she'd hoped.

Did things ever?

# FORTY-FOUR

'Let me through! Let me pass! *Let me go!*'

Alice's agony was palpable. Only vaguely, almost as if the landscape she passed through was a world in a dream, did she notice the numbers of men who lined the railings, and the fact that some wore constables' uniforms and carried their batons in their hands and were assembling, forming a ring round the green swathe of parkland in which the troupe was camped.

What did this matter to her now? What did anything matter? She pushed past them . . . she shouted at them coarsely, nothing but a gypsy girl with a child slung on her back in the gypsy fashion, a shawl pulled over her head and a basket over her arm. Their instructions were to wait for the signal and then to surround the field and move in. They were to look for a lady and her nurse – the fugitives might be disguised – but the most important reason for their offensive was to capture the rogue, the trouble-maker and wanted man, Luke Durant.

So when this thin, wasted creature with the desperate eyes pushed past them they let her through before moving back to close ranks once again. Edward Brennan was talking to the officer in charge of the enterprise, giving the descriptions once again as they sat in one of the horse-drawn vans. He was jumpy and nervous. He was not even looking in Alice's direction as she passed not yards below him. He checked his watch for the fiftieth time . . . twenty minutes to go.

Alice hailed a cab, pressing a handful of coins into the grunting driver's hand. She commanded him, 'Take me to Drury Lane,' which was the only name in London she knew. The journey passed in a confusion of sights and sounds, some real, some straight out of her memories. The cab halted and the driver called

411

down. She opened the door and stepped out, realizing that because of her simple garb and the area they were in, he probably thought her a prostitute.

Behind the house-fronts Alice discovered a London she had only glimpsed when Luke had taken her into the city two days before. Menace was everywhere . . . this strange place was sinister and dangerous and Alice might just as well have found herself in a jungle. There was no knowing what dark alley you were going to find yourself in next or in which dingy court. Alice was afraid of the drunken women who lurched in the door-ways of the public houses, she was wary of the men who loitered beside the openings of the dark tunnels, of the raucous street-hawkers who eyed her as she passed by and she was terrified of the thin, pocked man with the face like a rat who followed her as she hurried along, not knowing where she was going or what she was searching for.

She only knew she must get away . . . and she knew something else, too. As she grew nearer to the shabby heart of the city every footstep she took told her that she was coming to her place; the shame and degrada-tion she saw all about her was hers . . . the humiliating poverty, the hopeless indignities, the screams that came from the slatternly women who stretched from between their grubby sheets in the darkest courts to box children's ears . . . she identified with all this now. At last she was home. This was her place. All her life she had been lonely, and she told herself now that it had not been a loneliness caused by a lack of company – but a yearning for her own kind. People who loved her for what she was, people for whom she need not pretend. Well, at last she knew herself for what she was and she was one of these people. She could hide herself somewhere here and never be found.

She hadn't thought twice about bringing Davy. She had acted from instinct. He was a real child, a real baby, not like the first one, not like the baby that hadn't been real at all. 'It's all in your own head, that's where you're doing it. Nothing has happened between you and Garth. Nothing!'

'Oh, but Milly, Milly, please listen to me, it has!'

Davy was hers, and their future, good or bad, ought to be shared. She would do her best for her son, the only child she had left. She would do whatever she had to, suffer for him if necessary, but she would love him in the kind of way she would have liked to have been loved. She had rushed into Mika's caravan and grabbed him blindly as soon as Milly's back was turned. She had taken one of Mika's straw bags to carry him in, and she'd fled.

She stepped round a pile of rotting vegetables in which some ragged children were scavenging. A man tilted his grimy hat and grinned at her tipsily, and a notice in a churchyard told her to 'Trust in the Lord'.

The street names meant nothing to her; she only saw that they grew dirtier and dingier and harder to read the further she walked, tinny and spindly as if they resented being nailed to the brick-chipped walls, contorting themselves as they pressed against the corners of these smoke-begrimed alleys. And the buildings grew taller until they spiralled right up to the sky, enclosing her in a yellowish light. She climbed a spindly metal bridge and found herself over the railway tracks. She stared about her. To her right flowed the river, its banks strewn with decay and a mist of pungent effluent steamed off the surface of the water as if the slow-moving sludge was on fire underneath. To her left, facing on to the Strand, the Globe Theatre rose like a smoky cliff over the ranks of slates and chimneypots. A train came, and the bridge seemed to flutter and tremble in the same way as her heart. But nothing could really hurt her. This was, after all, only a dream. She hung tightly on to the thin band of straw as the vibrations thundered underneath her, taking the weight of Davy in her hands, fearing he might be torn from her in the black rush of the approaching train.

She hurried on again as she saw that the man with

413

the rat face and the limp continued to follow her.

It started to drizzle. She took shelter in the doorway of a moneylender's shop and stood there, shivering, while she watched the procession of customers go in and out of the tavern opposite. She was going to have to ask for help. She was going to have to *speak to someone*. She felt no self-pity, no reproach; she had brought this situation on herself and there was nobody but herself to blame. Milly was right, as Charlotte had been right and as Edward had been right. She ought to have stayed in Deale – her children were better off without her. Perhaps she should not have brought Davy. She was mad. She had no control over her own feelings and, after all these years, she had given away her love again. Blindly. Foolishly. Shamelessly. *And she had believed that Luke loved her!* All those words he had spoken, those precious confidences, all those special touches and glances . . . she would have laughed out loud as she stood there, if her face had been warm enough to move, if her expression had not been frozen by cold, fear and horror. She was an unnatural woman and she had never been any different and this place and these people, they went well with her darkness.

She remembered how pathetically she had tried to please them – the people with the power – as a child, as a married woman, as a prisoner in the Asylum. You had to act the way they wanted you to act or be hurt.

Dimly, as she began to grow up, she had realized that one day she would lead a different life, that there was a world beyond this one and that she would one day find another self other than the one she was forced to live in daily. The realization of this had come as a kind of miracle, a release from the suffocation of the grinding training in humiliation, in suppressing herself. Fragile, sensitive, frightened and longing, she had been prepared to love Edward because she had been told it was all right for her to love Edward. And always she had searched for approval, for an image of herself in the eyes of other people.

Charlotte had been quite right to warn Edward about her. They had been right to punish her and curtail her behaviour. They had been right to take care over what she read or where she went or to whom she spoke. They had been right to remove her from her children – especially her little girls – the effect she might have had could have been terrible.

And quite probably she had started to take money . . . to move things and yet deny she had done it . . . to be told that guests were coming and then to forget she'd been told. So convinced of her own lack of worth and her guilt and failure, she saw that it was quite probable that she would be inadequate in other spheres of her life.

'Put that down, Alice, why are you wandering around stroking that ornament? It is not alive . . . it is not a pet . . . it is an expensive piece of porcelain,' – that was Charlotte.

'I just like the smooth cool feel of it in my hands,' Alice had replied. But then she had watched the expressions they exchanged.

'What are you attending to the fire for? Don't you know we pay servants to do that?' Edward's voice was always stern . . . the measured, heavy voice of the judge.

'I didn't want to bother them, it's late. And I like to arrange the pieces of coal myself, I like to direct the flames with my own fingers.'

More exchanged glances, and small frowns.

'You surely have not been outside without your coat, Alice? Not in this weather!' This was Milly who couldn't help talking like that, but suddenly the interpretation was different.

'I had not planned to go out, only I saw the snow and I wanted to rush out and run in it before someone else put their footprints there.'

And Charlotte's voice, laden with condemnation, over Milly's shoulder, 'Take the children upstairs, please, Milly, while we make sure Alice changes into something sensible. We don't want them to hear her talking like that.'

'We are not expecting visitors, Alice, so whatever possessed you to dress in that flamboyant gown?'

'I felt like looking pretty tonight.'

And she realized, before she spoke them, how foolish those words sounded.

And so she also came to understand how Edward and Charlotte, forced into coping with her, day in, day out, and finding the process such a struggle, had come to depend on each other. But it was years before she realized that Edward went to her sister's bed. Because Edward was so disgusted by sex, because, whenever he came to her, the experience was obviously so repulsive, so obnoxious and nauseating to him, Alice had assumed that he felt the same way about all women. And she had never considered Charlotte to be a sexual person . . . that thought was too ridiculous, it had never entered her head.

Alice was not hurt by her discovery, made by accident one morning when she rushed into Charlotte's room without knocking in order to search for her needlework box which she'd lent her the previous evening. No, she wasn't hurt when she saw Edward's face next to Charlotte's on the pillow, when she saw how they glanced at each other then, when she saw Edward's dressing gown on the bedside chair. She was astonished. She was confused. So it was not all women he loathed . . . but just her . . . just Alice.

When Alice told Milly, expecting shock, Milly said she already knew.

'But you kept it quiet from me? You decided I ought not to know? You made that decision?'

'I considered it was probably something you would be better not knowing, with you so upset and nervous all the time these days.'

'They love each other, Milly! And yet Edward was forced to marry me. How long have they loved each other? Could it be possible that even at the beginning Charlotte wanted Edward, and that's why she told him about me? Oh, no wonder they hate me!'

'And now you are being ridiculous. You do have this tendency to exaggerate, Alice. Nobody hates you. Goodness me, sadly, men have their needs, and Edward is no different from other men. After a while it is often the case that men get bored with their wives and need a change . . . '

'But Charlotte, Milly! So high-principled, so moral, so rigid, so cold. Charlotte has always disapproved of me and my past, and yet she gives herself to a married man – my husband!'

'Charlotte has always been the devious one, the trouble- maker.' Milly scratched her head and a selection of pins fell out. 'But I must confess this is most unworthy of her, and her in her sister's house. It is quite disgraceful.'

'This had never been my house, Milly. From the moment we came here Charlotte was mistress of it.'

'Only because you showed no interest. Only because you were either lost in a book or off walking on your own. Charlotte has a more dependable character than yours, less temperamental. But devious and scheming, oh yes.'

'They are close, Milly. They shut me out and will not let me in.'

'I warned you that your behaviour would bounce back at you one day. Edward has never been able to forgive you. You deceived him and unfortunately he found out. He does not understand you, my dear. Few people do, except me – you are so nervous and highly-strung.'

The result of Alice's discovery meant that afterwards, Edward and Charlotte made no secret of his whereabouts at night. Even when he'd made one of his rare and terrible visits to Alice's room . . . even after that he made no bones about the fact that he went, for comfort, to Charlotte. And as their joint attitude towards Alice became more severe, she began to dread the evenings when she was forced into their company. She implored Milly to spend more time downstairs, 'Because I can feel their hatred towards me, Milly. Sometimes it feels as if they are killing me. And their remarks are so cruel, especially in front of guests, and the servants. They seem to enjoy making a spectacle of me. You haven't watched them as I have. You have not had to endure the ordeal of all those silent evenings, those interminable mealtimes.'

So Milly had started accompanying Alice downstairs. And, in the end, Milly admitted that their behaviour was deliberately cruel. When the old man, Henry Brennan was alive, things were different. He was master of Winterbourne House and when he was present he ruled the roost. Charlotte and Edward retreated, temporarily. But then he grew doddery and old, forgetful. He started spending more time in his room and the onslaughts resumed; they became unbearable again.

'But why, Milly, why? And what can we do?'

Henry died.

Alice started visiting Milly's cottage, bringing the children whenever she could. It was her haven. But eventually Edward stopped even that. 'I don't like them being out alone in your company, Alice. We can never be certain of their safe return.'

'But Edward, I take great care of the children when they are with me! And Milly is there. Surely you can't be suggesting that, even if you consider me a bad mother, you no longer trust Milly.'

He refused to argue. He just looked at her sadly. And then Charlotte announced that she would give them their lessons, a pleasure that Alice had enjoyed in the past.

'You are far too lenient. Between you, you and Milly let them run wild. They are growing up without knowing the meaning of discipline. You are doing them no service, Alice!'

And Alice couldn't bear to watch how Nicholas'

happy little face used to crumple at Charlotte's strict words. How the atmosphere in the nursery turned oppressive when she entered the room. How severely she treated them . . . no songs, no stories, but dull pages of maths and Latin translations . . . lessons that Charlotte had taught herself during those long, lonely hours of their own childhood. 'Control yourself,' became the two words most often spoken. And long hours of sewing for Laura and Kate who were still too tiny to thread their own needles. Alice's heart cried out against it. She cringed when Charlotte chastised them for the laughter of excitement, for the giggles of fun and the shouts of joy, or when they ran to their mother when she came through the door, hanging on to her skirts and swinging.

Milly disapproved of Charlotte, too – the nursery should be such a happy place! Controlled, of course, but relaxed. Milly tutted her firm disapproval but she plodded out and turned her back, helpless in the face of it. For it had come so gradually upon them, and they had been unprepared for any of it.

But, shame on them both, they had done nothing. Two powerless women in that cold, mean house and neither a match for Charlotte's bitter tongue. Even the servants were on Charlotte's side. Even the servants suspected Alice.

Milly, bewildered and hurt, took the easy way out and retreated further and further into her own world, into the safe comfort behind her cottage door. She did not understand what was happening. And Alice, unable to follow her there for fear of punishment, fled back to her books, to that fairy-tale place where nothing really happened, or if it did there was always the happy ending to look forward to. To cling on to. Charlotte was quick to confiscate the books, calling them immoral and unsuitable. 'Servants' trash!' she said.

Oh, if only Alice had been in a position to pick up her children and go. The situation became so intolerable that living was a daily torture. Nicholas, growing up, tried to rebel against it, for he remembered happier times, but Charlotte and Edward were severe with him. Alice knew they told him things . . . things about his mother . . . disturbing insinuations that upset him dreadfully.

She caught phrases of the things they said, 'It is better if . . . '

'She has never been . . . '

'In some ways more irresponsible than . . . '

And was she? *Was she?* Wasn't it because of her behaviour that all this had come to be? Wasn't it because of what Edward called her own unhealthy desires, her inability to control herself as she should? The needs that took her rushing out into the night, that made her dance in her room alone, that made her cry when she heard sad music . . . There was something wrong. There had always been something wrong. The stirring within her had never died; no matter how she tried to numb them, her yearnings had never gone away.

She cringed in corners. She blamed herself.

'You need help,' said Edward one day. 'Charlotte and I think you should see a doctor.'

'I am not ill, Edward.' She was afraid of him, afraid of his meaning.

'Charlotte and I have decided.'

'You want me to go, Edward, don't you? You want to be rid of me so that you and Charlotte can marry. That has always been what you wanted and I think it has been that way right from the start.'

'You can be such a fool, Alice!'

'Why do you not ask me for a divorce? If that's what you want, why not do it?'

'Because I know you would not agree to it, Alice. You would not agree to give up your rights to the children. And you are bad for them. It is important to me that you are distanced from our children if possible. You upset them, particularly when you are in one of your states.'

420

'What states are you talking about, Edward? I do not get into states.' She was firm. She held herself straight. She tried to hold his eyes. She felt like a madwoman already, she thought she stared like a madwoman stared and everything she said sounded crazy.

'All that hysterical weeping, not eating, sullen behaviour, wild accusations, going around the house like a ghost, sad-eyed, making everyone nervous, not knowing what your next action is going to be.'

'Is it any wonder I go round sad? I have little left to be happy about. You and Charlotte never leave me alone with your criticisms and scoldings. Whatever I do I can do no right! I have tried to please you both, Edward, God knows I've tried. I know you don't want me as a wife, I fully understand that and I understand why. I did not come to you chaste, as a wife should, and for that you have never forgiven me . . . '

'You don't know, Alice, do you? *You honestly don't know!* You are so deranged you are quite unaware . . . '

And she couldn't reply because she didn't know what he was talking about.

She pleaded with him, sensing an increasing threat in the atmosphere that terrified her and tasted of rank poison. She wrung her hands and stepped back from him, requiring more space between them so that she could still breathe. 'I could take the children and go, if you would be prepared to help me. Milly would come with me. We would none of us bother you further. You would be alone with Charlotte, which is what you desire. I would not stand in your way. I would agree to a divorce if I could stay with the children. Edward, you must see that to part me from them would be cruel.'

And it was then that he repeated himself, very gently. 'I want you to see a doctor, Alice, and I have made the necessary arrangements.'

Alice shivered. Soon Davy would require a feed and where would they spend the night? There might be a

421

frost. Her breath was cloudy-white on the grey winter air of this late afternoon. The gas-lamp beside her spluttered sadly, while the lights from the tavern across the way beckoned brightly.

She would go in and enquire. Someone would give her food and a bed; someone would offer her work. She was young, strong and healthy. Of Luke she could not yet bear to think . . . of his great betrayal. She should have known that a man like that could never love her.

What was she? Nothing.

What had she ever been? Nothing.

She felt right standing there on the street, frightened, cold, but right, with the child on her back . . . needy, almost a beggar. The sharper the cold and the greater the fear the more easily she could blank out the pain. How pleased Luke must have been when he realized who she was, when he saw this perfect opportunity for revenge present itself to him on a plate. And that's exactly what she had done . . . again . . . on a plate . . . offered herself and all that she was to someone who didn't want her.

Look at her! She caught a reflection of herself in the dull window of the moneylender's shop. She looked evil, in black like that, a thin, bedraggled, evil shadow. Alice tugged at the cord that held Davy to her back and held up her skirts before stepping across the cobbles towards the brightly-lit door of the tavern.

She had given herself away before, that's what Milly called it. So why not now? What, after all, was the difference? At least she'd be able to count what she got in return. Count it on her hand, not feel it slipping from her body, from her hiding place in the dank straw where she had once loved and clung so desperately to Garth.

Yes, she'd been sick, and ill. Her body had grown in strange ways that she had to hide from everyone . . . from the sharp, prying eyes of Charlotte, from the disapproving, furious eyes of Milly. Her body was punishing her as Milly had done. 'Nothing has happened,

422

Milly, nothing is happening. It is in my head. I make things up and I dream dreams.'

And it was easy during that long, cold winter to wear more wraps; everyone discarded the fashion and took to voluminous skirts and pinafores. She was thin to begin with and she ate little; she preferred her own company and she was safe because she had always insisted on bathing alone. Milly understood all about that. Milly had never betrayed that first childhood secret and even Charlotte, who seemed to find ways to know everything, never found out. She felt weak and ill. She was often sick. She preferred to stay in bed and wrap herself up, wrap herself away from the world and its angry faces.

This was merely the pain of Garth coming out, the loneliness growing inside her body because it couldn't find anywhere else to escape. She grew and bulged with sadness and loneliness. 'He never said anything to you! He never touched you.'

'No, Milly, he never touched me. He never kissed me. He never said kind words.'

It was let's pretend, it was make believe. And Alice understood make believe.

Even that night, on and on until a weak dawn came scattering splinters of winter amongst the blood on the straw, it was make believe. She tried to smile through the pain, she whispered, 'It's all right, Alice, it's all right. You are making it all up.'

Just an image of hands, an image of lips, an image of words that were always lies.

There was no baby really, just a scrap of a pale blue dream in the morning. She cut herself free with the sharp iron hook amongst the tools on the tackroom wall. She didn't kiss it, no, nothing like that. She wanted to whisper a nursery rhyme – Evangeline, her favourite doll in the frilly pink crib – but she didn't have time and it would have felt like telling nursery rhymes to herself.

But the next day she was drawn back to the stables

and, of course, the little doll baby was gone. It had never been there and you do not mourn for the children of fairies.

Alice entered the public house and the door swung closed behind her.

# FORTY-FIVE

If Luke Durant had heard those fatal words from anyone else he would not have believed them. Even Nathaniel – if Nathaniel had told him Luke would have suspected some terrible, tasteless joke – unlike Nathaniel, yes, but that's what he would have thought.

But it was Bella. And the anguish he saw in her face as she recounted, gently and kindly, Milly's warnings, made him close his eyes against an awful sincerity he could not challenge. He reeled from her deadly attack, hopelessly wounded, but he listened gravely, nodding sometimes when Bella stumbled, finding it impossible to go on. At last it was all out . . . all there, spread out before him . . . insanity, murder . . .

'When did she tell you these things?'

Bella shifted her large frame as she sat in her high-backed chair in the leading caravan, surrounded by bunches of coloured bunting and hand-bills, her pipe loose on her lap as if she'd lost the energy even to suck on the much-bitten end. Wisdom, huh. The smoky-coloured crystal ball in the corner laughed at her, the pack of well-worn playing cards was high on the shelf, abandoned. How did one learn not to feel lost and inadequate when people turned out to be not what they seemed? Especially someone like Luke, who was so wary of love. Bella would rather be anywhere else in the world than here; she would rather be talking to anyone else but Luke. She had spent the last two hours in something akin to purgatory, going round and round in her head, wondering whether to keep quiet . . . this would destroy Luke. But if nobody told him the truth and his relationship with Alice was allowed to deepen . . . She had come to her decision reluctantly, for she did not believe in interference. Her voice was quick and gruff. 'Milly Toole came and told me this early this morning, when you were making arrangements to leave. She was greatly upset, poor soul, and she decided that the burden of keeping her secret was too heavy to carry. She has protected Alice all her life, she's been a good friend, a mother. I have never understood why Mrs Toole has been so interfering and vigilant – now I know. If what she says is true . . .'

'Then you think it might not be?' he asked quickly. 'Good God, is this real?' He looked around him, appealing to Bella when he repeated himself, spreading his hands in supplication, 'Am I hearing right? Is any of this real?'

Bella's black eyes were shrewd and unyielding and she confronted Luke squarely. Her red flannel petticoats were spotted with candlegrease and she had done nothing this morning with her tangled, soot-black hair. She heard her own deliberate voice say: 'I have no reason to disbelieve Mrs Toole. The last thing in the world she would do would be to hurt her darling, Alice. And I have come, quite surprisingly, to like and admire the woman.'

'That is no answer. I want to know what *you* think. The things you have told me are incredible. Is it possible that Alice could be so sick? Is it possible – and how could I not have known it?'

Bella hated the way she was speaking, like a tolerant schoolmarm trying to explain a place on a map – old, worn words, such poor vehicles at a time like this, when all she wanted to do was not speak at all, but lean over and take Luke in her great, comforting arms and blank it all out.

'When we're in love we see what we prefer to see. We don't stop to look for the flaws. And your love, Luke, it blossomed so quickly – you recognized something in Alice that answered a need in yourself. Perhaps it was her helplessness, the deep sense of innocence – the madness itself that attracted you. We all have mad-

426

ness in us. We're all frightened, yet intrigued by it. And I think that you could have been dazzled, and yes, it is possible that you were mistaken.'

Luke let his head fall in his hands. He moaned, 'You have not told me the truth. You are not telling me what you, yourself, thought about Alice Brennan. Why aren't you telling me this? Why are you using other people's thoughts and words? You don't sound like yourself any more, Bella. And that frightens me.'

'I use other people's words because I don't know Alice. I wish I did. I wish I had spent time talking to her so that I could help you now. I have seen the close way Mrs Toole watches her. I have spent long hours listening to the old woman's concerns for her. I have seen the puzzling way Alice loves her child one moment and then leaves it. I have sensed her fear and yet not been able to place it . . . she laughs one moment and cries the next; she behaves like a child and yet she is not a child.' She did not want to offer hope in case there was none.

Luke raised his head briefly in order to say, 'She had much to be frightened about. Edward was following her. A life back in Deale Asylum was threatening her . . . '

'She was frightened of loving you, Luke. That was the source of Alice's greatest fear.'

'She was always so jealous . . . afraid I might leave her or look at some other woman. She could not bring herself to watch me perform on a stage.'

'Had she cause to fear you, Luke?'

He shook his head despairingly. 'Any fears of that kind came out of her own head. I spent hours trying to reassure her.'

'Perhaps you should talk to Milly Toole yourself,' said Bella under her breath, quivering under a great surge of pity as a shaft of feeling moved between them and stabbed her with Luke's own pain. She looked at the hurt and bewildered man, at the curly black hair,

427

stubborn and crisp, the square brown face, blue round the chin and unshaven. She saw the naked need in his eyes and longed to answer it with the right words. But she could not find them.

'Milly Toole does not trust me. She dislikes me. She is frightened for Alice.'

'In what way?'

Luke's eyes met Bella's for one thoughtful second and his voice came in a whisper when he said, 'I do not know in what way.'

'I know you loved her, Luke,' said Bella inadequately, drying her hands on the rough folds of her petticoats. 'I think I know how much you loved her.'

'I loved her, yes,' said Luke. 'And I love her still. Nothing can change that.' And he smiled a singularly sweet and warming smile as he got up quickly, parted the frayed damask curtains and left the caravan. She did not attempt to go after him. But it was that smile that worried Bella Pettigrew Lovett more than anything else that had passed between them. Nothing could stop him now.

'Where is she?'

Milly Toole's mouth hung slackly open before she could pull herself together to answer, 'I don't know! I have searched everywhere. She has gone. And Davy – she has taken the baby with her! Oh Luke, I did not mean this . . . I was so afraid that the birth of her baby had started all this off.'

'A little late for meaning, a little late for plain speaking!'

He strode away from the caravan not wanting to hear any more. He had heard enough. He made quick enquiries from a group of Romanies who were warming the oats before mounting his horse, adjusting the stirrups, and fastening his cloak across his chest. He swished the whip down on the stallion's haunches and it was only as he was limbering up to a canter, approaching the opening of the park, deep in thought,

428

that he saw the close ranks of men lining the six-foot railings. Spiked railings, lethally sharp.

Their devices were pathetic! He took it all in at one glance, then rode round in a small circle, murmuring to the horse under his breath. He paused to shorten the stirrups, clenched his knees and sat tight in the saddle. He gripped his reins. He brought down the whip.

All he saw as the horse took the jump was a row of white faces that fell back in a wave at his unswerving approach. He thought he saw Edward Brennan's face, tight and whiter than all the others. He thought he saw an arm stretched out, a wild finger pointing and a mouth that was opened wide in a shout. He thought he recognized those slovenly henchmen, Corbett, Callow and Duffy, as astonished as their master as they grouped uneasily round him. But Luke saw all that in one piercing flash amidst total confusion, roaring motion. And the shout was probably in his own head as the air rushed past his ears and the horse thundered powerfully beneath him. There was no sense of triumph, no exhilaration that he had outwitted them, just a dull, bruising certainty that had settled on his chest. Nothing could stop him – only death could do that. Ah yes, death, and he was prepared for that . . . but only in his own time, as it should be.

He would never have dreamed of leaving Alice alone and unprotected, especially as the trap pulled tighter. All those times when they had to be parted, Luke, ever anxious, ever aware of the cunning of Edward, had set the most sly, the most devious, the wiliest gypsy he knew to protect her. A lean, mean individual with small darting eyes. 'Never relax your guard,' Luke had told his thin-faced, tight-lipped friend. 'Never for a moment drop your eyes. She is the most precious person in my life and I am not prepared to lose her. If you let me down you answer to me, and God help you.'

The limping, surly Caleb Cavil had closed one knowing eye and smiled, in his own way. He owed Luke . . . many people owed Luke, who was more tolerant, more likely to offer help and understanding on delicate matters of law than their rather fearful employer, Pettigrew Lovett, who could turn on them one minute and be laughing with them the next. And if Cavil had got away with more than his share of skulduggery, if he had managed to pay his fines and stay out of gaol then it was Luke who had advised him, Luke who had saved him. The lean and morose Cavil had more dark deeds marked up against him than most other men . . . it was a way of life for Cavil . . . it would seem that other people's property, and Cavil, could not be parted. He had held his grubby knife at more drunken throats down dark alleys than it was worth counting and yet he maintained to the world that the money that weighted his pockets came from the sales of his highly debatable bottles of hair tonic.

Alice, desperate no doubt, and unhinged – Luke flinched – imagining that her worst fears were about to be realized and that Luke would desert her, had blundered off with Davy to God knows where, giving Cavil no time to alert him. But there was no doubt in Luke's mind that Cavil would be close behind her. She would come to no harm with Cavil so tight on her trail.

It was a cold afternoon. Frost began to glisten on the surface of the cobbles and the lamps were being lit early. Luke shuddered as he travelled nearer, hoping against hope that he was right and refusing to dwell on the worst terrors, refusing to imagine what might happen to Alice here, lost and alone. Cavil was there. He could trust Cavil. As he rode his horse through the streets, growing calmer, forcing himself to think more clearly as every minute went by, Luke guessed that Alice would want to hide herself, make for the bustling, teeming places where she could lose herself in a crowd. How had she travelled? Did she have money? What was in her mind at this moment? If only he knew. If only

430

she had been able to trust him. And if only he knew where to look first.

Life had never been safe and easy for Luke. For as long as he could remember he had had to fight. For all his good thinking, Mathew Durant was a violent man, quick to anger and intolerant of dissent. Luke's mother was afraid of him and his servants avoided him. Luke could remember wishing he was bigger, stronger, wanting to protect his mother against his father's outbursts of vicious rage. But his mother had her own ways of protecting herself, with poetry, music, her friends. She filled Castle Bellever with people. They clustered round his mother as if to suck at her wit and beauty . . . she'd been charming, cultured, alluring. There had not been much room for a child, not much opportunity of protecting her.

His was a peculiar childhood. He'd spent much of it alone, too highborn to play with the local boys, too strange to be invited to the houses of the nobility. So Luke used to roam the wild, unkempt grounds and go fishing with Seaton. Happy? Yes, he'd been happy. But he remembered most clearly the desperate way he had always yearned for something or someone of his own . . . someone he could love and protect and grow close to, rather than someone who smiled and nodded and danced and flirted, pretending that nothing was wrong.

There had been something between his father and mother which eluded him, something that kept him out, something he could never break through.

Seaton, kind and gentle and with all the patience in the world, sometimes helped him with his small menagerie of wild animals – a rook with a broken wing, a rabbit with its foot crushed in a trap, the blind toad, the fox cub abandoned by its mother. But when they were mended he let them go. He had never kept them as pets . . . it was cruel to do that with wild things,

Seaton said. His pony was his own, but that did not need him. It was a spoilt, wilful beast with a mind of its own and greedy for oats, happy to soften its eyes at anyone who gave them. His father's dogs were sophisticated, long-nosed disdainful creatures, too luxurious for loving and mindful of their sleek, glossy coats.

At sixteen he had discovered a certain kind of love was easy to find. Women liked him! After his initial astonishment he revelled in his luck, but the kind of warmth and companionship he really craved was much harder to find. When he'd first met Milly Toole, sitting comfortably in the kitchen at Venton Hall, he experienced a gust of betrayal when he compared her with his mother and wished that aloof, wonderful creature of whom he was so much in awe was homely and plain and as easy to talk to, as available to him as Milly Toole was. He loved the warmth and the bustle of the kitchens at Venton, the good smells, the laughter and quick wit of the maids, the numerous chairs at the table. The kitchens of the castle were not like that . . . the main kitchen hall was a high, vast, vaulted greystone place, with myriads of outhouses, dimly-lit passages and cold stores. It was more like being outdoors than in. Even in summer it was stony cold and the smells never lingered in that comforting way. They steamed away, up to the ceiling with the heat and got lost there. He was never welcome in it. He was shooed out of it.

He insisted on riding out with his father that fatal night: he demanded it. He decided his childhood was over, that he find a way in . . . through manhood.

But it hadn't been like that. He had not felt like a man – no, not at all. He had felt confused and frightened, not properly understanding what it was all about, only that his father must be right. And then to see his father fall like that, wounded, possibly dead? The great man covered with blood, no voice, just pleading, anxious eyes . . . Luke had been terrified of that.

And the eyes of that other boy mirrored his own. The same startled fear was in them . . . wondering why . . .

Life seemed suddenly to have ended.

He was an outlaw. No home. No safety anywhere. His father had killed his mother; through his absence in gaol, his wife had been murdered, and if Luke had stayed home at Castle Bellever he would have had the chance he had craved. He might have been able to protect her, save her life – *but would she have wanted that?* Would she have wanted to live, with Mathew no longer there? Luke had never been able to answer that question, and it haunted him.

He had never visited his father in gaol – he could not. He would be captured if he went near the place. And he wasn't sure if he wanted to go. Then it was too late.

Nathaniel Pettigrew Lovett – every year the theatre called and made camp in the courtyard, performing for his mother and her guests in the great hall. Sometimes they'd let him take small parts. He had dressed up, had painted his face. He'd been good at pretending to be someone else, he'd found it easy, simpler. Nathaniel, that great bear of a man, had told him in his great booming voice: 'You have great talents, my boy. You would make a fine actor!' Luke remembered how once he'd made his mother laugh.

After the massacre there had been nowhere else to go. Seaton told him to ride out and find Nathaniel. 'He will take you,' said Seaton, somewhere in the panic, in the horror and the chaos of it all. 'Go now . . . find him. He is a good man, the only man who is big enough, strong enough, to entrust with your life.'

That was a long, long time ago – and much had happened to him since. He had seen the world, acted on most of the world's great stages . . . oh, not under his own name, but as the man they called Robert Melville. Some small progress had been made in the English courts of justice. It was a process of whittling away at the red tape, they said, of whittling away at outmoded

433

prejudice. They said it would not be long before his name was cleared and his estates returned to him.

A long, long time ago. Luke had discovered much, had experienced much, had learned much about life and about people.

But until he met Alice he had never found love. And then he had known. Instinctively, at first sight of her, he had known.

But she would not let him in.

Wooton Street, Richard Street, Sutton Street – into the taverns and gin palaces he went, ignoring the painted, beckoning women and watching the men, searching for the riff-raff that were Cavil's types and who might have a message for him. It never occurred to him that he might not find her, that his task was as impossible as searching for a needle in a haystack. The seedy under-world of this city was meat and drink to Cavil. He drew breath from it, he had spent his childhood in London, there was not a soul he did not know or had not known, once, as he went about his dubious business. Through this criss-cross network of small criminality Cavil would somehow reach him. Through Griffin Street, York Street and Addington Street Luke went, letting himself be seen in each public house before turning and leaving as swiftly as he had come, as the night darkened and grew colder, rubbing his hands against the chill and tying his horse to the most convenient lamp-post.

If it took him the rest of his life he could search and go on searching. As he rode he scanned the pavements through aching eyes, brushing the sleet from his eyelashes with an impatient hand. He saw his moving shadow rise and fall against the walls, towering tall one minute, shrunken and almost disappeared the next, and that's the way his hope went.

And then there was the shrivelled little man in the corner, under the burnished pewter beside the fire-place, who called him over with a jerk of his head and

434

a wink down his long, shiny nose.

'Lookin' fer someone, guv?'

'Caleb Cavil.'

'Yep.' The man eyed Luke suspiciously over the foaming top of his mug. 'Cavil came in 'ere, scuttled in 'ere more like as if 'e were 'bout ter wet 'is trews. An' then orf out again quick as yer please. 'E's in the Bunch o' Grapes in Derry Street . . . '

'How long ago was he here?'

The man took a lick at the foam. His tongue flicked in and out, like a snake's. 'One hour . . . two . . . 'ard ter swear fer certain.'

And Luke nodded, threw a guinea down on the table, and it was still twirling on its edge when he left.

The sleet turned into snow, and the flakes were falling gently, thickly as Luke quickly dismounted, tied up his horse and pushed open the tavern door.

He saw her immediately. The parlour was small, cosy and well-lit. Under a heavy black mantel a coal fire blazed merrily. Alice, with Davy in her arms, was sitting in one of the windsor chairs to the side of the grate. A heavy man in a shiny black hat was conversing with her from the other. Cavil was sitting up at the bar with his dirty cap askew on his greasy grey ringlets. Shining glasses and pewter mugs hung above him.

Luke's gaze was the gaze of the pirate who has, at dear last, found the treasure. When he reached her he touched a strand of her hair, moving his finger to her cheek, her lips.

She smiled but her eyes had gone pale. The bulky man coughed, patted his stomach and got up to leave. 'We were just investigating the possibilities of doing a little business, your pretty little friend and I.' That face would stand one punch, only one, and then it would split, thought Luke.

He hoped the man wouldn't speak again, for his explanations would be too distasteful. He stared at the fat man coldly, watching him, never dropping his threatening stare until he left the room.

Cavil sidled over. 'Thought you wuz gunna be too late, guv,' he said, tipping the back of his cap with his finger so that it leaned further down over his nose. 'Another few minutes an' I wuz wonderin' what ter do next like.'

'I owe you, Cavil,' said Luke. 'Remember that.'

'Oh, I will,' said Cavil oilily, over one raised skinny shoulder as he slid out of the bar.

'That terrible man has been following me all night!'

Luke raised his eyebrows. 'Then Cavil is losing his touch.' He sat down in the now-vacant chair. 'And now we must talk. You must tell me what this is all about. Is Davy all right? Do you need to find a room for him?'

She said straight away, 'You were using me, Luke. Milly told me. You never explained about the personal vendetta that exists between you and Edward. You were using me for your own revenge, to even the score between you.' Her words accused him in the most expressionless voice he had ever heard.

He took her hand. It was passive, small and cold, in his own. 'That is simply not the case. What happened between me and Edward was long, long ago. I did not tell you because I feared you would jump to that conclusion. The time was inappropriate, and now you have to believe that any hatred I had on that score is gone. The matter is of no significance to me . . . '

'I am sure Edward does not think so.'

'I am not Edward. I do not see things in the same way as Edward. I do not think in the same way as Edward. I am not prepared to lie and pretend . . . '

'You do that every night when you act in your plays. You deliberately deceive . . . '

It was no use. He looked at her. He looked at her fragile hand . . . *a hand that had killed!* He heard the desperate plea in her voice and he felt his heart break. He knew what she had been prepared to do, if he'd arrived a few moments later. He knew what she would

436

have done with herself . . . such a lonely little suicide. And he knew that whatever he did, no matter how long he lived, he could never convince her of his love for her. She was too wounded.

All this hurting had to stop.

'I am taking you home, Alice,' he said softly. And he touched Davy's head with extreme gentleness. She looked down at her child, as if astonished to find herself in sole charge, and alarmed by it. And Luke said, 'We cannot go back. They are waiting for us there. It is cold, it is dark, and it it nearly Christmas. It is time that we all went home.'

# FORTY-SIX

Apart from a few short cuts, they took the road they had followed only weeks before – could it be merely a month ago? – but this was a very different journey. Alice, bruised from hours in the saddle, her face tight and sore from the battering wind and driving sleet, buried her face in Luke's coat and clung to him tightly. Davy was strapped in a basket on her back, and it was because of him that they could not travel at the speed Luke would have chosen. Alice was grateful for that and Davy, wrapped from head to foot, only a sliver of his face showing, was lulled by the constant rocking motion, and slept for long hours at a stretch. It was only when he woke that Luke let up and was willing to pause for a rest while the child was changed and fed. At night, weak, cold and weary, Alice fell into whatever bed there was available, the baby cuddled beside her, and her sleep was deep and dreamless.

Once, she woke in the night, leaned over and lit a candle, pulled her shawl around her and, sitting on the edge of the bed, gathered Davy into her arms. The flame settled. She ran her finger over his head. He didn't wake. She stared at his face, feeling wonder and marvelling at his beauty, perfect down to the last detail. There was a warm flush of love for this child which was hers in a way none of her others had ever been. He was helpless, totally dependent upon her and he was real. She could not hand him to Milly on a whim; she was not expected to leave him in the nursery while she went to her cold room and dressed, ready to go downstairs, feeling that ache, that awful ache, that terrible dead space in her arms. Davy was real, he was hers.

Why had she agreed to go with Luke when, only hours beforehand she'd been so determined to lose

438

herself in the grimy tenements and courts of London which had seemed the only real home left to her then? And she'd been on the point of earning some money – the first real money she'd had of her own. A room, spartan but clean and not far from there, the man had promised her, and a special breed of customers who would be happy to pay over the odds for an hour with a lady. But Luke had arrived as she was on the point of agreeing, and she was disgusted with the ease at which she'd allowed herself to be persuaded to give up her plans and go with him. Disgusted, but resigned because what did it matter anyway? And even now with him hurting her so she would rather be with him than alone in her dreams.

'Why have you come for me? Why must you go on pretending, Luke? It would have been kinder to leave me . . .' Alice had wept. 'At last I have taken a decision in my life and I know I could have carried it through . . .'

'I am not leaving here without you. I love you, Alice, and I don't care whether you believe me or not. You are not staying here.'

And oh, his lies were so very convincing. To look at his face, to hear him was almost to believe that Edward meant no more to Luke than a rather irritating insect, something that must be disposed of, slapped down before he could proceed on his way, for certainly he harboured no grudges. The last thing in the world she was, he assured her, was a weapon for revenge. But that was one of her greatest flaws – she always believed what men said. She wanted to believe, so she did.

The dream was deepening. Her words came slowly. They were difficult to form in her mouth. 'There is no future for us, Luke. There is nowhere for us to go. You tell me you're taking us home, but what is home, and how long can we stay there before they come for us both? And when Edward takes me back what will you do? Will I cease to matter to you then? Or if you avoid

439

capture will you come for me, obsessed with outwitting him, determined to bring him to his knees?'

'I am not concerned with the future, Alice. This day is the only time that matters. Today you are coming home with me, and the reason you're coming with me is because we are in love with each other.'

She wanted so much to believe in true love, she wanted to go with him. Even knowing that he would desert her when he'd finished with her, when her purpose was used up, knowing this she still went with him. She despised herself for her weakness, but she went. Nothing was real. Nothing was happening.

'We cannot leave Milly,' was as far as her feeble protests took her.

But Luke said, 'You had no difficulty with that problem when you set off on your own only hours ago. Milly will be well looked after and when the hue and cry has died down we'll find her again. We can't return to the troupe and put everyone there at risk. As it is, when Edward's men close in Nathaniel will have trouble denying the fact that he's been harbouring a wanted man.'

'But Bellever, Luke – won't that be the first place the authorities will look?'

'That will be the very last place – I so rarely go there. They'd expect me to travel north . . . and they wouldn't go seeking for you in a place so close to Edward, Charlotte and home.'

Alice continued to protest, but weakly. 'Bella told me the legal procedures were nearing a conclusion and that you were keen to be in London when the final judgements were made. This must be most inconvenient for you at such a time.' She would have gone on mocking, but Luke interrupted her bluntly.

'The final message, good or bad, will eventually be passed on wherever I am.' And his laugh was a cold one, his smile bleak and she thought he was angry because she'd run away, because she'd not trusted him.

'What did she tell you, Luke? *What did Milly say?*'
Luke was different – sadder, serious. There was a grimness about the set of his mouth and his easy manner had disappeared.

'Milly has told me nothing at all.' But his face was hunted and tense. And then, gently, 'Why, what are you afraid of, Alice?'

She did not answer because she could not. She only knew that he was different.

He was determined to get on; she had never seen him like this before. However many miles they covered their progress did not satisfy him. Alice would have liked to linger beside the inn fires in the early mornings when it was still dark outside and there were white fern patterns crimped on the windows and frost on the grass. The thought of more hours in such uncomfortable circumstances, holding so tight that her arms became cramped and numb and every bone in her body was bruised, the thought of more of that became intolerable. But he would not listen to her complaints. 'We have to get off the road. Only when we reach Bellever will I feel safe. I have to get you and Davy home. I can't protect you in these wide open spaces. I have to get home.'

And so they travelled on, and it wasn't the cold that made her feel, sometimes, that Luke had been turned into stone. The country roads were iron-hard and icy, scarred by hoofmarks, the surfaces scored by the undulating ruts of cartwheels. They paused briefly at turnpikes where Luke, muffled to unrecognition by his high collar and scarves, clapped his raw hands and called impatiently to the keeper who came grumbling out of his cottage, his breath steaming on the frosty air. Luke threw down his coins, kicked on the horse and they moved quickly on.

And for Luke? Their love couldn't be, but he couldn't stop loving.

It was with grateful lungs that he gulped down the

freezing air of every new morning. He embraced the discomforts of the road and the grim task that he had set himself. He could not turn his eyes to right or to left. There was only one road and whatever he did he must follow it. Luke's grief possessed him. Every day, when he saw her, it overwhelmed him again. It was an agony that seized and bound his spirit so that he was engulfed by his anguish and could see no other way out of it.

He loved her. No matter what she was or what she had done, he loved her. And he would protect her until the end.

Nearer home now, and the familiar, steeply-angled pastures were covered with heather and broken by granite spurs. Tangled thickets of sycamore and ash filled the crevices in the hills and formed furry dark islands on top of the smooth contours. The tiny light grew larger as they approached the castle through the gloom and Luke gave a great sigh as he allowed all his breath to leave his body, in spite of the fact that this arrival held a frightening relevance for him. There'd been times when he'd feared he might not find the energy to make it. Past the gatehouse and under the bridge and there was Seaton, old, wispy, frayed and shuffling but still the same Seaton with the same fond look in his eyes. And the same old question, his grumpiness betrayed by the half-smile on his face, 'Why didn't you let me know you'd be coming?'

'Has anyone been?'

'Nobody has been near nor by.'

Seaton helped Alice from the horse, regarding Davy with a twinkling eye but making no comment save to urge them, 'Get indoors quickly, out of this crippling cold. At least I have a fire there, and some mulled wine beside the hearth.' He sniffed and gave a far-away stare. 'There's snow in the air, I can smell it. 'Twill be on us by tonight. Take her inside, Luke, take her in. I'll deal with the beast and there's no luggage to speak

442

of, I see. Will this be another fleeting visit?'

'No, Seaton, not this time.' Luke patted his horse. 'He's completely worn out. I've ridden him near to death. Take good care of him, Seaton.'

'Are we to stay for a while then, Luke?'

He did not answer but helped her through the massive door – its frame was mantled with ivy, the door itself crusted with moss – indoors and up the winding steps to the well-lit tower room that was Seaton's. Alice had been here only once and yet it did feel like home.

It was silent in Seaton's tower room and after the constant assault of the noise of the journey the silence was welcome. Not even the weather breached it. The tower room was vast and round with three arched doorways leading from it. The uneven stone floor was covered with piles of Turkish rugs which lapped and criss-crossed each other. Thick tapestries draped near-ly every inch of the granite walls. The tiny windows were shuttered, and a coat of arms and crossed swords gleamed above the fireplace. The furniture was of dark brown oak, ancient and worn to the hue of ebony. Magnificently dilapidated luxury, impregnable safety.

She sat in the chair beside the fire and Luke covered her with rugs so she felt squashed, like a bundle. She felt the rocking motion still . . . in her head she was still travelling. It took concentration to relax the muscles in her arms and her legs. Painfully and slowly the feeling returned to her hands and her feet. Luke took Davy from her and laid him on a rug in the alcove beside the fire. He slept. Seaton disappeared through one of the narrow doors while Luke reached for the red-hot poker and put it into the earthenware bowl resting on the slates before the monstrous fire dogs. The spicy red wine steamed and bubbled. He ladled a spoonful into a long-stemmed goblet, came and knelt before her, straightened her hand and folded it back round the shape of the goblet. 'Sip some of this. Slowly, for it will be hot. You'll soon feel better.'

Alice was now able to move her face. The mask which had frozen it stiff was melting. She was weary, travel-stained and ugly. Her heavy hood fell back from her hair and, seeing Luke staring so hard at her like that, with her free hand she smoothed it. It was tied back in a simple bow, but tatty ringlets of gold had blown across her face and were stuck there. Luke looked no different, unruffled as always. He had thrown his hat on to a chair knob, flung his caped overcoat over the back; he wore brown corduroy breeches and a thick brown waistcoat over a cream-coloured flannel shirt. Round his neck was the bright red neckerchief with which he'd covered his mouth on the journey. She smiled at him because she was thinking she had never seen a man so tall, broad and handsome. How he would laugh at her if she said that, yet he could be a farmer's boy with his rugged, weather-beaten face and his black curly hair coiling over his forehead like that.

If only they had been able to love. If only their love had been real.

Seaton crabbed his way into the room bent double over a tray. Three wooden bowls held a steaming brown broth, golden with grease on the surface, and chunks of bread torn from a loaf were spread thickly with butter.

'Goose giblets,' said Seaton in his crackly voice, smacking his lips with pleasure. 'Full of goodness, and onions and turnips and bits of all sorts of odds and ends, herbs and spices. Taste it . . . smell it . . . I think it's one of my best.'

'Goose?'

'It is Christmas Day tomorrow.'

But Alice hadn't known that. She'd forgotten about time and the outside world, about ordinary occasions and normal events. Her children's faces were clear before her as she put down her wine and obediently took Seaton's proud offering. Oh, how she missed

444

them! Oh, how she longed to see them and hold them again.

They talked while the tree-trunk of a log that stretched across the fireplace slowly burnt down and every now and then spat into the conversation. Luke was easy with Seaton, he trusted him utterly. Alice listened while Luke told Seaton her story. She found it hard to believe it was she they were talking about . . . had she imagined so much? Had she travelled so far in her head, seen so much? And all the time Edward and Myers had stayed hot on their trail, 'Plotting and planning,' said Luke, 'and I was never sure if he'd recognized me, and what he intended to do. Until the end. No doubt he'll be cursing on his way home . . .'

'He might decide to stay in London,' said Alice sleepily, from her fireside chair.

'No point in that now,' said Luke. 'Even Edward must realize that he'd never find us in London. And he wouldn't know which way to follow us out of it. No, I'm sure he will be coming home, with his sour-faced retainers clustered around him.'

'Charlotte will be unbearable,' said Alice, managing a smile. 'I don't know how he'll break the news to her. She won't let him give up, Luke. She'll never allow that. Charlotte won't be content until he has wed her. That is what she has always wanted. Right from the very beginning that's what she planned.'

And Alice noticed that Luke said nothing in reply to that.

'Poor Milly, she'll feel sad this Christmas, on her own and in a strange place with Davy not there and nothing of her own around her.'

'Milly Toole is in her element.' Luke surprised Alice with his certainty. 'Nathaniel and Bella will take good care of her. You must have seen how she warms to the life as each day goes by. She is always first by the fire, she has learned most of the songs and dances, she has made close friendships and she has never, really, been

445

so contented. For Milly Toole, life is just beginning!'

'She doesn't show it,' said Alice, conjuring up Milly's large, worried face.

'She is not content unless she has something to moan about.'

But Alice said, 'Poor Milly,' and Luke looked at her sharply.

After Davy was fed and changed Alice was almost asleep. In her head she still rocked, she heard endless hoofbeats, clanking, metallic on an icy road. Seaton led them along a narrow, dark passage; they followed the wavering flame of his candle that sent a halo round his wild mane of hair. Down three stone steps and into a musty chamber. The bedroom was deep and dark like a cell but the bed must be climbed, like a mountain. Luke had to lift her on to it. She sunk into the mattress which was warm and aired and shaped itself round her. Luke climbed in beside her and she fell asleep fully clothed, thinking of nothing, warm and comforted in his arms.

While Luke lay awake all night beside her, staring down at the face that he loved and holding together his breaking heart.

# FORTY-SEVEN

And then, in the morning, 'There's something special I'd like you to see.'

Alice yawned, stretched and rubbed her eyes, languishing in the luxury of waking up beside him. 'But Luke, it's still dark outside! Even Davy is not awake yet.'

That urgency of the road was back and he was closed against her. He was still angry then, unable to forgive her for running away. How easy it was for her to slip into the belief that all this was really happening. Still, she would follow him. Right to the end she would follow him. And when he was finished with her it would all be over. This time, when it was over there'd be nothing left. And until that time she must savour every hour; she must will herself to believe that this was all true.

He was up and round to her side of the bed. She sat on the edge and slipped into his arms. He kissed her softly. 'Happy Christmas, Alice,' he said.

She followed him down the passage and back through the tower room in which they had dined last night. All was dark. All was silent. No sign, yet, of Seaton. They clad themselves in their travelling clothes. He made sure she was well wrapped up, 'For it's freezing out there.'

'But where are we going? I can't leave Davy!'

'If Davy wakes Seaton will hear him, and Seaton is very good with children . . .'

'He is not a child yet, Luke, he is a tiny baby!'

'Don't underestimate Seaton. I've never known a problem to beat him yet.'

Luke picked up a small sack which Seaton had given to him last night. Alice didn't know what was in it. She hadn't been able to hear Luke's instructions given so quietly to the old man before they retired to bed. Clutching the heavy sack in one hand, Luke took hers in the other and led her purposefully down the twisting staircase, through the door and out into the courtyard. Why didn't he speak? She wished he would speak. He was frightening her this morning.

'Oh look, Luke! Oh, look at that!' And then she stopped, staring. Luke watched her. Her face had never looked so sweetly childlike before, nor her eyes so enchanted. She looked as though she was stuck in a dream, blinking, trying to deny it but unable to do so. She whispered, 'I have never seen anything so completely beautiful.'

The master of Bellever was home and, according to the ancient tradition, Seaton had tied candles to the giant oak tree. Now a hundred tiny lights burned, silvering the snow that frosted its branches and settled, clean and level on the courtyard floor. There was no life, no movement, nothing lived except them. Little whirlwinds of snow spun off the turrets and landed softly at their feet. Everything was eerily silent, transformed by a queer snow-light. Against the dark of the morning sky the candles dazzled their magic, turning the world into soft white velvet.

Their footsteps were soundless as they neared the tree. Wordlessly, beneath the branches, he wrapped her gently in his arms and kissed her. She thought him remote, unreachable when he said, 'I love you Alice,' and she tried to pull him closer but could not.

He was tiring of the game, she could tell. Soon he would tire of her. Soon it would be over and she would wake. She had given her heart for the last time. She had been a fool but she had this moment . . . this sight . . . this feeling, something to last for ever and ever.

'Where are we going?' she asked.

He did not answer but pulled her across the courtyard, over the wooden bridge of the moat and down

448

the bank beside it. She tensed. The sky was whitening in the distance, the sun would soon be up. An icy breeze ruffled the tops of the trees below them, scattering the snow. She tasted it in her mouth, she licked her lips and melted it where it touched her. They went down a narrow, uneven track, and it was slippery here but Luke steadied her.

'On Christmas mornings we used to come here before breakfast. Everyone in the castle used to come here and skate on the moat if it was firm enough. It's easy to sweep away the surface snow with bundles of branches . . .' She could hardly hear him because his back was to her, but she thought he was saying they were going skating.

Shivering, but not with the cold now, she stood back and watched him as he worked, as roughly he wiped the sprinkling of snow from the ice of the hollow moat. The exposed ice was silver and black in parts, and this was a shadowy, echoing place, right down below the castle walls, at the very roots of the castle itself. It towered above them, formidable from here, and ageless, and Alice could smell decay . . . the fairy tale was not here. There was only a narrow pathway round the edge of the water, and thick black undergrowth poked its head through the crust of snow here and there, thorny and brambled.

'You skate, Luke.' Alice stood and watched him and hugged herself against the tunnel of cold wind that channelled its way down from the steep stone walls. She shivered and said, 'You skate if you want to. I'll watch you from here.'

'No!' he called back to her, his face red with exertion, unable to concentrate on anything else but the work in hand. 'We must do this together.'

'But I have never skated before.' Had he heard her? Was he listening?

'No matter. It's easy. I'll teach you.'

Soon he had cleared a wide patch of ice. The moat

wound away, round the walls and off out of sight. He banged his hands together as he came back and clambered up the bank towards her, pushing aside the undergrowth with his rough broom of branches. She looked down at his approaching head: flakes of snow had settled on the blackness of his hair.

He sat on the grass and pulled her down beside him. He untied the drawstring of the sack and took out two pairs of skates. Quite numb now, she could not resist. He took her feet on to his knee, one at a time, and strapped the skates on before he did his own, grunting against the cold. There was something wrong . . . he never looked at her! She wasn't here, close to him like this; Luke was alone and she just a shadow at his side.

'Now,' he stood up and caught her hand, pulling her with him. 'I'll help you down.'

Her words echoed inside her head. 'I can't, Luke! I can't!'

'Come on,' he encouraged her, but his voice held no reassurance. 'I am with you. You are safe. I would never let anything harm you.'

'I cannot do this.'

But they were down the short bank and on the edge of the ice. He steadied himself and turned to reach her. She jerked away her hands and put them to her ears. Her shoulders hunched. Her eyes closed tight. She screamed. She screamed so that her brain reeled from the animal sounds that she made. She screamed, unable to form the words that she wanted. 'I cannot do this! Why don't you listen to me? Why can nobody hear me?'

She heard him through the noise. *'Give me your hand!'*

He could not reach her from his position on the edge of the ice, so he took a step towards her. He reached out his arm, but again she pulled back. He was desperate now and intent on reaching her, and yet nowhere near as desperate as she. She fell in the brambles, felt herself slipping towards the water. She clutched the cruel black thorns that tore at her skin, and she retched.

He came to stand over her, staring down. So this . . . this was the face of true madness. Tears rolled down his cheeks. He could not let this moment go; it was this moment – now, or never. *Mad. Mad.* She rolled on the ground like a creature in torment. He could not see her this way. He could not! He hit her. With the full power of his sorrow he hit her. He slapped at her face with his powerful hands and there was no mercy in Luke's anguished world.

Finally she stilled. She was silent. He had stopped the awful noise in her mouth, he had forced her eyes wide open. His face was waiting, Luke was waiting, unable to move any more. The hand that she held out to touch him was trembling. She traced his face, she stared at the tears that she took on the ends of her fingers as out of the deepest, longest sleep she asked, 'Luke?'

He couldn't move. His power was all spent. He wanted to sleep. He was so terribly tired.

There was nothing to say. All that was left was, 'I love you, Alice.'

Childlike, she formed her words like a series of questions. 'I am frightened of the water. I have always been frightened of the water. Nobody knew. Nobody ever knew except Milly . . . and now you.'

He was tempted to laugh because what did any of this matter now? Childish confidences, foolish terrors . . .

'I would like to skate with you. But I cannot go too near the water,' she whispered.

Afraid. She could kill her own sister and yet feel afraid . . .

His stare changed. He gripped her shoulders. She thought he was trying to force her again and she cringed away from him, her back to the ground, rigid, determined . . .

His voice was rough and thick when he asked her, 'How long, Alice? Think carefully! You said you had been afraid of water since you were a child. How long?'

She shook her head. Perhaps he would understand if she said just a little bit more but oh, it was hard to speak of the secret she'd fought so desperately to keep. She'd been so afraid that they might make her overcome her horror, like Papa did when he knew she was nervous of horses. But the water, the water was very different. Milly had promised. Milly swore as she rocked her. She said, 'Trust me, my darling. Milly understands and Milly will never tell. Especially not Charlotte.'

Alice stuttered, 'We once had a nurse called Agatha. She used to hold my head under when she gave me my baths and she made me go with her when she tried to drown the kittens. I watched them die. Then, later, when she'd gone, I went and rescued Abernathy. I hid him. One of the kitchenmaids helped me until Agatha went. I have never got over it, Luke. I have never been able to bear to be near to water.'

'But Lucinda was drowned. Lucinda was drowned, Milly told me, in deep water.'

'What has this to do with Lucinda? Lucinda took her own life. I told you about that! She took her own life when she knew that I was to marry Edward. She was in love with him, Luke . . .'

'And the child, Neville? The child they believed was murdered?'

What was this? Alice undid the skates with trembling hands. She struggled to her feet. She turned her back on Luke and walked, slipped, hurried up the pathway back towards the castle. What was the matter with him? What was he saying? What had happened? He caught up with her; he tried to stop her and turned her round. She stood before him, she shouted: 'I do not know what you're saying! Of course my brother was not murdered! Who told you that? He was prematurely born, and he died and my father took his life because of it. You know this. Oh Luke, leave me alone now! I have woken up. I know you are real! You are not part of an unending dream but now I feel as if I am back with Edward and Charlotte again . . . I am being made to feel stupid, I no longer understand what is going on around me! What are you trying to do to me, Luke?'

But he wouldn't give up, not now. She pushed herself free but he followed her. He mused, 'And the cat – how did the cat die? Somebody strangled the cat!'

Alice stopped and turned to face him. 'Charlotte accused me of killing Abernathy. She stood there and screamed and accused me! I could never answer Charlotte when she was in one of those moods. She was angry, wild, full of fury. No one could deal with Charlotte and so we all just put up with her, or tried to avoid her. But what is this all about, Luke? Why are you trying to upset me like this by mentioning such things?'

He stopped when they reached the courtyard oak. He gripped her tightly and looked staight down into her eyes. Very slowly he said, 'I will never forgive myself.' She was amazed by the pain she saw on his face. In a hoarse, broken voice he told her, 'I believed all that Bella told me! I believed you had done all those things . . . and worse than that . . . so did Edward! That is why, Alice, don't you see! That is why your husband behaved so strangely, that is why he tried to commit you. He really believed you were mad. He wasn't pretending, or setting up some foul plot. He was fooled by Charlotte, who took her time and played her demented games over half a lifetime, so eager was she to get her revenge!'

Tense, and her face ashen, Alice asked, 'What revenge? Why would Charlotte need to take her revenge on anyone?'

'Because she was plain and ill-natured and not the firstborn. Because she felt cheated. But none of these reasons really matter. The most important fact is that you were never ill, it was Charlotte who was deranged! It was Charlotte who inherited the madness in your family and because you were not the prim little moral girl you ought to have been, because you strayed and went looking for love, you made it so easy for her! Oh, Alice . . . can't you see how easy it was for Charlotte once you had made your fatal mistake? And she had to kill Lucinda . . . she had to make sure that you married Edward so that she could stay close to him . . . influence him and one day, finally, marry him! If Lucinda had refused to give Edward up, then Charlotte's dreams would have been ruined. She killed your sister! Alice . . . please stop shaking your head and listen to me: *Charlotte drowned Lucinda!* Charlotte killed your brother, out of sheer, uncontrollable jealousy, and Charlotte killed your cat because taking him away from you hadn't satisfied her. She had not hurt you enough by doing that, so she had to remove him from you completely.'

Alice gazed up at Luke, still unable to comprehend the enormity of the words he was speaking. 'And you, Luke, you believed I had done these things!' Alice could hardly ask the next question. 'Did Milly tell you I had done these things? How could Milly believe them?'

Luke shook his head. Above him the candlelight flickered, answering the brilliance in his dark brown eyes. 'No, Alice, Milly did not believe them. How could she, when she knew you were frightened of water? No, Milly merely wanted to part us for her own misguided reasons and recounted the whispers she'd heard in that house, believing, as always, that she knew best. She had seen you hurt so many times, she had seen you unhappy, she couldn't bear to see it again. No, Milly tried to part us in the only way she knew.'

Alice hesitated as though she was trying to remember a terrible dream. 'Those were the stories Charlotte told

454

Edward about me? That I had killed? That I killed Neville? That I drowned Lucinda? *And he believed her?*'

'Driven to gullibility by guilt. Unable to live with the possibility that Lucinda killed herself because of his rejection of her, he preferred to believe anything but that. Edward was vulnerable, and there was Charlotte offering him a way out. He clutched it, he couldn't let go. How could he?'

Alice spoke quietly. 'And because he pretended to love me I clung to him, believing, daring to love him back. Oh, I tried to love him on our wedding night, that dreadful, dreadful night, and all the while he believed I was mad. No wonder I repelled him! No wonder he flinched from me when I tried to touch him. No wonder he couldn't wait to leave me and get back to Charlotte!'

'Yes, and since then she has tightened her grip, hounding you, making your life one long misery, and finally convincing Edward you were too sick to remain at home. Naturally he wanted you gone. A weak, troubled man, he wanted to bind himself to the woman he loved and depended on so desperately. She cast a spell over your husband, Alice, she drove him with her own madness, insatiable, demanding, withdrawing her love and protection every time he came near to letting her down. Once, when you were fourteen years old, you broke the strict code which society demands of women and the consequences of that have proved terrible.'

'But if Milly knew the lies Charlotte was telling, if she knew that Charlotte was accusing me of Lucinda's death, why didn't she go to Edward and tell him the truth?' Alice stared up at Luke with confusion. 'Knowing about my terror of water, Milly could have proved my sanity, my innocence.'

'I don't think Milly knew any of this until your escape from Deale when she probably decided to start listening at doors. Until then Charlotte was merely suggesting the kind of unstable behaviour it is always impossible to label. And Milly was always worried about you, Alice. She must have had reasons for worrying about your state of mind . . . reasons I still don't quite understand.'

And so there, holding each other tightly under the tree, protected against the cold by each other, Alice told Luke about Milly's horrified reaction to her affair with Garth. The denials she was forced to make. With faraway eyes, dimmed with pain, she spoke for the first time in her life of her firstborn child. 'A daughter. She was real, Luke, wasn't she? Oh yes, she was real. As real as all this is real – this castle, you, me . . .' And of the desolate year that followed when, 'Yes, I was a little mad then, struggling to control my emotions, keeping my secret, not understanding what was happening to me and certainly not knowing what would happen in the end. It was an awful, cruel kind of innocence we shared. We were old enough to love, it was no good Milly denying it. Even Lucinda, she loved, too. And yet we were not thought old enough to know what the consequences would be. It is incredible.' Alice stared through the snow-laden branches with tears in her eyes.

'And yet Milly did not know that you were pregnant?'

'I'll never be able to answer that, Luke. I always believed she did not know, but I can't be certain. It could be that she did know, she knew but it was too much for her to accept. I'll never know the truth of that. I just can't be certain.'

'And you left the baby where she'd been born, in the stables. What happened to her? Is it possible that one of the servants found her?'

'I can't answer that, either. I know how badly you need to know that, I know you are thinking of Lorna, but I can't answer you, Luke. And does it really matter now?' Wearily she faced him because there was one

456

impossible question she needed to ask him. 'You be-lieved Milly's story. You say that you love me, and yet you believed every word that she said to Bella. What were you going to do, Luke? Why did you decide to take me skating? It was nothing to do with tradition, was it? It was to do with nothing but you and me.'

He couldn't speak, but the forlorn desolation of the last dreadful days showed clearly in his face.

She said, 'And what right did you have to decide?' Her lips were blue, pale with the cold.

'I had the right of loving you. I had the right that came from the belief that I could not protect you for ever, Alice, because one day, wherever we went, they would come for you, and dying for your protection would not be enough. And yes, I did believe Milly. You were often so strange, far, far away, and jealous, so uncertain. Now that I understand it is all terribly clear, but then . . .' His eyes left hers when he said, 'I decided that we should die together. You would not have suf-fered and I know where the ice is thin . . .' and his voice trailed away into the wind, into the misty dis-tance.

'You would have died with me, Luke?' she asked him softly.

'I could not have lived without you. You should have known that.'

What greater proof of his love could he give? And there might have been time for joy, then, for the relief of understanding. Alice could have gone to croon over his words in some quiet place, but there wasn't time. She clutched him and cried, 'But Charlotte is at home, alone, with my children, and Edward still miles away! Dear God we must go there, we must fetch them. She is mad enough to do anything . . .'

Luke was himself again – calm, cool, the man she had seen in the churchyard and had fallen in love with from the beginning. This was reality . . . it always had been. He led her indoors. 'You have been through

457

enough. I'm going. You cannot come with me and Davy needs you here.'

She shouted, tugging on his sleeve, in danger of holding him back. 'To involve yourself in this is to ask for tragedy. They might catch you and take you . . .'

She rushed out after him, but he was across the courtyard and into the stables. She followed him, arguing her cause. 'I must come with you. Let me come . . .'

'I ride much faster alone.'

She was forced to stand and watch as he saddled his horse, mounted, scuffed a whirlwind of snow on the crisp white surface of the courtyard, and cantered out over the bridge. The world fell silent behind him as he disappeared into the distance.

She squeezed her hands together and prayed. 'Oh, let him come back with my children. Let them be unharmed. Whoever you are, listen to me! Dear God on this day of all days I beg You to let them come safely home.'

# FORTY-EIGHT

Charlotte turned like a cat and then stood, dead still, on the stairs. Only one hand, clenched tight on a fold of her skirt, betrayed her tension. She was pale, and when she turned round her cold blue eyes were strained when she stared at Luke.

'What do you mean by . . . and who are you?'

But Luke's smile chilled. This is the woman who applied the torture. Day after day she turned the screw and this is the house where it happened. Nothing blinked to give it away, for the house was as blandly serene as its mistress. He passed over the threshold of the great entrance hall, spacious, palatial, the marble columns signifying order, their whiteness suggesting the greatest of calm. His boots clicked over the black and white tiles, neat, regular, but austere, like Charlotte. Remote.

He had not bothered to knock or to wait for the door to be opened for him. Assuming it would not be locked he turned the handle with both hands and flung it wide to pass through. Swirls of snow accompanied him, disturbing the fire and gusting a shroud of smoke which sat like a veil on the atmosphere, a fog in the air.

Was the woman who stood so still, watching him, was she aware of the enormity of what she had done? And suddenly he was struck by the extreme smallness of her.

Four stairs up, and she turned round completely. She faced him with curbed animosity and asked, 'Who are you?'

He didn't bother to answer but said, 'It was the unforgivable sin, wasn't it, Charlotte? Loose, wanton behaviour. It shocked and disgusted you, no matter

459

that it was by its very nature, innocent and sad.'

Charlotte drew herself up, her face went tighter. 'I have no idea to what you refer.'

Luke stepped forward, repelled and fascinated by the creature on the stairs. The niceties of introduction were not necessary now; all he wanted was to understand why. 'And you must have loved Edward. In your own twisted way you loved him from the beginning, Charlotte, didn't you? It must have been very painful, living without hope for so long. First he was Lucinda's, then he belonged to Alice. But then you saw your opportunity and you grasped it. You had already killed out of jealousy – the cat, your newborn brother – it can't have been too difficult to kill your own sister, especially when she had confided in you all that happened between her and Edward before she died. Lucinda came to confide in you, didn't she? Milly was probably busy telling her not to be silly, to control her wayward emotions, to deny them for ever. So Lucinda came to you. She wanted comforting, didn't she, and she told you exactly what you wanted to hear. Because you had him then. You understood Edward's weakness, his terror of women, his inability to love, and you knew very well that his guilt would be something he would be unable to handle. Killing Alice would be a waste of time because they would never have allowed him to marry Lucinda, or you. Neither of you would have gratified Henry Brennan's passion for prestige. And you were terrified that if Lucinda had lived she might have convinced Edward to elope with her and then you would never see him again . . .'

He felt nausea twist in his stomach when she interrupted with that bitter peal of laughter and her cold eyes brightened. What was she? What was this? Her small hand gripped the banister, banded with tiny veins; the lips drew back, the eyes penetrated as he continued, 'And it was so easy for you, Charlotte, wasn't it, because of Alice's mistake? Madness was as good an explanation as any. Even poor Milly, in her well-meaning way, was an unconscious accomplice, even she was for ever watching and dreading a repeat of the unreasonable behaviour. Even she believed Alice to be a bad mother, not to be trusted with the care of her children – a child who had never grown up. Oh yes, Charlotte, once you had started on your course of action you found it quite simple to persevere . . . '

Charlotte gave a short, wounded cry. 'Alice was never worthy of Edward! She was never worthy of any of the love she was given because I knew how she seethed underneath those sweet, dainty ways, those perfect manners! Underneath all that, I knew, oh yes I knew she was nothing but a monster . . . '

'Because she had feelings! Because she reached out for love?'

'She was impure!' Charlotte shouted the words so they reached the vaulted ceiling, and hung there, dripping with malice.

Words were useless. He could not get through to this woman wrapped in the brittle armour of fanatical self-righteousness. 'But you didn't know, did you, about the flaw in your plan, the flaw of which Alice was so foolishly ashamed – the fact that she couldn't bear water!'

Charlotte laughed again, a chilling sound in the vast, silent space. 'My love is what Edward needed. My love . . . me . . . the plain, homely woman, her in the background who never mattered. And yet it was me he needed. He would never have been happy with Alice.' And her hand clenched convulsively as she turned to move up the stairs, her back straight, her head held high with a peculiar kind of dignity, dismissing him.

He began to follow her up. 'And now, if you do not want your evil behaviour to become known you must use your influence over Edward in a very different way. Alice's children must be returned to her. They will be returned to her, whether you like it or not. I am taking

461

them with me now. And if Edward's voice were added to the other ones clamouring for my pardon I am certain he would be listened to.'

Charlotte whirled on him. 'Your small concerns mean nothing to me. Why do you come here and bore me with them? You think you can bargain with me like that? You think that with your pathetic little piece of proof – Alice's supposed terror of water – you can undo all my years of work, and that Edward is going to believe you? Whoever you are, I can see that once again Alice has found herself a fool. Why would I bother to influence Edward? I have no interest in you, or in justice. And do you honestly think that Edward will listen to a man like you?' She laughed again, but when they reached the first landing a small, trim woman, flustered and anxious, rushed towards Charlotte with her hands out before her as if she were carrying an invisible tray, too heavy, that might unbalance. Charlotte stopped dead in her tracks. She held up a hand to shush the maid but the woman came forward and spoke in a rush.

'It has been three days now, madam,' she said, but her pleading eyes were on Luke. 'And I cannot allow, no, not even for the direst punishments, those little girls to be kept in their room any longer! 'Tis cruel, madam, can't you see, and I have to say I am worried about their health shut up in there with no heat, nothing but bread to eat and water to drink. I am sure if the master were here he would not agree . . . '

'Hush, Jane!' Charlotte raised an arm, about to strike. There was a livid red spot on both her cheeks – the only colour about her, for her lips were white as the rest of her complexion and her dress was a metallic grey. 'Can't you see that we have a visitor and that now is not the time!'

Jane fastened her eyes on Luke. 'I don't care about the time or the place any more, madam, I'm that concerned.'

'Where are the children?' Sudden fear made his heart feel hollow.

Jane bowed her head, would not look at Charlotte when she said, 'Follow me, sir, although I do not have the key. God help me, if I had it, I would have let them out the day before yesterday.'

'The lack of a key does not bother me.' Luke followed Jane at a near-running pace along the landing and up a second flight of stairs to the closed door of the nursery. He looked at her enquiringly, and his eyes and the nurse's were haunted with worry. 'Kate and Laura are in there?'

'They have been in here for far too long, sir, and nobody else having a say in any of it, and me not even being told for what or for how long she intends to keep them in there. I am their nurse and yet I'm not even allowed to speak to them.'

Luke called out, 'Laura! Laura, can you hear me?'

There was no answer. The stout oak door was too thick to let sound through. 'Is there an axe?' he asked the ashen-faced Jane. 'Can you fetch me an axe from outside, and quickly?'

'I'll find you an axe.' For how long had this good-looking young boy been hiding there, listening? It seemed that this house was haunted by watchers and secret listeners.

'Nicholas?'

'Yes, I am Nicholas. I heard all you said in the hall and I'll fetch you an axe.'

He left, and Jane confided hurriedly, 'He was going to ride off in search of his father today. Neither of us knew what was best to do. It has been quite awful. Her heavy-handed discipline is one thing but since the master went away neither Master Nicholas or I have known what's been going on from one minute to the next! She won't discuss anything with either of us and the rest of the servants, well, they're going round like shadows terrified of her cutting tongue and her vicious punishments. Only yesterday she slapped poor Nancy so hard round the face that the girl fell against the fireplace and cut her head open. A doctor had to be called. I can't tell you how relieved I was to see you this morning, sir, I just can't tell you,' and the woman collapsed in tears.

A small rustle at the far end of the corridor attracted their attention. Jane's hand flew to her mouth. 'Charlotte,' Luke called softly. 'Would you make this much easier for everyone and allow me to have the key, please.'

The thin woman in grey moved silently forward. 'Who are you?' she asked, in a dull, expressionless voice.

Jane recoiled. She would have disappeared into the wall had she been able. Luke told Charlotte his name and once again asked for the key.

'You're the one!' said Charlotte, licking dry lips and ignoring his request. 'You are the man who took Alice, who attacked Doctor Myers at the cottage, who has harboured her all these weeks, who has kept Edward from me . . . '

'Yes,' he told her gently. 'I am the one.'

'Alice has been making up vile stories against me.'

'No.' Luke stared over Charlotte's head, urging Nicholas to hurry. 'Alice has said nothing against you to me.'

'Then how have you come to these conclusions?' She was almost lifeless, except for a pulse that throbbed in her forehead.

'Charlotte, it wasn't hard. I was slow to understand, for like everyone else I was thrown by your sister's emotional behaviour, but once I understood it was not hard.'

'You can't know Alice,' muttered Charlotte fervently, chattering in near-silent prayer. 'She behaves like a little girl still. Nobody knows Alice. She won't let anyone through. She is a contrived performance from start to finish. So how is it possible that you

464

care so much? How did she convince you of her sanity?'

'Charlotte, the awful truth of it is that I do know Alice, and that I love her, mad or not. So I hope that answers your question.'

Nicholas would have given the axe to Luke but he nodded and let the boy go on. Grimly he stood back, raising the weapon high before bringing it down on the door. A panel splintered. They watched as the axe came down, a second, a third time, cracking an awful silence, while sweat sheened the boy's earnest young face.

Luke thrust his hand through the gap and turned the handle but it was Nicholas who pushed past and was first into the room. It was to Nicholas that the children, cowering beside the window, rushed when they saw him. How like Alice they were – tiny, perfect images. Nicholas scooped his sisters up in his arms. He wheeled around to face Charlotte. 'Never!' he shouted at her. 'Never again will you get within yards of them!' And then, more quietly, but with eyes sparking metal he said, 'I will kill you first, Charlotte.'

And Charlotte, still with that deadpan expression on her face, looked up at Luke and quietly explained, 'See,' she said. 'See, he is just like his mother. He is mad.'

'How many more would you have destroyed, I wonder,' said Luke, staring down pensively in disbelief. She swayed slightly and he heard her quick breathing. 'And for how long would you have got away with it?'

Jane, full-bosomed and crooning like a nesting dove, cuddled the children. They still clung to Nicholas, refusing to let him out of their sight, and after assuring herself that they were all right, the nursemaid hurried down to the kitchens for food. Charlotte left the room, ordered out of it by Luke. There was time for a bag to be packed, for warm clothing to be collected together, 'Because I am taking them straight to their mother who is waiting,' said Luke, 'and frantic with worry by now.'

Luke and Nicholas stood beside the nursery window. A mantle of snow covered every inch of the ground; it was innocent, white, covering the pain and the failure. 'These girls belong with their mother.' Luke hoped the boy would understand because there was no alternative and he must realize that. 'They certainly cannot stay here, and when your father returns he has much to settle and sort out. He can never obliterate what he has done. He is not a stupid man and yet he behaved like a fool and there is no excuse for that. There is much he can do to make amends and I know that he'll want to do that, once he fully understands what has happened, once he knows what he did to his wife. You have a straight choice, Nicholas: to come with us and make a new start, to help us create a new home, build up the walls and fill it with love, or you can . . . '

He was afraid of the boy's answer. He knew there would be resentment and yet there was not much time for decisions and Alice would be broken-hearted . . .

Nicholas tried to hide his tears by turning his head. 'You won't understand. She won't forgive me.' His voice was a broken sob coming from a very bleak place. 'You see, I half-believed what they said – it was me who told them she was planning to escape from Deale. I didn't know what was happening. My father endorsed all that Charlotte said and I saw that Mama did act strangely sometimes . . . compared with Charlotte.'

How like Alice he was! They needed each other so badly just now. Luke said, 'I understand very well, Nicholas, because I share your guilt, for I was almost convinced myself and so now we both have some

466

making up to do. I hope you will come with us, for you can't travel two roads any longer and neither of yours is going to be easy after this. Your mother loves you deeply, and she needs a chance to tell you so before you are too grown up to listen.'

Nicholas' decision did not take long to make, nor did it take the two riders much time to cover the short distance between Winterbourne House and Castle Bellever. There was no sign of Charlotte when they left the house, burdened by bundles of clothing, blankets and the two small girls, lively and excited by the prospect of seeing their mother. And when Jane sidled up to Luke to ask, 'Should I not accompany you? Won't the children be needing a nurse?' Luke tried to be kind when he said, 'Not for a while, they won't. Alice needs time on her own with her children, but I'm sure there'll be times when you're needed, Jane. The children are going to want to see you frequently and when we are ready we will send for you.'

Jane gestured anxiously up the stairs. 'But what of my mistress? How are we to handle her now? Where has she gone and what is she doing? I'm telling you, none of us can stand this much longer with the master away.'

'He'll be back today or tomorrow, Jane, and I think you can leave it to him to deal with your mistress in whatever way he sees fit. Meanwhile, my advice is to ignore her completely, and to keep your distance. Whatever she is, whatever she has become, she has destroyed herself before she had the chance to destroy anyone else, thank God.'

'But only just in time, sir,' said Jane, as they rode away.

The cold white air streamed off the castle walls. It shimmered, lost in a frosty smoke as they approached. Laura, her arms clutching Luke tightly, called out, 'We're here! We're here! I know this place!'

But Nicholas, overawed by the extraordinary sight of the towering walls over the tree-tops, pulled up his horse. Kate, muffled with a hood obscuring half of her face, insisted on being lifted down. 'I know the way,' she said, 'and I want to go on my own.'

They let her lead the rest of the way. Her small legs slipped and slid on the snow and when she reached the moat she stopped and stared, puffing like a deflating balloon. Nobody heard what she said because it was said far too softly, and her words were too childish to understand. 'These are the shadowlands, and I knew they were here all the time, and I knew that Mama would be waiting.'

Alice stood beside the door.

Kate started to run, a bundle pounding across the drawbridge, and when she saw her mother she screamed and held out her arms. She flung herself into Alice's arms, a travelling snowball and Laura, shy, slipped in after her, shuddering with pleasure and lighting up with quick little smiles of delight. Nicholas slowly led his horse over the bridge to the waiting group. Luke, still mounted, watched from a distance as the family which had never been a family, united.

Alice turned her face to her son and Luke saw the love in it. Nicholas shuffled forward, head down, clumsy, confused, not knowing what to say or how to respond because it was not easy, he was not a child. Nothing was simple any more. With her daughters at her skirts Alice held out her arms and just stood there, dark against the snow in the bright red cloak which Seaton had found. There was nowhere for Nicholas to go except forward. And Luke heard Alice say very quietly, 'Oh Nicky, it seems as if I have waited all my life for this moment.'

Somehow Seaton had found himself a banquet to prepare. The Christmas meal was splendid, the conversation furious, excited, and occasionally hysterical with laughter. Sometimes Kate looked up in wide-eyed wonder, staring at one lively face, then another. What had happened to all the rules, to proper decorum? And the games they played afterwards were wild and funny. Mama rolled on the floor, limp with laughter, and nobody looked at her crossly. Kate tried it. They danced and they sang while Seaton dozed in a chair in the middle of telling a story, with Laura trying to arrange his hair, sitting on his knee.

In the afternoon they sledged. They kept well away from the moat because Mama said she'd always been afraid of water and lots of other things, too, but she'd never said it before because it sounded silly. People often call important things silly. Before it grew dark they went round the castle walls, making plans. Luke said it would take three years for the work to be complete, and by then they'd be married.

'But we must wait until the theatre comes by,' Alice told him firmly. 'Then we can do it by gypsy law. And Milly, how Milly would hate to miss it. Do you think she will ever come home, Luke? Back to her cottage again?'

'She'll have a choice but I don't think she'll be able to give up the travelling life, now she's tasted it. And Bella Pettigrew Lovett will knock some of that damn commonsense out of her.'

But it was in the evening, while they sat by the fire, that Laura said, 'Papa might be lonely, all on his own with just Charlotte.'

Alice looked quickly at Luke but it was Nicholas who answered. 'Some people need people, others don't. And I suspect Papa won't even want Charlotte any more when he gets home and hears what happened. He'll be happy to see us sometimes, just as we'll sometimes be happy to see him. It won't be much different, really, from how it used to be.'

'And you're sure they will pardon you now, and everything they took will be returned?' Alice took

469

Luke's hand. 'Can we trust this happiness? Won't something come and whisk it away?'

'The case was nearing conclusion before this happened. And once Edward realizes the grotesque part he has played in this business he will certainly put in a good word. His children are still important to him . . . he won't want them spending the rest of their lives travelling round the countryside, homeless. After all that has happened he'll know that there's no way, now, of getting them back.'

'He has always hated to lose,' Alice worried.

'Quite. And now he has only one way of winning.' Luke was positive. 'If he does not behave like a gentleman he knows full well that I'd be happy to bring this whole scandal out into the open – everything, from start to finish – and his part in it.'

'And Charlotte? What do you think will happen to Charlotte?'

'She should be hung, drawn and quartered,' said Seaton, drunkenly.

Luke said, 'Edward has only two options. Either he can keep her at home and watch her sink quickly into total madness, or he can send her to be cared for in Deale. I know which option I would take.'

'Poor Charlotte. I wouldn't wish that experience on anyone.'

'She not only tried to destroy you, but she would have destroyed Nicholas also. She had already started her ghastly games, suggesting to Edward that he was mad because of his rebellious nature and his natural concern for you. That's why Edward was so keen to retrieve little Davy – an heir to replace the one already doomed. Nicholas was getting too clever, not easy to influence like Edward himself, and most of all, most dangerous of all, because he loved you, Alice. No, Nicholas would have been next . . . Madness or murder – in Charlotte's sick mind which one she chose never really mattered.'

When Alice and Luke made love that night beside the fire, after everyone else was in bed and asleep, he traced her body made gold by the firelight and he told her, 'You are more beautiful than I have ever seen you. You hold yourself in a new way; some other part of you is alive and I fear you no longer need me to love you.'

Alice smiled, remembering Unity Heath and Lottie, and all those other brash, proud women who flaunted themselves with such abandon. Yes, there was something of them in her now, brave and brazen and proud of it. Proud to be herself, proud to be choosing the man to give herself to, knowing she was special because of who she was.

She thought of the half-grown girl who had loved all those years ago . . . the same person . . . the same body. She had stayed a child for so long, waiting to learn how to love herself over all that heartbreak, all that pain. All that need.

Wrapped in a blanket she moved from the fire, crossed the room and unlatched one of the heavy shutters. She pulled it open and gazed out of the window. She looked out over snow-crusted turrets, the statuesque oak, the softly-blanketed walls and off into the thick, snowy night. The snow descended softly, covering every ledge, every lintel, tendering the world, blurring it. It didn't matter how many snowflakes fell, the sky stayed full of them. When she closed her eyes and tried to remember all that had happened her mind felt sore, so she let it fill with the soundless snow, hushing and lulling its way to the ground. New to her, and sweet, a love for life rose up inside her until the tears came. And her love for Luke, it engulfed her so that she wanted to do things for him she could never do before . . . dance . . . write songs . . . write poems . . .

She had lived with so much loneliness and now he offered her a drawbridge. He beckoned, and she knew she would never see, in Luke's eyes, the bright narrow corridors of nightmare through which she

471

had travelled, or herself, debased and humiliated, small and frightened with nothing to bring him. He had set a value on her, a high price and one on which she could build up her pride and self-respect. She would survive.

Gently she closed away the night, she crossed the floor and knelt beside him. He said, 'Hello Alice,' as he reached for her hand and held it tight. 'Welcome, welcome back from the world of make believe.'